P9-DFY-477

"FASCINATING PSYCHOLOGICAL SUSPENSE."

—San Francisco Examiner & Chronicle

What police detective Sam Purdy had to say to Dr. Alan Gregory was simple enough:

"My problem, Alan, is that I don't happen to know any other psychologist I can rouse out of bed at dawn a few hours after a good friend of his is murdered. I want your help, okay. I trust your opinion. So just put on your shrink hat and come to the theater where the murder occurred and *notice*. Feel the killer. Taste him. Smell him. How he did it. What he felt while he was planning it, doing it. What need it met. It's all there. And that kind of stuff is your business."

Sam Purdy was right about one thing. It was Alan Gregory's business, in more ways than one. But he was wrong about where Alan had to go and the gamble he had to take. For there were deeper questions than who killed Peter . . . there were questions about a man's secrets and the harrowing truths of his haunted heart. . . .

HARM'S WAY

"Serpentine and sexy." —*Kirkus Reviews*

"Breakneck riveting suspense . . . a top-notch thriller." —*Just Books*

"A nifty thriller." —*Rocky Mountain News*

"Intricate, engrossing murder . . . convincing." —*Publishers Weekly*

PRAISE FOR STEPHEN WHITE AND HIS NOVELS

HIGHER AUTHORITY

"Sinister and scary."
—*New York Times Book Review*

"Absorbing, intriguing, chilling . . . a most
engaging thriller."
—*San Diego Union Tribune*

"A plot as intricate as it is mesmerizing . . .
Stephen White keeps on getting better."
—*Denver Post*

"A powerful piece of storytelling . . . tense
and chillingly real."
—John Dunning

"Stephen White scores again . . . fast-paced . . .
a captivating read!"
—*Milwaukee Journal*

PRIVATE PRACTICES

"A captivating thriller . . . murderous mayhem
and superb action scenes . . . clinical psychology
as a dangerous profession . . . book us
for another session, please!"
—*Kirkus Reviews*

"A can't-miss read!"
—Larry King, *USA Today*

"Intriguing . . . this psycho-thriller provides
solid, satisfying entertainment."
—*San Diego Union Tribune*

"An intriguing plot and believable characters . . .
will keep you guessing to the end."
—Phillip Margolin

"Engrossing . . . Stephen White is a first-rate writer."
—Aaron Elkins

Get a $2.00 rebate on
Stephen White's new hardcover,
REMOTE CONTROL!

Available in April 1997

█ █

To get your $2.00 rebate, mail:

■ Your original dated sales receipt for REMOTE CONTROL
(hardcover) with price circled

■ This rebate certificate

■ Write in book UPC number _____

To: REMOTE CONTROL REBATE
P.O. Box 8046
Grand Rapids, MN 55745-8046

Name: _____

Address: _____

City: _____ State: _____ Zip: _____

This certificate (original or photocopy) must accompany your request.
Void where prohibited, taxed, or restricted. One rebate per household.
Allow 4-6 weeks for shipment of rebate in U.S. funds. Offer good only in U.S.,
its territories, and Canada. Offer expires **June 30, 1997**. Mail received
until July 15, 1997.

Signet

Dutton

Printed in the USA

HARM'S WAY

—◦◦◦—

Stephen White

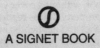

A SIGNET BOOK

SIGNET
Published by the Penguin Group
Penguin Books USA Inc., 375 Hudson Street,
New York, New York, 10014, U.S.A.
Penguin Books Ltd, 27 Wrights Lane,
London W8 5TZ, England
Penguin Books Australia Ltd,
Ringwood, Victoria, Australia
Penguin Books Canada Ltd, 10 Alcorn Avenue,
Toronto, Ontario, Canada M4V 3B2
Penguin Books (N.Z.) Ltd, 182–190 Wairau Road,
Auckland 10, New Zealand

Penguin Books Ltd, Registered Offices:
Harmondsworth, Middlesex, England

Published by Signet, an imprint of Dutton Signet,
a division of Penguin Books USA Inc.
Previously appeared in a Viking edition.

First Signet Printing, March, 1997
10 9 8 7 6 5 4 3 2 1

Copyright © Stephen W. White, 1996
All rights reserved

Ⓤ REGISTERED TRADEMARK—MARCA REGISTRADA

Printed in the United States of America

Without limiting the rights under copyright reserved above, no
part of this publication may be reproduced, stored in or introduced
into a retrieval system, or transmitted , in any form, or by any
means (electronic, mechanical, photocopying, recording, or otherwise), without the prior written permission of both the copyright
owner and the above publisher of this book.

PUBLISHER'S NOTE
This is a work of fiction. Names, characters, places, and incidents
either are the product of the author's imagination or are used ficti-
tiously, and any resemblance to actual persons, living or dead,
events, or locales is entirely coincidental.

BOOKS ARE AVAILABLE AT QUANTITY DISCOUNTS WHEN USED TO
PROMOTE PRODUCTS OR SERVICES. FOR INFORMATION PLEASE WRITE
TO PREMIUM MARKETING DIVISION, PENGUIN BOOKS USA INC.,
375 HUDSON STREET, NEW YORK, NY 10014.

If you purchased this book without a cover you should be aware
that this book is stolen property. It was reported as "unsold and
destroyed" to the publisher and neither the author nor the publisher has received any payment for this "stripped book."

for Rose

When it comes to racing with death,
all men are not created equal.

—Norman MacLean
YOUNG MEN AND FIRE

A warm Friday night in April, the air still and perfumed by lilacs.

Emily had to pee. I fingered her leash as she circled and sniffed the ground for whatever peculiar scent would tell her she had found the right spot.

Peter was on his way out the lane. He slowed his old Volvo and thrust his left arm through the open window in greeting. "Hi, Em," he called.

I returned his wave and watched the wagon's lights trail away. Emily cocked her ears as she squatted in the dust.

She would have preferred that we continue on for a walk but I was eager to get back inside, where my wife waited for me with chilled pepper vodka, a video-cassette, and a cozy spot on the couch.

When it became important that I know, I had to speak with a lot of people before I understood what happened later that night.

The Community Hospital Emergency Department records show that at 2:10 a.m. two men carried Peter through the door of the ER. He was immediately stretched out on a gurney covered with sheets already bloodied by a fourth-grade casualty of a school-bus crash near Allenspark. One look at Peter made it clear that there was no time for clean linen. In seconds he was surrounded by exhausted ER staff.

"He's got a faint pulse. Hurry, please! He's lost a lot of blood!" yelled one of the two men who had carted Peter from the Boulder Theatre to the nearby hospital. The man was burly, with thick arms and short legs and unruly hair that was a memorable mix of copper and silver. His face was flushed red from the exertion, and his tiny eyes communicated urgency. The man had been a medic in Vietnam and he swore that he'd detected a faint carotid pulse when he'd found Peter in the theatre when he arrived to do his after-show cleanup. Experienced in triage, he had decided that there was no time to call an ambulance and had rushed Peter to the hospital in his own car, an old El Camino with a sleek golden cover over the back.

The ex-medic had corralled a university student off the sidewalk adjacent to the alley behind the theatre to ride in the back of the El Camino with Peter. Earlier, the sophomore had been at a party at one of the fraternity houses on the Hill and gotten so blitzed he'd lost his keys and had to walk home to his apartment on Spruce Street. At the time he was shanghaied he had been taking a brief respite from his hike home in order to vomit in the alley.

In the frantic atmosphere in the ER the inebriated kid from the university looked bewildered. He shadowed the ex-medic wherever the man moved.

"I don't get a pulse. Anyone getting a pulse?" called a tall gray-haired nurse who had been the first to appear at the head of Peter's gurney in the wide hallway outside the treatment rooms.

An ER doc arrived at a trot and scanned Peter slowly from head to toe. "Bag him. Where's the bag? Do we have an open room?" he said in an even, air-line-pilot voice.

"In your dreams."

"Get some O-neg. BP?"

No one answered at first; then someone said, "Not yet, I'm trying."

"Call cardiac over here. Get me a line wide open."

"Respirations are zero. Still no pulse. No pressure."

"Stay with the CPR. We're going to need a central line. *Get me a room!*"

Down the hall, someone yelled, "Is cardiac three open yet?"

"When did you have that pulse? How long ago?" The ER doc, a guy in his forties with acne scars, a receding hairline, and a ponytail, looked squarely at the big man with the red face.

The ex-medic barked, "Five minutes, sir! That's all, maybe four. I know this one, sir! He's worth saving." Blood stained the man's clothing and his skin. It was Peter's blood, and it had started to lose its sheen. The pasty film was cracking and sepa-rating on the thick red hair of the man's forearms. The ex-medic had been Peter's friend. Now he stood at attention, crying. Wearing painter's coveralls over a sleeveless T-shirt, drenched with Peter's blood, his eyes illuminated as though they were powered by the sun, he was somehow the most dignified person in the ER.

He sobered everyone in his presence.

* * *

My dear friend Adrienne, Peter's wife, was the urologist on call for the ER that night. She was just completing a difficult catheterization of a ten-year-old girl who had a pelvic fracture from the bus accident. She heard the commotion in the hall outside the trauma room, knew instinctively there was a code, and concluded that one of the casualties from the school bus had crashed. As soon as she finished inserting the cath, she stripped her gloves and went out to see what was going on.

Adrienne was five feet tall in spike heels. Maybe. From her vantage point she had no chance of seeing over the half-dozen people surrounding the gurney, so she squeezed into a tiny space left open near the patient's feet. The ponytailed emergency-medicine doc leaned over the body, counting silently while he performed CPR. A nurse kept time with the breathing bag she pressed firmly over her patient's mouth and nose. With thick wads of gauze another nurse sopped amber blood from countless short, linear wounds. Needles were being plunged into his veins—"I'm not getting a flash, nothing. This guy's got no pressure, zero"—plastic bags of fluid were being hung, and leads were being taped with remarkable precision to newly cleaned places on Peter's hairless chest.

"He's going out. Damn. Anybody got a pulse?"

Adrienne couldn't tell who said that. The voice she heard was tired, not urgent. A female voice, she thought. But no one at the table responded to the open question.

From down the corridor, someone called, "C-three is open."

"Stay with the CPR. We're moving into cardiac three. Everybody together, let's go. One, two, *now!*" The ER doc, the one rhythmically thrusting his weight onto Peter's chest, spoke clearly, expecting his directions to be obeyed.

Cardiac three was in Adrienne's direction. She hopped back to keep from being bowled over by the wheeled table and its multiple attendants.

As the gurney sped by she saw her husband's open eyes looking right at her. Through her. Her heart dropped to her toes.

She said, "Oh, Jonas, your daddy."

I

Borrowed
Time

You think you know someone.

Peter Arvin had been my neighbor for almost ten years. I'd dined with him a hundred times. I'd helped him build fences, dig holes to plant shade trees, clean gutters. For hours I'd watched him shape and smooth wood in his studio. He'd comforted me after my first wife left me, and he soaked up my tears when my dog died. When his baby was born, I was there next to him. He had invited me to hold the cord while he cut it. I did, although I never knew why.

In Peter's company and at his insistence I'd finished many bottles of his good wine that I had no business finishing, and run a handful of 10Ks that I had no business running. I had never beaten him at tennis. Not once. I doubt it had ever crossed his mind to let me win.

Peter liked being the best.

He liked being an anachronism, too.

The music that blared constantly in his studio always came from old records. LPs. Creedence Clearwater, Grand Funk, Cream. Early Airplane. Peter relished an opportunity to serve Tournedos Rossini or Beef Wellington to a dining room full of Boulder cholesterol phobics. He drove a 1976 Volvo station wagon with an AM radio. If he ever owned new clothing I never saw it.

Peter loved the backcountry and the mountains and yet had married a woman who thought the *city* of Boulder was a wilderness. He camped and hiked alone, usually in the Indian Peaks, and on days when inspiration avoided him in his studio, he could often be found hanging at some gravitationally defiant angle on a rock face in Eldorado Canyon. Peter was a regular practitioner of "free-soloing"—which involves climbing high rock faces without ropes or safety gear. I wouldn't have gone near those same vertical walls without scaffolding.

One night at a dinner of fiery jerked shrimp that Peter had prepared shortly after he and Adrienne had gotten pregnant, she asked him to give it up. Just like that.

"No more free-soloing?" he said without looking up from his meal.

"That's right, Geppetto. No more free-soloing. The guys that do it are, literally, a dying breed. I want you around to change diapers."

He exhaled before asking, "Can I still sport-climb?"

Adrienne nodded. Sport-climbing meant ropes, and hardware, and if Adrienne got her way, a helmet. To me, the difference between free-soloing and sport-climbing was akin to the difference between swimming with sharks unarmed and swimming with sharks while carrying a penknife. But no one asked my opinion, and I kept it to myself.

Adrienne nodded again. She said, "Sport-climbing's okay."

Peter's eyes smiled but the corners of his mouth never turned up.

I was only an observer that night, but the interchange had appeared to be a graceful marital contract negotiated without rancor. Over the next year, though, I heard through mutual friends that more than once Peter had been seen on the Diving Board or Tagger, or another world-class climb in Eldorado, no ropes, no helmet.

A colleague, a clinical psychologist like myself, who had witnessed one of these remarkable solo climbs reasoned that every successful ascent Peter made was really nothing more than a failed suicide attempt.

Peter Arvin wore his blond hair down to his shoulders and shaved once a week, whether his wispy beard needed it or not. His smile was that of a leprechaun, and he was miserly enough with it that you knew it was special when he directed one your way. His eyes were one shade more golden than hazel, and they always seemed sadder and wiser than everyone else's.

Even in metaphysical Boulder, Peter could bring a roomful of locals to awkward silence with his musings on the meaning of some aspect of life that none of us had ever considered thoroughly. He was big on extraterrestrials one year, on phantom governments the next. The rain-forest problem had him stumped.

It was always something with Peter, who was as spiritual a man as I had ever known. The nature of his spirituality was personal and idiosyncratic and at times plain weird, but Peter's determined sense was that there was a higher energy at work, a deity, at least

in-the-making, somewhere in the universe. He talked
about his spiritual beliefs constantly, as other people
might speak about politics, or sports, or the weather.
"If there is actually a God—a single God," he'd told
me one spring while we were working manure into
his wife's vegetable garden, "I think we're talking
about an adolescent. It's got to be a kid-God who's
trying to take care of this planet. Face it, there's just
too many fuckups for this to be a full-grown Supreme
Being with four hundred million years of experience. I
mean, losing the dinosaurs, for instance—can you
imagine a God who's actually paying attention allowing
that to happen? Sorry, no way.

"This planet is being run like it's something somebody's doing on the side, when what they're really
interested in is the celestial equivalent of getting laid
or starting a rock-and-roll band."

He preferred to read biographies to anything but
science fiction, which he called "anticipatory nonfic-
tion." He loved the theatre—from Shakespeare to
Broadway road shows to local rep companies. He was
always an enthusiastic groupie and eager volunteer,
and at times a generous benefactor.

In his studio he was a magician. He fashioned wood
as though only he knew the meaning of the grain and
the whorls. Acclaim for his pieces was widespread,
and he had recently been profiled for his work in the
Denver newspapers and in *Colorado Homes and Life-
styles*. Peter didn't feign modesty about his carpentry.
"The right piece of wood is a piece of wood that's
waiting to become a chest, or a bed, or a chair. The
wrong piece you have to *make into* a chest or a bed or a

chair. I find the wood that is waiting." His work was usually commissioned a year in advance. He never charged enough for any of it.

Becoming a father had seemed to change him in intrinsic ways. Not enough to shake his character, but he was five degrees less frivolous here, ten degrees more responsible there. He was more focused. He smiled more.

I knew all these things about Peter. In retrospect, I didn't know obvious things. I didn't know much about his life before he moved into the house up the hill. I knew little about his family in Wyoming. I didn't know if he had ever been a Cub Scout or played second base in Little League or puffed into a clarinet in the high school band.

Still, I lived next to him for ten years with the illusion that I knew him well. But then so did Adrienne, his wife.

After he was murdered, we both found out we didn't know shit.

Saturday morning, a little after six, I watched headlights carve a winding path down the lane that led to my house. Since the guy who delivered the morning paper had come and gone, the car, I surmised, was evidence that Adrienne was getting home from what I knew had been a particularly gruesome night at the hospital. The front page of the newspaper was covered with the story of the Allenspark school-bus crash.

I walked through the house and opened the front door to greet Adrienne on our shared driveway. My plan was to offer her the option of unwinding from her overnight ordeal at the hospital by commiserating with a sympathetic friend—me—instead of just going home and sleeping off the night's horrors the way a drunk sleeps off a bender.

But the approaching car wasn't Adrienne's minivan. It was a familiar Ford sedan. The front tires crackled to a stop on the gravel five feet from where I was standing. Sam Purdy got out. I tensed at the sight of him. Police detectives, friends or not, arriving uninvited at the cusp of dawn tend not to be bearing good news.

Emily followed me to the door. She was a big bear of a dog whose color was the dusky brown of clay dirt after a rain. She'd lived with Lauren and me only three days. I had just adopted her, an orphaned show-reject, at a breeder's near Cheyenne. In her brief stay with us, Emily had yet to develop any proprietary interest in either our little house or our safety, so she didn't bark at the arrival of a stranger.

The first time Sam Purdy had ever arrived at my door, years before, he'd come to interrogate me. The last dozen or so times, he'd come as a friend. This time, Sam looked miserable. His clothing told me he was on the job. He wore his trademark herringbone sportcoat over a plaid shirt. His stained tie was loose at the collar.

"Hi, Sam. This doesn't look good—your being here." I assumed he had come to talk with my wife, who was a deputy DA. "You want coffee?"

"I could use some, sure, if it's made." He squatted down and greeted Emily, who took a step back from him. "You got a new dog? That's great. What's her name?"

"Her name is Emily. Just got her a few days ago. She's two. So far, we think she's wonderful."

"She's the same as the other one, isn't she?"

"Yeah, she's a Bouvier, just like Cicero."

Sam examined my face curiously, the way people do the day after I shave off my beard and they haven't yet figured out what's different.

In the next breath, he told me that Peter had been murdered.

I don't know how much time passed before I felt his hands guide me to a chair. Sitting, I stared at him in disbelief, and made him repeat what he had said.

When he did, and the words were exactly the same, I turned away and stared outside in vacant denial. My impulse was simple. I wanted to run across the drive and ring Peter's doorbell five times, ten, however many times it took until he answered. Sam's voice finally cracked once again into my conscious thoughts. He was trying to tell me what had happened. Twice I interrupted him and asked if he was sure it was Peter.

He was. Slowly his story began to register, and I let myself get consumed by the details.

"No? Just like the Denver thing?"

"Maybe like that. Too soon to tell."

"But it looks the same, Sam? The same guy killed Peter?"

"Yeah, like I said, maybe. As far as what I know from reading the papers. It looks the same. We've got a call in to the Denver homicide people. See if the details match. But it looks like it might be the same MO as the Denver theatre murder."

The horror was still hovering—unreal, distant. "Does that mean that Peter was killed by a serial killer? Is two enough?"

"Hell, it always starts with one, doesn't it? FBI criteria say you need three to call it a serial. But there's no doubt in my mind after what I've seen in the last few hours that we have to consider we have some kind of ritual murderer on our hands. That is, if the details check out."

"This wasn't like ... a bungled robbery or something?"

"No. This was a fucking freak show. A psychopathic fucking freak show." He remembered something that caused his face to contort briefly. "No robbery this time. Last night's show was some New Age musical crap. Sold out in advance. Only cash on hand at the theatre was concession receipts. It's not like at a movie theatre that has an on-site box office. Manager says he doesn't think anything was stolen, anyway."

"I don't believe this." *Oh Peter, what did they do to you?*

My thoughts again refused to budge from the living, and I saw Peter's face as clearly as if he were in front of me. He wasn't smiling. His eyes sparkled with a wealth of secrets but were also darkened by shadows. I tried to comprehend the fact that he would never see Jonas walk or hear him sing. That he would never drink any of the fine wine in his basement, or fulfill his dream of trekking in Nepal.

"You haven't talked to Adrienne yet?" I said to Sam. If I couldn't embrace Peter, at least I wanted to be with her.

"His wife?"

I nodded.

"Swallow *this*. She was in the ER at Community last night when he was brought in. She saw him there, stood by during the attempt to resuscitate him. It was awful, apparently. She spent a half hour alone with his body, then went back into the operating room to work on a kid from the school-bus crash. I called the hospital on the way over here—she's still there. You know about the school bus?"

"Yes." I couldn't imagine what last night had been like for Adrienne. "I just don't believe this," I said.

*   *   *

I was dressed and ready to go five minutes later.
Lauren was numbed by the news of why I was waking
her and rushing out of the house. She pulled on a robe
and hugged me, her arms full of comfort. We held
each other for a while. She came upstairs to lay eyes
on the messenger and to encourage Sam and me to
head off without her. She would get dressed, she said,
check on Jonas and Lisa, his nanny, and then go find
Adrienne.

Like a vapor, Sam Purdy's portly frame seemed to
expand to fill whatever space was available. Half the
time I was in his company I felt that I was surrounded
by him. Sitting in his department car that morning
was a suffocating experience.

I felt a tear in my eye. I brushed it away with the
back of my hand and asked Sam what he wanted
from me.

He was trying to turn left from Spanish Hills onto
South Boulder Road, but even on weekend mornings
the traffic into Boulder from the eastern suburbs was
stretched out like a rope. After about forty-five seconds of feigned patience he plopped a magnetic light
on top of the Ford and pulsed the siren three times
until he succeeded in edging out into traffic. A quarter
mile down the road he turned off the electronics and
answered my question.

"If—let me repeat, it's a big 'if'—but if this is a ritual
killing, and if this was done by the same asshole who
butchered that guy at the Performing Arts Complex in
Denver last month, I'm going to be needing to look at
the crime scene in special ways. Psychological ways. I

have to be prepared to start profiling this killer from the get-go. What I want from you, Alan, is your perspective, your point of view. I want you to examine the scene as a psychologist, see what strikes you, see if you can tell me anything about this creep."

When the argument he expected from me failed to materialize, he continued, "See, what usually happens—with rituals and serials—is that the forensic shrinks have to work from photographs of the early crimes. Because for the first couple of murders, the homicide cops usually don't know they have a serial on their hands, so they don't call in shrinks to examine the scene. But I want you to see this one, live and in person, just in case my hunch is right."

I was staring across the front seat to the south, past the Flatirons, toward Eldorado Canyon. It's where Peter loved to climb, that's what I was thinking. I said, "Sam, I'm flattered at your faith in me, but you know I'm not a forensic psychologist. I don't know anything about serial killers."

He turned his big head toward me. He said, "Come on, Alan." His tone was admonishing. It focused me. "Don't crap out on me. You know about sociopaths?"

"Yes."

"You know about psychopaths?"

"Yes."

"What's today? Friday?"

"Saturday, I think."

"Whatever. By Monday, with what I'm gonna give you to read, you'll have completed a postdoc in ritual murder." His tone softened as rapidly as it had sharpened. He said, "I don't want to turn to a stranger for this. And I don't think you want me to, either. You know about profiling, right?"

"I know what it is. But it's a specialized skill, Sam. One I'm not trained in."

With undisguised sarcasm Sam said, "My problem today, Alan, is that I don't happen to know any other psychologist who *is* adept at profiling who I can roust out of bed at the crack of dawn a few hours after a good friend of yours is murdered. Fuck—I want your help, okay? I trust your opinion. I trust your bullshit threshold. So this morning, please, just put on your shrink hat and come in to that theatre with me and *notice.* Pay attention to what some asshole did to your friend. Feel him. Feel the killer. Taste him. Smell him.

"Somehow, he left himself all over the stage of that theatre. They always do. What he did. What he didn't do. How he picked Peter. If he got his rocks off. How he got his rocks off. How he planned it. How long he waited. How much control he had. How much control he lost.

"Maybe the guy thinks he was a ghost last night. He wasn't, I promise. There's traces of him still in there. And I want to find every last trace."

He turned right onto Broadway.

"What that asshole did to Peter Arvin, it's there. *How* he did it. It's there. What he *felt* while he was planning it, doing it. What *need* it met. It's all there. And that kind of crap is your business. I want you to do an intake on a ghost this morning. And this one, I can fucking assure you, ain't named Casper."

The Boulder Theatre graces Fourteenth Street just off the brick-paved paths of the Downtown Boulder Mall. The theatre is adorned with a charming art-deco façade and its retro ambience never fails to yank me back to preadolescent memories of Jujubes, pubescent bosoms, and sweaty palms in the balcony. In its various incarnations since being constructed as the Curran Opera House at the turn of the century, the Boulder Theatre had been a legitimate theatre, a first-run movie house, and a third-run movie house. Lately it had been a music hall and, on occasion, a community theatre.

Driving up to the police barricade that morning with Sam, I was still praying that he was wrong, that this was not going to be the first time that the victim of a homicide at the Boulder Theatre didn't get right back up.

I didn't know what else to do. So I sat down.

I chose an aisle seat on the left side, maybe halfway to the stage.

A few years back, the theatre had been remodeled to accommodate rock and roll, dancing, and the sale of alcoholic beverages. The long rows of wooden theatre seats that had held fannies for decades had been replaced with unremarkable aluminum-framed, fabric-cushioned chairs. The rear of the seating area had been carved out to make room for a bar, and a part of the lobby was now open to the orchestra section. A parquet dance floor hugged the front of the stage.

The theatre reeked of alcohol and old beer. The mustiness of the cavernous space was heady and unpleasant. Glare from the houselights scalded the room, highlighting every scar. Circles of fossilized chewing gum dotted the floor. The ornately painted ceilings and walls were in good repair, but lower down, where the patrons could do their inevitable damage, the paint was scratched and filthy. Theatres, it seemed to me just then, stashed all their charm in the dark, like saloons.

Dark or light, though, this room knew no time of day; noon and midnight were absolutely irrelevant where I sat. I exhaled and imagined midnight, the previous midnight, and tried to drink it all in.

Three people, two men in uniform and a woman wearing a long, black raincoat, were huddled stage left. The acoustics of the theatre let me know that they were whispering but didn't let me know about what. The woman waved to Sam Purdy. He took a final glance down at me, wondering, I thought, whether he could risk leaving me unattended, shoved his hands in his pockets, and continued down the aisle to join the huddle.

Yellow crime-scene tape marked off the whole proscenium and two discrete areas in the orchestra. I watched Sam step over the tape and become a fourth whisperer onstage.

The crime-scene specialists had apparently already come and gone, taking with them certain and uncertain residue of Peter's murder. How they were going to decipher what dust, which hairs, and which fingerprints were important was beyond my comprehension. Last night, this room had been filled with hundreds of people, every one of them shedding, sweating, sneezing, touching.

In the end, though—late—there had only been two people here. Peter. And Peter's killer. I knew one. I was supposed to help Sam find the other.

At first I told myself it wouldn't be too hard, what Sam wanted me to do. One look at the stage filled me with false confidence; I guessed immediately why Peter had been here so late. He had been installing or modifying sets he was building for a benefit performance of a local production of Noël Coward's *Present Laughter*. Peter donated a generous amount of set-design and construction time to local theatre groups. I specifically remembered his mentioning that he was helping with this production, a benefit for the local AIDS hospice.

From my seat I could see a couple of partial sets in the wing stage left. On the stage itself sat a single wheeled unit that was raked slightly toward the audience. Because the piece was center stage, and because I sat in a pretty good seat in the orchestra, I had no trouble believing that the dark stains on the set were just part of the scenery.

So I was actually surprised when I realized that I was probably looking at Peter's blood.

I still didn't know how he had died. But sitting there, my breath shallow, the silence and the clear white light chilling me, I began to wonder if the killing had been a sexual thing.

Certainly not sex the way my more disturbed patients might elucidate the act in their fantasies. This would have been sex on the edge of a knife, sex in a dark world I didn't know and had never wanted to visit. This would be a place where the balance between aggression and eroticism has shifted, where rage subsumes lust, where ferocity devours passion.

Although I made a guess, the precise location where Peter had been found by the custodian wasn't clear. The scenery onstage looked to be a partial set of a living room. I surmised that it was the centerpiece of a triptych of scenery that Peter had constructed to come together as a parlor for the play.

The dominant piece on the set was a white piano. Grand? Baby grand? I don't know pianos. But if the blood was a reliable clue, that's where Peter had been killed. On that piano. Dark stains—from my vantage point I couldn't call them red—started in numerous places on the top of the piano and then followed the angle of the rake as the lines narrowed like tributaries into two discrete trickles that had plunged onto a white carpet below. The dripping had stopped hours ago.

If someone just dimmed the houselights and brought up the spots, it would be so easy to believe that it was all just paint or whatever it is that theatre sorcerers use to fool the eye into seeing blood.

While I sat mesmerized by the bloody piano, Sam Purdy was suddenly next to me, his appearance instantaneous and magical, like a special effect. "When the custodian found him, Peter was on the piano. He was naked, faceup. As you can see, he'd lost a lot of blood by then."

I couldn't bear to speak out loud about the details of Peter's murder. "How were the lights set?" I asked, curious at my own inquiry.

Sam said, "Hmmm." He reached into his sport-coat, retrieved a notebook and pen, and jotted something down.

"Was that Lucy up there? The woman you were talking to?" I asked. Lucy Tanner was another Boulder Police detective, a protégée of Sam's.

"No, that's a homicide detective from Denver. Came to check for similarities with their crime. Maybe point some things out to us."

New patients like to tell stories that attempt to explain how and why they have ended up sitting and talking with a stranger who is charging them two dollars a minute. The stories they tell are usually poignant, often tragic.

Sam wanted this theatre to tell me a story, to tell me what had happened that had drawn me here early on a Saturday morning. Here to seat 11, row J. I knew I could be, and ultimately would be, cruelly captivated by the story of Peter's murder, but there were other things I needed to absorb first.

Pay attention, Alan. The killer was *here.*
Find him.

My reluctance about being in this cold theatre with Sam had vanished. My reluctance about probing the distant mind of my friend's killer had disappeared. To my complete surprise, I had surrendered to this task. I wanted to be there and I wanted to find the murderer.

I wanted him.

"Why are those seats marked off with tape?" I pointed to two rectangles of a dozen seats, one rectangle third- and fourth-row center, the other the first two rows in the balcony. Again, center.

"A tip from the homicide cop in Denver. It looks like this guy changes roles. First he's director, then actor. Finally, he's audience. Maybe he sat in both those sections of seats. Afterward. To admire the work he'd done onstage. But you can't go in there. The crime-scene investigators are on their way back to process those areas for prints and trace evidence—and other things."

"Can I walk around?"

"Wherever you need to go, except those two areas, and don't go up onstage without me."

First I went back to the lobby and this time reentered the theatre with different eyes, feeling instinctively that the killer didn't come in this way and find Peter alone onstage fussing with the carpentry on the sets. That would have been too haphazard an entry. Peter could have run out either of two nearby fire doors. No, I was guessing that this production had been scripted much more carefully than that.

"The murderer attended the show last night, didn't he?"

Sam had apparently approached the same conclusion himself. At first he said nothing in response to my pronouncement. Then he asked, "Do you want to know what we know?"

"No, I don't think so, not yet."

"Good. I think that's better."

I approached the rectangle of seats marked off in the balcony. I sat in the first seat outside the yellow tape and gazed down at the piano. I imagined Peter being cut, being tortured, bleeding to death. The image flickered; I couldn't hold on to it.

Moving to the lower rectangle, I chose another seat just outside the yellow tape, front-row center, and tried to refocus my imagination from there, from the best seat in the house. The outcome was the same. Flickering, strobe-lit images. Trails.

"Can I go up onstage?"

"Sure, come on." He led me stage left and lifted the yellow tape. I scooted under it and walked up the stairs. The uniformed cops and the raincoated woman were nowhere around. I had not noticed them leaving.

My hands were deep in my pockets, my shoulders slightly hunched. I didn't know what the hell I was doing. For me that's not a particularly novel state of affairs, and clinically I actually thrive on it. Patients walk into my office with new stories all the time, wondering how many times I've dealt with similar things before.

"My husband likes for me to squat over him and

pee on his face. Do you have any experience with that?"

No, but I'm willing to learn. Teach me.

"You should probably know that Peter was tied to the top of the piano. One limb to each leg."

I looked at the piano and felt I could suffocate in the image of Peter being tortured there. I wanted to find a phone and call him so he could tell me that this was all a mistake.

"Where are the—?"

"We've got them. They'll go to CBI. We have photos of what it looked like when we go there. You can see them whenever you want. But you need to keep in mind that everything we're doing here is complicated by the fact that the scene was contaminated. Peter's body had already been moved by his friend, a custodian. He's the one who found him and brought him to the ER at Community."

Sam had invited me here for answers, and all I had were questions. This was beginning to seem familiar, almost exactly like clinical work.

Why had Peter been chosen for this role? How had he been coerced into mounting that piano and permitting himself to be drawn and tied? What dance had preceded it? How was he being threatened? With the knife? Was it a knife? Did he know his killer? What? *What?*

For a short while, perhaps a minute, I cried. Sam stayed next to me, quietly.

I wiped my eyes. "Where else were they? I mean, together. Where else did they go?"

"This stays here, right?"

"Yes."

"We think just up on the stage. Maybe over there, by those other two pieces of scenery on that side of the stage. Then back on the stage. With the piano. Except for a trail outside, when his friend carried him to the truck, the only blood we've found is either on the piano or on the rug. So we don't think Peter was moved once he started to bleed. The murder took place center stage, right where the piano is now."

Four crime-scene investigators pounded through the doors from the street into the lobby, puncturing the silence. They carried heavy equipment in molded plastic cases. The woman in the black raincoat appeared behind them and directed them to the taped-off areas in the first two rows of the balcony and at the front of the orchestra.

I watched two of them get started with 35mm cameras. Then a floodlight for video washed the rim of the balcony. I noticed a glint of light reflect off the glass of two projection rooms high at the back of the theatre.

"There're a lot of little rooms up there, behind the balcony. We think maybe that's where the offender hid, waiting for the theatre to clear out after the show. Or maybe downstairs—there's a mess of dressing rooms downstairs."

"How did he know someone would be here? How did he know he would have a victim?"

"That's one of our questions."

The two criminalists with the video equipment came down the balcony stairs and began to film the other area, the one close to the stage.

Sam said, "You know about George Paper?"

"No. Should I?"

He shrugged. "Theatre manager told me about George Paper. Seemed to think I should consider him a suspect."

"You already have a suspect?"

He cracked a grin. In these circumstances, it looked almost evil.

"George Paper was the first projectionist the theatre ever had, a lot of years ago. An old guy, white hair. The story goes that he hanged himself, right over there." Sam raised his arm and pointed to a jumble of thick ropes on the wall of the theatre twenty feet from the other side of the stage.

"Suicide?"

"Some say suicide, some say accident, some say 'Who knows?' Theatre manager says George is still here, hanging around, so to speak. He's seen him a few times himself."

I patted him on the shoulder. "This is great, Sam, it sounds like you've already got yourself either a suspect or a witness. With George Paper's help, this investigation should be cake. You don't need me."

He led me down a staircase into a hallway lined with dressing rooms, grungy lounges, and utility rooms. I poked my head into each space.

"What?"

"I just want you to get a feel."

"Were they down here?"

"We don't think so." He led me back upstairs.

I pointed to a door on the south side of the orchestra. "Where does that go?"

"A little courtyard. It's enclosed. The only exits are here, to the alley. And the front doors to Fourteenth Street."

I glanced toward the doors. "No exit alarms?"

"No."

I turned to Sam and said, "Take me home. I want to go see Adrienne and see how she's doing. And I need to decide if I'm going to help you with this. If I say yes, I want to see that stuff you have for me to read. Everything you have. After I digest it, you can tell me what you guys have already figured out. Then maybe we can talk. *If* I say yes."

The corners of Sam's mouth rose. He figured he already had me.

Sam knew what he was doing. This field trip to the theatre had short-circuited my shock. Now I was getting angry. And Sam wanted me angry, angry enough to savor the opportunity to do something— anything—to get even.

———◁◦▷———

"What was he like? Peter?"

When we left the theatre and got into his car Sam didn't start the engine right away. He had asked me a simple question and he was waiting for an answer. I knew that in another circumstance, with another cop, this conversation might have started with "Did the deceased have any enemies?"

How often do we think about what our friends are like? Especially old friends. Dear friends.

"Peter was smoke, Sam. Underneath, something was always smoldering, but when you were with him, he was always just smoke."

I was still waiting for him to start the car. "That's it? The guy's your friend, your neighbor, for ten years, and all you can tell me is that he was 'smoke'?"

For no reason I was aware of, I smiled. "I can tell you a thousand things. A million Peter stories. I can tell you what he liked, what he loved, what currently baffled him. But I can't really tell you what he was like. Because there wasn't a single soul that Peter trusted with that. Not one. Maybe Adrienne. I don't know, maybe not even her. And Jonas—his baby— Jonas is the only human being that Peter really let in."

Although my grief had set me rambling, Sam was trying hard to be patient. I appreciated it.

"And?"

"Before Jonas, Peter never let anybody depend on him. He once told me that reliance is a breath away from dying. He and I talked about it, well, a lot."

"You guys were close?"

"We were friends, Sam. We spent a lot of time together, mostly doing stuff. Like you and me. But are *we* close? To be honest with myself, I would have to admit that Peter and I were never that intimate. I never had the illusion that Peter was vulnerable to me. My opinions might have amused him, or enraged him, but Peter was insulated from rebuke or praise, mine or anybody else's."

Sam finally started the car and said, "I know you're trying, but so far this isn't particularly helpful."

"Peter was like no one else I know. In some ways, he was a nut. In others, he was a genius. Like with wood." Sam turned the corner. My thoughts changed. "He was a loner, too. That may be important. Being at the theatre by himself late at night, that's Peter. All of his favorite things he did alone. Carpentry, rock climbing, backpacking, running."

We were caught behind an RTD bus at the corner of Spruce and Broadway. It seemed to me that the diesel fumes were being injected directly from the bus's exhaust into the passenger compartment of Sam's car.

When the light changed, the bus blessed us with a final blast of sickly air, and Sam turned right.

"Where are you going?"

"You said you want to see your friend, Peter's wife. I'm betting she's still at the hospital."

"God, I hope not."

He returned the conversation to Peter. "So far, we've arrived at the fact that he was a loner."

"Yes. Except for sex and tennis, he preferred to do his favorite things alone."

"You know about his sex life?"

"I know about the tennis. The sex-life part is conjecture. Witness Jonas."

"The marriage, how was it?"

"I thought Adrienne had an alibi."

"Humor me here."

I weighed my response. "Don't take this the wrong

way, but what they had wasn't my kind of marriage. But it was steady and constant and not disagreeable."

"What made it not to your liking?"

"Sometimes couples have individual differences that complement each other. You know—one is quiet, the other is a talker. With Peter and Adrienne, you never felt the complement. They were like parallel lines."

"What was the glue?"

That was easy; I didn't even have to think about the answer. "Respect. They respected each other. Infinitely."

———৩৩৩———

While Sam and I were busy at the Boulder Theatre, Lauren had walked up the hill to Adrienne and Peter's house and awakened Lisa, the nanny, to check on Jonas. Lisa was shocked and uncomprehending at the news of Peter's death, but promised to stay with Jonas as long as necessary. Lauren's next stop was the lounge outside the Community Hospital operating rooms, where Adrienne was assisting a vascular surgeon who was repairing a fresh bleed in one of the young school-bus crash victims. Lauren thought she heard a nurse say it was a kidney.

Sam dropped me off at the hospital, and I tracked

Lauren down in the lounge. I relieved her so she could return home to be close to Jonas.

When Adrienne finally finished up in the operating room, she accepted a long embrace from me, immediately adding that she needed to make rounds on the kids she had treated since the bus accident the previous evening. I suggested that one of her partners would gladly take her place. She said no, she would do it.

I started to argue. She warned me off with her eyes and with a curt "Not yet, Alan. Not now."

My impulse was to comfort her. To hold her. To say silly things that might soften the shell of her grief. She had ministered to me at times when I needed *her* touch. But she wasn't ready for my help.

Frustrated, I accompanied her to the pediatric ward and then to the ICU and waited nearby while she chatted with the injured children and their parents, read chart notes, jotted down orders, and sniped at the nurses. The sniping wasn't stress-induced, some understandable genuflection to the pressure of Peter's murder. It was just Adrienne being Adrienne. It worried me that Adrienne was behaving—well, normally. It would have worried the nurses if Dr. Adrienne had been acting any other way.

Rounds completed, and no more easy excuses not to go home available to her, Adrienne agreed to let me drive her minivan back to Spanish Hills. On the way, I offered her every opportunity to talk. She said she couldn't. "Maybe later," she said.

Lisa had taken Jonas into town to pick up warm bagels from Moe's, and she greeted us at the door with an aromatic offer of a hot meal. Adrienne declined. Lauren had watched the minivan arrive home, and in two minutes she, too, was at Peter and Adrienne's house. She and Adrienne hugged. We all said some banal and forgettable things, and when I embraced Adrienne again, I moistened her hair with my tears. She smiled ruefully and touched me on the side of my neck. Then I watched as she plucked a fading Jonas from Lisa's arms and retreated upstairs to her bedroom to rest. She and her baby. As though an explanation were required, she said, "I don't want to sleep long. He'll be my alarm clock. Lisa, you'll stay?" and bounced up the stairs. Yes, *bounced*, her always-abundant energy seemingly undiminished.

In the midafternoon she descended the stairs to discover her house had begun to fill with friends.

Over the course of the day a few dozen people stopped by to be with Adrienne and to be respectful to Peter's memory. I knew about half the callers, and considered a handful of those to be good friends. Diane, my partner at work, and her husband, Raoul, came. Two of Adrienne's urological partners. Our mutual neighbor down the hill. Many of the guests brought food. As the numbers increased, Lisa went downstairs to Peter's basement wine cache to retrieve something to serve the many guests. Peter, I'm certain, would not have endorsed her choice of refreshments. Fifteen-year-old Talbot would hardly have been the wine he would have selected to accompany the bagels, cold cuts, salads, and covered casseroles.

Shortly before dusk, as the sun bent to kiss the layered clouds above the mountains, Lauren and I strolled hand in hand across the dusty driveway to our house.

Adrienne had refused our offer to join us for dinner. She said she needed to be alone.

———❧———

Lauren parked herself in front of the television and got lost in the hacked-up network premiere of a forgettable movie starring Meg Ryan. I made us both some tea, left a small bowl of mai tai–flavored jelly beans next to her on the couch, curled up in the living room in my green leather chair, and dug into *Sexual Homicides: Patterns and Motives* with an ardor I could not have previously imagined. Besides the book by Burgess, Douglas, and Ressler, the grocery bag of material that Sam Purdy had left on my doorstep also included a number of government documents on the psychological profiling of violent criminals, mostly generated by the Investigative Support Unit of the FBI at Quantico. From his personal library, Sam had also provided me with Ginsburg's *The Shadow of Death*, *Beyond Murder* by Philpin and Donnelly, *Whoever Fights Monsters* by Ressler and Schactman, and a whole file of reprints from the *Law Enforcement Bulletin* and other cop-journals.

I read transcripts of interviews with serial killers. I read Ted Bundy's words, David Berkowitz's

meanderings, theories about Jeffrey Dahmer's up-
bringing and the Boston Strangler's rage. I read
about the carnage inflicted by organized killers and
the chaos and mayhem left behind by disorganized
ones. I read about child abuse and the worst families, about child abuse and the best families.

I looked at crime-scene photos of brutality that
almost numbed me. Almost.

I was a student again. It had never been my best
role. But I voluntarily descended into a world that was
more vile than any I had ever imagined.

And I was engrossed.

When she was tired, truly tired, Lauren's voice
assumed a pebbled texture, like a gravel road's, but
softer and stickier, as though the surface were slick
with honey. On those rare occasions when she was
both chatty and exhausted, I loved listening to this
late-night burr, found it at once erotic and maternal. I
sometimes postponed sleep just to keep her talking a
little longer. But this Saturday night I was ambivalent
about Lauren's soliloquy, because her sandpaper-and-
syrup tone sang a lullaby of despair, each verse
recounting for me some part of Adrienne's manner of
grieving, or not grieving, for her dead husband.

Our bedroom was cold, and Lauren slept naked.
Although the consequences of multiple sclerosis caused
her, generally, to be phobic of heat, this night the duvet
was pulled tightly to her chin. She was on her side,
facing me, her hair inky and dense on the pillow. A few
long strands feathered up from her head, as though
they had been blown by some breeze that had gusted

from the foot of the bed. As clearly as if it were a gentle beast hovering in the shadows, I knew that slumber hung close by, waiting for the tiniest of openings to spring out and capture her for the night. I knew, too, that I could thwart her dreams if I wanted, with a touch or a kiss. Instead, I waited. In the middle of a sentence—something poignant about Adrienne's resolve to raise Jonas as well as if he had two parents—her eyelids closed slowly and sleep took her hostage. I kissed her shoulder and lay back, quite awake, my head propped by two pillows.

I returned to the books and journals and continued to read. Within an hour I had come to the conclusion that the term "sexual psychopath" had the truest ring of all.

This literature spread on the bedclothes all around me also referred to these violent repeat murderers as other things, most often "serial killers." But that identifier felt inadequate to me. Not necessarily wrong, but misleading. Because, as a label, "serial killer" seemed to focus almost entirely on the linearity and incremental nature of the killing, as a flat stone skipping on water might be described as causing serial splashes.

Lauren startled me. In a husky voice that husbanded the sleep she was guarding, she asked, "Are you going to be done soon?"

"Yes. I'm having trouble with the nomenclature in this literature. I don't like 'serial killer.'"

"What on earth are you talking about? What time is it?"

"It focuses on the repetition too much." I shared my analogy about the stone skipping on water. "Focusing on the repetition misses the point. For me, as a psychologist, what's interesting about these assholes isn't that they might commit one gruesome murder and then another and another. Hell, after three hours of reading this crap, that's the only part of it that makes *any* sense at all. The serial part of serial killing—the repetition—takes place because the killer is somehow rewarded by the act. That part's simple."

"Rewarded?"

"Sure. These killers are rewarded, whether by pleasure, by decreased tension, by isolation of affect, by sense of accomplishment, by reduction of the compulsion of some fantasy—by *something*—from there on, it's a no-brainer, psychologically speaking, to understand the desire for encores. Hell, even the *need* for encores."

She reached a warm hand out from below the covers and touched me on the arm. "That's nice. Now please, why don't you go to sleep? You can puzzle this out tomorrow."

I barely heard her plea to shut up because I selfishly needed to continue. "One more minute. The baffling part, see, about these guys who do this again and again is that they *do* enjoy the act, that they *are* rewarded by it. And if I'm going to be of any help to Sam in profiling Peter's killer, that's where the money is. I have to discover why this guy enjoyed the act. And what piece of it he did enjoy."

Lauren pulled up the covers. "Fine. Good luck. Good night."

"Good night. I love you."

I kept reading. The act of killing, I was learning, was

sometimes incidental, not intrinsic. The fantasy before the murder was intrinsic. The torture was intrinsic. The killing, though—sometimes the killing was a convenient and sure way to quiet the solitary witness to the fantasy and the torture.

Time passed. Pages turned. Once again Lauren rolled toward me, shading her eyes with her hand. I guessed that she had been awake, this time, for a while.

The cushion gone from her voice, she said, "Tomorrow. Do it tomorrow. Go to sleep."

"Listen to me for a minute more. Please." I wanted her to argue with me, to assist in focusing my thoughts.

"No. Either go to sleep or take that stuff someplace else. Having this in bed is too weird, even for me."

Although I knew I wouldn't go right to sleep, I threw the papers on the floor and turned off the light, the whole time acutely conscious of the proximate pulse and the shallow breathing of a naked woman with whom I was very much in love.

The incongruity was stupendous.

Peter, can you hear me?

Who did this?

Guide me.

I leaned over and kissed Lauren on the cheek, holding my lips to her warm flesh until she stirred.

The stirring, that night, it was important.

I finally slept, and dreamed not at all about killers and rapists.

II

Amateur Hour

By nature, Adrienne isn't a calm person. A house-fly trapped by a window appears sedate when compared with her intensity. So, although my decision to honor her request to walk to the Downtown Boulder Mall and buy her a double espresso seemed a bit like giving in and introducing Sleepy or Dopey to a dealer who could supply him with a few more Quaaludes—compassion and friendship prevailed over reason.

Her welcome invitation came Tuesday, the day after Peter's funeral. Sunday, Adrienne had been forced to endure lengthy interviews with Sam Purdy and his partner, Lucy Tanner, and had hibernated with Lisa and Jonas for the balance of the day. Monday brought the social responsibilities of the funeral services and burial. She had family, hers and Peter's, to cope with at all the services, and I thought she managed her many roles remarkably. Not with any grace, though; that wouldn't have been Adrienne. Let's just call her stoic and competent, always sarcastic, and occasionally borderline rude.

Adrienne was aware that I was helping Sam Purdy construct a psychological profile of the murderer who had left her husband to bleed to death on the stage of the Boulder Theatre.

Her reaction when I first relayed that news had

been characteristically Adrienne. "What, you? The police can't find someone who has done this before? Like even once?"

I had assured her that my unstudied efforts as a psychological profiler weren't intended to suffice. The FBI's seasoned criminal-profiling experts at Quantico would also construct a profile of Peter's murderer.

"Why amateur hour, then, Sherlock? Are you like an intern? An apprentice? What?"

"Sam wanted a second opinion. He knew he'd be getting a profile from the FBI. He thought I would be particularly motivated because I was Peter's friend. And I was available to see the crime scene; the FBI guys wouldn't see it, so Sam figured I might be able to tell him something useful before he hears definitively from the feds." When I looked over to assess her reaction, she seemed unconvinced by my argument. So I changed my approach. "And I'm pretty smart, Adrienne. I'm as good at what I do as you are at what you do. People are often eager for my help, and, believe it or not, they're usually grateful that they got it."

She froze me with her dark eyes. "You don't know from grateful, sweetie," she scoffed. "You help somebody feel less depressed, or even if you fix a man's broken arm, you might get 'grateful.' But if you fix a man's dick, you get a friend for life. Believe me, that's *grateful.* I know from grateful."

Adrienne and I were old friends. Ten years before, when she had first moved up the hill from me into the grand house that had belonged to my landlady of many years, we initially greeted each other warily.

Her view of westerners seemed to have been filtered through images of John Wayne and Ronald Reagan.

For a few awkward weeks, our houses were separated not only by a wide gravel driveway, and a wider disparity of property values, but also by an uneasiness accentuated by good old-fashioned mistrust and ignorance.

Peter, on the other hand, walked from west to east as though he had never noticed a frontier. He was Adrienne's prototypical western man. They had met while she was in medical school and had somehow connected romantically. Upon the completion of her residency, Boulder had been the compromise location they chose for establishing her practice.

If they were going to be in the West, Adrienne would have preferred a real western city, which to her seemed limited to Chicago, or, for some reason I could never comprehend, Portland. Peter insisted on proximity to the mountains. Adrienne could find only one place that met their criteria: the Front Range of the Rockies. Without trying too hard, she got an offer to join a growing group urology practice in Boulder.

When they came to town and moved in up the hill, I was still single. She and Peter were already married, and before long she had grown quite committed to "fixing dicks," as she occasionally called the healing activities of her urology practice.

Maybe because our cynicism seemed to flutter on similar wavelengths or maybe because she found me such a receptive audience for her irreverence, Adrienne and I soon developed an intimacy that transcended our backgrounds, which differed many degrees in gender, culture, religion, and geography. I loved her dearly and was greatly troubled by the fact that we hadn't spoken compassionately for more than a moment since the tragedy at the theatre.

That's partly why I agreed to buy her the double espresso.

She chose Chucho's for her coffee fix. To get there from my office on the west end of Walnut, we had to walk past the Trident, Peaberry, the Book End Cafe, and at least a couple of other coffee bars on the mall. I didn't mind the pleasant walk at all. But to test her mood, I asked, "Why Chucho's?"

"Because they don't treat the act of drinking coffee as though it's something new and important and because it isn't full of people with tattoos I don't understand and precious metal shoved through visible body parts." A four-block detour to avoid being affronted by trendiness. Not always easy in Boulder, but for Adrienne a small price to pay.

The outdoor mall that anchors Boulder's downtown was resplendent in floral affirmations of early spring. We were walking from west to east, enjoying the bricked-in gardens that were already dense with neat platoons of tulips. The trees had begun to leaf out with the pale green promise of what I hoped would be an early and enduring end to winter.

Adrienne drank her double espresso European-style, standing at the varnished bar, which barely reached the top of her bosom. She dumped two sugars into Chucho's best, and I watched her down it in about three swills. My longing for a leisurely cup of coffee with my friend drained as fast as did her cup. She said, "Let's walk."

I took my coffee to go. She turned back to the west purposefully, as though she had a destination.

The mountains vault up four blocks away from Boulder's downtown with a stunning abruptness. When the sun is high and the trees aren't yet fully leafed out, the foothills of the Rockies define vertical space with defiant wonder, daring eyes to the heavens. A thousand miles away, the ocean urges eyes to the horizon with the same insistence, making everything seem limited and limitless all at once.

"You're being patient with me. I appreciate that. Waiting for me to talk, I mean."

Adrienne sometimes disarmed me when she was agreeable. I squeezed her hand. "I miss him terribly, Ren. I can only guess what it's like for you."

She removed her hand from mine and touched her eyelid with her fingertip. "I've been prepared for him to die, Alan. Really, I never thought Peter would last this long. But, you know, I always thought it would be the damn mountains that got him. An avalanche, or a rock-climbing accident, some whitewater, a stupid grizzly bear. I didn't know what up there would get him, but I always thought it would be the mountains. He wanted to die up there. I was always sure about that. I used to joke with him, ask him which mountain would be my widow's peak. Then Jonas was born. Jonas changed everything for Peter."

I nodded, assuming I was endorsing some universal truth about the effect on grownup lives of the arrival of the young.

She noticed my reflex and immediately rejected it. "I'm not in a platitude mode here. Pay attention.

"It started as a joke, you know. Jonas. His name. I called myself the whale when I was pregnant. We called Jonas 'Pinocchio' while he was in utero. But in the fairy tale, Jonah is the one who is reborn. That's what attracted Peter about the name. Not just the baby's birth, but the chance for rebirth. Peter's reaction surprised all of us. Maybe mostly me. I thought cherishing Jonas was going to be my thing."

"I don't understand what you mean."

She didn't appear to care. She continued with her monologue. "Until Jonas was born, death was going to be an incident for Peter. An interesting one, I think. Like doing a fourteener, or taking a week off to play around in Canyonlands. But I think he viewed it like it would just be something that happened. You know how Peter was. He talked about this shit all the time, about dying, the meaning of life, all that existential crap. I mean, while he's putting away groceries, I swear, we would have these long talks about the meaning of decay. Like it's on some cosmic plane right up there with yogurt."

She returned a wave from someone across Broadway, then looked down at her tiny feet. "For Peter, being married to me was never a reason not to die. There was none of that 'I couldn't stand to go through eternity without you' crap or any 'Adrienne needs me, I can't climb mountains anymore, it's too dangerous.' Peter wasn't romantic. And he didn't want me dependent on him. He could not have cared less about material stuff, possessions, but he was always encouraging me to make enough money to support my desires, never to get dependent on what he might provide. It's why he never charged enough for his work. He didn't want me to get used to the money or the security. It's like he always knew he was about to check out. In an odd sort of way he was protective of me, I think."

"He loved you, Adrienne."

She raised her dark eyebrows. "You're sweet. Naïve sometimes, but sweet. This isn't about whether or not he loved me. I know the limits of what Peter and I had. What I'm trying to talk about here is what changed when Jonas was born, what changed inside Peter that allowed him to let someone need him. Because he did let Jonas need him. I still don't understand that—that transformation. And I want to. It's part of saying goodbye to him. Maybe most of what it's going to take to say goodbye to him. Does that sound silly?"

We had talked through a complete cycle of green and red and yellow. The cross-traffic provided a constant buzz. I was distracted by a conversation ten feet away; a city cop was trying to explain downtown Boulder's no-dogs ordinance to a hefty woman with a dachshund on a short golden chain.

"No," I said, "it doesn't sound silly."

"Good. Then I want you to help me," Adrienne said. "I can't do it myself right now. I don't have the energy. I don't have the time. I don't want to upset Jonas's schedule. So I need your help."

"You know I'll do whatever I can, Ren. Lauren and I both will."

I followed her across Broadway. "Apparently I'm not being clear. This isn't an affirmation-of-friendship conversation we're having. I do want your support, sweetie. I do. But what I'm asking for right now, what I *really need*, is some big-time help."

"You want a favor? Sure. Whatever I can do."

She knew I still wasn't getting it. But she was absolutely not averse to taking advantage of my confusion. "Good. Then help me find out why for all those years when he was so willing to die, Peter didn't. And then help me find out why when he was finally so eager to live, he couldn't."

"Why now, Ren? Why not let the dust settle a little?"

"Because I know Peter's family too well. When the dust settles again, they will let it obscure everything. Now's the time to see what was there that he didn't want me to see. I want to know what he left behind. I want to know what formed him." She paused. "And I want to know if Jonas still has a family there. If we're welcome."

—◦◦◦—

Adrienne's visit to my office and her request for help had been a welcome surprise. But, as is often the case where his work is concerned, Sam Purdy's request for help later that day felt more like a summons.

Sam met me at my house in Spanish Hills. Although this was his day off, the reality seemed to be that "days off" were a technicality for a detective investigating a homicide. Sam had agreed to make the drive to Denver during rush hour only because of my schedule. I didn't finish with my last patient that day until five o'clock. Sam's initial response when I told him I would meet him at five-thirty—and not at two, when he wanted to go—was a suggestion that I just cancel my "damn appointments" so that we could be down to Denver and back before traffic clogged the turnpike and the Mousetrap.

The traveling Broadway production of *Miss Saigon* was closing its two-month run at the Buell Theatre the next weekend. Before the road show packed up for Seattle, Sam thought it was important for me to get familiar with the details of exactly how the murder that had preceded Peter's had taken place at the Buell. The Denver murder had been committed on the stage of *Miss Saigon* just about five weeks prior to Peter's death. Sam insisted that making sense of the details, most of which had been kept under wraps, required that I understand how the production of *Miss Saigon* was set up inside the Buell, including how the scenery was installed and how the stage was designed.

After a drive that took most of an hour we arrived at the threshold of downtown Denver. I turned into a side-street canyon shadowed by a few of the buildings of the mammoth Denver Center for the Performing Arts. The many theatres and the adjacent parking garage of the huge complex were loosely connected by a wide concourse of concrete, stone, and brick. Those meandering walkways were covered by a vaulting

glass and aluminum canopy that was intended to be
evocative of the Galleria in Milan.

It wasn't.

Sam told me where to park.

The administrative offices of the DCPA were
housed through a poorly marked and uninviting
entrance that somehow seemed to go upstairs from
the sidewalk and still end up in a basement. As I followed Sam inside to a security door and waited for us
to be buzzed into the adjacent waiting area, I guessed
that the room we were in was somewhere in the
bowels below the blond brick cube building that was
Boettcher Concert Hall, the home of the Denver Symphony. Water pipes, ventilation ducts, and thick con-
duits snaked off in every direction from where Sam
and I stood on scratched linoleum. A fire-alarm panel
the size of a small billboard provided most of the
room's charm. My fantasy that this was going to be
the beginning of a glamorous journey into the arcane
world of the theatre began to suffer some serious
erosion.

The receptionist greeted us without looking up. His
attention was focused on a problem with the keyboard
of his computer and apparently its intricacies were
best assessed if he pushed his black glasses as far
down his long, thin nose as possible. His desk sat
behind a thick glass panel, and I began to wonder,
given the recent murders and all the security, whether
the theatre business wasn't much more dangerous
than I had ever imagined.

A minute or two later, Sam and I turned simultaneously as the sound of footsteps echoed down a wide

corridor. A black man, easily three inches taller than my six-one, walked toward us with long, slow strides. His gaze was directed at the floor and his hands were in the pockets of the trousers of a stylish double-breasted suit. His head was shaved and the skin of his skull glowed like polished copper under the fluorescent glare of the industrial lights. His scalp was almost exactly the same shade as his shoes.

The man looked up suddenly, as though he had just remembered why he was there. The smile that lit his face was as warm as summer sand. He said, "Sam, Sam, so good to see you again," holding out both his arms in greeting. He shook Purdy's hand with one of his own and squeezed his shoulder with the other. A thin mustache graced his upper lip like jewelry, and his dark eyes were laced with pale streaks the color of birchbark.

I was captivated by his voice. Crisp and authoritative, it bore no trace of an accent. If he had been reading from the Koran, I would have been tempted to convert. Each word took its time coming out of his mouth. My impression was that there was no hurry anywhere in this man. Confidence, but no arrogance. I hadn't even been introduced and I liked him already.

I could tell that I was in a wonderfully objective frame of mind. Just perfect for conducting a murder investigation.

Sam said, "Charles Chandler, this is Alan Gregory. *Doctor* Alan Gregory." I couldn't tell whether or not Sam was being sarcastic with his use of the appellation.

"Call me Charley. It's a pleasure to meet you, Alan." He began walking back the way he had come, and I

felt one of his hands on my lower back, gently urging
me along with him. "If you want to see the stage in the
same configuration it was in when Lonnie was killed,
we're going to have to move along a little. The crew
will be here soon to get ready for tonight's performance, and they'll change everything around to get
ready for the curtain."

He led us down a basement corridor and then up a
staircase that emptied into the lobby of the symphony
hall. From there we walked through a connecting
vestibule that housed snack facilities and a bar and,
finally, made our way up a ramp into the festive lobby
of the Buell. The upper levels of the theatre spilled out
onto mezzanines and balconies that were suspended
over the spacious lobby. Staircases to the upper levels
snaked boldly up into the light.

Charley stopped in front of a pair of double doors
that led to the orchestra seating area. "Sam, to be certain I understand, you want me to go through the
whole show again? I know you've been through it
before with Dale."

"I haven't told Alan anything, Charley. I want him
to see it the same way I did. So give him the whole
performance. No Cliff Notes."

Charley nodded and smiled; then he opened one of
the double doors and motioned for us to precede him
into the seating area at the back of the orchestra. The
light from the open door provided the only illumination in the theatre. With the door closed, the light
faded, then disappeared.

I couldn't even see my hands. I tried.

"This is what the theatre looked like that night.

Dark. Very, very dark." Charley Chandler's robust voice sounded as though it were amplified. "If the curtain goes up on time, *Miss Saigon* ends right around ten-forty. Most of the cast and staff are gone as quickly as they can get out of here, certainly by eleven, and the last of the crew are history fifteen minutes later. Twenty, max."

I heard, but didn't see, Charley turn and push the door open behind us and felt some relief as light from the lobby washed back over us. "This way, now, please," he said, and led us briefly back out into the lobby and then down a wide concourse that paralleled the main orchestra seating area. We proceeded down a flight of stairs, through a couple of sets of doors, and finally into another dark room. The place was a maze, which I think was Charley Chandler's point.

This new space was not inky black, but instead illuminated by caged blue lights mounted high up on the walls at intervals of about fifty feet. The blue hue revealed silhouetted shapes jutting up from the floor and hanging like apparitions in the air.

Charley moved away and reached behind a couple of large square objects that I guessed were storage crates of some kind. The blue lights went dark.

So did the room. From a few steps away, I heard Charley's voice.

"We're actually in the stage area, now. Specifically, we're in the wing, stage left. As the audience sees the show, it's the right side of the stage. The Buell is designed with much more space stage left than stage right. The large doors behind us"—he flipped the blue lights back on, barely illuminating two overhead doors ten feet behind where we were standing—"lead directly to an indoor loading dock. We can unload two semis simultaneously, right onto the stage. Please stay here for a moment and don't try to move. I'll turn on the worklights so we can walk around. The stage is treacherous in the dark."

I counted his footsteps as he walked away. Four.

Sam was so silent I wasn't sure he was still with us.

Lauren and I had seen *Miss Saigon* twice. Once in New York when she was living there receiving treatment for her multiple sclerosis, and once during the second week of this run at the Buell. That had been only six weeks ago; our seats for that performance had been about twenty rows back on the left side of the orchestra.

An array of bright lights flashed on from above. The matte black floors, stage, and walls were all devoid of luster and seemed to swallow the light. Suddenly I realized that the dark cavern of silhouettes concealed a riot of shapes and colors. I recognized sets crowding every inch of floor space. A big portion of the U.S. Embassy in Saigon sat incongruously next to peasant dwellings from Vietnam and a whorehouse from Thailand. Everything was disembodied, the theatre equivalent of a jumble of mannequin limbs.

A go-go cage hung right above my head, and barely above eye level a dark, painted sign read, HOT STUFF FOR LOVERS.

Charley spoke. "We entered the stage this way because I wanted you to get a sense of how difficult it would have been to navigate this area in the dark, especially if the murderer was unfamiliar with the stage as it is set up for a production as complex as *Miss Saigon.* The lights were off when the killer started. The stage and both wings are densely packed with scenery. And the switches I've just used are extremely difficult to locate. If you didn't know where they were, it would take half the night just to find them."

I was mesmerized by the clutter. "I had no idea the stage was so crowded."

"The other wing is just as congested as this one. And more of the theatre's battens and pulleys are in use than for any other production that has ever gone on the road."

"What are battens?"

"The battens are the overhead mechanisms—heavy pipes, really—that support the scenery, which is lowered directly onto the stage. Have you seen the show?"

"Yes."

"The embassy fence, for example, is hung directly above the stage and is lowered right into place when it's needed. It's hung on a batten. It's controlled by an old-fashioned counterweight system that's run from the fly floor. Some of the other battens are controlled electronically, curtains and transparent screens and such. I'll show you the fly floor in a minute."

"And the pulleys?"

"The pulley and cable system is motor driven. It raises and lowers the hanging sets that are stored above the stage." He pointed up at the myriad pieces suspended above the wing. "As the pieces are lowered, stagehands manually guide them onto knives that protrude from tracks on the wings of the stage deck. The knives—"

"What do you mean, 'knives'?"

"They're heavy iron blades that are attached to the cables below the stage. They lock into scabbardlike sheaths on the scenery. When the knives are pulled along on their cables, which are under the deck, the sets get pulled along the tracks on the stage. During a show, the movement of the knives—and therefore, the scenery—is preprogrammed and is entirely controlled by computer."

Charley moved over to a twenty-foot-long bank of electronic equipment and computer keyboards and monitors. In front of him three black steps led up onto the stage. "One of these keyboards controls deck cues—those are the instructions for moving the stage-mounted sets and any scenery that travels on the motorized cable-knife track system. The other computer—this one—controls the motors for the battens and pulleys that haven't been set up for manual control from the fly floor. As I said, for this production some of the batten controls are manual, some are computerized. Each keyboard has two monitors, one for use with natural light, the other for use with infrared light for those times when the stage lighting is too dark for standard video cameras. Either computer can back up for the other. But if both of them were out simultaneously, the show couldn't run. The timing required to move all this scenery is much too sophisticated to be handled by humans."

We walked from the wing onto the stage proper, which was empty. "Stand here for a moment. Please don't move until the lights come back on." Ten seconds later the worklights flashed off. Five more seconds and the blue lights followed.

Sam Purdy was next to me in the dark. He spoke for the first time since we'd entered the theatre. "This is what it was like when the murderer arrived onstage." His voice was a whisper, as though he feared being overheard by a phantom audience. "Overnight security is shit, basically consists of three patrols by a solitary guard between the hours of eleven p.m. and eight a.m. The first custodial people don't arrive until around eight in the morning. I'm betting the murderer knew that. He waited until the pre-midnight security check was over, and then he came in and started his private show."

The worklights flashed back on. Sam and I were standing at the front of the stage, near the orchestra pit. The pit was covered with lightweight netting and was jammed with chairs and large musical instruments.

Charley called to us to join him at the back of the stage. Crammed into tight areas behind an opaque screen were the signature sets of *Miss Saigon*. The helicopter from the embassy evacuation, a huge statue of Ho Chi Minh, and the stunning Cadillac from the "American Dream" sequence were stored together in a tight jumble.

"The same knife and cable track mechanisms move these pieces," he said. "Except these sets are too heavy and delicate to be hoisted by the cable and pulley system. So they are moved onto the knives manually. This will be important."

We followed Charley to the wing stage right and

meandered carefully through the same kind of congestion we had encountered on the other side. Sets and scenery were hung above this wing, too, and some big pieces were stored on the floor awaiting mounting onto the knife tracks. On the far wall were the dozens of heavy cables that controlled the battens. Our guide exited the wing through some dark doors and climbed two flights of stairs. We followed and entered a catwalk above the stage. The long wall of the catwalk was lined with heavy cables that ran vertically into a black abyss above the stage. Each long cable was anchored to the wall by an imposing metal claw. Even to my unsophisticated mechanical mind, it was clear that if you released the claw, the weight of the cable was going to send something heavy flying somewhere.

"This is the fly floor. This," he said, "is where I think it all began that night."

A high-pitched chirp resounded around the fly floor. All three of our right hands reflexively jumped to our respective right hips. The pager in question belonged to Charley. He pulled it from a holster and read the digital message.

"Excuse me, please. You'll be okay here for a few minutes?"

Sam nodded.

I said, "Of course."

––⟪∾⟫––

"Who's Dale?" my back was to Sam as I asked him about the unfamiliar name that Charley had mentioned before he departed the fly floor to respond to his page. I was examining the mechanics of the controls of the counterweight and pulley system.

Heavy plates, not unlike those used by bodybuilders, were placed on the cables that vaulted up to the battens high above the stage. Each cable had a different amount of weight hung on it, just enough, I assumed, to counterbalance the mass of whatever was hung at the business end of the batten. It seemed much too simple and low-tech when I compared it to the sophisticated computer setup I had seen stage left, which had more in common with the deck of the Starship *Enterprise* than it did with my conception of "theatre."

"She's the Denver homicide detective who's heading the investigation of this murder. Dale Hunter. You saw her at the Boulder Theatre, remember? Tall, pretty. Good name for a dick, huh? Lucy Tanner thinks she's the best thing that's ever happened to women cops. The guy who got killed here, by the way, was named Lonnie. Lonnie Aarons."

I knew something about Lonnie Aarons. After his grotesque murder, the local news outlets had repeated the man's name until the dead musician had become a folk hero. It was way too big a price to pay for your fifteen minutes, was what I had thought at the time. Partly because of the morbid media saturation following Lonnie's high-profile murder, I hadn't turned on the news since Peter's death. I couldn't stand to watch whatever the video voyeurs were doing to him.

I said to Sam, "I take it that it's significant that this Denver detective's not here with us, right?"

Sam looked at me, then away, and found a stool on which to lean his ample weight before he answered me. "You're quick, Alan. You know, before—I mean a few years ago—when we first met and I was still thinking you were an asshole, I just considered you to be lucky sometimes, not really smart. But over the years you've actually begun to surprise me. You have a reliable sense of what is bullshit and what might be important. An astonishing trait, I might add, in someone who voluntarily spends as much time listening to drivel as you do."

Sam Purdy had complimented me without answering my question. The only novelty in that equation was the compliment.

"So why is Charley Chandler—and not Dale Hunter—conducting this private tour of the murder site for me?"

He smirked. "Because Dale doesn't give a shit what you have to say. She would trust a politician before she would trust a shrink. Anyway, Charley's got a perspective that I find interesting. A theatrical perspective, if you will. He manages this whole complex, which I guess makes him a bureaucrat, or at least a businessman. But his background is theatre. His undergraduate degree is in theatre arts from UCLA. And he's got an MBA from the executive program at CU Denver.

"But Charley's secret love, apparently, is mysteries. He reads 'em by the dozen. He's even writing one, he tells me. Asked me for some advice about a detective character he's working on. You know, a true *he-ro*."

Sam stopped his discourse right there, as though sufficient explanation had been provided.

"But why isn't the Denver detective here?"

"She knows I brought you here to look around. She'll stop by if she gets a breather."

From our perch on the fly floor, I was looking straight across the stage from stage right to stage left. My focus was on the heavy battens, which hung in neat parallel lines in an immense rectangular cavern above and across the stage, the bottoms of the suspended scenery pieces at rest just a few feet higher than the top of the curtain.

"You think Charley's figured this out? He knows how Lonnie Aarons was killed?"

"He thinks he knows how. Though I doubt if he's right. But he does know his way around the stage and around this theatre. He understands all this mechanical and computer crap and knows what it took to pull this crime off. The details may all be wrong, so take them with a grain of salt. But when he talks about all the theatre shit, listen." We heard footsteps on the stairs. "Hear him out, the guy tells a hell of a story."

Charley's suit coat was fully buttoned when he returned. "Sorry," he said. "Where were we?"

"The fly floor?" I said helpfully.

Sam said, "Tell him what you think, Charley. About the murder. What it took to do it."

Charley smiled warmly at Sam. He walked the length of the narrow fly floor, finally stopping at the end that hung above the rear of the stage. His back was still to us when he began speaking. There was no hesitation in his presentation.

"Lonnie was killed by a theatre person. I'm not certain yet whether that person is, or has been, part of this particular road production of *Miss Saigon*, or whether that person just studied this production and became familiar enough with it to manage to do what he did onstage while preparing to kill Lonnie."

Charley turned to face us. Sam turned to me.

"Alan doesn't know any more about Lonnie's murder than what he's read in the paper. Walk him through it, Charley. Just like you did for Dale and me that first time."

"Not here. Let's go someplace a little more comfortable."

He led us down from the fly floor, through the right wing, then backstage. He stepped aside to allow us to precede him into a large lounge filled with overstuffed chairs and sofas. "The green room," he announced.

"Nice," replied Sam as he chose the cushiest chair.

Charley remained standing. "Permit me to set the stage," he said, amused at his own affectation.

In the distance, we heard a solo piano rehearsing.

da da da da da da DA

The heat is on in Saigon.

Charley had it like this:

"See, it all starts when the killer falls in love with the show. Maybe it happens during its Broadway run in New York. But by the time *Miss Saigon* gets to Denver, I'm thinking, this guy has already attended a lot of performances.

"*Miss Saigon* mesmerizes the guy. Imprisons him and doesn't let him out on parole. Why? Got me. The music in this play is fine, that's all, fine. The sets and the production are stunning, sure. Extravagant enough to warrant a return performance? Yes, absolutely. For the murderer, though, the attraction is beyond the glitz. There is something about the theme, about the love story, maybe about Vietnam . . ."

I was beginning to feel apprehensive that my tour of the theatre was about to become a sinister replay of my morning in the Boulder Theatre. I was aware at a deeper level of why Sam had brought me here. To my surprise, I was learning about this guy. This *killer*.

"Tell us about Lonnie Aarons." The words were Sam's.

Charley faltered, seemed rattled that he couldn't tell the story his way. "The attraction for the killer isn't Lonnie. See, Lonnie . . . Lonnie spends his time down in the orchestra pit playing show tunes. People tell me he was an above-average string player. But Lonnie wasn't flamboyant. There's a clarinetist who looks like Fabio; he's flamboyant. Lonnie was quiet. He had acquaintances among the other orchestra members, but no enemies, and no friends. Somebody said that if you asked the other members of the orchestra, half would say that Lonnie Aarons was gay, half would say that he was straight. That's the kind of guy Lonnie was."

"Then how was he chosen?" As my lips formed the words, I knew I was asking as much about Peter as I was about Lonnie.

"Good question," added Sam. "Noticing Lonnie at all took some effort. He's skinny. He's balding. He's down in the damn pit. Why pick him out?"

Charley was ready. "The play crystallizes some fantasy for the guy. Who knows what? But I think something in the play triggers something in his mind that makes him take his fantasy out for a walk and then he just lets it run. And when he does, shit, it's a rabid pit bull on parade."

I said, "You think the murderer just plugged Lonnie in?"

"Yes, exactly," Charley says.

Sam was getting frustrated either with the pace of Charley's story or with my interruptions. "Go on," he said to Charley, "tell us how you think it happened."

---✎✎✎---

"They're in the theatre. Don't ask me how they got here yet, but they're in the theatre, now, and they have time. Overnight security is nothing. Remember how dark it is. The guy walks straight to the switches and turns on the lights. Maybe the houselights. Maybe the worklights. Maybe the theatrical lights, some spots. Imagine whatever you want. Then comes the tape. Lonnie gets gagged and bound with packing tape and gets set on a stool. The killer rolls the stool to the center of the stage.

"The guy leaves Lonnie and comes up to the fly floor. I see him in my head. This part's fast for him, like MTV. He's real excited now, there's a spring in his step. He has to fight to control himself, to remain patient. He lowers the cable that controls the batten that secures the embassy fence and then locks the cable back into place once the fence is suspended all the way to the stage floor."

Charley stopped and froze me with a shy smile. "You following?"

"Yes."

"Okay, this part is *irony*. The chain-link barrier that protects the evacuees and the marines at the U.S. Embassy from the instant refugees they leave behind in Saigon, now it's all that's protecting Lonnie Aarons from his killer.

"The killer's done upstairs for now. He hurries down from the fly floor and walks to the left wing, where he boots up one of the two computers, the one I showed you that controls the cable-knife track system. With me?"

I nodded.

"He uses the motor and pulley to lower the go-go cage from the Bangkok street scene to the stage. He locks it onto its knife. Perfect. Now, shit, he's getting more confident. Lonnie is still on that stool, as much a prop as that go-go cage. The guy goes back to the keyboard. Just a few strokes accomplishes what he wants.

"The go-go cage rolls onstage, stopping in its pre-programmed location. Imagine this, now. Against the caged steel backdrop of the fence sits a terrified man taped to a stool. The whole scene's looking porno-graphic, in some weird, sixties, fraternity-hazing kind of way."

To me, Sam says, "See how complicated this is? Get what I'm saying?"

I nodded.

Sam says, "Maybe this is where he takes a break, Charley. Maybe here?"

"Maybe. . . . But as each piece of his fantasy falls into place, the dude's *flyin'*. He's back at the keyboard. He's Oz now," Charley says, his voice rising. "He orders out half of Dreamland, then the hotel bedroom where Ellen meets Kim. A piece of the prostitute's shack where Kim and Chris first do it—he sends that out, too. The stage now has two beds, half a Saigon saloon, a security fence, and a cage full of strippers."

"You're the shrink, Alan, what do you think?" The question is Sam's.

I'm flabbergasted and don't respond.

Charley laughed softly, almost a cough. "It's crazy. Psychotic. It's whoring and horror and home and dishonor. And in the center of it all is Lonnie Aarons, hunched over, eyes saying everything his gagged mouth can't. *Imagine.*"

I thought, *Oh Peter.*

But the killer wasn't done with Lonnie.

No.

da da da da da da Da

━━━━━⁂━━━━━

Behind me I heard quiet clapping.

Charley's face suddenly took on the embarrassed resignation of a nine-year-old caught smoking in the school john.

Sam broke in, "Hey, Dale. Thought you couldn't make it tonight. Sit down, sit down. We're listening to Charley's thoughts about what happened here last month."

"I got done early, figured you guys would screw things up without me. And I never have been able to stay away from the stage." She faced Charley. "I think what you mean, Sam, is that you're listening to Charley's *fantasies* about what happened here last month."

To my ear, her voice carried more levity than criticism.

Charley didn't seem so sure. With defensiveness in his tone he said, "Sam said it would be okay to tell Alan what I think went on." Something, I conjectured, must already have transpired between Charley and Dale that had left Charley on edge.

Dale's tone danced between annoyance and amusement, as though it were her intent to keep Charley off balance. "If Detective Purdy says it's okay, hell, it must be okay." She took a seat on the arm of a sofa. "Certainly won't be the first tall tale to be produced in this place," she said, mostly to me. "Charley, here, is a fine theatre manager and a great storyteller, but his version of the *Miss Saigon* murder is not exactly supported by truckloads of evidence. By the way, I'm Detective Dale Hunter, Denver Police Department. You must be Sam's shrink."

Sam's shrink? The thought filled me with angst. I stood and said, "Alan Gregory. Nice to meet you. I think I saw you at the Boulder Theatre."

"Oh, that morning, yeah. I'm sorry about your friend."

"Thank you."

"Please understand that my permitting Sam to bring you here is pure courtesy. I'm not a believer. Nothing personal, so please don't hold my skepticism against me, Doctor. The FBI's already sent one of their own guys, straight from Quantico. The guy cost me hours of staff time I couldn't afford, at a time when I particularly couldn't afford it. Sincere guy, wore nice sweaters and great socks. He ends up telling me the *Miss Saigon* killer is a bright, strong young loner with an old grudge. Somebody who would fit into society, at least marginally." She winked at Sam. "That shrink was a fucking genius, I'll tell you."

Dale Hunter was dressed in good slacks that flattered her long legs, a button-down guy-type shirt that I would never call a blouse, and a blue blazer with those brass buttons that make it all seem nautical, as though the next thing she was going to do was hop a plane to Martha's Vineyard and spend the weekend with Walter Cronkite on his yacht. She was an athletic, strong-looking woman. Her shoulders and upper legs filled the fabric of her clothing. Although she was not thin, she was toned. I guessed she was a swimmer. I guessed low body fat.

Her face was attractive, with wide-set eyes. In my book, cops should be weathered, but Dale Hunter's skin was the color of peach flesh, and despite Colorado's desert dryness her complexion was rich and moist. She wore small gold earrings and only a little makeup— maybe a touch of blush and some eyeliner. The dominant feature of her face was her lips. They were full and robustly pink, and I couldn't be sure if I detected any gloss on them or not.

I noted that Sam was staring at the small triangle of exposed flesh below the hollow of Detective Dale Hunter's throat. When she turned to face Sam, he averted his eyes a second too late. She had caught him staring. She smiled, obviously not offended by his appraisal. The smile was expressly for him, right smack back his way.

Charley's beeper sounded again. He seemed relieved to have something else to do.

"Sam, you know the rest, you can tell it," Charley said, his voice suddenly without life. Charley stood. "Tonight's show is about to start. And there are a few things I need to take care of first. Come on." He led us a few steps to the wing, stage right.

It was almost curtain. The director, or somebody, called for attention.

Bikinied bar girls and khakied and fatigued GIs prepared to go onstage. Dressers made final adjustments to the costumes. One young dancer released her bikini top and leaned over from the waist to refit it over her breasts.

I watched her complete the task, then moved to a position where I would have a better view of the stage for the opening number. I was standing next to Dale Hunter. I whispered, "You've got your hands full. This guy's going to be hard to catch, isn't he?"

Her head was in deep shadows that made her short hair seem lighter in color. Her voice was lively. She said, "Oh, I'll catch him. This guy was ambitious. Flamboyant, even. This fantasy he played out here was like halftime at the Super Bowl. The guy tried to cram too much in. Even though he was careful, he left us a lot to work with. So, yes, I'll get him. And, yes, it might take a while. He's a bright guy. Though, given what happened in Boulder, there's signs he may be disintegrating. If that's the case, he'll be getting more sloppy. My goal is to find him before he does this again."

I considered the likelihood that arrogance was a universal trait among homicide detectives, as it was with Adrienne's surgeon friends.

Without a change in tone, Dale Hunter continued, "Sam says you just got married."

"Yes, I did, last fall. You married?"

"Divorced. From a social worker, God help me. You probably know that marriage isn't easy for cops. The stress, the hours, the crap. Takes its toll on everybody. Job gets old, I've got to find something else to do."

"Sam says it's tough. Sometimes I don't know how he does it."

"You know Sam well? You guys friends?"

"Yes, we're friends."

"What about *his* marriage? It's okay?"

Was this honest concern I was hearing? "Sure, as far as I know. He has a kid, a son."

"He's happy?"

Happy? I'd never thought about it. "I think so."

"Does he—never mind." She laughed. "Don't mind me, I'm a new single woman, and I'm always checking on the inventory out there. My radar tells me things, you know?" I couldn't tell if I heard another little chuckle from her.

Inventory? Sam? The reality was that Sam could have been unfaithful to his wife a dozen times since I had met him and I wouldn't have suspected a thing.

Ten feet upstage he stood with his thick arms folded across his chest. The corners of his mouth were turned up under his mustache in a smile. He scratched at his ear with his left hand. He didn't wear a wedding ring.

In that instant the music started. The sounds of the overture resounded off the flagstone walls of the theatre. I found myself listening intently to try to isolate the wail of the violins.

I wondered if Lonnie Aarons was missed in that pit below the stage. I wondered if other musicians ever walked home alone anymore.

As though they had been switched on electronically, the actors stretching in the wings suddenly became dancers. They bounded to the stage. The overture pealed thick as meringue. Excitement streaked through the wings.

da da da da da da Da
The heat is on in Saigon.

<hr />

Sam and I stood backstage at the Buell until the fall of Saigon. The call of a saxophone from the orchestra pit was haunting and lazy, like a big cat on the prowl. I wondered for the first time whether the killer had used the story or the score of the musical in his scripting.

Before leaving the wing, I whispered a goodbye to Charley Chandler, asked for his business card, and offered my own. In my mind, I was already generating questions I would run by him later. How much did the murderer know about the theatre? About computers? About lighting? How does someone learn those things? Could a nontheatre person know them?

Dale pulled Sam aside; he followed her away from the stage, and they talked privately for a couple of minutes. While they were having their homicide detective tête-à-tête, I waited in a busy hallway lined with dressing rooms and frantically changing, half-naked actors. When Sam and Dale returned, I thanked her for permitting me to visit the theatre; then he and I proceeded down the deserted corridor of the Actor's Walk, down some outside stairs, and found my car.

Neither of us seemed to want to talk. I was engrossed in the complicated exercise of trying to separate what about my evening had been theatre and what had been reality. The dark stage, Charley's compelling presentation, the show, the music, the odd conversation with Dale Hunter—all felt like jumbled fragments of a choppy night's dreams. But my mind kept returning to a single image: Peter on the piano.

Had Peter endured the same kind of torture as Lonnie Aarons? The thought dug at me like a needle searching out a splinter.

Ten minutes later, as we approached the interchange of I-25 and the Boulder Turnpike, I was trying to figure out some way to inform Sam that Dale seemed inordinately interested in him. Before I found the right words he asked, "What did you think of Charley Chandler?"

I said, "Nice guy. I liked him immediately. He's got flair."

Sam sighed. Just a little, enough to let me know he hadn't really been asking for a social assessment.

"I think he's bright, Sam. I think he's given this a lot of thought."

"Yeah, he has done that. Though I'm sure he's whiffing at some of the details." The inside of the car was dark. When I looked over I could occasionally see the left side of Sam's face illuminated by the head-lights of a passing car. "Dale doesn't put much weight on it," he said.

"On what Charley says?"

"Yeah. On what Charley says. She calls it 'fantasy land,' too much conjecture. And she also isn't going to put much weight on whatever you're going to have to say whenever you finally get around to saying it. She said the FBI shrinks told her that their profiles are right about seventy percent of the time. She thinks so far in her career she's seen nothing but the other thirty."

"What's your point, Sam? We're not doing this for her, are we? This is for Peter. We don't have to con-vince Dale Hunter of anything."

"Do I always have to have a point? I'm just talking here."

The timing was right. "You know, I think she likes you."

He shifted on his seat. "Ahh, shit, Alan. Give me a break."

I was enjoying needling him. "It's true. I think she might be interested. I thought you would want to know."

God, but I wish I could have seen him better in the dark car. From Sam's voice, I could tell he was intrigued by whatever, if anything, had transpired with Dale. But I couldn't tell whether the intrigue was just his ego feeling good about an attractive woman's interest or whether he was actually sniffing the bait.

"I'm just a fat cop, Alan. Women like Dale want men like you, not men like me."

"Which means what? That you shouldn't be flattered?"

A light rain had begun to fall, and I heard nothing but the intermittent clapping of the wipers on the windshield and the buzz of the tires as they shredded through the thin film of moisture on the street. Not a word from Sam while he considered my question. I checked my speedometer and slowed down to sixty. There's always a damn speed trap going through Westminster.

Finally he said, "I'm from northern Minnesota. This wouldn't happen there. No way in hell. We'd have a summer without mosquitoes first. Can you believe women these days? I can't take this kind of shit. Jeez, don't I have enough on my mind? Isn't this sexual harassment or something? Maybe I should get myself a lawyer."

―◆◇◆―

Sam had left his car at our house. I invited him in for a drink. He accepted. Before going inside, I glanced down the drive toward Peter's studio. It was dark. I still harbored a fantasy that one night it would be bright again, full of the symphonic sounds of old rock and roll and whining power tools.

Emily greeted us at the door without barking, her chocolate nub of a tail shaking like a metronome. I knew that someday very soon, her little dog brain would identify our house as her house, too, and Lauren and me as members of her pack, and she would bark at every visitor as though they had come to steal her puppies. But not yet. We were all still just pleasant curiosities to her.

Lauren was awake and, unusual for her at that hour, upstairs in the living room. It was a little before ten o'clock. Teasers for the soon-to-start late news were running on TV.

Although she knew I wouldn't be home for dinner, neither of us had expected me to be this late. She seemed miffed, either that I hadn't called or that I had dragged Sam inside with me. Maybe both.

She said hi to Sam, then, "I was sitting here waiting to see whether your flaming deaths were going to be the lead story on the ten o'clock news."

I leaned over and kissed her, lingering a second on her soft lower lip to let her know I was glad to be home and didn't want her to be angry with me. Right when I was about to pull away, I felt her tongue and then a gentle bite and I knew things were going to be fine.

Pointing to the phone, I asked Sam if he wanted to call Sherry and then turned and walked to the kitchen. I came back with a bottle of vodka and three glasses.

After watching me pour for Lauren, Sam said, "You got a beer? I'd rather have a beer. You always have great frou-frou beers."

I returned to the kitchen and brought Sam a frou-frou beer.

"Like it?"

He took a long swallow. "Tastes like beer," he said.

I poured myself some vodka and said to Lauren, "We learned a lot tonight."

"Yes? Tell me." Lauren grabbed the remote to flick off the TV. Although she was a Boulder County deputy DA, Peter's murder wasn't one of her cases. But it was high profile and she knew plenty about it from work and from me and from Sam and from Adrienne. And Sam knew that whatever I was learning, Lauren would know soon enough. He had voiced no objection to her being part of this conversation.

Sam said, "Leave the TV on. Just turn the sound down."

She did.

I started recounting the story the way I felt it, which was a confusing jumble of the romance of the theatre and the horror of choreographed torture and murder. Halfway through the retelling of Charley's version of events I drained my vodka and refilled my glass and got another beer for Sam. Lauren still cradled her half-full glass on her lap.

My shoulders were tight. I raised my arms to stretch my muscles while I examined the dark mist in the valley to the west. Someplace in the rain I managed to discover a conclusion. I said, "You know, I don't think the guy who murdered Lonnie Aarons was the same guy who killed Peter."

Sam's attention had been split between my soliloquy and the soundless TV news. Now it was all on me.

"Go on," he said. He was encouraging me, not challenging me. I felt as though I were a graduate student who had just stumbled onto the track of the correct answer to a long-puzzling research dilemma.

Lauren looked back and forth between us, trying to make sense of the interaction. "You don't think it was the same guy?"

"No, it wasn't—I don't think it was." I was aware of forcing extra assurance into my tone, as I might intentionally overstuff a suitcase. "Maybe it was a copycat-type thing that happened to Peter, or maybe it was totally unrelated. But, no, it wasn't the same guy."

"Don't stop, Alan. Talk it through." That was my dissertation chair speaking.

"The Denver murder was a production. It was planned—no, no, no—it was scripted. Carefully laid out. Scenery, computers, lighting—everything was just right. I wouldn't be surprised if murdering Lonnie Aarons took almost as long as the play. Peter's murder was, by contrast, almost uninspired. No theatre, no drama. The differences between the two murders are like the differences between Ziegfeld and a fifth-grade Christmas pageant."

Sam's second beer hadn't yet arrived at his lips. He tilted it back and drained a quarter of the bottle. "You sure you're not just reacting to the glamour of *Miss Saigon*? The Buell isn't exactly the Boulder Theatre and the Broadway production of *Miss Saigon* certainly isn't the Flatirons Players production of *Present Laughter*."

I thought about it. The first thing I thought about when he mentioned the glamour of the theatre, I'm embarrassed to admit, was the young woman shaking her healthy breasts back into her bikini top just before the curtain of *Miss Saigon*. When I managed to think about other elements of the glamour equation, I said, "I'm sure it's an influence and I'll have to factor it in, but my gut reaction is that Lonnie Aarons was killed during the course of a carefully planned production. Lonnie was only a casualty of what the murderer did in the Buell. The play was the thing. The fantasy ruled.

"But with Peter, that night in the Boulder Theatre, death *was* the production. And Peter's murder *was* the thing.

"All that stuff I've been reading says that a serial killer's fantasies become more complex, more twisted, from killing to killing. But Peter's killing was much *less* complex than the one at the Buell.

"And the damn literature says that a serial killer's ability to stay in control during the act tends to degrade over time. The pressure of the fantasy eventually erodes the control. But Peter's killing never got anywhere near as frenzied as the one we heard about tonight."

"My, we're the instant expert, aren't we? Sam, what do you think?" Lauren's playful voice had begun to take on that honey-and-gravel texture. To me, right then, she looked like sex. Sam and I each had a chair, and although she had the sofa to herself, she was curled in one corner of it. One hand held her narrow

glass of vodka in a grip that was wonderfully evocative, the other was between her legs. The light was soft
on her black hair.

"I dragged him to Denver so he could get an uncontaminated look at what happened down there. I've
tried not to influence him a whole lot. And I don't
think he's off base, Lauren. Ever since Dale Hunter—
she's the homicide detective in Denver—and I talked
after Peter's murder, and she told me what actually
had happened during the murder at the Buell, I've
had my own doubts that it was the same guy. But
Dale's convinced it's a serial, a new serial—a virgin—
one who's breaking out of his shell. And Lucy—"

"Lucy?"

"My partner, Lucy Tanner—she and the rest of the
team investigating Peter's murder with me tend to
agree with Dale and the Denver team." He smiled at
me. "So Alan's my very first ally. Ain't that peculiar?"

Lauren sat up straight, and her sudden proper posture yanked me back to the present. She challenged
him with her tone. "Why are you in such a minority
on this, Sam?"

He knew the game had changed. This was no longer
a late-night bull session among friends. This was
Deputy District Attorney Lauren Crowder wanting to
assess the quality of Sam's evidence.

"You know that cops tend to differ on how much
weight they put on profiles of violent criminals. Dale
and Lucy tend to fall on one extreme—they don't like
the touchy-feely crap. I'm kind of in the middle. I'll
listen; if it makes sense, I'll buy it. That's where we
differ. On this issue I'm kind of a flexible guy."

Lauren smiled at Sam. "God, you're good, Sam Purdy. You almost had me. What is it you don't want us—or, more accurately, don't want Alan—to know yet? You bullshitter."

The corners of Sam's mouth turned up into the edges of his mustache. He said, "I don't know what you're talking about."

"Bullshit. You're trying to get Alan to pitch his tent in your camp before you dump a piece of evidence in his lap that he can't explain. What is it? What do they have that you can't make sense of?"

Sam drained the second beer and eyed the vodka bottle longingly. "Well, there is some semen."

"Some *semen?*" She pushed her hair back off her forehead. "What about the semen, Sam?"

"There's some semen that creates a little problem with my two-killer theory."

"Such as?"

Semen? I was sitting up straight now, too. I was also just beginning to acknowledge the ramifications of the discussion. If there were two killers, someone might have had a motive to kill Peter.

His murder might not have been random.

"Such as . . . see, here's the problem. The murderer at the Buell spent a little recreational time in the audience. Either during his production or after. Enjoying his work, enjoying it a lot. He jacked off. At least a couple of times. The crime-scene people found semen in two locations in the theatre. One in the orchestra, one in the balcony."

"And I bet you found semen at the Boulder Theatre, too, didn't you?"

"Yeah, we did."

"And it matches?"

"Yeah, it seems to, so far. Same type and secretor status. There's more serology pending, DNA if we need it. But I'll grant a match so far, based on what we got."

"That's quite a distinctive signature this creep leaves behind. And this little problem with your theory, Sam? It's kind of like the *Titanic*'s little problem with an iceberg."

"Yeah, kind of like that."

Lauren stood up languidly and gave Sam a soft, affectionate hug and a kiss on his forehead. Into his ear, she said, "That's one of the things I like about working with you, Sam Purdy, you never let a little forensic science get in the way of the thrust of your investigation." She headed downstairs to our bedroom.

The dog was at her feet.

I was totally in love with Lauren.

Despite the fascinating dialogue I had just been listening to, I wanted Sam to leave so I could get downstairs to be with my wife before she drifted off to sleep.

I would think about somebody else's semen tomorrow.

One of the things I do when I'm faced with imponderables is to get on my bike and get lost in road rhythm. On a sunny afternoon of a spring day with no breeze and clean roads, there is nothing more cleansing to my mind than a high spin and a good thirty miles at speed.

To confound routine as much as possible the day after my visit to the Buell, I rode southeast from my house and ended up circling behind the Jefferson County Airport on a maze of back roads that I didn't know. I stumbled upon the world headquarters of Up With People and mused that Peter would have found some unique meaning in that serendipity.

When I got back home I still hadn't figured out anything new about the theatre murders.

The aroma of freshly baking bread permeated the house. The lilt of some Bach I might have known the title of ten years ago drifted from the living room, waging a gentle battle for my attention. My memory of the Bach catalog was as illusory to me as was this bucolic vision of marriage that I was living.

My ability to identify music had, I thought, faded over the years, lost to the end of some youthful ideal, when time and energy were devoted to such things. In a similar way, my illusions of blissful marriage had been sacrificed to the realities of a bitter divorce.

For me, this second time around, marriage was a whole new enterprise. I'd entered into it without caprice, conceding from my "I do" that the romantic formula Lauren and I had scraped together would probably never yield tidy sums. I expected to have to toil at this union. I expected to be making allowances for her baggage and voicing apologies for my own. But now, to my surprise, I was in love and I was in bliss and it all seemed so easy.

The irony didn't escape me; I was aware at least a few times a day that my life had begun to glow in unexpected new ways just as Peter had begun to turn to ash.

Twilight lingered as the mountains stood proud to the west. I showered away the sweat from my ride.

Lauren had boiled up a big pot of red beans and rice with plenty of Cholula to go along with the fresh baguettes she had baked. I helped her carry the food to the living room. Where, single, I had once had a serviceable dining-room table with an exquisite view of the Continental Divide, Lauren and I now had a tournament-quality pool table with an exquisite view of the Continental Divide.

We did much of our dining at the coffee table.

A moment after I got comfortable on the floor, Adrienne knocked at the door and let herself in. In her tiny hand, apparently for Emily, she gripped a dog biscuit the size of a femur.

Adrienne declined to join us in the red beans and

rice, which, upon clinical examination, she seemed to be having trouble believing was actually comestible. She did eat a good-size hunk of warm bread, however.

Finally, growing impatient with our leisurely approach to dinner, she asked, "Will you guys come with me to the studio? I haven't been there yet, you know, since the thing at the theatre. I don't want to go out there alone the first time. The police have been through it, and I don't know what I'll find. Lisa can only stay another hour with Jonas, and I think I want to go and look around."

She tore off another chunk of bread. "Please?"

Fifty yards of gravel-studded clay separated our front door from the entry to Peter's studio.

The barnlike shack had started its existence as the tack house for a ranch that fifty years before had spread out over a few hundred acres of the eastern Boulder valley. When I moved onto what was left of the original property as a live-in handyman during my graduate school days at the University of Colorado, the shed was nothing more than a decrepit depository of exotic insects and neglected tools. The building was drafty and cold and miserable in winter, searing and stuffy and miserable in summer.

Right after he and Adrienne bought the big house, Peter launched a frontal assault on the barn, displaying an abundance of enthusiasm and spirit that I rarely saw manifested in him again. He rented a big truck and carted out years of accumulated equipment and debris. He brought in flatbed loads of lumber and windows and skylights and doors and conduit and electrical and mechanical supplies.

After a few weeks of basic structural renovation, Peter disappeared, arriving back with a different rental truck, this one a big Ryder that was full of his real tools, his shop tools, his planers, and saws, and sanders, and drills, and he began to move into the place that everyone soon called Peter's studio.

Except for Peter. He called it his shop.

The original structure was the shape of a small barn. Over the years some owner had added enclosed areas under shed roofs on two sides, and the total size of the renovated structure probably was close to two thousand square feet.

Peter had filled the space with tools and life and old-time rock and roll.

Sometimes people called him a carpenter. Sometimes a cabinetmaker. Or a builder. And he had found wry delight in the corners of his eyes for those times that some prospective customer who didn't know him well called him an artist. I never asked him what he called himself, though once I had heard him answer a question on the phone with the phrase "I make stuff." Pause. "Out of wood, mostly."

That night we all stopped five feet from the double doors to the studio. Of the three of us, Lauren was newest to bunking on the ranch and certainly had known Peter less well than Adrienne or I, so her hesitance probably carried the least meaning. But I sensed something significant in Adrienne's reticence and my own. Mine had to do with anxiety about what I'd find. I felt as though I were about to walk on a newly harvested field that I'd seen only in its lush, planted state. My fear wasn't just that it would feel empty, barren of fruit. My fear, even approaching the door, was that the studio would feel as though it had been plowed, the residue of Peter already turned under.

With an unexpected vertical leap of about three and a half feet, a jump completed with a well-executed one-eighty, Emily broke the spell that had us all cemented to the ground. "I guess she wants in," said Adrienne, smiling. "Let's go." She jangled keys, threaded one into the deadbolt, and opened the left-hand door.

Everybody stopped again. At least, everybody human stopped again. Emily ran inside. I reached in and hit a couple of switches to illuminate the arrays of big lights that hung from the ceiling of the white-washed interior.

"Did he always leave it like this?"

Lauren's question could have been answered had she just looked at either my face or Adrienne's.

Everything was shrouded. It looked like a big house in the Hamptons that has been closed up for the season. The shrouds skipped the power tools, instead Peter seemed to have reserved them for finished or in-progress pieces of woodwork that lined the perimeter areas of the space.

"He used to cover stuff sometimes. Especially when a client was coming over and he didn't want to answer questions about something that he was still working on." I nodded as I silently agreed with Adrienne's explanation. She frowned as she continued, "But I've never seen this much stuff covered up. Have you, Alan?"

"No," I said. "This is different. He didn't say anything to you, Ren? About something different he was doing?" A breeze blew past us and stirred the air within the barn. The sour smell of fresh lumber drifted back our way.

Adrienne said, "No."

Lauren seemed to recognize that her position on the periphery of intimacy with Peter might grant her some psychological latitude that Adrienne and I were having difficulty mustering. With a softness that found just the right amount of entreaty in it, she said, "Why don't we all go take a look. See what Peter was up to."

Lauren led Adrienne in by the hand. I followed, and as I made a cursory visual examination, decided that other than the profligate shrouding, Peter didn't seem to have been up to anything particularly unusual. I moved to the far end of the shop and gingerly lifted a corner of a large sheet of sailcloth from a major work in progress.

"Wow," I said under my breath, "that's gorgeous." The piece that I had revealed was, I guessed, an eight-foot-or-so section of cabinetry, the part that would be installed above counter height, behind a bar. The style was nineteenth-century western saloon, and the woodworking, though unfinished, was stunning.

"Was he doing a restaurant, Adrienne?" This piece was of a scale too mammoth for a private home.

"Yeah," she said, tapping her forehead with her

index finger. "I think he was. For a casino in Black Hawk or Central City, maybe Cripple Creek."

"I thought he had decided not to do any more big commercial projects."

"I'm trying to remember what he told me. I think somebody Peter knew from college asked him to do it. Someone I don't know. He's with one of the big out-of-state casinos that have moved into Central City. I think Peter told me he was charging the guy an arm and a leg, was going to buy a zero-coupon bond for Jonas's college fund. We didn't talk about Peter's customers that much, unless it was a piece he was excited about making. Commercial work usually bored him." Adrienne was standing close to the table saw, near the center of the room. She seemed reluctant to approach the finished carpentry.

Finally she waved her arm toward the piece I stood next to. "Is it done?"

I looked again. "Close. It looks like he'd finished the carpentry on it, anyway. It needs to be stained and sealed. But this is only a section of something much bigger. It isn't enough. There have to be more pieces that go with it."

Across the room, Lauren lifted another sheet of sailcloth. "Here's more, looks like the same style."

I examined yet another piece. "It's all the same project. Just waiting to have the finish put on. He didn't do that anymore, did he, Ren? The finishes, the stains?"

She shook her head. "Rarely. Certainly not on a big commercial installation. He'd sub it out. Too toxic. Probably would have trucked this stuff to Tony Celli.

You met him on Saturday, maybe? He looks like a Marine, tight T-shirts, jeans that always seem too short. Tattoo of a dragon on his arm. Doc Martens with white socks."

"Maybe," I said. I didn't recall meeting Tony Celli, but Saturday—the whole weekend really—had been a blur. I had a vague recollection of Peter's mentioning Tony before. I made a mental note to call him, see if Tony would help us get some finish slapped on these pieces, get them disposed of, get Jonas's zero-coupon funded.

The mood in the room was lightening up appreciably when Emily decided, for the first time since she'd moved to the ranch, to let us know what her bark sounded like. I'd had another Bouvier before her, so I knew the vocabulary, which ranged from a throaty I-don't-think-I-like-this "woooo" to a thunderclap roar that I felt could register on the equipment of the National Earthquake Information Center in nearby Golden.

This bark was Richter-scale material. A single clap that resounded in the tight space like a hand slap on concrete.

Adrienne reacted by saying, "Oh shit!" and spinning around in a circle, her eyes canvassing every inch of the studio. I was sure she half expected to see Peter, or his ghost.

Emily ran to Lauren, who said, "What is it, honey? You hear something? You know you have a very ferocious bark for a little girl."

"I think my heart stopped," said Adrienne, who

was clutching her chest with both hands, gasping for breath. Her face was flushed.

Finally—after a week when her life had been altered as though its orbit had been changed by a meteor strike—finally Adrienne spun slowly to the floor, let her shoulders sag, and started to cry.

Emily walked over to her, leaned in close, and said "Woooo."

Across the drive I spied Lisa standing in the open front door of the house, one round hip cocked north, Jonas's sleepy head pillowed on her shoulder. There was something even more languid than usual about Lisa since Peter's death. As Adrienne grew more manic around the house, she seemed to be draining Lisa of something essential.

Lisa wasn't classically beautiful. Her heart-shaped face was a little too full, though Rubens would have judged her thin; her cheekbones were undefined, her chin was small, and her long hair was too sandy to be blond, too washed out to be brown. Although I suspected an innate intelligence, signs of her sagacity rarely surfaced. She lacked ambition. Still, she was one of the most visually sensuous women I had ever met. My bride, Lauren, loved to needle me about my reaction to being in Lisa's presence. I thought I tolerated the teasing with élan, and was content just to be in Lisa's vicinity occasionally.

I held an arm lightly around both Adrienne and Lauren as we walked in the direction of Lisa and the baby. My skin felt as though it had been floured with the fine grit that perennially dusted Peter's shop.

Halfway across the yard Lauren kissed me on the cheek and broke off to go back to our house. "I'll try to wait up," she whispered, then, louder, she said, "Good night, Adrienne. Whatever you need, okay?" As she turned away, Lauren patted herself on the thigh and called to Emily, who tagged right along next to her.

For Lauren, it was medicine time. She was going home to prepare her injection of Copolymer I. The ritual she followed was symbolic and spiritual, an offering of hope to a scientific promise of prophylaxis against future exacerbations of multiple sclerosis. If the little twenty-seven-gauge needle found a vein on its half-inch journey through her skin, a spot or two of blood would be spilled. More symbol, more sacrifice. She would wince as she lowered the plunger and forced the viscous medicine to pool in her sparse layer of subcutaneous fat.

Under her breath, she would say, "I'm so lucky."

In my mind, I translated her words into something like "The only thing worse than doing this is not doing this."

I knew that she had left Adrienne and me behind because she preferred to perform her ritual alone.

Through thick, unattractive sniffles, Adrienne called good night to Lauren, and then said to me, "Thanks for coming out there with me. I really didn't want to go by myself. God, I hate crying."

I was about to say something reassuring, when she continued, "Don't even think about saying what you're about to say, Alan. I don't need your permission to cry."

"You know me too well."

"Yeah, I do. Actually, what's closer to the truth is that I probably know you a little less well than I knew Peter. And I'm beginning to feel that he was even more of an enigma than I thought."

"When someone's gone, it's easy to focus on the missing pieces, Ren."

She kicked the dirt with the heel of her shoe and, with a familiar teasing tone in her voice, said, "For God's sake, would you shut it off for a second? This isn't going to be like having a conversation with M. Scott Peck, is it? Are you actually going to pay attention to me here?"

We had almost reached the porch. Lisa shifted Jonas's weight and cocked her hip in the other direction. Apparently she noticed Adrienne's red eyes or heard her sniffling. She asked, "Was everything okay out there? Adrienne?"

Lisa wore jeans that were tight on her ass and hips, full and loose on her legs, and a long-sleeved top with a scoop neck. All in all, only a few square inches of white flesh were revealed. But Lisa could have been shrouded like the woodwork in Peter's studio and, in my mind, couldn't have managed to look modest.

"It's fine, Lisa. Just like he left it." Adrienne smiled as we reached the porch. On tippy-toes she kissed her son's lips. He scrunched his closed eyes, and for that moment I saw Peter alive in his progeny's face.

"Do you mind putting him down for me, Lisa? I'll only be a couple more minutes."

"Sure, happy to." Nanny and child turned to retreat inside.

Adrienne said, "Oh wait, does he need a bath?"

"I gave him one already. Do you want me to spend the night?"

For some reason, Adrienne looked at me before she said, "No, it's okay. Go ahead home, I'll see you tomorrow."

"Good night, Lisa," I said.

She smiled at me over her shoulder.

Adrienne pulled me to the porch swing, sat me down, and punched me in the arm. "What is it with men and Lisa? Shit. I'm constantly embarrassed for your gender. I'm tempted to dissect a dick someday and find out what the hell gives it a life of its own. And why the hell it's so stupid. I'd win a Nobel fucking Prize. Speaking of prizes, who knows, if you get lucky, maybe Lisa'll let you join the bake-off." She squeezed herself onto the end of the swing as far from me as she could manage.

"What's the bake-off?" I knew I shouldn't ask.

"Lisa has these men who have been after her *forever*. She's been shining them on for the longest time. Now she says she wants to pick one. There's three of them she sort of likes. And those three are going to be the finalists in the bake-off. A grad student, a professor, and a computer nerd who looks like Gilligan.

She's having each of them make her dinner so she can see who cooks the best."

"This sounds like something you would come up with."

"I've had some input. The woman can't cook a lick. Sometimes she ruins Jonas's baby food, and it comes in a damn jar. The bake-off is a proven survival method for the kitchen-resistant woman. Worked perfectly for me and Peter."

"You chose Peter after a bake-off?"

"No. But if I had, he would have won."

She was right. Peter could cook up a storm. "Do the guys know they've been entered in this contest?"

"No. They're oblivious. They're just lathered up over the possibility of getting to sleep with the prize. You know, I really don't get it. I love Lisa and she's saved my life a dozen times since Jonas was born and God knows I don't know what I'd do without her now. But she's not *that* pretty—"

I scoffed audibly here.

"—she's not exactly a conversational genius, and she's got no ambitions that I've ever been able to identify. Why are all these high-powered men lining up at her toes?"

Putting more prurient thoughts aside, I said what came second to mind, "She's safe, Ren. Maybe it's the same reason that Jonas loves her. Maybe grownup men just want some of what he gets."

"Jonas gets to put his hands on her boobs any time he wants."

"Like I said."

She reached out and touched my face, then examined

her fingers. "You're covered with sawdust, too, aren't you? I'm going to have to take another shower." She brushed at herself for ten seconds. The act looked maniacal, reminded me of the Three Stooges. "So what did you decide about the favor? Will you do it? Go learn about Peter for me? Find out if Jonas and I belong? I can't go now. I just can't. And if I wait, I'm afraid life will go on and what seems so important now will just fade away and I'll never know if there was something else I should have known, and that's not fair to Jonas."

I watched a light flash on, then seconds later off, in the kitchen in my house across the drive. A quick bath completed, her flesh warm and soft, Lauren was retrieving the vials of medicine from the refrigerator.

I turned my head to the right, to the north. "Go where and learn about Peter?"

"I guess where he grew up. Talk to his family and his friends."

I was beginning to understand the request a little better. Adrienne and her mother-in-law had never warmed to each other.

"So you think the answer is in Wyoming?"

She nodded, scooted down so her feet could touch the ground, and gave the swing a push. It rocked unevenly.

"Has to be. I've looked everywhere else for it." She gave the ground another shove with her extended foot. "It's a big fucking state isn't it?"

"Wyoming?"

"No, confusion. Come on, even if you think this is stupid, humor me."

I wanted to go home and be with Lauren. Sometimes she liked it if I completed the injection ritual for her and disposed of the syringes in the empty plastic milk bottle in the cabinet above the washing machine.

I said, "Okay, Adrienne. I'll go. I'll do what I can do," having quickly decided that Adrienne's errands would complement the ones that I'd been drafted to do for Sam, anyway.

She reached into her back pocket and slapped a folded airline ticket envelope onto my lap. "I knew you'd go. Those are coupons good for trips to Jackson Hole. Take the prosecutor with you if you want. Jackson is real close to where he grew up. Peter loved it up there in the spring. But he never took me. Find out why. Find out why he never took me."

Lauren was in bed when I got home. I locked the doors, took a quick shower, and brushed my teeth before crawling into bed.

"Something's not right," she said as I finger-kissed that impossibly soft skin between her hipbone and her pubic hair.

I said, "I know. Any ideas about what?"

"No. Just a sense that Peter's death wasn't a simple tragedy."

I explained that I'd agreed to do the favor for Adrienne.

"She told me what she wanted. I knew you'd do it."

"So you want to go to Jackson Hole for the weekend?"

"Thought you'd never ask."

We made love. The day felt complete.

Since he hadn't suggested that I had any official status within the police department, as far as I knew I was functioning as an unofficial consultant to Sam Purdy. Which meant that I was about as close to the vortex of the official investigation of Peter's murder at the Boulder Theatre as Denver International Airport is to Denver. My only direct contact with the police department so far had been Sam, and I found it convenient, and familiar, to labor under the illusion that he was functioning like Dick Tracy, a solitary, valiant crusader for justice.

At another level I knew, of course, that many additional people were involved; Lucy Tanner, another Boulder police detective, had been at the Boulder Theatre the morning after the murder, and I assumed that, in addition to Lucy and Sam and the team they had assembled, a whole range of technical and forensic support people would be involved in an investigation with as high a profile as this one.

When Madeleine Aurora—I always assumed that was not the name her parents had graced her with at birth—from Sam's office paged me three times in a row while I was with a patient the next morning, I figured something important had broken in the case. Maybe an arrest was imminent. Actually, when I returned her call between patients, I discovered that Madeleine was laboring under Sam's instruction to get me to attend a meeting at the police department at three o'clock that afternoon.

A year and a half earlier I had enjoyed brief employment as a temporary investigator for the offices of the Boulder County coroner and had become acquainted with Madeleine during that time. Sam was so reliant on her ability to organize his life and keep him out of administrative trouble within the department that he treated her with the kind of respect one accords a coiled cobra, always wary she would strike at him, turn on him, and then desert him, leaving him to die a slow, painful bureaucratic death.

I, on the other hand, always found Madeleine sweet and accommodating. She was an aging hippie who made no secret of the fact that she would rather be chasing Jerry Garcia across North America than keeping Sam Purdy out of trouble. She was also one of those people who have an intrinsic understanding of complex organizational systems, which is to say that, bureaucratically speaking, she could cut through bullshit as effectively as she could spread it. Those skills made her both invaluable and dangerous to Sam, whom she played as adeptly as Wynton Marsalis plays the trumpet. For me, it was special fun just to watch Sam bow down to somebody.

When I told Madeleine that I had a three-thirty patient and couldn't make the meeting across town and still have a prayer of getting back to my office in time for my session, she went silent. I guessed that I was causing her serious logistical problems. "Are there a lot of other people involved, Madeleine?"

"Too many. I've been chasing chickens around the barnyard all morning."

After extracting her promise that she wouldn't tell Sam about my largesse, I called my three-thirty and offered to see him over lunch. He jumped at the chance.

So by midafternoon I was across town, being escorted to the first-floor offices of the Boulder Police Department detective division.

I saw Madeleine before she saw me. She wore a jeans skirt that barely reached her kneecaps, Birkenstocks, and a "Hate Is Not a Family Value" T-shirt. My legs had been shaved more recently than hers. When she spied me, she walked up and took my arm and said, "Hi, honey, I owe you one. Follow me, I'll show you where everybody is waiting."

I trailed in her wake, which was scented with the unmistakable aroma of patchouli oil. She led me upstairs to a western-facing room full of rugged, uncomfortable chairs arranged in a classroom configuration. Big windows with drawn miniblinds overlooked a parking lot and, in the distance, the Flatirons. A table in back of the room had a scratched and dented brushed-aluminum coffee urn and a box of grocery-store doughnuts.

I watched Scott Truscott, my old boss from my days as a coroner's consultant, approach. Scott was the chief medical investigator, the second-in-command in the office of the Boulder County coroner.

"Scott, good to see you. I wasn't sure you'd be here."

"I didn't know you would be here, either. Are you—hold on a second—" He extracted a Celestial Seasonings teabag from the inside pocket of his sportcoat and called out to Madeleine before she got away, "Madeleine, is there any hot water around here?"

"Try the squad room," she sang back, not slowing her exit for a second.

"The coffee here sucks. So how have you been doing? Practice going okay?"

"Practice is going better all the time, Scott." I held up my left hand. "I got married; I'm doing well, too."

"Yeah, I heard you and Lauren got married. That's great, congratulations." A suspicious look passed rapidly over Scott's face, darkening his expression like a squall line darkens the plains. "Wait. Sam's not planning on foisting you off on me again, is he?" He tried to make a face that might convince me belatedly that his question had been a joke.

I smiled. "Not to worry, Scott. I'm just helping him assemble some psychological clues for a profile on the murderer at the theatre. Strictly volunteer. Peter, the victim, was a good friend of mine."

Scott was momentarily at a loss as to how to respond, seemed grateful for the opportunity to wave hello to Lucy Tanner, who had just entered the room and was walking toward us.

Seeing Lucy among her colleagues reminded me of how much I didn't know about her. To me, she always seemed young, late-twenties young, but I figured I was wrong about her age. She possessed much too much wisdom and patience to actually be that fresh, so I pegged her at around thirty-three. She dressed rich, and acted comfortable being rich, her style and sense of fashion reminiscent of my ex-wife the TV producer, not of a detective for a small Rocky Mountain city where style is more likely to be defined by Patagonia and Columbia than by Chanel or Lagerfeld.

Her features were severe. She had intense blue eyes that were set far apart and weren't quite large enough for her face. She wore her eyebrows in their natural splendor, thick and full, big, slashing accents on a face with all the classical attributes of beauty—high cheekbones, narrow chin, wide forehead, full mouth—yet everything was somehow cut too acutely.

Lucy and I had crossed paths before and I knew that she was a resourceful cop who was totally loyal to Sam. I also knew from observing her efforts that she could lie and mislead with the best of them. Sam said he trusted her more than any other detective on the squad because, one, she was sharp, and two, she didn't want a desk. She didn't want sergeant's stripes. She didn't want to do anything but catch perps. Sam liked her, I decided, because he thought she was like *him*.

Lucy poured herself a cup of coffee, seemed to stare down a doughnut that she suspected was going to jump right out of the box into her mouth, and walked over to a pair of detectives who were talking in front of the blackboard across the room.

"Hey, Luce," one of them said.

"Hey, guys. How are the fat boys?"

Sam walked in then, looking rushed and harried.

He was with a person I didn't know who was pushing a cart with a TV monitor and a VCR. The man with Sam was the only person in the room who wore a suit—a real one, where the trousers match the jacket. He wore it well, managing not to look overdressed in a room full of sartorial sloths, and managing not to make the same statement of sophistication that Lucy made when she entered just about any room in Boulder.

I asked Scott Truscott who the guy was.

"That's Michael Martin. He's the forensics maven."

Michael Martin plugged the electronics into the wall and walked over to the others at the front of the room. Sam broke off from the group, crooked a finger at me, and I joined him by the windows.

"The kid has disappeared."

"What kid?"

"The one from the theatre, Kenneth Holden, the drunk CU student who helped get Peter to the ER? He's gone. Middle of the fucking semester. His roommate doesn't have a clue where he is. His family is freaked."

"When?"

"Nobody's seen him since yesterday morning. I called him this morning to get him to go over what he saw one more time. Got his roommate, who thought I was the cop Ken's parents had called about their son being missing."

"Do you think it means anything, Sam?"

"No, probably doesn't mean shit. But I don't like it. I'd interviewed the kid twice already. Once that night, which was damn near pointless. He was really plastered when he got pulled off the sidewalk to help get Peter to the hospital, didn't remember half of what happened when I first talked with him. I thought then and I think now that the janitor's a much better source of information. Which, unfortunately, isn't saying much."

"The janitor's the one who knew Peter, right?"

"Yeah, I just called him again. He never saw the kid before that night, and he hasn't been in touch with him since. Doesn't have any idea where he might be."

"What are you going to do?"

"I'm going to ask the guys in missing persons to pay a little extra attention and let me know if they find anything. The kid's car is gone. They'll put out a bulletin on it. Talk to his friends, the people he works with. Other than that, nothing. Wait."

As I was pondering the news that Kenneth the college kid was missing, Elliot Bellhaven entered the room. Given that Elliot was the deputy district attorney assigned to the prosecution of Peter's murderer, his presence at the meeting didn't surprise me. It didn't displease me, either.

I liked Elliot. For a while, our relationship had been hovering in that odd limbo that exists between acquaintance and friendship. He was smart. He had a politician's heart and a politician's smile. He remembered everyone's name and everyone's spouse's name. He acted as though he wanted your vote in the next election *and* he acted as though he deserved it as well. It was a nice trait in someone who had never run for office.

In addition to everything else he had, Elliot Bell-haven had the HIV virus.

I was, I guessed, the only one in the room besides Elliot who knew that last fact. Elliot's sexual orientation was a matter of some curiosity in Boulder's political, law enforcement, and gay and lesbian communities. It wasn't the sort of thing Lauren's colleagues would wonder about over a crowded table at a dinner party, but rather the kind of thing—"So, do you think Elliot's gay?"—that might be spoken casually into the wind to a friend as someone risked public censure by sneaking a cigarette on a host's deck between courses.

Elliot didn't know that I knew his HIV status. And I couldn't tell him that I knew. I'd read about his exposure in his sister's psychological record after her therapist's death had left me access to his patient charts. Elliot's secret should never have been mine to protect. But it was. And my awkwardness about what I knew probably contributed to the state of limbo that marked our relationship.

Elliot strolled around the room shaking hands and counting heads, and when he reached Sam Purdy, he looked at his wristwatch and said, "You ready to get started, Sam?"

I wondered who was going to grab the podium. Detectives and district attorneys sit together atop important investigations like two heads atop a single body. The relationship was, in theory, supposed to be cooperative, but there was always an adversarial edge.

Sam hesitated for a split second. Mistake. Elliot

blew past him. "Good afternoon, everyone. Thanks for coming. Let's get this started."

Except for Sam, everyone moved to a chair.

Elliot again thanked everyone for coming. "This is an unusual meeting to deal with an unusual crime. The purpose of this meeting is threefold. First and foremost, this meeting is for the purpose of developing a criminal profile of the murderer of Peter Arvin. Second, it is an opportunity for each of you to informally present your findings to your colleagues. In your reports, you can't theorize. Today, you can. Third, it's a chance for all of us to put our experience together and see if we can come up with something new to guide this damn investigation. Sam?"

Sam stayed put, leaning against a narrow shaft of wall between the blackboard and the window.

"In my memory, we've only done this a couple of times before in Boulder. But I think it was clear to everyone in this room as you walked onto the stage of the Boulder Theatre in the middle of the night last weekend that this murder wasn't what any of us are used to dealing with. So consider this an atypical response to an atypical crime.

"For those of you who don't know him, I'd like to introduce Dr. Alan Gregory. Alan's a local psychologist who has agreed to volunteer his services to help us assemble a criminal profile of the killer. I'm also going to use today's meeting to gather the information necessary to fill out the VICAP forms for the FBI. So we'll do our best here today on our own, and then we'll get a fresh, unbiased view from the feds.

"Alan has seen all your reports and has developed

some preliminary impressions about what happened at the theatre and about the type of offender who might be responsible.

"Any questions? No? Okay, let's start by reviewing the case history and profiling the victim. Alan will supplement the victim history a little later. Luce?"

Detective Lucy Tanner walked to the front of the room and scooted herself up to sit on a table, facing the group. She crossed her legs at the ankle and seemed unconcerned with her skirt, which was riding up near the territory where knee definitely ends and thigh definitely begins.

Sam grabbed a chair by the windows and straddled it.

I sat in the back row, off by myself, and listened as dispassionately as I could manage as Lucy described the events that had transpired the night of Peter's murder at the Boulder Theatre. She reviewed all the cop stuff—when they got the call, who responded, how the scene was secured, et cetera, et cetera, et cetera. I assumed the minuteness of detail she presented, which was not at all revelatory, was to convince her colleagues that procedures had been followed properly and that nothing had been missed. I digested her almost biblical description of Peter, "a self-employed carpenter married to a physician," and wondered if there was an echo of derision lurking in there somewhere.

As soon as Lucy Tanner finished, Sam spoke without getting up from his chair. "Luce has been in touch with the Denver homicide people—she has a 'friend' who works down there—so she'll also be presenting the similarities and differences between our homicide and the crime that occurred last month at the Performing Arts Complex in Denver. She'll do that at the end, after everybody else has finished."

I wondered, then, why Dale Hunter hadn't been invited to present the case at the Buell herself. Probably too busy.

Michael Martin was next to speak. I pegged him as about my age. His hairline had receded back onto his temples and up his forehead to square off and box his face. He was skinny, not in a particularly athletic way; rather, he was probably one of those guys who eat five thousand calories a day, have an "active metabolism," and consider walking the Downtown Mall to be exercise.

His presentation was funny. Martin was never disrespectful to Peter, which I appreciated, but it was apparent that he was someone who loved having an audience. He walked the front of the room like a stand-up comic, his range of facial expressions as varied as the Colorado weather.

The only problem was that Martin's delivery was much better than his material, because the reality was that the forensic evidence that had been collected on the case was either noncontributory or not yet analyzed. Martin's conclusion: the killer had been methodical, prepared, wary about leaving trace evidence behind, and knowledgeable about how to avoid leaving trace evidence behind.

In the parlance of all my recent reading, Peter's murderer was what psychological profilers call "organized."

"So what do we have? To be honest, not much. It's

one of those cases where the lack of trace evidence and fingerprints is more significant than anything we have in terms of hard findings. This offender knew what he was doing. Although I wouldn't testify to it, I'm guessing gloves, tight cotton clothing, and a hat. He brought his own knife and it has not been recovered. Although the coroner can address this as well, the wounds give us a pretty clear idea that we're looking at a small knife, no more than a four-inch blade. Sharp. Could be folding, could be paring.

"Fingerprints? I've got dozens, maybe close to a hundred, from a half-dozen likely locations around the theatre, and at the entrances and exits. So, in the unlikely event that the offender wasn't gloved, we have something to work with for matching if you guys come up with a suspect. We've run what prints we could through the computers and developed three leads."

He called a question over to Purdy. "Sam, did any of those check out?"

"Lucy?" Sam said, turning toward her. "Nothing there, right?"

"Just some cons who were at the show that night. Two of the pricks were with the band, if you can believe it."

Michael continued. "Stage area was dusty enough in many places to capture shoeprints or at least partials. We lifted what we could and identified eleven different ones plus the victim's. We have a pretty good idea which shoeprints belong to the offender by tracking the victim's prints around the stage and backstage areas. If we're right, the perp has small-to-average feet, eight and a half or nine, and wears an old model of running shoe we think might be Avia. Not much wear on the soles. I doubt he ever used them for running. No noticeable limp or gait defect is apparent, but CBI is far from done with the analysis. The surprise to me, here, is that he wore running shoes and left us with the prints when he was so smart about not leaving other traces around. So, I'll bet you a thousand to one when you find him you won't find these shoes anywhere.

"What else? The best signature we have is from serology. Guy whacked off in two locations in the theatre, left nice fresh semen samples behind. Based on help from the Denver PD lab we already know the guy is an AB-negative secretor. We'll order DNA profiles as soon as you find us somebody to match them to.

"Hair and fibers? We got lots. Enough hair to make a toupee. Enough fibers to weave an afghan. The stage area of the theatre was filthy. I'm sure something we gathered is useful for future matching. The problem is we don't happen to have any magical way to determine the useful from the useless at this point. There was no fiber transfer to the victim. And the only hairs on his clothing were, on preliminary analysis from CBI, his own and his son's.

"Lastly, we have the ligatures. We think the murderer brought them with him. The ropes themselves are nothing special. New, nylon, commercially available at a thousand outlets. The knots used were not distinctive.

"We've collected fingerprint, shoeprint, and hair

samples from everyone we can place on that stage in the eighteen hours prior to the murder. That includes almost two dozen people, including the janitor who found the body and the kid from CU who helped carry the victim to the hospital."

The kid from CU. Kenneth Holden. Missing.

"Crime-scene photography is thorough and available. Videotape of the scene is clean and comprehensive. I want to take a few minutes now to show the videotape and review the crime-scene photographs. See if anything new strikes anybody with a fresh look."

Just then, Madeleine floated through the door and knelt next to Sam's chair. She cupped her hand over her mouth and spoke directly into his ear for about thirty seconds.

Michael started the videotape of the crime scene. I watched about ten seconds of orienting shots.

Sam stood and walked out of the room. I'd seen the videotape twice before, though it felt as if it had been ten times. That was enough. I joined Sam in the hall.

He looked at his feet before he looked in my eyes. "They just found the kid's car. Kenny Holden's. At a trailhead in Rocky Mountain National Park."

Kenneth had become Kenny. It was now official, we were worried about him. "Where is it?"

"Fern Lake Trailhead. Apparently the trailhead isn't far from the Big Thompson, which runs high and fast from snowmelt this time of year. You know the area?"

"Yeah. I went there a few times in graduate school to commune with nature and get naked."

"Figures, you pervert. Well, that's where the car is."

"You think he's gone camping, got hurt, maybe, or lost?"

"It's possible, but, no, I don't think so. This smells. Let's just say I have a feeling Kenny didn't go for a hike."

"Why?"

He shook his head. "I'll tell you later. I may drive up to the park this afternoon if we can get this meeting wrapped up on time. You can come if you want and if you promise to keep your clothes on. You ready to present to our esteemed panel?"

"I'm ready."

"Let's go. Please be brilliant. This case is getting fucking complicated."

—∾∾∾—

Scott Truscott was on next. Scott's boss, the Boulder County coroner, had done the autopsy on Peter. Everyone in the room that day had already read the narrative postmortem findings that the coroner had dictated as he examined Peter's corpse. Scott's role today was to translate his boss's remarks into lay terms and to provide the coroner's interpretations of his findings to the other investigators.

Following Michael Martin's audiovisual lead, Scott set up a poster board plastered with autopsy photographs alongside a large diagram of the wound-pattern distribution that had been found on Peter's body. I noticed that Lucy Tanner seemed to be growing restless as Scott relayed the coroner's impressions of the meaning of the pattern and nature of the knife wounds on Peter's body.

The coroner's interpretation of the wound pattern, which had not been included in the autopsy narrative, was that the killer had used the knife methodically. In only one of the wounds was the blade buried with enough force for the hilt to bruise the adjacent tissue, and the pattern included little of the random angles of entry and differing depths of wounds that are typical of a frenzied killer. None of the cuts was slashing. None of the knife thrusts was intentionally disfiguring. No attempt had been made to disembowel or amputate. The pattern of cuts did not suggest either a sexual focus or a fetish-like attachment to any particular area of the body, including the genitals. The entrance wounds were surprisingly uniform in size and shape and all but two were within thirty degrees of perpendicular.

Peter had been stabbed sixteen times with great care.

The conclusion the coroner reached was this: the Boulder Theatre killer was controlled during this homicide. Although he had not placed the information in his report, the coroner told Scott that the wounds were not inconsistent with torture.

Scott anticipated what the response would be from this skeptical audience. To postpone his challengers, he held up a hand and said, "Hold on, please, everybody. I asked the coroner about this impression specifically. Given what we know about the other murder—the one in Denver—and given that we have a positive serology match for the semen collected in both locations, I asked how consistent his findings were with what we knew about the murder in Denver."

Someone interrupted. "What kind of torture we talking?"

"Who knows. Either to serve a fantasy or for information, I guess. Hold on—the coroner admits that the picture is not consistent. The use of the knife in the Denver murder was frenzied. The killer got lost in that attack. There was a genital focus. This homicide was methodical. The killer never got lost in this one. The coroner's general opinion—and most of you have heard it all from him before—is that the physical-evidence inconsistency is your problem to explain, not his. He is not concluding that these are definitely different offenders. He is only suggesting that the pattern of injuries inflicted during the homicides on these two victims *may* be inconsistent with a single offender acting in a fashion consonant with serial sexual homicide."

I listened carefully to the discussion that followed Scott's presentation of the coroner's findings. In remarkably even tones, everyone jawed back and forth about what meant what. Lucy sat with her arms and legs crossed and offered only a sarcastic "That's quite a stretch" to the argument. Sam was quiet, too, but remained attentive. I assumed he was mulling over the quandary presented by the apparent disappearance of Kenny Holden in Rocky Mountain National Park.

When all the arguing had concluded, the bottom line seemed to be the same one I'd ended up with after my own musings on the same dilemma, that the discrepancies in behavior between the two murders were easier to explain away than the consistency in the semen.

The most efficacious conclusion: two murders, one murderer. This guy was two strikes on the way to a serial strikeout.

My job was clear. It just wasn't easy. How was I going to profile this killer? How would I explain this murderer, one who grew less rather than more impassioned? *Because his passion should evolve.* How would I explain this killer, one who grew more rather than less controlled? *Because his control should decay.*

As Lucy Tanner returned to her perch on the table to present a summary of the similarities and differences between the Denver and the Boulder homicides, I became less and less sure that I had anything intelligent to add to this investigation.

Lucy covered no new ground. Her bias was clearly visible now. So was her admiration of Dale Hunter's work. Perhaps in an effort to counter Scott's presentation, or in anticipation of needing to counter-balance mine, she stressed that the physical findings—particularly the serology reports, the MO, and the consistency of the type of knife used in the homicides—were absolutely clear evidence of one killer's having committed both crimes. Any proponent of an argument to the contrary, she said, bore primary responsibility for explaining away that evidence. She eyed Scott Truscott as she voiced her final challenge.

When her gaze shifted away from him, it came to rest firmly on me. She tugged at her skirt and then slid her fancy pumps to the floor.

Now it was my turn.

A lesson I'd learned during graduate school was to start my class presentations on pedantic, noncontroversial grounds. Offer the unarguable first. Spring the contentious stuff after I had lulled the audience to sleep with the expectation of a diet of tedium.

I was tempted to start this meeting the same way I'd begun dozens of inpatient case presentations over the years: *The patient is a thirty-seven-year-old, married, Caucasian male, self-employed as a carpenter. He has a one-year-old son.*

I didn't. I had already decided to try to can the shrink stuff and to use cop-talk as much as possible. This was an audience I couldn't afford to alienate with professional arrogance, especially given the fact that this was my first stab at profiling.

If not experienced, at least I was prepared. My homework was done. The rudiments of criminal profiling are not high science.

"We have a single homicide," I began. "I will defer for now the question of whether this single homicide is the work of a nascent serial killer. As you all know better than I do, the FBI requires a sequence of three separate homicides with windows of time between each event to categorize an offender as a serial killer. So even with the Denver murder included, we've only got a pair, and that leaves us at least one ace short of three of a kind.

"I'll start with victim risk. If we assume that this is a

targeted-stranger homicide, and thus far the investigation is leaning in that direction, the risk of this particular victim's being chosen in this case can be considered to have been moderate. Peter was known to prefer solitary activities and to frequent local theatres at odd hours to assist in set construction. He was a small man who was not physically imposing.

"In regard to apprehension risk, the chances of the offender's being caught during the commission of this homicide can be considered reasonably low. The theatre was deserted, and the homicide took place at an hour when the building could be expected to be empty. The possibility has already been discussed, however, that despite the low risk of apprehension, the arrival of the janitor on the scene caused the crime to be interrupted prior to its intended conclusion. From the point of view of using judgment effectively, the offender showed reasonable wisdom in his choice of location to commit his crime. Conclusion: we're looking for a smart guy; this offender is not impulsive.

"There seems to have been no evidence discovered that contradicts the conclusion that this victim was abducted at the theatre and killed on the piano. No transportation of the victim to or from the death scene was necessary."

I took a deep breath and tried to stem an itching anxiety. Tension displayed itself in many ways for me, one of which was that I would speak quickly, and end up using words like "nascent" and "mitigated." "That covers all the easy parts of my analysis. Now comes the hard part. It's the hard part because I'm talking here about the murder of my friend. And it's also difficult

because no matter how I shape and mold and finesse
what's in front of me, I can't get the evidence you've
collected so far to fit a coherent profile."

I had already decided to cushion the impact of my
conclusions by presenting them early on. Before this
group started arguing with me about specifics, I
wanted them to know that I couldn't make this suit fit.

"Peter was a man who lived a defiantly independ-
ent life. He didn't care what anybody thought about
his lifestyle or his choices. He made a living as a carpenter but was so good at it that in any given year he
could have made twice or three times what anybody
in this room makes. Peter's primary recreation was the
mountains. He rock-climbed in summer, ice-climbed
in winter. He did cross-country hut tours in the high
country and kayaked rivers that even fish avoid. He
had climbed tough routes on McKinley and Shasta. He
did many of these things by himself. As a man, he was
resourceful. He was resilient. And he was self-reliant.

"What's the point? I'm not sure exactly. I guess that
I want you to know the victim in this case. Because
this victim wasn't chosen for his naïveté, as Lonnie
Aarons was in Denver. He wasn't chosen for his plia-
bility, as Lonnie Aarons was in Denver. And he wasn't
chosen for his susceptibility to charm, as Lonnie
Aarons might have been in Denver.

"Peter was immune to charm. Peter was almost
immune to influence. In the face of charm, Peter was
about as likely to be seduced as a blind man is to be
aroused by a stripper."

As soon as the analogy left my mouth, I found

myself staring straight into Elliot Bellhaven's eyes. It seemed that he was amused.

I walked around the table that was in front of me and scooted myself up into the same position that Lucy had used during her talk. "Peter has a year-old baby. The birth of his baby was the only catalyst I had ever seen have significant impact on Peter's life. He became less rigid, less defiant. He took on work, commercial work—work he hated—to set aside money for Jonas's college education.

"Peter was a fighter, he was tenacious as hell. I'd seen him carry a recreational tennis match to three hours in the July sun. I'd seen him take chess games to five hours.

"Although I know there is no evidence of his having suffered resistance wounds and no evidence of Peter's having defended himself from a close-range assault, I guarantee you that I've been unable to think of a single circumstance where Peter would voluntarily disrobe and climb on top of that piano to be bound and tortured. It's even hard for me to imagine Peter doing that because somebody had a gun pointed in his face.

"We have to explain that anomaly. We must. And so far we haven't."

Anomaly. I was still anxious.

"I'm going to move away from discussing the victim now and talk about the perpetrator, the killer. You've already heard the detailed crime assessment. You know what Peter was up to that night prior to the assault. You know how we think the offender spent his evening, as well.

"There is no doubt—none—that we are looking for an organized offender. We can also safely assume that the offender had a way to get Peter to be cooperative. Perhaps the method was as simple as a gun. I don't know.

"The murder was staged, but the crime scene wasn't. The dramatic aspects of the crime were plotted out beforehand. The nakedness, the ligatures, the piano, the slow cutting, the masturbating—all part of a script. There is no evidence that the crime scene was set up in a particular way to mislead the investigation. However, it is my opinion that the janitor who came in to clean the theatre did interrupt the killer. So even if the offender had planned to rearrange the scene in some fashion that would disguise something about the crime, he didn't have time to pull it off.

"What about motivation? What drove this homicide? The most cogent assumption is that the crime was sexually motivated. The victim's genitals were prominently exposed. The offender masturbated in excitement over his work. Not once, but twice. Given the functioning of the human penis, we have to consider the likelihood that he stopped for self-abuse at two different periods during the production."

I looked over at Scott Truscott before continuing. "Obviously, as Scott has already stated, a sexually motivated crime is inconsistent with one of the coroner's alternate hypotheses about the nature of the knife wounds—that is, that the homicide possibly related to torture unconnected with the sexual pleasure of the offender."

One of the muscular cops Lucy had called "the fat

boys" interrupted me. "What if it was both? What if the homicide involved not only elements of torture for information but also elements of sexual sadism?"

Sam finally broke his silence. He had remedied his slouch and was sitting up straight, interested. "Hold on a second. Isn't it a fair supposition that if a victim is being tortured for information, it isn't too damn likely that he was chosen at random? Doesn't this whole line of reasoning undermine the working assumption of a stranger killing?"

I watched, fascinated, as Lucy Tanner's face displayed her realization of what was happening. "Oh, no, you don't," she said, turning in her chair so that she grabbed everyone's attention. "Isn't our job, gentlemen," she said, "to find the most efficient explanation for the facts? What you guys are doing here is adding layer after layer, trying to accommodate facts that your theory can't explain. You're building a house of cards, not a criminal profile." She smiled a conciliatory smile. "This one's a lot simpler than you're making it. Do what's natural, guys. Let the dicks do the talking. Follow the damn sperm."

Sam chuckled. Then he nodded once, opened his eyes wide, and clenched his fists. I imagined a lightbulb above his head flashing on at about a zillion watts.

What had clicked for him?

I finished my presentation with a recounting of the differences of the dramatic qualities of the two productions, Denver and Boulder. As an amateur profiler, even if I could account for those differences, which I couldn't, I faced other dilemmas. How did I explain the change in the knife wounds—pattern, distribution, intensity—between the two murders? How did I explain the increase in organization from crime to crime? And how did I explain the dispassionate nature of Peter's murder when compared to the killing of Lonnie Aarons?

Barring the presence of the identical semen at the two crime scenes, I told the group, my conclusion would be that we were dealing with two different offenders. With the semen, my conclusion was that I needed more data.

"So this is what we have so far—based on the single-suspect theory and based largely on sexual homicide offender probability data gathered by the FBI. We're looking for a white male, eldest or only child, of above-average intelligence. Data suggest that offenders who perform serial sexual homicide are usually between twenty and thirty-nine. Given what he has accomplished so far in life, I would use the middle of that range as a minimum; I think he is in his late twenties to late thirties. This offender is more successful than you might expect, and probably holds down a reasonable job, but one below his skill level. Norms show that he has only marginally successful, superficial relationships. Given the choice of victims and the sexual activity at the scenes, he may be homosexual, but is just as likely to be confused as to his sexual orientation. He might be dating occasionally, for appearances, or out of reluctance to accept his sexual preference. He likely lives alone. If he's with a roommate, they're not close, and the arrangement is for financial reasons.

"I'm guessing that he doesn't have a history of serious criminal offenses. I would be surprised if he has previous convictions for rape or sexual assault. He's new at this. Remember, he's smart; smart enough to know that his signature—killing on stages in theatres with knives—leaves him vulnerable to apprehension.

"He's connected to the theatre. He may be an actor or otherwise involved in theatre production—stage management, lighting, design. He may have studied theatre in college. He may just be an aficionado. I wouldn't be surprised to see his bedroom decorated with theatre paraphernalia—posters, programs, souvenirs, whatever. You may find that souvenirs from the crimes have been added to the collection. I would guess that he took photographs, perhaps even video-tapes, of what happened. When you catch him, you may find them.

"He's computer-sophisticated. I would imagine that computers are either integral to his vocation or are a serious avocation for him.

"He drives his own car and lives somewhere in the metro area; his mobility is certainly not limited by walking distance to either theatre. Sometimes, with killers like this, there's a pocket of chaos someplace in what, to outward appearances, looks like an organized life. Maybe his car is a hovel. Maybe his room. Maybe his desk.

"The offender's family background started off stable. Both his parents were in the home. He suffered losses early, but I'm betting not *too* early. He remembers something. It's the fuel for his fantasies, for his anger. The easiest guess is loss. Maybe one parent died or left him, maybe both. His anger is focused on males. Both my friend Peter and Lonnie Aarons were slight and blond. I wouldn't be surprised if there was a paternal resemblance. I would imagine the offender suffered moderate to severe abuse on at least a few occasions growing up.

"Moving to the dual-suspect theory, what I've got to offer"—I paused—"is nothing."

With that I asked for questions or discussion. We talked, we argued a little, we got nowhere. I promised a written report by late the next afternoon.

I hung around until everyone but Sam had left the room.

"Great work, Doctor," he said. "I have a feeling you've just provided additional credibility to Dale Hunter's thirty percent profiler-bullshit theory."

He was smiling. I couldn't tell if he meant it.

III

*Road
Show*

It wasn't the sex, which was great, even better than the premarital version had been.

The surprise about being married had come from other unfathomed, inconsequential things.

One night I commented while snuggling up to Lauren in the exalted fortnight right after our wedding that I loved the feel and smell of clean, fresh sheets. From that day forward, twice a week, fresh, crisp linen appeared on our bed. Not a word was ever said about why.

The gesture was a simple gift that was renewed each time it was granted, and each time I got into our bed and felt the tight, soft weave of freshly laundered bedding, I also felt loved. So simple.

The marriage was like that from the start. A dreamy quilt woven of ordinary scraps of love.

Sometimes, on those days when she finished up in her office before I was done in mine, she would sit in my waiting room on Walnut Street and look at back issues of *The New Yorker*. When my last patient departed, she would come into my office and do her best to read me to see what kind of day I'd had, and she would embrace me, or kiss me, or walk me downtown to the West End Tavern and buy me a drink. Or two. Once she walked in, seductively removed her blouse and her bra, lay down on my sofa, and said she desperately needed a back rub.

I obliged.

I grew to know her strength better and better and to respect it and honor it without comment. That was important to her. Her thighs and buttocks were, I knew, sore and bruised from years of injections. Often, too often, I watched the steel door slam shut on her as she was imprisoned by one or both of the twin jailers of heat and fatigue, which would cause the residue of old exacerbations of her multiple sclerosis to revisit her like reruns of old, annoying TV shows.

Before Peter was murdered, as our first married spring approached, I brought a contractor in to air-condition the house as a surprise. When she came home that day and spied the work that had been done, she had tears in her eyes, and she caressed the new thermostat as though I had just presented her with a string of the finest jewels.

What can I say? I was in love with the woman.

The ring of the phone startled me. So did Adrienne's voice, which seemed compressed with labored calm. "Alan, can you come down to the studio right away? I mean *now*."

It was midnight. I was propped in bed next to my sleeping wife, scribbling corrections on a draft of my report for Sam. The damn thing was due the next day. Madeleine had agreed to retype it for me if I had it on her desk by lunchtime.

I said, "Of course, what's going on?"

"Just hurry," she replied, and hung up.

I scrawled out a quick note to Lauren and left it on my pillow, pulled on jeans and a heavy sweatshirt, found some shoes I could tolerate wearing without socks, and headed for the front door. Emily was right with me. I was grateful for her company.

Adrienne had the studio lit up like Coors Field for a night game. I'd expected she would be waiting anxiously at the door. She wasn't. Saying, "Yoo hoo," as I walked in, I found her hunched over Peter's desk, sifting through stacks of files, matching sketches with bids, and finished pieces with invoices, a jigsaw puzzle that when finally put together would probably close the book on the financial aspects of Peter's art and craft.

"Hi, Ren," I said softly, approaching the desk. "You find something important in Peter's papers?"

"On, yeah, I found something important. But not in the papers." She seemed distracted. "You know what I did today? You know what I *found* today? I found a potato. A goddamned *russet.*"

I stopped waiting for her to lift a sheet of paper from the desk and offer it to me in explanation. As she was prone to do, Adrienne was, I sensed, about to take me someplace I had never been before. I knew my next line. "You found a potato?"

"I'm finishing an operation this morning and I get a call from the ER. There's a young woman there who claims she has a tree growing out of her vagina. Nurse tells me she thinks the woman is psychotic. I say, like, really, what was your first clue? Woman won't cooperate with a pelvic. Nurse says there's a terrible odor and a foul discharge and wonders if I'll take a look under anesthesia. I say, hell, why not, I'm a damn tree surgeon, right? They get permission and get her prepped and I get a speculum in, and sure enough, she's got an entire Idaho stuffed in there, sprouting like Jack's goddamn beanstalk."

I didn't know what to say. "Why didn't they get a gynecologist to do this?"

She smiled at me. "Gynecologists don't do potato extractions, they only do the other root vegetables— your parsnips, your turnips, your rutabagas."

I made a quick judgment that the tuber story wasn't the reason I had been beckoned in the wee hours.

"What's up about Peter, Ren?"

Ignoring my question, she stood up and greeted Emily with some baby talk before she walked over to the sailcloth shrouds that still blanketed the big finished pieces on the west side of the room. With crisp motions she yanked them off one by one, revealing the carefully sculpted components that someday soon would come together to be a bar in a saloon in yet another unnecessary fake Old West casino up in Black Hawk.

Nothing looked amiss with Peter's work. Adrienne ducked around the biggest of the pieces and said, "Not there, back here."

Emily immediately ran and joined Adrienne, sniffing at the edges of many things that caught her canine fancy. I followed, squeezing into a narrow corridor behind the uncovered saloon pieces.

Another shroud, this one older, dirtier, and caked with dried paint, covered a long piece that Peter had shoved against the wall. We hadn't seen it during our cursory search the other night, but thoroughness had not been our aim then. Adrienne looked me in the eye in a way that pierced through any of my post-midnight malaise that might have survived the potato tale, then yanked on the shroud. The big cloth formed a billowing cloud that soon deflated at her feet.

When I looked back up I saw that Peter, the carpenter, had constructed a casket. It was elegant in its simplicity. The wood was pine, lodgepole, and knotty. The lines of the coffin were square, except for the lid. The long box narrowed at the feet, flayed out at the shoulders. The lid was bowed up and the rounded center section was carved in intricate relief.

Peter had once told me that he had toyed with, then given up, the practice of woodcarving long before we met. The design on the casket was complex but not particularly inspired; and it helped me understand why Peter had eschewed carving for carpentry.

Before I could say a word to Adrienne in reaction to the coffin, I heard the shuffle of footsteps behind me, and turned to see Lisa, sleep etched in her features, standing in the doorway to the studio. Jonas, awake but somnolent, was in her arms. Lisa had apparently pulled on some sweatpants to go with the long T-shirt in which she slept. The shirt was wrinkled.

Emily offered a tenor "Wooooo," to greet the two intruders. The bark succeeded in bringing Jonas to tears.

I said, "Emily, quiet."

She said "Wooooo" again, as though she were definitively establishing the parameters of my influence over her.

Lisa ran her fingers through Jonas's thick hair. "Adrienne, I think he's got a fever. He's tugging at his ear again. Do you have your otoscope home?"

"Yeah, I think it's in my bag. I'll be up in a few minutes to take a look."

Lisa appeared not to hear. She was staring straight at the part of the unshrouded casket that was visible from the doorway.

Adrienne found her way out of the narrow space by the coffin, then kissed her cranky son and felt the flesh on his face and abdomen. She dismissed Lisa quickly. "Take him back up and give him some Tylenol for now. He's probably got another otitis; we may have to get him to Dr. Amy tomorrow. Take my bag up to his room, too, okay?"

Lisa said, "Sure," in a thin voice. I sensed that she wanted to stay, or to say something, maybe about the casket. When she finally mobilized her feet to move, she looked over her shoulder at me, gazing back with a dolefulness that momentarily made me forget the coffin that Peter had made.

"Earth to Alan."

"What?"

"The coffin. We're talking life and death, here, sweets, not young flesh and cleavage like the Royal Gorge."

Adrienne had misread me. My focus on Lisa at that moment wasn't particularly lascivious, but was, rather, perplexed and curious.

"Did the police see this when they searched?" Sam hadn't said anything to me.

"I don't know. They mostly seemed interested in his

paperwork. I think they just kind of looked around the shop."

"What's this carving on top?"

"It's mountain shit. Peaks and trees and the call of the wild. You know Peter." Not "You knew Peter."

"What's it mean? Who's it for?"

"*Hello.* That's why you're here. He told me he got rid of this thing years ago. Obviously, he didn't. This is Peter's unconscious talking to us. So interpret. That's what you mindsuckers do, isn't it? Interpret the unfathomable? Go ahead, interpret the great mysteries of Peter's mind for me." She stood still and defied me with her eyes. I reminded myself that when she was in a better mood, Adrienne was a kind woman who actually referred patients to me.

"Do you think it's Peter's? I mean, did he intend it to be used for himself?"

"You can bet your ass it's Peter's. Given his preoccupation with death I'm surprised there's not one for me in here somewhere. Or some version with gussets for Jonas."

"But you knew about it?"

"Years ago, before we even moved here, he told me he had built it and asked me if I wanted to see it. I said absolutely not, that I thought it was macabre. He said he'd get rid of it."

Just like he said he would stop free-soloing.

My mood had grown almost as dark as Adrienne's humor. "But why didn't he show it to you recently, in the last few years, so you would know he still wanted to be buried in it?"

Adrienne moved close to me. The top of her head

barely reached my shoulder. She looked up at me, her eyes dark. "You need to attend a few more funerals, Alan. That's not a burying coffin, it's a burning coffin. That wood is pine. The occupant of that box was destined to be cremated."

A few days earlier, Peter's body had been placed in a fine cherry box and lowered into the dense clay of the cemetery out on the Diagonal Highway. I recalled no hand-wringing about the relative merits of cremation versus boxed decay.

"Did you know that Peter wanted to be cremated?" Then, before she answered and because I'd never had reason to ask before, I continued, "Did he leave a will? Like with instructions for what he wanted done with, you know, what he wanted done with his—"

"Are we talking assets or remains here? The answer is no. No will, no funeral instructions. The best I ever got him to do was agree to sign a notarized statement that spelled out our wishes about a guardian for Jonas should both of us die. A will? You mean how to divide up his power tools? Who gets the world's second-oldest operating Volvo? No, not Peter. Not my Peter."

Who makes himself a casket?

A carpenter philosophically preoccupied with death, of course. But why? If my guess about the dating of Peter's last woodcarving was correct, why build a casket so many years ago and still hang on to it? And if Peter did go to all this trouble, why not at least tell his wife he had kept the damn thing so that his final wishes could be respected?

"Adrienne, you and Peter kept your businesses, your work lives, to yourselves, didn't you?"

She glared. "You're asking why I didn't know any-thing about the box? Or about the saloon? Or all these stupid pieces of paper on his desk, or anything else, right?" The frustration was apparent in her voice. I thought she was close to tears.

I nodded.

"He didn't know shit about my practice, either. How many patients I see, how many surgeries I did, what my secretary's name is. He wasn't interested. If I wanted to talk about a case that was on my mind, or a patient who was making me nuts about something, or some colleague who had just convinced me that the phrase 'ultimate asshole' was an oxymoron, Peter was a good listener.

"At times he was a little too mystical for someone like me, but still a good listener. As far as his work went, he'd mention a new client or bring me down here occasionally to show me a piece he'd completed that he was really proud of, but mostly our work lives were separate.

"It was a funny ritual, but every spring, he'd fill out an income-and-expense sheet for our accountant, and a few weeks later I'd stick a 1040 under his nose and show him where to sign, and he'd sign. He never looked at our income. Or my income. Never. Asking him how much money we made each year would have been like asking him how the Broncos did last season. He just didn't care."

Gazing up at my face, she sighed. "Well, now I've finally got you making interpretations, haven't I? And you're right. Our marriage wasn't normal. Why should it have been? I'm not. He wasn't. How the hell could our marriage be normal?"

This woman left me speechless more often than anyone I have ever met in my life.

"Alan, please go find Peter for me, so someday I can tell Jonas who his daddy was."

We locked eyes. "I'll talk to Lauren and see about going to Jackson this weekend, Ren. Call his mom and tell her we're coming, okay? Can I have the keys to the shop, too? I'm going to want to look around some more, if that's okay with you."

She tossed a key ring to me before trotting out the door. Her parting shot was "Remember Miss Potato Crotch? As soon as she's stabilized on lithium, I'm going to refer her to you for psychotherapy. You can talk to her about her momma." Adrienne didn't turn back for a last look.

The coffin still held my attention. I walked past the bar cabinetry to examine the box against the wall. The casket was Peter-sized, there was no doubt about that. And the carved panel in the center of the lid was definitely *Call of the Wild* material. A river, a mountain range, pine trees, and, in the upper right corner, licks of something else. I couldn't tell exactly what.

I opened the box. The lid lifted without a creak and locked at ninety degrees. The interior of the box was unfinished, rough, and splintery. No fabric covered the wood, as though Peter had decided that his last resting place should be a kind of splintered purgatory.

Emily barked. Not an early-warning "Wooooo," but a bark. A crisp one. This meant "intruder present."

I turned at her warning and saw Lisa standing ten

feet from the open door of the studio, her arms crossed in front of her. The long T-shirt, the long, straight hair.

But for this visit, she hadn't even bothered to pull on sweatpants.

At first she seemed oblivious to my presence. Her eyes didn't meet mine, but went past me. For a second I thought she was about to say something. I followed her gaze, turning back toward the casket, and drew in my breath at what I saw.

When I turned to face her again and opened my mouth to speak, she was gone.

Blindly, with my left hand, I reached up and tenderly traced the carving on the underside of the lid. I looked at the inscription. It read: "July 10, 1982."

The words were carved right where Peter's eyes would have been had he ever found his way into this box, as though the vision of that day in July is what he had planned to carry with him through eternity.

My first patient the next morning was due at nine o'clock, so I slept in till almost seven and grabbed a quick breakfast with Lauren before she headed to court.

She wasn't surprised about Peter's pine coffin.

"You know, I would never have predicted it, but on

the other hand, it's not unlike him. Peter talked about death more than anyone I ever met. I mean, even with me, and he didn't know me very well."

She was in a hurry to get to work, yet her kiss lingered for a few seconds. She pulled away, hugged the dog, and ran out to start her ten-minute commute to the Justice Center. I finished my coffee and read the local paper, noting that no progress had been made in the search for Kenny Holden in Rocky Mountain National Park.

After a quick shower, I walked with Emily back to Peter's studio.

I knew Sam was concerned that Kenny's disappearance was related to Peter's murder, but what nagged at me that morning wasn't the possible connection between Kenny and Peter, but instead, an intense sadness for Kenny's parents, who, the paper reported, had flown in from a suburb of Milwaukee to assist with the search.

On another day, I would have used the extra morning time at my disposal to indulge my favorite luxury, a bike ride, but my negligence about following up on some mundane things I had meant to do in the wake of Peter's murder was troubling me, and I had pledged to myself the night before that I would do my best to clear the list before the day was out.

I had not remembered, despite my best intentions, to get in touch with Tony Celli to arrange for him to come to the studio to pick up the pieces of the Black Hawk casino saloon and put a finish on them. And I had not discovered the name of the casino, or the identity of Peter's contact there, so that I could arrange to have the work delivered and Jonas's zero-coupon bond funded.

The first thing I did when I walked back into the studio was to put the shroud back in place on Peter's casket. That done, I could then sit reasonably comfortably at his desk. Peter, bless him, made my search for Tony Celli easy; Tony's name was on a speed-dial button on Peter's phone. I punched it and ten seconds later was talking with Tony Celli himself.

I explained who I was and why I was calling. Tony seemed distracted.

"You're lucky you caught me, I'm never here this late. Never. You're calling about my bud, huh? Peter, Peter, oh, my my. Can you believe what they did to him? I mean, can you believe it? It's fucking tragic, I'll tell you. Such a talent. Ain't nobody to replace him. Nobody." Tony paused, then, honestly quizzical, asked, "*Who* are you?"

"I'm his friend, his neighbor. Had he mentioned this project to you, Tony? I think it's cabinetry for a saloon. Uppers and lowers, probably forty, fifty feet of each."

"Really? Like a bar? Peter didn't do crap like that much anymore. A dozen different commercial companies could knock that off at a third what Peter would charge. Peter used to say he was tired of making fucking boxes with doors."

Peter was not particularly profane. He might indeed have said that he was tired of making boxes with doors. That sounded like him. The "fucking"—I was pretty certain—was a Tony Celli embellishment. More to the point, the news that Tony didn't know who Peter's client was on this job was truly discouraging. It probably meant that to solve my puzzle I would have to descend into Peter's files, a deep dive I wasn't looking forward to.

"Well, for whatever reason, Peter apparently did this project, Tony. I'm sitting in his studio right now, and I'm surrounded by the stuff. It's beautiful, but it sure looks like cabinetry for a saloon. His wife thinks it was for one of the casinos in Black Hawk."

"Whatever. Peter was a surprising guy. I'll come by and take a look at it. You want to leave the shop open for me, or what?"

I didn't want to leave the studio unlocked. "I'll leave a key with the nanny. Her name's Lisa. Is that okay?"

"Hey, whatever."

"Will you give Adrienne a bid to stain the cabinetry? Is that how this works?"

"No, no, no. Peter didn't like to include finish costs in his bids, just made life more complicated for him, which he wasn't fond of. I'll bill the customer myself, that is if I want the job."

"You mean you might not do it?"

"Depends. What the client wants me to do, if I like 'em, if they're cheap fucks. Peter and I are the best. We pick our customers, they don't pick us."

Adrienne, who was lucky she never had to make a living organizing someone else's life, had stuffed Peter's papers back into their files in a markedly haphazard manner. After fifteen minutes of straightening and flipping and checking dates and customer's names, and trying to match sketches with the pieces in his shop, I was stymied by the paperwork. I didn't know how I was going to identify the lucky casino customer whom Peter had selected to fund Jonas's first year at Stanford.

I had one last brainstorm to try before I made my way downtown to my office. I called directory assistance and asked for the numbers of a couple of big casinos already established in Black Hawk—Harrah's and Bullwhackers—and discovered the exchange for Black Hawk. I then looked to see whether a similar exchange was scrawled on any of the note sheets that cluttered Peter's desk.

Bingo.

The exchange in Black Hawk was 582. But the notes littering the desk provided no matching prefix. However, one solitary circled phone number written on the border of Peter's desk blotter started with those digits. I didn't have time to call right then, so I jotted down the phone number in my appointment book, yelled to Emily to come with me, and half ran to my car to get downtown to see my first patient.

I was halfway to Baseline Road when I remembered that I had neither locked the studio nor left a key for Lisa to give to Tony. A quick glance at my watch told me I could either go back home or get downtown in time for my appointment. I couldn't do both.

I made a U-turn.

After locking the studio, I drove to Adrienne's front door and rang the doorbell for Lisa. She answered in a fashion that in less pressured circumstances I might have called leisurely. I explained that Tony Celli would be coming by to appraise the bar cabinetry and asked if she would help out by letting him into the studio so he could take a look at the pieces that were ready. I held out the key.

Lisa was without Jonas. I guessed he was upstairs sleeping off his otitis.

Lisa's eyes were bright, and her skin still had an early-morning radiance. She displayed no awkwardness about our brief visual encounter the night before.

She palmed the key. "Sure, that's fine. I know Tony, no problem." She held the key back out to me. "I know where Peter's spare key is. You can keep that one."

"You know Tony?" Of course she would know Tony. She had worked for Peter and Adrienne full-time for over a year. Lisa had been around during the day, when Peter did most of his business. She probably knew most of his cronies.

"Peter liked him. Said there was nothing smooth about Tony but his finishes." She smiled, exposing a thin line of gum above her upper teeth.

Lisa's almost-blond hair was parted in the middle and fell past her shoulders in a long, straight shot. In the sixties, women would iron and peroxide their hair for that look. In the current fashion climate, I didn't know whether straight hair and rich full bangs were style liabilities or to-die-for assets.

I suspected that Lisa didn't know, either. I liked that about her.

If I hadn't had a patient awaiting me downtown, I probably would have stayed to question her further about Peter's friends, her appearance at the studio the night before, and her reaction to the coffin. Instead, I said, "Thanks for helping out," and raced back to my car.

To my back, in a voice louder than I had ever heard her use, Lisa said, "The cabinets, Alan, if you're wondering, I know who they're for."

I stopped in my tracks. "You do?"

She nodded.

One look at my watch told me I had run out of flexibility in my schedule about ten minutes earlier. "Who?"

"His name's Grant Arnold."

It meant nothing to me. As good as Lisa's news was, I knew doing anything with it would have to wait. "Where does he work?"

"That's all I know. Just a name."

"Listen, I want to talk with you some more," I said, "but I need to go, I have a patient waiting. You going to be here all morning? Can I call you in an hour and a half or so?" I had back-to-back appointments scheduled, forty-five minutes each, to start my morning.

She nodded again and closed the door. I thought I heard Jonas crying upstairs.

Despite her earlier assurance, Lisa wasn't at Adrienne's house when I called around ten forty-five. Nor was she home when I tried back at twelve-fifteen, two patients later.

As I hung up from leaving Lisa a message on Adrienne's answering machine at twelve-fifteen, my friend and partner in clinical practice, Diane Estevez, poked her head through my open office door.

"You want to grab some lunch? I'm meeting Raoul someplace for curry, his newest rage."

I was more than tempted. Diane was a dear friend,

and Raoul, her husband, was a constant source of wonder for me. They would be a great antidote to my current preoccupation with the sequelae to Peter's death.

"Unfortunately, I have to drive across town and drop a report off for Sam Purdy at the police department. Otherwise I'd love to have lunch with you guys."

"What kind of report?"

I told her.

"You're kidding. When did you learn that? You know how to do that stuff?"

"I'm learning now."

"Odd time for Sam to hire an intern, isn't it?"

"Thanks for your confidence in me. Actually, my initial conclusions seem to be in direct contradiction to the physical evidence, so Sam's faith in me may well have been misplaced. The FBI is doing its own profile. Pretty soon I'll be able to compare notes with the real profilers and get officially humiliated."

Diane redirected the conversation, something at which she was wonderfully adept, and soon had me talking about Peter, and how it felt to be involved in the investigation of his murder, and how was I doing with all this, anyway? A few minutes later, when she glanced at her watch and sprinted away to meet Raoul, I knew that I felt a hell of a lot better than before her appearance in my doorway.

Sam was at Madeleine's desk, bent at the waist, pointing at a handwritten list, when I arrived at the police department.

Madeleine smiled a greeting to me and indicated with her eyes and with a quick shake of her head that I should keep the profiling paperwork to myself for the time being. She didn't, I surmised, want Sam to know she was typing it for me.

"We've got news on two fronts," Sam said. "The searchers in Rocky Mountain National Park found a campsite set up with Kenny's stuff. His pack, his tent—everything but his camera."

"That's important, I take it."

He spared a second or two to glare at me. "All his friends say Kenny was a photography nut. Would never go into the mountains or anywhere else without at least one camera. His roommate and his girlfriend both say he didn't really like to camp or hike; apparently he only did it because it gave him opportunities to take some pictures."

"So he must have it with him, right?" I asked, distracted by Madeleine pointing to the trash can beside her desk, gesturing at my coat pocket with her eyes. She was behind Sam, who couldn't see her pantomime.

"No. He doesn't. That's what's interesting. Kenny didn't take any of his cameras with him. His roommate says all his photography equipment is accounted for in his apartment."

As casually as I could, I pulled the folded papers with my report on them from my sportcoat pocket and dropped them into the trash. Madeleine would retrieve them after Sam and I left.

"Maybe he bought a new one, or borrowed one."

"Maybe. And maybe a spaceship landed and the creatures took his camera from him and hurried it back to their craft so they could analyze it for rare metals."

I could have returned the volley. I didn't. Of Sam's repertoire of moods, this sardonic one wasn't my favorite. I decided to leapfrog to the conclusion. "You think the campsite, the car, everything's a setup to cover up a kidnapping?'

"Yeah, today, if I had to bet, I'd say that I think Kenny was abducted and probably killed. And somebody has done a ninety-nine-point-nine percent perfect job of convincing us he wasn't."

"And you think it's because he saw something the night of Peter's murder and the murderer is busy covering his tracks?"

"Gosh, you're smart," Sam said. "The other piece of news I've got is more difficult for our investigation to digest, given the prevailing evidence that says Peter and Lonnie Aarons were killed by the same guy, and our point of view that maybe they weren't."

"Yeah? What?"

"The lab guys at CBI may have a match. Somebody in Denver is pulling some serious strings to get this thing rushed. Anyway, two hairs found on the stage of the Boulder Theatre, near the piano, match a hair found on the computer keyboard at the Buell."

"DNA?"

"No. You need a root and forever for that. That would give us a one hundred percent match. These are only shafts. So it's only ninety percent sure."

"What kind of hair?"

"Long and blond. Pretty distinctive, apparently—so says CBI. Michael Martin says their hair guy is a wiz and he's pretty damn certain that all three hairs are from the same offender."

"But it's not definitive?"

"No, but it'll be close enough for a juror who's looking for a reason to convict somebody."

I looked hard at Sam. "It seems that we may be wrong about two different killers. The little boat we're in seems to be sinking. I think it may be time to abandon it and see if there's any room left on that nice big ocean liner that's sailing nearby with all our friends on it."

"Tell that to Kenny's parents. And don't forget your initial conclusion after you saw what you saw at the Buell and heard Charley's version of the murder. That nice cruise liner may be popular and cushy, but that doesn't mean it's going to the right places." He looked away and stared at his assistant. "And Madeleine, when you're finished typing that damn report for Dr. Gregory, I want to see it."

Sam looked warmly at me and laughed. "God, I wish you were the killer, Alan. You're so fucking inept, I'd have solved this damn case in less time than it takes me to trim my toenails."

Elitch's had moved to the Platte River Valley, the Rockies were home playing the Giants, and open parking spaces near Coors Field in Denver's LoDo were an endangered species. Lauren and I lucked upon a metered slot way down Wazee, near Speer, and strolled hand in hand back through the reclaimed splendor of Denver's century-old warehouse district in Lower Downtown. We were on our way to the Oxford Hotel.

Five years earlier we would have been scurrying from the illuminated arc of one streetlight to the illuminated arc of another, gazing warily into the entryways of the many boarded-up, derelict buildings of the district. Now we window-shopped at elegant stores and strolled past dozens of new restaurants and bars. Although LoDo had been on a slow economic ascent before major-league baseball came to town, the advent of the new ballpark at Twenty-third and Blake provided a golden cornerstone for the resuscitation of Denver's storied old district of wild boys and bad girls, warehouses and whorehouses.

Our destination that night was the Cruise Room in the Oxford Hotel. Although I'd never been there, Lauren knew the place well from the time of her first marriage. Her ex-husband's family's money came from railroads, and when I asked her, on the drive into Denver, why he preferred that particular bar, Lauren commented that she thought that her ex "liked to drink close to his money." Union Station was only a short block away from the Oxford.

If Coors Field was the impetus for the completion of the rejuvenation of LoDo, the renovation of the Oxford had been the first seed actually sown. A glorious old hotel built to serve the genteel railroad trade of another era, it had slid into disrepute and disrepair by the time Denver's urban business center had migrated a dozen blocks up Seventeenth Street, away from the brick and stone and humane scale of LoDo, and into the glass-and-aluminum ostentation of the downtown skyscrapers.

Although the Oxford's renovation had turned out to be a financial debacle for its developers, it had been an equally stunning aesthetic success, especially the restoration of the fabled Cruise Room to its original Art Deco splendor.

Lauren and I had made good time on the drive in from Boulder and arrived at the cocktail lounge before Charley Chandler made his way over from his office in the Performing Arts Complex ten blocks away. I'd called Charley that afternoon and asked him if he minded having another meeting to talk about the theatre murders. He had sounded pleased to hear from me and suggested cocktails at the Cruise Room after work. Lauren was delighted to join me.

She and I waited for a table to clear in the long, narrow lounge. The dimly lit space reminded me of an elegant, windowless Pullman that someone with an ample budget had outfitted seventy years ago for leisure and pleasure. The room had a small bar fronted by chrome stools, and the red-neon-illuminated walls were lined with booths.

The crowd was a mixture of self-absorbed couples, post-workday singles in Armani knockoffs and Ferragamo pumps, and pregame, don't-like-the-sports-bars singles in Levi's and Timberlands.

Every seat was taken and standing space was

minimal. I felt grateful when a booth opened in the middle of the room and Lauren tugged me to a soft upholstered bench. She flagged down a waitress and ordered a vodka martini for me and a gin version for herself.

Martinis were not our typical cocktails. Lauren explained, "The Cruise Room is a martini place. It'll be right, trust me."

We sat quietly, taking in the chatter, the flirtatious hits, offensive misses, and simply bad pitches being made all around us. It was early, not yet seven, and the energy in the room was cheerful; as yet, no one was more than mildly concerned about going home without a phone number or a partner.

Our drinks arrived quickly, and the waitress deposited the cocktail napkins and tall, classic martini stems on the table rather perfunctorily. I took a long sip and smiled at my wife. "You were right, this is perfect," I said to Lauren, who was intently browsing. The Cruise Room was an elegant place, full of pretty people. If social circumstances dictated that you had to be on the hunt, this was like getting to do it in the Serengeti.

Lauren apparently thought so, too. I watched her eyes lock onto someone behind me. She was so intent on whomever she was gaping at that she didn't even notice me look to see the focus of her attention.

I turned back to face her. "That's Charley Chandler, hon. Our date for tonight."

She held her breath for a second, then exhaled after processing my words and apparently recognizing them as English. "Wow," she said in a whisper, "he's cute." She looked down for a split second, then back up.

Charley Chandler's slow, confident walk and brash good looks turned a few more female heads and a couple of male ones before he spotted me, nodded in greeting, and slid onto the bench across from Lauren's.

I made the introductions.

"Hello," he said.

"Nice to meet you," she said. She was blushing.

I wondered if I seemed this inane around Lisa. I said, "I really appreciate your taking the time to talk with me again, Charley."

"My pleasure, absolutely, Alan. Especially since you brought your gorgeous wife. You've ordered? Let me get something." The cocktail waitress appeared at his side before he had a chance to look around for her. He ordered a neat Irish whiskey and a water back.

"So, you're hooked, too?" he said to me, without preamble. "I'm not surprised, it's actually kind of nice to have the company. Personally, I can't get this whole thing out of my head. I think about it. I write about it. I talk about it. I only hope that Dale and Sam catch this guy soon, so I can start thinking about something else. My wife says if this jerk doesn't get the death penalty, she'll kill him herself for what he's done to our marriage."

"Charley's been writing a mystery," I explained to Lauren.

He made a dismissive gesture. "Mostly I love to read them. I'm just a dreamer with the writing I'm doing. But so far I'm loving that, too." He turned to face her. "What do you love to do, Lauren?"

What a disarming line, I thought. I felt like getting up from the table and sharing it with the people at the bar who were still struggling with their come-ons.

I was about to respond to Charley's question by commenting that Lauren seemed remarkably content just to be staring into his eyes, when the two of them began a long conversation about what it's like to be a DA and to prosecute violent criminals. Charley had a dozen questions about the investigatory role of a prosecutor and the nuts and bolts of interrogations. Lauren responded in great detail about a subject that she usually finds tedious.

Great detail.

I finished my vodka and nodded affirmatively to the waitress's endearing pantomime as she queried us from across the room about another round.

Charley's tenor snatched my attention back to the table. "Lauren says that the forensic evidence is mounting to support Dale's theory of a serial killer. What have you got in Boulder? Anything I don't know?"

I'd already decided to tell Charley about the hair match that had recently been discovered, an act of indiscretion that Sam Purdy would fillet me for if he heard about it. But if Charley was going to be of any help to me, this was the least of the secrets I was going to have to share with him.

"They've matched hairs found at the two murder scenes. The one from the Buell came from the computer keyboard, the one you showed us that's used to control the knife tracks. And two more matching ones were recovered from the stage of the Boulder Theatre. Both the Boulder hairs were found close to where the victim was killed."

I heard myself say "victim" and wondered at the depersonalization I was foisting on Peter.

Charley ran one of his large hands from forehead to neck over his glossy head. "Well, that's a relief—a hair match—rules me out as a suspect. Do the lab rats have follicles to work with, or just shafts?"

The question wouldn't have surprised me from Lauren. But it was Charley's.

"Just shafts on the Boulder hairs. There's no genetic material to analyze. The hair from your theatre has a root, though, so they could do DNA, I guess. But there's nothing to compare it with, since the others don't have follicles."

"So they're not certain about the match."

Lauren jumped in, answering patiently. She explained how a prosecutor could successfully use the hair evidence to build a circumstantial case even without the DNA backup that would come from root analysis.

"But they could compare the genetics from hair that has the root with the seminal fluid, right?"

"Sure. But what would that tell them?"

Charley tasted his whiskey, closed his eyes, then drained the little glass.

I leaned forward. "You walked me through the entire scenario of how you think Lonnie Aarons was killed, Charley. I'd like to take a turn now, and tell you how I think my friend Peter was murdered. Is that all right? Then I'd like to hear your thoughts."

"Of course. I'm all ears." He drained his glass and moved his hands to his new shot of whiskey.

Charley's voice for storytelling was much better than my own. And he had a flair for the dramatic that I couldn't match, even in my dreams. But mostly what he had, we all realized as I shared my tale, was a vastly superior story to tell.

No matter how much the forensic evidence managed to distract me, the simple truth I had to face was that the murder of Lonnie Aarons had been much better theatre than the murder of Peter Arvin.

Charley's appraisal of my presentation was straightforward and confirmed my own impressions. "The material is derivative, not terribly inventive. Our guy appears to be losing his touch. Unfortunately, it happens to playwrights all the time. They take a lifetime to develop their first plot, a few months for their second. In the first one they make the dialogue sing; the second has no life, no body. No *meat.* Just a bare carcass. Two acts and some scraps they managed to sweep up from under Tennessee Williams's table."

Charley's assessment intrigued me. I hadn't considered the possibility that the relative lack of dramatic flair shown in Peter's murder, when compared with that employed in slicing up Lonnie Aarons, might actually be evidence of the decreased planning time the killer had allotted for the second crime and not evidence of a different MO and, therefore, a different perpetrator.

"Please go on, Charley. Keep talking."

"Even if what I'm about to say may sound inconsistent?"

"Join the club."

"Lonnie's murderer knew modern theatre, what I call 'spectacle theatre,' inside and out. I mean technically. Big, complex sets, blinds, computers, knife tracks, and—I'm guessing here—lighting and maybe sound, too.

"But the killer you're describing from the Boulder Theatre not only showed relatively limited creative flair, he also demonstrated virtually no technical knowledge of the theatre. Actually, unless I'm missing something from your story, he demonstrated *absolutely* no technical knowledge. Well, that doesn't add up. As much as I know about the theatre, from college, from being an actor, from working in administration for years, I couldn't have pulled off what Lonnie Aarons's killer did on that stage; I wouldn't have known enough. In a larger sense"—Charley opened his arms and curled his fingers toward the ceiling— "the theatre itself is this guy's weapon. As he killed Lonnie, he used his ability to manipulate the technical and mechanical systems of the Buell as precisely and as ruthlessly as a butcher manipulating his boning knife.

"Your friend, on the other hand, was tied down and stabbed to death. Yes, on a *stage*, in a *theatre*. But in my mind the similarities between the crimes end there."

"No," Lauren said. She waited until she had our undivided attention before she continued. "The similarities end with this guy's semen and this guy's hair.

He may be an inconsistent killer, and he may indeed be losing his flair for the dramatic, but so far he's been remarkably consistent about having distinctive blond hair and about being a secretor with great markers."

Charley gazed at her with the understated warmth of the setting sun. Then he glanced my way. "I hate technical advisers," he said to me, "don't you? I say, ban them from the stage. They ruin everything."

After Charley left the Cruise Room to go home to Cherry Creek, we took his recommendation and had a quiet dinner down Wynkoop at the Ice House Cafe before starting toward Boulder. We didn't talk shop during dinner. We talked about Lisa.

I told Lauren about Adrienne's idea for the bake-off, which amused my wife, and asked her how well she had gotten to know the nanny. Lauren had moved onto the ranch after Lisa had started watching Jonas.

"Oh, not well. I ask her how's the baby? She asks how's my job, do I want kids, do I like being a lawyer? I tried to recruit her once for Diane's softball team. I got the impression she had never actually worn a baseball mitt. It's that kind of thing. She's not a woman's woman, honey. She's a man's woman. Lisa's not girlfriend material, not for me, anyway. Maybe you can have that role with her, since it's one you seem to be lusting over." She teased me with her eyes when she said that.

This "woman's woman" and "man's woman" delineation was one I seemed to have some dispositional reluctance comprehending. Lauren and I had been over it before in regard to other women. With Lisa as the paradigm, though, the discrimination made some intuitive sense.

On the drive home, we got around to talking more shop.

I wanted to know Lauren's opinion regarding the disappearance of the college kid who had helped transport Peter to the hospital. She thought that Sam's appraisal of the sinister nature of Kenny Holden's disappearance had some merit.

"Sam has to consider it seriously, Alan. Coincidences happen, but not nearly so often as crimes do. Besides, this kid's being kidnapped or murdered isn't dependent on the truth of one particular theory of the murders. It's the only development so far that would be congruent with either scenario."

"Why?"

"If the kid was really a witness, whoever he saw coming out of the Boulder Theatre would be vulnerable. Whether it was the person's first murder of the year or his tenth."

"What does Elliot think?" Elliot Bellhaven was Lauren's colleague in the DA's office. She respected him, and considered him to have impeccable style to go along with his damn good substance.

"Elliot's holding his cards close to his chest, so far. Sam's out there by himself on this one, which is nothing new for him. Lucy Tanner has apparently fallen under the spell of that Denver investigator—what's her name?"

"Dale Hunter."

"Yes, her. And Lucy has the rest of Sam's team convinced that coordination with Denver is the way to go.

If Sam weren't so stubborn, I think there would already have been a decision to subordinate this investigation into the one at the Buell."

"What if it were yours?"

"If it were mine? God, I owe Sam a lot, so I'd probably give him some rope. But I'm not as political as Elliot is. Solving a serial-killer saga is much juicier than solving a local murder. Elliot would like to be part of it. And the voters would remember him for it when the time comes for him to run for DA or the city council."

"If the forensics are so good, why hasn't Elliot hooked his wagon to Dale Hunter and Denver?"

"It's a good question. Look, I don't know her, but I imagine it's because Dale Hunter doesn't have anybody to match all these forensics with. If she had a suspect, Elliot would probably jump off the fence and pressure Sam into running a joint investigation. I'm guessing she doesn't have anyone who looks good as a suspect and Elliot is reluctant to hook his wagon to hers until it appears that her wagon has some horses."

Lauren's assessment made sense. So did her conclusion, that Sam's latitude to run parallel investigations in the face of mounting forensic evidence that argued to the contrary would soon be limited by his superiors. That fact was simple political reality.

We drove on in silence. The highways from Denver to Boulder bleed first through thick industrial landscapes, then through a series of gradually thinning suburban portraits, places whose personalities are indistinguishable from each other when viewed from the freeway. We were somewhere in the obscure boundary territory between Westminster, Broomfield, and Arvada when Lauren spoke again.

"Alan," she said softly in the dark car, "what if you've been right all along and there is more than one murderer? But what if they're a team, what if they're acting together, not alone?"

I didn't get it. "A team? What do you mean?"

I heard her swallow and inhale.

"This may sound nuts."

"That's okay, I'm good with nuts."

"What if the two murders are the result of a type of avant-garde theatre—you know, like for a live audience? What if the murderer invites an audience into the theatre to watch what he does and how he does it? As a show."

"Performance art? But across the line, like a snuff film, but live?"

"Yeah, like performance art. What if it's being done like that?" Her voice was hesitant and whisper-soft, as though she were wary of her own thoughts.

I was instantly energized by the novelty of the hypothesis. The proposition was terrifying in its cruelty and menace, but so simple and elegant that I immediately saw how it could account for virtually all the anomalies that the investigation had produced thus far.

Without thinking any of it through, I started talking. "The troupe could be taking turns onstage with the knife, right? There could be different killers for each theatre, which explains all the problems I'm having matching up the profiles. The Buell killer could be an expert on the technical aspects of theatre. Peter's killer might not know shit about that. But the ensemble itself, the audience, could be the same each time, which explains the serology matches of the semen and the matches of the hair. Shit. It fits. How many of them do you think there would be?"

"I just had this idea. I don't know how many, this whole thing just now came to me."

"At least two, though, right? But as many as—"

"Only as many as could keep the secret. That would be crucial."

"So not very many."

"No, there couldn't be very many. I'd say three, max. More than that would be too risky."

"Unless the leader has an incredible hold on his group, you know, like Charles Manson and his family and the Tate and La Bianca murders."

"There were a lot of them, weren't there?"

"Yes, but I think this would be smaller. Two people are more likely than three."

"Yeah, they're taking turns."

"No, that's not right. There has to be at least three. The guy who masturbates hasn't been onstage yet. It's his turn next. Or soon."

"Do we know the hairs aren't his? Those hairs were found onstage."

"No, we don't know that yet. The DNA hasn't even been ordered."

"So it could be only two of them?"

"I'd say two or three. More would be impossible, unless it was a cult, like the Manson family. Two would make the most sense, though."

The possibilities inherent in Lauren's new theory left me almost breathless.

"You know, you have a very strange mind, honey."

"Yes, I do. It worries me sometimes."

———⚬⚬⚬———

A pretty pink envelope was gracing our front door when we arrived home from Denver. The salutation, in purple ink, read: "Allen." My misspelled name was underlined three times.

Lauren sniffed the missive for perfume. She smiled as she said, "Lisa." She pronounced the *s* as softly as if it had been knitted from clouds.

My dear wife opened the door and hugged Emily as I opened the envelope, which had been sealed only at the very tip of the flap, apparently with just the slightest touch of a barely moistened tongue.

Inside there was no further greeting. Lisa wrote in a large, full hand; mature, but lush. "I think Grant Arnold is with the Silver Streak Casino in Black Hawk. Peter didn't trust him. Lisa."

Lauren stared, watching me read. She teased, "So do you have a date tonight, honey? Or should I go ahead and find my diaphragm just in case you're free?" As she spoke, she was unbuttoning her blouse. The bra she was slowly revealing was the tangy orange of early-summer lilies. I had never seen that particular piece of lingerie before, but I liked it.

I handed her the note and started assisting her with the remaining buttons. "The guy Peter's cabinets are for—Lisa says he didn't trust him. She knows where he works."

She murmured, "Does your friend Lisa know how to do this?" Her hand was at my belt, and the button of my jeans.

"I imagine she does."

"What about this?" Her movements were quick, her cool fingers were deep down inside my trousers now.

"Probably," I said on a sharp inhale.

"And this?"

Through a half moan I said, "I can't say for sure."

"Well, you just keep on imagining, buster."

I followed her as she slowly descended the stairs to our bedroom. She continued to shed her blouse as she went, and I watched the black of her hair against the ivory of her skin and marveled at how someone could be so sick and so healthy all at the same time.

Distracted by the slender lace bands of the tangerine bra, I said, "I think I prefer reality to imagination," just as she reached the landing at the foot of the stairs.

"That's too bad, love, because tonight—tonight I'm specializing only in fantasy."

An hour later, as I fought the onset of sleep so that I could further savor a wonderful evening, I decided that Lauren and I were going to have to socialize with Charley Chandler more often.

I reached to turn off the bedside light and noticed that Emily was standing silently by the bedroom door.

Oh yeah.

Still naked, I climbed the stairs and let her out the front door. While she sniffed the ground and circled, I spied bright lights in Adrienne's bedroom and a dimmer beacon where Lisa slept.

I found myself wondering what it meant that Peter hadn't trusted Grant Arnold.

The phone number that I had copied from Peter's desk blotter belonged to the Grubstakes Development Group, Inc., not to the Silver Streak Casino. I asked the woman who answered the telephone if I could speak with Grant Arnold, but half expected not to find him, either because my information was faulty and Grubstakes wasn't developing the Silver Streak Casino, or because, at eight-thirty in the morning, I was calling too early.

"May I tell Mr. Arnold who's calling?" asked the receptionist.

"Alan Gregory."

"And you are with?"

"One of the subs working at the Silver Streak."

"Just a moment, Mr. Gregory." Her voice had the hard singsong of New Jersey. Maybe, I thought, Grubstakes Development had started to gather its fortunes in Atlantic City before coming west for greater riches after limited-stakes gambling was approved by Colorado voters for a few Colorado pioneer mining towns.

A sharp, somber voice, without any discernible New Jersey heritage, greeted me with unexpected familiarity. "Alan, what can I do for you?"

Instantly, I surmised that Grant Arnold was a

lawyer. I knew a lot of lawyers. I was married to a lawyer. I was entitled to the supposition.

"I'm calling on behalf of Peter Arvin."

A brief pause ensued while Arnold digested my vague explanation. "Are you representing Pete?"

Good, he had heard; at least I wouldn't have to explain about Peter's murder. "No, no, his wife is."

"I thought his wife was a doctor. She's a lawyer?"

I had no way of knowing which one of us was more confused. To me, it sounded like a toss-up. "She *is* a doctor. But she's also his personal representative. I'm a friend doing her a favor. That's why I'm calling."

This pause was longer than the first one had been. "She's his personal representative? Like his executor? Pete's dead?"

"Yes, Peter's dead."

"What happened?"

I asked him whether he had heard about the theatre murder in Boulder a week before. He said he had.

"The victim was Peter."

"You know, when I heard about that thing, I didn't pay much attention to the victim."

There was a metaphor lurking somewhere in there, I was pretty certain.

Finally, Grant Arnold added, "Shit, that's awful. I cannot believe this."

I waited. Grant filled the void as I had hoped he would. "Pete and I were old friends," he said. "*Old* friends."

I wondered whether Grant was stressing the past tense in reference to a dead friendship or in reference to a dead friend. Adrienne had said that she thought that Peter had agreed to the casino project as a favor to a college buddy. Had Grant and Peter stayed close over the years? I didn't think that he had ever mentioned Grant to me, and Lisa's note said that Peter didn't trust him.

"Were you? You grew up together?" I didn't think they had, but ignorance is a much better conversational lubricant than assumption. Anyway, my partner, Diane, maintained that I had a natural talent for playing stupid.

"No. We met in college. We rock-climbed together. Pete's dead? God, it's hard to believe it."

"You went to Montana with him?" I asked. Peter's alma mater was the University of Montana.

"No, we were at UNLV." He chuckled a little. "Though it seemed that we spent most of our time in Yosemite."

"I didn't know Peter went to UNLV." I really hadn't known. I'd thought—I'd assumed—he'd spent all of his college years at Montana. The Yosemite part didn't surprise me; Peter had talked often about the great climbing he had done there.

"No, his first two years in college he was at Nevada Las Vegas. We were roommates. He left, transferred." He said the last three words, I thought, as though Peter's departure still perplexed him. "He left after the fire."

What fire? "A fire at school?"

"No, no, not at school. It's a long story."

"Yes?"

One Grant didn't want to tell.

I said, "I'm sorry about the way I broke the news,

about the murder, I mean. I was his friend, too. It's been a difficult time."

"Well, you probably guessed that I already knew that Pete was the victim."

I guessed that, given the media saturation about the theatre murders, everybody knew. "Yes, I figured you already knew."

"I bet you're calling about the work that he was doing for us, aren't you? It looks like I'm going to have to decide what to do with a half-finished saloon, right?"

"Actually, no. I think Peter's work on the cabinetry is mostly done, Mr. Arnold. We've measured out the pieces and they seem to match right up with Peter's sketches. The cabinets aren't stained or sealed yet, but Peter wouldn't have done that, anyway. And you will have to get someone else to install it and trim it out. But to my untrained eye, Peter's work is finished, Mr. Arnold."

"It's done? God, I'm relieved to hear that. I went out on a limb with Pete on this. Financially, I mean. Certainly not artistically. And I'm surprised, truly. Delivery isn't scheduled until August. Pete said this project would take him most of six months to complete."

"Look, maybe I'm wrong, maybe there's more work to be done that we just didn't find sketches for. It probably makes sense for you to have somebody come to Boulder and take a look at the pieces, make sure everything is right."

"Yeah, I should do that. I'll have the general

contractor send someone by." He asked for directions and a phone number. I provided them.

Grant seemed ready to hang up the phone, to move on to the next challenge of his day.

"I told his wife I would ask you about payment."

This question generated the longest pause yet.

The lawyer voice returned. "Mr. Gregory, Pete was advanced his material costs, which were substantial. The bar is all imported fruitwood. As a personal favor to him, I also agreed to pay him sixty percent up front, much more than is customary for this kind of project. The remaining forty percent will be paid upon delivery. We have documentation for our disbursements, of course."

Of course. "The remaining forty percent? For his wife's information, it's about how much?"

"I don't have the breakdown in front of me, but the entire cabinetry package for the saloon was over ninety thousand dollars. We probably still owe Pete—or his estate—in the vicinity of thirty, plus or minus. Please tell his widow she doesn't have to worry about the money." He chuckled. Grubstakes was loaded, I guessed.

I thanked him for his time, hung up the phone, and out loud, said, "Ninety thousand dollars? My God, and I thought shrinks charged a lot."

Lauren and I had a date, weather permitting, to have lunch on Pearl on the narrow sidewalk outside Caffè Antica Roma, just a few blocks from my office. She had promised me that she would be there early enough to get us a table. The morning had broken

warm and sunny at first light, and strolling downtown
at noon I was remarkably content with my day. For
the first time since Peter's death I felt that I was
making some progress in completing the tasks for
which Sam Purdy and Adrienne had recruited me.

I now knew whom to deliver the cabinetry to, I
knew how much money Peter was owed for his work,
and I was tantalized by the new theory that Lauren
had developed, which would make my psychological-
profiling efforts for Sam Purdy appear reasonably pre-
scient, as opposed to stupid.

Lauren had told me at breakfast that she planned to
call Sam as soon as she got to her office that morning
to propose her theory about the theatre murders'
being part of some perverse performance art.

I had expected a call or two from him this morning
to discuss Lauren's revelation. No calls had come.

When I arrived at the restaurant, I found out why I
hadn't heard from Sam. In the shade, not ten feet from
the bright springtime sun of this Rocky Mountain
day, he and Dale Hunter and Lauren were sitting
together, waiting for me, in the outdoor dining area of
Antica Roma.

So much for our date.

I kissed Lauren and shook hands with Dale Hunter,
whose grip was softer than her manner. In greeting
Sam, I placed my hand on his big shoulder and
squeezed the fat tendon by his neck as hard as I could
to let him know how I felt about his crashing my lunch.

He laughed.

Two chairs were free at the table. I grabbed the one
between Lauren and Detective Hunter and wondered

about the other empty one. I guessed that it was reserved for Elliot Bellhaven, the deputy DA who would be prosecuting Peter's murderer when the cops identified and arrested a suspect.

Sam must have seen me eyeing the spare chair. "Lucy's going to try to join us," he explained. "She's got some strong opinions about this new theory. But she's in court."

Turning to Lauren, I asked, "Not Elliot?"

She said, "He's out of town. Roy asked me to sit in. I'll brief Elliot when he gets back tomorrow." Royal Peterson was Lauren's boss, the DA.

"This place is wonderful. It looks like a movie set. I love having excuses to come to Boulder. What's good here?" Dale's question was, of course, directed at Sam, who looked uncomfortable with her attention.

Lauren said, "The bruschetta's great and they usually have a good ravioli special. I hope you like garlic." The air around Antica Roma was often thick with garlic, much the same way that the air around McDonald's is redolent of French fries.

Garlic was better.

"Love it."

The waitress took our drink orders and soon returned with a trayful of tumblers of iced tea. We ordered food and she left again; the whole time the conversation hovered in awkward banalities. While Dale and Sam bitched about some delay in forensic analysis, I told Lauren about my conversation with Grant Arnold in Black Hawk. Over her shoulder I could see the marquee of the Boulder Theatre. BIG HEAD TODD—ONE NIGHT ONLY was what it read.

Dale finally balked at the pleasantries. She turned to Lauren and said, "Tell me your idea about our murders. I'm intrigued."

Dale and Sam listened attentively as Lauren explained her theory. Dale asked good, probing questions; Lauren provided good, coherent answers.

The food arrived in a timely fashion—never a certainty at Antica Roma—and everyone started eating.

Lauren picked at a big salad and moved solidly into the category of proponent. "See, it fits. You guys have all been doing somersaults trying to explain the inconsistency in the MO while at the same time trying to make sense of the laboratory and forensic evidence that indicates you're dealing with a solitary offender. This theory is particularly efficient in accounting for those differences."

I had been silent through most of the meal while the professional crime fighters talked. Sam, too, had been quiet, especially for him. I thought he seemed awkward around Dale, which was understandable, considering her previous overtures. But I also thought that he was a little flirtatious himself, with his eyes and with his manner. I couldn't tell what he thought about Lauren's hypothesis, though the fact that he and Dale were at a Pearl Street café on short notice, listening to Lauren's ideas, at least supported the supposition that either he or Dale Hunter took the new theory seriously.

But it soon became apparent, to my surprise, that Dale Hunter was not an advocate. While listening to her questioning of Lauren, I had thought that the Denver detective was viewing Lauren's idea approvingly. I was wrong.

"The theory is cohesive, I'll grant you that, Lauren."
Dale was mopping olive oil and garlic from her plate
with a chunk of bread. Her voice was kind and dismissive simultaneously, the type of voice adults use to
inform children that despite all their hard work
they've come up with the wrong answer. "The
problem is that it's just not necessary. The only reason
to complicate the underlying assumption of our investigation of the murder at the Buell with this ensemble
theory of yours is if I sign off on the psychological-
profiling effort of your husband or the dweeb who visited me from the FBI." She smiled at me. "And
although I'm sure he is a wonderful husband, Alan
has no particular credibility as a criminal profiler."

I was about to interject that, in Dale Hunter's world-
view, "credible profiler" seemed to be an oxymoron.
But she continued before I had a chance to speak.

"As in any investigation, I think the best explanation is the one that fits the facts as we know them
without twisting them into a pretzel."

"And in this case, that is?" Lauren asked evenly.

"Same guy, different circumstances. Lonnie Aarons's
murder was well rehearsed, the guy really got off on
it. Peter Arvin's murder was more spontaneous, the
guy didn't plan as much or as well. He didn't have as
much fun. The signature's the same. The semen's the
same. Pretty simple. No mirrors. No pretzels."

Dale turned back toward Lauren. "This ensemble
idea is too unwieldy. How do you recruit for this kind
of group? And it seems to me there would be way too
many potential loose lips. Have any of you ever read
or heard about a troupe of serial killers? I sure haven't.

I know there have been some pairs, and some cults, but a whole traveling road show of serial killers? I've never hard of it."

Dale Hunter's point was valid. In all the recent reading I'd done, I had not come across it, either. Even serial-killer duos were rare, although the literature did document a few of them. An ensemble? Other than the Manson family, none in any of my research.

Sam's neutrality during the conversation puzzled me. If he disagreed with Dale, which I suspected he did, it wasn't like him to stay silent and not press his argument.

Lauren ordered coffee, which seemed to be a cue for Dale to look at her watch, excuse herself, and head for her car. Sam stared at her khaki-skirted butt as she departed.

"She doesn't like your theory, Lauren, but I do. I think it floats. I'm going to follow it, see where it goes."

"What about Lucy, what does she think?" I asked. So far in the investigation, Lucy Tanner seemed to be of one mind with Dale Hunter.

"Lucy'll do what she's told. She may not like it, but she'll do what she's told."

Lauren turned to Sam. Dale's arguments had scored some points with her. "Dale's right, you know, Sam. My new theory is exhaustive, but it's not the simplest explanation for the facts as we know them."

"I know that."

I asked, "But you think Lauren's theory is worth pursuing, anyway?"

"To my way of thinking, it's better than the alternative. I can't sign off on the idea that the same hand swung both of those knives. In my gut, it just doesn't feel right."

The coffee arrived. I asked Sam if and when he thought the troupe, if there was one, would present their next bloody performance.

He drained half his cup before he responded. "We've kicked that around a lot already, based on the single-killer theory. There were three weeks, give or take, between the first two murders. One was on a weekday, the other on a weekend. Serial killers, especially organized ones, are like submarines—they can stay submerged for an awful long time before they have to surface—so we could be holding our breaths, waiting, for weeks, months, years even."

"Or it could be tonight," Lauren said.

"Yeah, it could be tonight," Sam agreed. "Every theatre manager and every theatrical group on the Front Range has already been warned about this. We're doing everything we can. It hasn't been enough to stop them, but we're doing everything we can."

—◦◦◦—

The things I thought about during spare moments in those days after Peter's murder were not surprising. I thought a lot about my friends and what they meant to me. I thought a lot about loss, about the attrition of the objects of our love and attachment that is a natural consequence of age. I thought, especially, about Peter and Adrienne, and the remarkable impact of the arrival of little Jonas.

I don't think it was possible for a human being to work any harder than Adrienne did before Jonas was born. Twelve-hour days were the norm for her, and fifteen-hour days were not infrequent events. Supposedly, she took Thursdays off, but in reality a day off for Dr. Adrienne often meant no office hours, only a mere four- to six-hour stint at the hospital.

The tempo she maintained was, I had to admit, consonant with her character. I teased her about the pace, comparing her, unimaginatively, to a rat on a treadmill. She would always protest that she was making plans that would allow her to slow down and always had arguments about why her workload was necessary, the arguments mostly having to do with arcane aspects of the consequences of managed care. But the bottom line was that Adrienne ran through life at top speed because Adrienne ran through life scared.

The closer someone got to Adrienne, the more it seemed that she had to feel indispensable in order to feel safe with the proximity. Beneath her brash, cocky, quintessentially Eastern façade, Adrienne was a generous, sensitive, and good human being, and on rare days she knew it. Her friends suffered through those days, because when she was confident, her cockiness was unshakable and barely digestible. Most of the time, though, she didn't quite feel indispensable, wasn't totally sure of her value. Then, if she couldn't hold you at bay with her sarcasm or her cynicism, as an alternative she would dazzle you and engulf you with sheer speed or tenacity. And I knew from experience that if you weren't as nimble as an NBA point guard, she would be quicker than you, and if you weren't used to running marathons, she would shame you with her endurance.

After Jonas was born, things changed for Adrienne. When she wasn't with patients, she was with her precious baby, where her vitality served her well. In my humble professional opinion, her abundant energy bordered at times on clinical mania, and I always felt that she was only a few short hours of sleep away from a recommendation from a colleague—one who was fractionally braver than me—that she *maybe* just try a little lithium or Tegretol to slow her down. But Jonas benefited from her indefatigable nature; despite her frantic work schedule, he got plenty of time with his mother because she required so little rest.

Then there was her marriage.

Her relationship with Peter had always been the anomaly in Adrienne's life. Peter didn't need her, at least not in any conventional manner that I ever discerned. She knew she wasn't indispensable to him, never had been, never would be, and that fact left her teetering on the edge of an awkward emotional vertigo with him. I suspected that the lack of equilibrium was the foundation of their attraction for each other; they kept each other off balance in a way that was peculiar and addictive. The whole affair, I'd decided, was the romantic equivalent of Peter's love for rock-climbing—free-soloing—a death-defying act of scaling great affectional heights without ropes or safety equipment.

Their marriage, the one I observed across the gravel lane between our homes over a decade, was not one I would covet for myself and Lauren. Peter and Adrienne lived largely parallel lives and collided in brief, indefinable, yet somehow interdependent interludes, their consuming work and their appreciation of the emotional dangers they shared the main commonalities between them.

Until Jonas.

I keep getting back to Jonas because the baby seemed to change many things. Not everything— Peter was still ephemeral, Adrienne was still consumed. But the truth was that the baby provided a focus for the arrows from Cupid that their marriage, alone, could never quite target.

Adrienne made time for Jonas. She turfed surgeries to her partners, ignored the pleas of her many patients by cutting down on office hours, and refused the difficult reconstructive operations that she'd always found so rewarding, but that had a way of turning her ten-hour days into eighteen-hour marathons.

The transformation wasn't quite so immediate for Peter, though. As the father of a newborn, Peter was an awkward parent, hesitant and reticent. The cocoon of caution he initially wore when he was around the baby wasn't shed for weeks, and then one day he shucked it with sudden assuredness, and it seemed to me that from then on it was okay for Peter to need the baby and okay for the baby to need Peter.

Jonas catalyzed those changes, and he catalyzed a lot of contentment. From his first day on the ranch he was a sound sleeper and a robust eater. Except for an occasional ear infection, Jonas was healthy. He smiled early and often, and was generally the kind of baby all first-time parents need and few actually get. Within two months of his birth, the transformation he'd produced in the Ponderosa was apparent in both Peter and Adrienne—in their spirits, in their marriage, in their lives.

Then Peter was murdered.

Immediately, Adrienne's workload skyrocketed back to the stratosphere, as though her husband's death had been a torch on a very short fuse.

Whatever Jonas's birth had catalyzed seemed, to me, to be decomposing as rapidly as his father's flesh.

———✦———

After the working lunch with Lauren, Dale Hunter, and Sam, I rushed back to my office, used the bathroom, checked my mail and my phone messages, and called Adrienne, who had been pressing me for news about the intentions of the proprietors of the Silver Streak in Black Hawk.

Of course, the receptionist in the group practice said that Adrienne wasn't available. She would have said this, I felt certain, even if Adrienne were standing next to her pleading for access to the phone. I said, This is Dr. Gregory, could you please see if she will speak with me? The receptionist said, Doctor is with a patient, I'm sorry. I said, Please, this is an important matter, *Doctor* asked me to call. The receptionist sighed like someone who didn't like to grant exceptions to important rules and put me on hold.

Finally, I heard, "What is this *Doctor* Gregory crap? The title should be reserved for people who have earned it—physicians, not philosophers."

"Then make it easier for someone to get past your goddamn receptionist. And what is this crappy music you guys play while your patients are on hold?"

She was too smart to bite about the canned music. About her receptionist, she asserted, "Laura's good."

"Laura's a hard-ass. As rigid as wrought iron."

"That's what makes her good. My time is valuable."

"And mine isn't?"

"Don't start with me, Alan. What do you want?"

"I spoke to an old college buddy of Peter's, a guy named Grant Arnold, who is an executive of some kind with this casino in Black Hawk. The cabinetry is theirs, and they still owe you about thirty grand."

She whistled. "That's great, I'll buy that zero coupon for Jonas."

"They want to see the cabinets, make sure all the pieces are there. I told them it would be fine to send someone to check things out."

"No problem, set it up with Lisa, would you? Anything else? I don't mean to sound unappreciative, but I've got to hustle."

"Adrienne?"

"Uh-oh, there's bad news, too. Here comes the bad news. I knew it."

"Grant says that his company has already paid

Peter about sixty thousand dollars. The thirty grand is only the outstanding balance. Even after material expenses there should be a lot more money lying around. Did you find the rest of it anywhere, or should I ask him for receipts?"

"No, I haven't found that much money, but then I haven't looked, either. Peter kept his own books, his own accounts. I don't have a clue how much money he had stashed away, or where. I've got lots of worries these days, sweetheart, but money, fortunately, isn't one of them. I've got plenty of money. I'm a *doc-tah*, remember? And unlike you, a real one."

A light flicked on, indicating that my next patient had arrived. I should have hung up the phone and gone to work. I didn't.

"Do you know anything about a fire Peter was in, around the time when he was at UNLV?"

"Yeah, I know about it, why do you ask? It wasn't his favorite subject."

"Grant mentioned it, said he thought it was the reason Peter changed schools. I was just curious, I didn't even know he had been at UNLV."

"Peter used to work for an organization called Graystone, an Outward Bound–type place, in Wyoming. His group got trapped by a forest fire one summer. It was apparently pretty dicey, someone in the group was killed, a real rage-of-nature thing; he didn't like to talk about it. I can't imagine it had anything to do with his changing schools, though."

"Did he ever say anything negative about Grant Arnold? Lisa said she thought Peter might not have trusted him."

"No, I've never even heard the man's name before. Lisa must have overheard something. Ask her."

"Did something—"

"Listen, my little detective, I have a guy lying flat out on my examining table with his groin draped with sterile cloths waiting for a vasectomy from my magic hands. If I speak with you any longer, I might not have time to properly anesthetize his privates, which he might hold against both me and my dear firstborn, so can we finish this later? Thanks for the news about the cabinets, that helps ease my mind a lot. I was afraid for a while that I was going to have to build a restaurant to put them in or hold a garage sale to get rid of them."

We said goodbye. I walked out and retrieved my patient, who wanted to talk about his ambivalence about having his five-year-old vasectomy reversed.

Sometimes life's circle has a remarkably small circumference.

Lisa and Jonas were outside when I got home from work that evening. Jonas was playing with plastic urine-specimen jars in his sandbox in the yard on the north side of the house. Lisa was supervising, which seemed to involve evoking a stream of constant encouragements to her charge not to make a meal out of the sand with which he was playing.

The sun was low over the mountains, and the light possessed a late-afternoon intensity that required I either sit with my back to it or squint. I walked over and said hello and tried to engage Jonas in a cute little peekaboo game that he had found enchanting the last couple of times we had been together, but this time his sand toys were much more interesting to him than I was.

I sat on the grass next to Lisa and asked how she was.

She looked at me with curiosity in her eyes, assessing, I supposed, whether or not my question was sincere. She told me she was doing fine.

She was wearing cutoffs and a tank top. Her legs were curled under her. The day's heat was evaporating quickly as the sun set.

I gestured toward Jonas, who had pulled himself to a standing position, but appeared about as stable as the peso. "Is he walking yet?" I asked. Jonas was a legendary speed-crawler, and had not developed much interest in ambulation.

"He stands, takes a step or two, but he's still not concerned about walking."

"How's he doing otherwise? Does he miss his daddy?"

She gazed at him warmly. "Jonas is, um, good, Alan. He knows something has happened, that's for sure. It's like he knows that there is this big hole in his life and he's being extra careful not to fall into it. He knows his mother is very sad and a little crazy, and he wonders when I cry sometimes. At some level, he knows. Little Jonas is a wise man, like his father."

Lisa was wearing a perfume that she had used before, though ordinarily she smelled only of bath soap. The scent of the perfume was a memory trigger for me every time Lisa had it on. I'd once slept with a woman who wore it. She was a small woman with long blond hair and pale eggshell skin. I slept with her literally once in a spare bedroom in a big house at a holiday party in Boulder Canyon. Now I couldn't remember the name of the fragrance, couldn't even remember the name of the woman. But the olfactory triggers that fired from my memory of that night told me it had been a truly fine evening.

I thanked Lisa for her note and asked her what made her suspect that Peter didn't trust Grant Arnold.

Before she answered, she reached over and shooed away a bee that was hovering near Jonas, then looked me hard in the eyes in a frank manner that I wasn't accustomed to from her.

"I overheard them talking once, on the phone. You know how I used to take Jonas down to the shop to see his daddy once or twice a day?"

I knew; I had seen them going and coming back many times. Lisa, with Jonas in a Snugli, or later, once his muscles had developed as much tone as is possessed by your average teddy bear, perched spread-legged over Lisa's hip as they walked across the dust and gravel from the big house to the studio to spend time with Peter.

"Well, one day I had taken Jonas down to the shop and Peter was on the phone with this Grant Arnold guy when we got there. Peter's voice was raised; I could hear him even when we were still outside. Usually he was so quiet, you know?" She paused, examining my face, wanting me to remember Peter with her.

I nodded.

"Peter said something like, 'Right, just like last time,

Grant. You sure came through last time.' But totally sarcastic, as if Peter didn't really like whatever had happened 'last time.' I remember thinking that Peter sounded more like Adrienne than himself.

"That's all I know about Grant. That's why I wrote in the note that I didn't think Peter trusted him. I thought you should know; though I'm not sure why."

"Well, I don't know what it means, either, but I appreciate it. When I spoke to him, Grant Arnold hadn't heard about Peter's death and seemed genuinely upset when I told him. He didn't seem at all reluctant to pay Adrienne what his company owes her. He would like to send someone by to examine the pieces in the studio. I told them you would let them in. I hope you don't mind."

Her eyes were on Jonas as she said, "Oh, I don't mind at all. Anything I can do to help out. You know that."

Jonas turned to us and squealed in delight at something he had done. I watched for a moment and couldn't comprehend the reason for his enthusiasm. No matter; I clapped for him and laughed. Lisa's eyes seemed doleful below her bangs. She grinned sweetly, more at me than at Jonas, I thought.

That smile. Lisa's smile was crooked, and not only by five degrees or ten, but truly crooked. I found it charming. Lauren told me once that she thought I would find a cold sore the size of a hubcap charming if it was gracing Lisa's lips.

"I miss him," Lisa said, staring right at me.

"Me, too. He was a special friend, Lisa."

She shook her head just a little to tell me I wasn't

understanding her. "Peter said you were the one
who'd always know what to do. He was right, I think.
You have some of his light in your eyes. Not as much
of a glow as Peter had, but some. Look closely at Jonas
and you can see it, the light. It's his daddy's virtue
shining. Healthy spirits leave healthy glows. They're
like shadows in reverse."

I looked closely at Jonas and saw that he had managed to shove sand into orifices that weren't likely to
yield the grains during his daily bath. I saw a lot of
joy, but I didn't see Peter's light or Peter's virtue in
Jonas's big caramel eyes. For the first time, though, I
realized that Peter and Lisa were kindred spirits.

Lisa could speak in metaphysical circles as well as
Peter had been able to.

I guessed that there were at least ten thousand
people in Boulder who could instantly make sense of
what Lisa had just said to me about shadows in
reverse.

The problem was, I wasn't one of them.

"Whoa, whoa, whoa. Let me think, let me think."
Charley Chandler was silent for most of a minute as
he considered Lauren's hypothesis that an ensemble
of killers, and not an individual, might have committed the Buell and Boulder murders.

I was cradling the phone between my shoulder and my ear while I cut vegetables to throw on the grill. Lauren had called and left a message that she was going to be late. I was planning to barbecue some salmon for dinner.

"Alan, you still there? You know what? It works perfectly. Absolutely. Lauren thought of this? Geez, it's really beautiful, elegant; I wish to hell I'd come up with it. It even makes sense of the one piece that I've thought was impossible to explain all along. Would you ask her if she minds if I use it in my book?"

"What's the piece you've had trouble with, Charley?"

"The skills this guy possesses. The great range of skills. A single killer would have to know almost too much about the theatre—you know, too many different trades. But if there are two or three of them with complementary skills, the range of talent that was demonstrated here at the Buell becomes much more understandable. One of them knows about computers, another about sets and lighting, whatever."

"I hadn't thought of that angle."

"Well, Lauren's theory works, as far as I'm concerned. But what does it do to your psychological profile?"

"It annihilates it. I go from speculating about a quasi-social loner to proposing that we're looking for some dynamic group leader—some guy who can get others to commit murder in front of a live audience. I have to go back to the beginning and redraw the guy completely."

"But Lauren's idea makes sense to you, anyway?"

"I've been bothered all along with the way the two

murders were committed. Like you said the other
night, the Denver murder was better theatre, more
sophisticated. Serial killers enhance their fantasies
between crimes. This one was nothing compared to
the Buell's. Since you proposed what happened to
Lonnie Aarons there, I haven't been comfortable with
the single-killer theory."

"What does Sam Purdy think?"

I told him about our lunch in Boulder earlier that
day, that Sam seemed intrigued with the new theory
but Detective Dale Hunter's reaction to Lauren's pro-
posal bordered on outright skepticism.

"I'm not too surprised. Dale's got to be conservative
right now. I don't know if you read the Denver
papers, but she's under a lot of scrutiny. She's now a
month out from the murder without an arrest in an
incredibly high-profile case. The local press is pushing
her very hard; it would be risky for her to advocate
something as outrageous as Lauren's theory without
some concrete evidence to back it up. The media
would jump all over her for changing course without
good reason. And the political ramifications can't be
ignored, either. I don't know if you've heard but there
are rumors in town that Dale's being considered for a
Justice Department position that's open in the Denver
regional office."

"No, I didn't know that. What kind of position?"

"Something to do with community policing grants.
Anyway, if it's true, it would be a real coup for her
career. Dale's ready for a desk."

"So she needs this case closed?"

"In the worst way."

"But isn't it true that most serial murderers are never caught, Charley?"

"That's right. Dale's stuck between the proverbial rock and a hard place with this one. If she had collared this guy in the first few days, she would have looked great to everybody, a real hero. Now she runs the risk of just being another frustrated homicide cop who let the big one get away."

"She seems pretty cool about it."

Charley agreed. "That's right, Dale keeps her cool."

I thanked him again, and we said goodbye.

My thought as I hung up the phone brought a smile to my face. Whatever Dale Hunter's problems, political or otherwise, might be, they haven't interfered with her sex drive.

That smile broadened as I heard the tires on Lauren's car crunch gravel on the driveway. I pulled the salmon from the refrigerator and brushed on some olive oil.

Later, after dinner, I drank a second beer and watched Lauren play pool.

"You know, I hate to admit it," I said, "but at this point, I think that if Peter had been born and raised in Rock Springs, Wyoming, and not Jackson, I wouldn't be all that eager to make this road trip for Adrienne in search of Peter's roots."

Lauren finished lining up a shot and gently impacted the cue ball before she answered me. She didn't even watch as the solid ivory ball in turn clicked against the purple four-ball, which immediately followed a straight, gentle path down the length of the table into the far corner. Lauren knew it was going in. It was, I thought, as if the ball were being guided on tracks.

"Why? What's wrong with Rock Springs?"

"Ever been there?"

She shook her head, her attention back on the table.

"It's kind of like Limon," I said. "But without all the charm."

"I haven't been to Limon, either."

"Bakersfield?"

"No."

"Well. You'll just have to trust me on this. I think Jackson is going to be much nicer. You know, the Grand Tetons? Yellowstone? Mountain air?"

She smiled in a way that was slightly condescending and enormously affectionate. Whether or not she agreed with me, I was feeling certain that Jackson, Wyoming, was going to be a nice place to visit.

IV

Stage Fright

Sam told me later that Kenneth Holden's swollen remains had washed up on the sandy shore of the Big Thompson riverfront campsite of a family of evangelical Christians who were escaping the oppressive late-spring heat of Stillwater, Oklahoma. Led by the father, the family prayed over the discovery for about ten minutes before being guided to see the merit and wisdom of notifying the park ranger, which they did just before dark. By the time the Forest Service authorities arrived, the site had been trampled by about three dozen curious campers. The adolescents in the group, in particular, seemed endlessly fascinated about the aquatic and insect life that had taken over Kenny Holden's orifices in much the same way a squatter takes over a deserted cabin.

Sam got a call about the discovery of unidentified male remains in Rocky Mountain National Park about two hours later, near nine-thirty. Sherry, who was an experienced cop spouse and knew the routine, was busy packing him a corned-beef sandwich on rye and filling his thermos with coffee, and Sam was grabbing a sweatshirt in case the park was cold, when another call came in from the police dispatcher in Boulder.

The dispatcher was rerouting a call from the police department in Central City about a body that had just been found, apparently murdered, on the stage of the Central City Opera House in Gilpin County.

Later, as Sam recounted the macabre events related to the discovery of the two bodies that night, he remembered that he took a long minute to kiss his sleeping son, Simon, and stroke the boy's delicate blond hair before heading out the door to go to Central City.

Sam wasn't at all conflicted about whether to head north to Rocky Mountain National Park to see Kenny Holden's swollen remains or go west to Gilpin County to see a new and probably bloody atrocity. A fresh body told better stories than a decaying one. The choice was that simple.

Although his imagination could provide plenty of conjecture, Sam wanted to see for himself what the hell had happened on the stage of the Central City Opera House.

Lauren and I were home in bed when Sam called from his car to tell us where he was going. He said he wouldn't wait for us to get ready but wanted us to get up there as quickly as we could.

Lauren had fallen asleep early, exhausted, a not-uncommon state of affairs for her. She had awakened when the phone rang, and listened to my end of the conversation with Sam without opening her eyes. As soon as I hung up I filled her in on Sam's request for us to attend the murder investigation and offered to make the trip to the mountains alone. But Lauren was pulling on clothes and tugging a brush through her hair even before I was.

I took Emily outside to pee and told her to keep an

eye on the house for us, then climbed into my car and started the engine. A moment later, Lauren emerged from the house, bringing along a pillow still warm from our bed. She was asleep again before we reached Rocky Flats.

The mountain mining town of Central City, Colorado, owes its existence to speculators and gamblers and outsiders. During the town's first economic boom, in the 1860s, the attraction was gold nuggets and silver ore and the outsiders who speculated were miners. In its current late-twentieth-century rejuvenation, the lure was limited-stakes gambling, mostly slot machines and blackjack, and the outsiders who speculated were land developers.

Prior to the flood of investments that came with the beginning of legalized gambling, both Central City and its downhill sister, Black Hawk, were in grave financial decline. For years, the towns had been crumbling under the economic burden of trying to maintain their century-old infrastructures without a significant tax base. Central City's tourist appeal had been greater than Black Hawk's, and there is little doubt that even without gaming Central City would have managed to survive a little longer than Black Hawk.

Limited-stakes gambling was the cure the voters of Colorado prescribed for pioneer mountain town cancer.

I thought that day, viewing the town of Black Hawk for the first time since gambling had arrived, that the cure seemed to have worked. Even at eleven o'clock on this late-spring night, as I drove south down the

Peak to Peak Highway from Coal Creek Canyon and
saw the uplit towers of construction cranes, and the
floodlit churning waters of spanking-new sewage-
treatment facilities, and the halogen-scalded paved
acreage of asphalt parking lots, and the long rows of
fake Dodge City storefronts where there had never
been buildings before, I decided that Black Hawk
looked more like Frontierland at Disney World or Six
Flags Over the Old West than the decrepit old mining
town I remembered from previous leisurely September drives taken along the Peak to Peak to view
the aspen leaves changing color.

The cure for Black Hawk's near-fatal disease apparently included a hell of a lot of plastic surgery.

Just before arriving at the right turn that would take
us up the hill to Central City, I saw, on my left, a sign
indicating the construction site of the Silver Streak
Casino, which was the ultimate destination for the shop
full of cabinetry that Peter had left behind. The casino,
as I could tell by the concrete shell of the building,
would be large by recent Black Hawk standards, but
not immense. The site surprised me. The structure was
going up on the wrong side of the Peak to Peak, the east
side, in the mouth of a narrow canyon carved by a
small, snowmelt-driven creek. Almost all the other
gambling venues in Black Hawk that I could see were
on the west side of Clear Creek, clustered on the two
streets that were once the sole arteries of the old town-
site of Black Hawk.

In the parking lots flanking Clear Creek an armada
of tour buses was already loading Front Range gamblers for their shuttle rides back down Highway 6 to

Denver. Despite the late hour and the departing throngs there was no escaping the fact that the town of Black Hawk was thriving.

Previously, driving west from Black Hawk to Central City, I had always felt a sense of geographic separation between the towns, a sense of leaving one place before arriving at the other. No longer. Now the winding road up the hill was lined almost nonstop with new construction, most still unfinished. The scale of the new casinos dwarfed the few frame houses remaining in the canyon.

Central City had once been the pioneer capital city of Colorado. Its mining nickname, the Richest Square Mile on Earth, reflected the wealth of its boom times in the 1860s and '70s. Those two decades were the town's heyday, and a plethora of fine brick and stone buildings were constructed on the wandering streets of Central City during that time. Perhaps the finest of the structures was the incongruous Central City Opera House, built adjacent to the opulent Teller House Hotel.

Opened in 1878 at a cost of twenty thousand dollars, the eight-hundred-seat theatre enjoyed less than a decade of glamour before a big gold strike farther down south in the Rockies, in Cripple Creek, stole the thunder from Central City's fragile economy in the latter half of the 1880s. With the population declining and the standard of living plummeting, the opera house slid into disuse and was relegated to town-hall status until 1932, when it reopened for opera.

The night that Lauren and I were driving into Central City was a Thursday. I had read in the previous

Sunday's Denver papers that this year's season was due to start with a gala opening of *Manon*, by Massenet, on the coming Saturday.

Not unexpectedly, given the congestion caused by the number of police and emergency vehicles that are attracted to a murder, the narrow road in front of the opera house was closed to traffic. I stopped the car at a roadblock and was trying unsuccessfully to explain to a Gilpin County sheriff's deputy exactly why we needed to get up the hill when Lauren woke and pulled her DA's ID from her purse. The deputy examined it, seemed reasonably impressed, and told us where we could park. We left the car in a casino lot and in a few minutes were walking uphill past the Teller House, which was no longer a hotel, but now a Swiss-owned casino jammed full of slot-machine junkies.

Yellow crime-scene tape blocked our path to the opera house. Again, Lauren tried her ID, this time on an officer of the Central City Police Department who was manning the entrance to the perimeter of the crime scene.

He was absolutely unimpressed. He figured me for a reporter and wanted to see my press identification. I pulled out an old ID I'd kept from the time I was a coroner's consultant in Boulder County and showed it to him.

"This isn't Boulder County. What do you want?"

I asked him to please find Detective Sam Purdy, who I was certain would vouch for us.

"Who?"

"He's the big cop from Boulder who is probably acting like he thinks he's the governor."

"Oh, him." He sent someone inside the theatre in search of Sam.

The Central City Opera House is a stately, solid structure with deep stone walls and a mansard roof. A narrow, rounded balcony graces the central section of the façade and is flanked on each side by a simple block tower. The building is almost devoid of ornament. A sign centered high on the stone wall below the mansard reads simply OPERA HOUSE. Wide brick patios on each side of the building provide the structure with a sense of grand separation in this hilly canyon town where flat land is such a precious commodity.

Mobile crime-scene trucks and the coroner's wagon had been parked on the street side of the downhill patio. That meant that inside the opera house the criminalists were already at work on the crime scene and the coroner was probably busy examining the body. Out of the corner of my eye, across the street, in front of the Gilpin County Courthouse, I spotted a sign indicating the offices of the county sheriff. To my amazement, I realized that this murder had apparently taken place within spitting distance of the cops.

Jesus.

Chutzpah. Adrienne would call it chutzpah.

Lauren seemed anxious. She fidgeted with the strap of her purse while we waited for permission to cross the crime-scene tape. I didn't know whether her anxiety was similar to my own, which primarily involved dreading what I would see inside the opera house, or whether her nervousness was being generated by something else. Lauren was a seasoned prosecutor, and with the exception of certain atrocious crimes against children, she seemed to be able to assimilate criminal gore as well as could be expected from anyone.

She was particularly anxious, I was guessing, because the stage of the opera house probably held the clues that would substantiate the validity of her theory about an ensemble of serial killers.

Sam Purdy emerged from the lobby entrance that was farthest uphill, and farthest from us. He spied us quickly and came over with long strides. His hands were in his pockets.

He looked around to make sure no one else was within earshot. "It looks like our guy." He smiled rue-fully at Lauren. "Or guys."

"Can you tell for sure yet, Sam?" she asked.

He shook his head. "No. Can't tell for sure." He fixed me with his stare. "Are you ready for what's in there, Alan? The reason I called you up here is that I want you to do what you did in the Boulder Theatre that morning, okay? The same routine: see me, feel me, hear me. But this time there's a body and a lot of blood."

"Sure, I'm ready," I lied, not feeling at all prepared for what I might find inside. I seriously considered being honest with Sam and telling him that I would probably respond much more professionally if I waited until the body had been removed, or at least covered up. But I was embarrassed to ask to be excluded, and I didn't.

Behind me a pleasant voice said, "Hi, Sammy. We're back in business, huh? But we absolutely have to stop meeting like this, don't you think?"

Lauren and I spun simultaneously to see Detective Dale Hunter walking up the hill.

—◦•◦—

The four of us entered the building through the near tower doors, climbing stone steps into a modest lobby. Crime-scene tape blocked off a staircase next to a framed playbill with Lillian Gish's name adorning the top.

Sam didn't pause to allow me a moment to applaud the architecture or appreciate the history of the place. Instead he led us five or six steps up from the lobby to double entrance doors that if shut would close off the top of the orchestra seating section. But that night the doors were propped open and the houselights in the cozy theatre shone brightly above us. Too brightly, it seemed to me.

Reluctant, I didn't look down toward the stage right away. Lauren did, as I knew she would, and I watched her face and eyes for clues about what she saw. Her first gaze down the theatre caused a widening of her eyes, then a reflexive glance away. When she returned her attention to the stage, it was with a hard stare and taut lips. For this next examination her eyelids narrowed, like the gunnery slits on a pillbox.

She said, "Oh my God." Sam reached to put an arm on her shoulder, thought better of it, and left his arm floating in space.

The dominant colors in the theatre were burgundy and gold played against a landscape of soft cream, the color of vanilla custard. The chairs were old individual hickory chairs with red velvet cushions and loose pillow backs. The scale of the seating seemed lilliputian, charming and anachronistic by the standards of our future century.

In a soft voice, Sam asked me when I was going to be done admiring the place. Instinctively I knew that he wasn't criticizing me, that instead he was orienting me, bringing me back to the gruesome reality of why we were in this mountain mecca so late at night.

Lauren grabbed my hand as I turned my attention toward the stage. I said, "Oh shit," immediately closed my eyes and swallowed a geyser of vomit.

"Before we go any closer, we'll wait up here for a minute or two, I think," Sam said. "At least until you get your bearings."

My eyes still closed, I visualized the stage, my mind accommodating to the horror to which I had just become a witness by leaving a large black hole in the center—where the body was.

The stage curtain was up.

Of course, I thought—these assholes couldn't see the play they had produced if the curtain were down.

As I re-created it in my head, I realized that the stage set had seemed jumbled. The rear of the stage, both left and right, was covered with reproductions of stone stairs that seemed to lead upward to gardens. Farther forward on the stage were a stone well with a raised bucket and a tall signpost that for some reason reminded me of a gallows. Trees and bushes sprouted thickly from the wings.

The set was of a courtyard, or maybe a plaza.

I wish I knew more about opera. What the hell was *Manon* about, anyway?

Hung center stage was a huge expanse of windows. The windows seemed to be those of a Parisian loft, small panes in many rows, the mullions thick and heavy. A settee was placed incongruously toward the front of the stage, facing the vista of windows.

The set pieces on the stage had to be from different scenes, and even different operas. The Central City Opera was a repertory company; three different productions made up the summer season. Unless Massenet had been a surrealist, this oddly amalgamated set couldn't be from a single act of his opera. I was reminded of the Buell Theatre in Denver, and the strange mix of pieces from the scenes of *Miss Saigon* that had been assembled for Lonnie Aarons's murder.

The time had come to fill in the black hole in the center of my imaginings. I looked again at the stage.

The victim's body was hanging naked, head down and buttocks out, suspended by the ankles from the charming Parisian window. Blond hair stretched down an additional foot from the corpse, almost brushing the floor. The victim's arms were outstretched so they ran parallel to the stage. From where I stood, I couldn't tell how the arms had been fixed in that position. The hands were bent at the wrist and the fingers pointed limply toward the stage floor.

The feet jutted up through empty panes near the top of the window, both on the same row, an empty pane between the ankles. Something linear and dark attached the limbs, fixing them behind the grid of mullions. I guessed the ligature was a rope.

Later I would learn that I had guessed wrong.

The blood that had been spilled from this victim was dark and fresh and abundant, and pooled so near its owner that it could be mistaken for nothing else. Linear streaks, deep and gaping and obscene, ran down the body from heel to shoulder. The lines had been carefully drawn; the streaks were precise and formed the shape of two narrow hand fans that had been barely squeezed open.

A large dark pond—people certainly do hold a lot of blood—shaped roughly like a kidney bean was pooled directly below the body, as though ready for the victim to dive into it to reclaim what was rightfully his. Where this person's hair wasn't blond, it was congealed into thick rust-colored vines.

His hair? Or her hair?

From the rear, the victim's gender wasn't apparent. This person had been slight and blond. I looked for body hair and thought I saw blond fuzz on the thighs and darker thatches under the arms. But there was so much blood, I could not be sure from this distance. As Sam Purdy urged Lauren and me down the steps of the orchestra toward the stage, I kept wondering about gender.

"Who's here, Sam?" Lauren asked.

He knew what she meant and inhaled to prepare himself for providing a long list. "Central City Police, Gilpin Country sheriff, mobile crime-scene people from CBI, county coroner from Gilpin. There's a call in to the medical examiner in Denver to assist. He may be here already."

"He may be a she, Sam," Lauren corrected.

"Whatever. Her patients aren't picky. I won't be, either." He scratched his forehead once and brushed back his hair. "There's probably a DA type from Gilpin County. Me, you, Alan, and Dale Hunter. Probably the mayor and most of the city council and a PR type or two, you know, somebody to handle spin control for the casinos. That's about it, I think."

Many of the assembled investigatory players seemed to be clustered at the foot of the orchestra seating area, between the first row of hickory chairs and the opening of the orchestra pit. The stage itself was blocked off with yellow tape, as were all the seating areas of the theatre. Dale Hunter, who had spoken only briefly to Sam after greeting us on the street, had preceded us to the stage and was standing in front of the orchestra pit talking with two men and a woman. The woman, in uniform, was pointing up at something on the stage with the pinky of her right hand.

Three criminalists were hard at work in their pale jumpsuits. The tedious tasks of photographing, video-taping, and measuring must have been completed already, because one of the trio was dusting for prints while the other two were busy on their hands and knees identifying and collecting trace evidence. They worked methodically and, mostly, silently.

I was fascinated that everyone seemed to be functioning as though the body weren't there.

Another criminalist ordered the houselights turned off in the orchestra, pulled some goggles over his eyes, and began scanning the darkened areas of the audience with a flashlight of some kind.

Sam explained, "It's a 'cum' light. Semen fluoresces under certain wavelengths. He's looking for semen."

The scene I was viewing in front of me—the stage, the crawling criminalists, the yellow tape, and, mostly, the rusty scent of blood—reminded me of my visit with Sam to the Boulder Theatre the morning after Peter's murder. But the stage values, the production details of this atrocity, reminded me much more of what Charley Chandler thought had happened to Lonnie Aarons at the Buell.

A person, a human being—someone with a family and friends and projects to finish and dreams to dream—hung upside down, suspended from a stage batten thirty yards in front of me, drained of blood, surrounded by fake stone and false gardens, everything ever desired in his or her life now a hollow, never-to-be-fulfilled promise. In terms of pain felt and dreams crushed, whether the victim was a man or a woman didn't matter anymore.

I wondered if there were any children who would suffer as a consequence of this crime, any ancillary victims like Jonas.

My gut ached from my thoughts and from nausea. I held Lauren's hand in my clammy one and tried to remember why I was in the theatre, why I was in Central City, what job I'd been enlisted to do.

Suddenly, in my head, I heard the music.

From the Buell. From the play.

da da da da da da DA

The heat is on in Saigon.

For a split second I thought I knew. And just as suddenly, the awareness, whatever it had been, was gone.

The atmosphere in the opera house was both charged and oddly serene.

The crime-scene investigators seemed to pop out of the otherwise slow-motion crowd because they were busy, occupied with the impersonal details of the crime, its victim, and its perpetrator. Investigators from Gilpin County and Central City were busy, too, interviewing people and taking notes. But almost everyone else milled about the large room listlessly, speaking quietly in pairs or gathering in small groups, their roles in this tragedy in temporary abeyance as they awaited their turns inside the perimeter marked off at the proscenium.

When a tall, thin woman entered from the wing, stage left, wearing cowboy boots, blue jeans, and a heavy Swarthmore sweatshirt, the people milling around stopped what they were doing and attended to the developments on the stage as though Beverly Sills had just returned to Central City for a long-anticipated encore.

The woman paced across the stage with confident strides and snapped open a yellow canvas bag with CORONER stenciled on it in black letters. She unfolded a disposable jumpsuit and stepped into it as gracefully as a model dressing in an evening gown. She stretched paper booties over her cowboy boots and latex examination gloves over her hands. A few seconds passed while she stared at the corpse; then she screened her face with a pale-blue mask, tying it above the knot of a dark bun at the back of her head.

"That's Carmen Roja," Lauren said. "She's from DG."

I looked from Lauren to Sam. His face was adorned with a wry smile. He liked theatre. This was good theatre.

Dr. Roja, from Denver's coroner's office, was present, I assumed, because she was a forensic pathologist and the elected Gilpin County coroner was not. The Gilpin coroner—who I later learned was actually a slot-machine mechanic for one of the Central City casinos—had probably shown up on the scene, taken one look at this brutalized murder victim, and immediately called for backup from the closest forensic specialist he could find.

Dr. Roja went to work with a camera, and I decided not to watch.

"Let's move closer," Sam suggested, already in motion. Lauren stayed with him, step for step.

I edged back instead, and sat softly on a hickory

chair outside the tape perimeter. "I think I'll stay here," I said. Sitting was a tremendous relief.

Sam stopped and turned. "You okay?"

"What do you think? I'm fine. You two go ahead. I need to get a feel for all that's happening; I'm not as used to all this as the two of you. I'll get the details later." I gestured at the victim.

Those details.

Concerned, Sam and Lauren eyed me for a few seconds, then proceeded down the incline toward the stage.

I called out, "Wait. Sam?"

He turned. "What?"

"The victim? Is it a man or a woman?"

"It's a guy," he said after a brief pause. "A page, an usher. He was part of the company. He just graduated from a little college in Missouri, came here for the summer, like an intern. Everybody in the company liked him. They said he wanted to be in the soaps."

I was pleased that Sam had learned something about the dead man.

Over Lauren's right shoulder I watched Carmen Roja peering intently at the flayed wounds on her patient, who was still inverted and suspended from the fake Parisian window. The pathologist held a small recorder in her hand and spoke into it as she worked. It was fortunate, I thought, that she was tall; a small person like Adrienne would never have managed to get close enough to examine the body and still stay out of the pool of blood underneath it.

Repulsed but captivated, I forced myself to withdraw

my attention from the pathologist's work. I didn't want to watch, but I didn't want *not* to watch.

Just then, the awareness flickered again, like a lightning strike. Bright for a second, then gone.

da da da da da da DA

The heat is on in Saigon.

What?

My thoughts came sudden and fast—staccato, clipped, and unrefined. AK-47 thoughts.

What? That was Carmen Roja's question. Right now. What had been done to this young man? What weapon? What cause of death? What manner?

Who? That was the detective's question. Who did it? One, two, or three assailants? Who were they?

How? Another question for the detectives. How did they get in? How did they capture this young man? How was the crime committed? How did they get away?

Why?

Why? That was my question. I owned it. Why was this done? I had to concentrate on that simple question and let all the professional investigators do what they did best to answer the what, the who, and the how. I had to stop playing cop and start playing psychologist.

I had to figure out the why.

Why, for instance, were those seven notes playing in my head?

da da da da da da DA

Lauren and I hung around for a couple more hours, talking, being silent, holding hands, being alone, being together, trying to find a way to make this whole experience fit into some context that could be rationalized. I knew that part of her usual strategy for coping with atrocities such as this was to adopt a distant, professional demeanor. My presence, and our still-evolving intimacy, interfered with the natural inclinations of her defenses to try to remove herself by getting clinical.

Sam and Dale spent most of their time up onstage conferring with the local investigators, and probably, at least in Sam's case, offering advice. In my own way I was intent, too—on trying to get a feel for what had happened in the opera house that night. Part of doing that required that we wait for Dr. Roja to release the corpse to the homicide detectives, so that they in turn could finish doing whatever it was they needed to do, so that Sam and Lauren and I would be permitted onstage to look around.

The body of the young man was finally bagged and removed from the stage around midnight. A few minutes later, Sam came down to the orchestra seating area and led Lauren and me onto the stage, where he introduced us to the man from the Central City Police Department who had given Sam clearance to show us around backstage. I thought it was silly that the man considered it necessary to remind Sam not to touch anything, then realized that the admonition was probably for my benefit.

The backstage architecture of the opera house was similar to that of both the Buell and the Boulder theatres, with its main storage and open work spaces primarily stage left. The wing on the right was cramped and small, and, as at the other theatres, contained the controls—the pulleys and levers—that operated the overhead sets. Stage left was spacious by comparison but was crowded with scenery for the three different opera productions that constituted the repertory that season.

Numbered and lettered evidence markers littered the stage everywhere we walked, identifying the location of blood splatters, footprints, and specific places where various pieces of trace evidence had been collected. The controls of the counterweight and pulley system had been given significant attention by the crime-scene technicians. According to what I'd learned from Charley Chandler, I computed that the killer would have had to move the battens at least twice to get the victim, Mark Literno, suspended the way he was.

An impression—something just shy of a conclusion—was forming in my head as we moved from the stage into the attached building that housed the dressing rooms and costume-storage area. Sam's purpose in taking us there was to show us how easy it was to get into the building. Downstairs, below the stage, he showed us how many places there were to hide.

I paid attention and reminded myself to keep an open mind about all I was seeing.

My feeling—the conclusion I was fighting—was that this killing had been theatrical but not particularly sophisticated. If the Buell murder had rated four stars and Peter's murder one, this one was two, maybe two and a half.

To me that meant one thing. A third killer.

* * *

I didn't like the idea of driving home from Central
City at one-thirty in the morning. Almost anyone
behind the wheel of a car heading down the Front
Range at that hour was likely to have spent a significant portion of the evening drinking alcohol in the
Central City or Black Hawk casinos. The prospect of
sharing curvy mountain canyon roads with drunks in
the middle of the night held no attraction for me.

Sam was still conferring with Dale Hunter and the
Central City detectives investigating this newest
murder when Lauren and I said goodbye and made
our exit from the opera house. Given my trepidation
about driving and given her fatigue, we quickly
agreed to drive down the hill and take the first vacant
hotel room we could find. It turned out our choices
were limited; these gambling towns were still commuter resorts, not intended for overnight guests. One
big new hotel had just opened in the canyon halfway
down to Black Hawk. We stopped there, checked in,
and begged toothbrushes from a pleasant young
woman in housekeeping who was sincerely sorry that
she couldn't offer us any toothpaste.

By the time Lauren had washed her face and
brushed her teeth using some breath drops from her
purse, the adrenaline rush that had fueled her ener-
getic appraisal of the murder scene at the opera house
had totally dissipated. She crawled naked into bed
next to me and shivered once or twice before
becoming still. When she finally spoke, only half a
minute later, I immediately noticed, with some

delight, that her voice had taken on that honey and gravel murmur indicative of true languor.

She faced me, her head on her pillow, mine on my own, for a minute, examining my face for something that seemed terribly important; then she rolled over onto her other side and edged her ass back into the curve of my groin, her head on my pillow.

"My theory still works, doesn't it?" she asked with no enthusiasm at all about the prospect of being correct.

"Yes, in fact, it works even better than it did before."

"Why do you say that?"

She was squirming around trying to get comfortable on the hotel mattress and her slightest movement seemed to spur my reluctant arousal. It didn't feel intentional on her part. It certainly wasn't on mine, though, given the events of the evening, I welcomed the full contact with her flesh.

"Because this one doesn't have the same feel as the first murder at the Buell, and it certainly wasn't much like Peter's. This one was different. This one involved a third director, a third producer. Each time, each murder, something is qualitatively different. That makes your theory work."

"The sword thing was awful. It was certainly a disgusting new twist."

The victim had been a young man. Mark Literno's feet had been held in place behind the window unit, not by a rope tying them together behind the panes, as I'd first suspected, but rather by a sword that skewered him together at the ankles. After pulling Literno's feet through the window openings, the killer had shoved the entire length of the sabre through the tender skin directly behind one of Literno's Achilles tendons and then inserted it into the same spot on the other leg.

All I could say was "Yes, it was awful."

"But there was no semen this time."

I could have told her that I seemed to have only recently produced a drop or two of my own, but I didn't.

"How do you explain that, Alan? That lack of seminal fluid."

"Well, they might still find some."

"I know, but if they don't?"

Earlier, as the crime-scene tech who was wandering the audience with the cum light had concluded his futile search for semen in the seating areas, I'd begun to think about the repercussions if no reproductive fluids were found.

"I'd explain it one of two ways. First, the masturbator was onstage this time, not in the audience. It was his turn to kill, and that's why there was no semen in the orchestra or the balcony. Or second, he's developing some sexual impairment or inhibition. He couldn't get it up, or he couldn't get off. Maybe everything needs to be perfect, or maybe things need to escalate for him in some way and something wasn't right for him this time. The fantasy wasn't what he needed. The literature is full of examples of impaired sexual capacity during sexual homicides."

Lauren's mind had moved on. "I wonder what hair and fibers and footprints will show—if they will lead back to the other murders."

The trace evidence would probably show something

to confuse the issue, is what I thought. "Those results will take awhile to get back, right?"

"Yeah," she said, barely audibly.

One of the many surprising things I had learned about Lauren when she moved into my house was that she had a collection of opera LPs. I asked, "Do you know anything about *Manon*, the opera that was playing today? Do you know what it's about?"

"A little, I saw it once years ago, performed in French. Why?"

"I'm wondering if the themes in the story are relevant somehow. The final dress rehearsal for Saturday's opening performance was today at two. Sam said that about four hundred people were invited to attend. I'm curious about the possibility of a connection. Whether the story has anything to do with the choice of theatres. That sort of thing."

She reached around and rested her hand on my hip. "Let me think for a minute, my French was never that great."

"It's a morality tale, I guess," she said, after I had almost given up waiting, certain she had already drifted off to sleep. "Manon is a sensuous, spirited young woman who is being sent to a convent by her father. On the way there she falls madly in love with a young man and they run off to Paris to live together. His father learns about it and has his son kidnapped to break up the couple. Manon, it turns out, is a bit of a material girl, and she soon finds herself a rich lover who will let her live in splendor. But when Manon hears through the grapevine that her old lover is about to become a priest, she rushes to him and changes his mind. They return to Paris together, where soon they are accused of some crime. Manon is sentenced to be deported and, in the end, she dies a tragic death in her lover's arms."

I could almost hear the fat lady sing. "Nineteenth century?"

"Mmm, of course. When else?" She pressed back into me, wiggling a little.

"Are there any kids in the story?"

"What?"

"In *Manon*, are there any children in the story?"

"No, why?"

"I'm not sure. The child in *Miss Saigon* is so integral to the plot. I'm looking for parallels."

"I'm kind of tired, sorry. I don't think I can help anymore tonight. Good night."

When my wife rolled away from me, my eyes had adjusted to the dim light in the room. Her black hair hugged the soft curve of her neck and her chest heaved lightly. In the distance, I could hear tour buses revving their diesels to get ready for their descent to Denver. One giddy gambler kept laughing and saying she couldn't believe it, she couldn't believe it.

Lauren's return to her side of the bed had left me with warm sheets, confused thoughts, and an erection.

The erection, I knew from experience, would go away long before the confusion.

I woke the next morning before Lauren stirred. After showering I reluctantly dragged on my clothes from the day before, hung a do not disturb sign on the doorknob, and took the stairs to the first floor of the hotel in search of some coffee and a pay phone. At ten-thirty that morning, Lauren and I were due to depart from Denver for our flight to Jackson Hole, Wyoming. We weren't going to make it and I had to phone my travel agent to reschedule.

The travel agent worked her keyboard magic, and changing to a later flight was not a problem. Next, I called Adrienne's house and got Lisa. I told her Lauren and I were away and asked her to feed Emily and let her out into her dog run. She said she would.

A fancy urn in the hotel lobby turned out to be full of coffee that was the pale, cloudy color of iced tea that had been made from powder. I took a single cautious sip, tasted nothing at all, and left the full cup behind on the table.

The Denver newspapers both prominently featured the Central City Opera murder. The *Rocky Mountain News* ran the story as the solitary page-one headline. An accompanying teaser at the bottom of the page promised a sidebar on "Stage Fright; Local Theatre Companies Terrified."

The *Denver Post*, too, had the story of the gruesome murder above the fold. Below the fold, but still front page, was a story about the body of a missing hiker, a college student from Boulder, discovered along the banks of the Big Thompson River near Rocky Mountain National Park.

I read the Central City stories first, learning details that I hadn't been told the night before.

Mark Literno, like all the ushers who worked for the opera company, had been recruited for the summer from ads placed in *Art Search* magazine. The ushers worked hard and did everything from cleaning the theatre to singing and acting in cabaret performances and pre-opera events. The young men and women all lived together in company-owned houses that were clustered on streets near the opera house. Mark and his fellow ushers, both men and women, had performed publicly that afternoon prior to the dress rehearsal of *Manon* and then, adorned in their nineteenth-century costumes, had assumed their duties in the theatre, which involved assisting people to their seats.

The dress rehearsal had ended on schedule at five-thirty or so, and the cast and crew and the rest of the opera company were on their way to their temporary summer homes by six. A few company members remembered seeing Mark lingering behind as they were leaving the theatre. A while after the performance, he had been visiting with a seamstress friend in the upstairs hallway of the building adjacent to the theatre, helping her rehang costumes so they would be in place for the gala opening on Saturday night. One of the ushers told police that she remembered reminding Mark that they were having a barbecue at her place around eight. She recalled that Mark said that he would be there.

But by eight o'clock that night, Mark Literno was probably already dead.

I put down the newspaper and said audibly, "God, this was risky." A woman who absolutely should not have been wearing horizontal stripes took some offense at my mumbling and moved away from me in the lobby.

But it *was* risky.

Peter's murderer had planned his escapades in the Boulder Theatre carefully and optimized the circumstances of the crime in order to keep from being discovered. And Lonnie Aarons's murderer had gone to elaborate pains to be certain that he would be undisturbed during his ritual assault at the Buell. But, apparently, Mark Literno's murderer had carried out his early-evening savagery in a just-vacated opera house on a busy street in a town that certainly didn't roll up the sidewalks at sundown.

Why? Why the sudden capriciousness?

There it was again, the why.

The police had a guest list to work with. That fact was news to me, as well. The tickets for the dress rehearsal had been distributed as gifts by the Central City Opera House Association to company members, benefactors, volunteers, and local businesspeople who had supported the production company in a variety of ways. With that list, and given enough time, the police could probably track down most of the guests who had attended the performance. That meant that a small rural police force had about four hundred people to interview; more people, I guessed, than the Central City Police Department had questioned during the entire previous year.

The other story in the *Denver Post*, the one under the fold, was about the discovery of Kenny Holden's remains. To my amazement—and Sam Purdy's certain relief—the press had not yet made anything of the link between Kenny Holden and the events surrounding Peter's murder, so the report of his death was straight-forward and uncontaminated by conjecture and innu-endo. He had apparently gone camping alone in the national park. A campsite with his things had been discovered days ago. The autopsy was pending, though the patriarch of the family from Oklahoma told the reporter that it appeared to him that the young man had suffered from either a bad fall or a severe beating.

A spokesman said that the police were working under the assumption that the young man had fallen while attempting to descend a steep trail to the river, but the investigation was continuing. It seemed to me that the authorities were busy ruling out suicide, not homicide.

Getting up from the bar, I squeezed my hand into the pocket of my jeans and found three quarters. I dropped them into the closest slot machine and debated long and hard whether to push the button or pull the handle. I pulled the handle. Things spun. Little bells played. I waited. Nothing else happened.

The house, apparently, was up six bits. Next time I would push the button.

I knew that Lauren, if she was undisturbed, would manage to sleep until nine or ten. And disturbing Lauren's sleep was something I did with great reluctance. One of the many puzzles about multiple sclerosis is the fatigue that is so constant and so intrusive. Lauren would regularly grow listless and weary by late morning or early afternoon, and be forced to sleep. The curious and infuriating part for her was that there was absolutely no guarantee that ten hours of rest at night and two hours more in the afternoon would make any difference in her lassitude. "Sleep is necessary," she said once, trying to help me understand what the fatigue was like for her, "unfortunately it's not always sufficient."

After a few attempts, I despaired at finding a better cup of coffee than the hotel offered. Starbuck's hadn't discovered Black Hawk yet. But I had an alternate destination in mind. I walked east, away from town, crossed the Peak to Peak Highway, and hiked up a mountain of rubble to the Cyclone construction fence that surrounded the site of the Silver Streak Casino and Gaming Club, which was just coming alive with trade workers completing their commutes from Idaho Springs, Nederland, and Golden. For a good five minutes I watched, fascinated, as the crane operator climbed the long strand of ladders that would take him to his day's roost, at least six stories above the road.

I quickly decided that I did not want his job during thunderstorm season.

The concrete-form construction was rising about three and a half stories above the ground and, if the fancy painted picture on the sign in front of me was accurate, would someday soon top out at four floors. The same sign also promised that the casino would be open in October. Examining the building shell, I guessed at all the exterior and finish work that remained to be done and wondered, October of what year?

Lights flashed on in the solitary window of the big construction trailer that fronted the site, close to the highway. I hadn't seen anyone enter the trailer, but the doorway wasn't visible from where I was standing. I wondered if Grubstakes Development would maintain an office out here to keep an eye on the project. Probably not, I decided.

But my choices that morning were rather limited. I could either gamble or snoop. I decided to snoop.

"We're not hiring."

The portly woman who spoke those words to me upon my entrance to the construction trailer didn't bother to look up from her desk. She had disemboweled a stapler on her blotter and was intent on trying to reattach the spring mechanism. Her words to me had been unaccented; I quickly decided that she wasn't the woman from New Jersey I had spoken to when I first phoned Grubstakes asking for Grant Arnold.

"I'm not looking for work."

"You can't use the phone, either. Or the head."

"I don't want to call anybody and I don't need the can."

"We're not buying." She still hadn't looked up.

"I'm not selling." I was beginning to enjoy this.

The little spring from the stapler went flying across the room. "Then what the fuck do you want?"

She was young, late twenties, and polyestered from head to toe. Beads of sweat were already appearing in the fine hairs above her lip. The air in the trailer tasted as though it hadn't circulated since the Colorado gold rush.

"Can I buy you a cup of coffee?" I gestured at the commercial coffeemaker a few feet from the doorway where I was standing. A steady black-brown rope descended with an inviting tinkle into the glass carafe. The liquid was the right color for coffee. And it smelled like coffee.

I wanted some.

"I start my day with Pepsi." She was looking at me now. "But help yourself."

I pulled a dollar from my wallet and fed it into the bill slot of the nearby pop machine. "Regular or diet?"

"You being funny?"

I shook my head.

"Regular."

The can clanged into the tray. I poured myself a mug of coffee and sat down next to her desk. She had a full, inviting face and eyes the color of dirty snow. She took the Pepsi from my hand.

"Molly," she said. "Molly Newton."

"Alan. Alan Gregory."

"What the hell *do* you want, Alan?"

Since Black Hawk was a gambling town, I played my best card—actually my only card. I asked Molly if she had heard about what had happened at the opera house last night.

She had, of course, and—as I gathered from the fact that she momentarily stopped breathing and looked anxiously at the door—suddenly feared that she was sitting enjoying her first Pepsi of the day with the crazed murderer responsible for that atrocity.

In my most reassuring psychologist voice, I told her about my friend Peter and his murder at the Boulder Theatre and the gorgeous bar that he had made to be installed in the building that was going up outside.

Just then, two guys in hard hats came into the trailer and poured themselves coffee in styrofoam cups. One of them turned to Molly and asked whether the fax he was waiting for was in from the architects. Molly laughed a conspiratorial "Are you kidding?" laugh and told him, no, but she would send it out as soon as it arrived.

"Dumbshits," she said as they left. "The architects are in California. Those two have been here for almost a year and they can't get the time zones straight. Fax won't come in for two hours at least."

Molly leaned toward me across the desk. "Did you know the guy who—you know, the one who got sliced up last night?"

"No, I didn't know him." I paused and lowered my voice. "But I was there, in the opera house, afterward. I'm a consultant with the Boulder Police Department." One lie, one half-truth. Not bad before I'd finished my first cup of coffee.

"Jeez. Did you see him?"

"Yes," I said. "I sure did. It was awful. I wish I could tell you what was done to him, but I can't. The police don't want copycats, you know. Trust me, it was worse than you've heard."

Molly sat back and nodded. She knew about copycats and about discretion. "So then why are you here?"

"Just curious, I guess, to see what kind of project my friend was working on. I wanted to see where his bar, his last work, was going to be installed. Why does it seem to me like this place is on the wrong side of the highway?"

Molly laughed again. Her laugh, like her face, was pleasant and endearing.

"Grubstakes does gambling *clubs*; they're not really just casinos. High level of service, a dozen fancy hotel rooms granted gratis if you're losing enough money. The Silver Streak is set up to cater to serious gamblers, not the ones who lose five bucks and then casino-hop. I can tell you that the guys who are building this place aren't interested in the busloads of seniors who come up from Golden."

"But all the gambling up here is limited stakes. How serious can the money get?"

"For now, the stakes are limited, and still almost all the casinos up here are doing fine. But next year or the year after that, after a little lobbying with the legislature, who knows? These guys are gamblers, remember."

Interesting. "You know Grant Arnold, with Grubstakes?"

"Sure. He comes around regular, every week at least. Keeps his hard hat in here. He's from Tahoe, like most of them, but he's all right."

"He and my friend Peter, the one who was killed in Boulder, they used to be friends a long time ago."

"Death sort of follows you and Grant around, don't it?"

Molly was quick.

"I don't know about Grant, Molly, but I do seem to be seeing more than my share these days. Where's Grant's office? Is it around here?"

"Yeah, across the street, up the hill, about halfway between Black Hawk and Central City. You want me to call, see if he's there?"

"No. I'm not sure what I want to do. I appreciate the conversation, though, and am more grateful for the coffee than you could know."

"Well, thank you for the Pepsi."

A glint in the filthy carpet caught my eye. I bent down and picked up the truant spring from the stapler and handed it to Molly.

She thanked me.

I walked outside into a surprisingly warm morning. That congenial Molly Newton thought Grant Arnold was all right was important to me, though I wasn't at all sure why.

As I was climbing up the hill to the hotel I noticed a painted sign for the local offices of Grubstakes Development. The lettering was not distinctive and the placard was about the size of a manila envelope. The marker was intended purely as a locator, not as an enticement to visitors.

In its Rocky Mountain incarnation, on the second floor of a narrow-frame building that seemed to be listing downhill while awaiting demolition to make way for another casino, Grubstakes Development looked suspiciously like a struggling local realty company. Before I rushed to judgment about the nature of Grubstakes' fortunes, though, I tried to keep in mind that the construction project I had just visited a few blocks away was costing somebody quite a few million dollars.

I climbed an exterior staircase that looked as if it had been tacked onto the side of the building as an afterthought. The stairs creaked and swayed just enough to get me to hurry my ascent. I entered a small, dark reception room crammed with a desk, computer, plain paper fax, copy machine, and two chairs. The young lady with the memorable New Jersey accent greeted me from the desk skeptically, as though she was pretty sure I was lost. Or hoped I was.

"May I help you?"

I reminded myself that I probably didn't look my best. I wasn't wearing any underwear, although hopefully that wasn't apparent, but otherwise was dressed in the same clothes I had worn the day before. I hadn't gotten enough sleep, hadn't shaved, and hadn't had the two cups of coffee I required to appear humanoid in the morning.

"I was hoping to find Mr. Arnold."

"Really? Is he expecting you?" In her voice there was a firm twang of disbelief that Mr. Arnold could possibly be expecting the likes of me.

"I don't have an appointment, but we've talked. Please tell him it's about Pete."

She got up from her desk and walked through a doorway into the adjoining room. While she was still seated, I'd noted that she wore a linen blazer that seemed to intentionally reveal the borders of the black lingerie beneath it. When she stood, she tugged down a short skirt and trod off in high, high heels. Maybe three inches' worth. I allowed a couple of assumptions to form: that Ms. New Jersey didn't do a lot of recreational walking on her lunch break, and that when she took this job, she somehow managed to confuse Central City with Las Vegas.

In a moment a man appeared in the doorway and said, "Hello, I'm Grant Arnold." The man was thin and average in height. He appeared to be the right age—Peter's age. His clothes were casual—nice slacks and a tasteful V-neck sweater over a polo shirt. His shoes were black and heavy and sensible, okay for here in the office, sufficiently sturdy for a visit to the construction site if a problem arose down there requiring his attention.

"Alan Gregory," I said. "I'm a friend of Peter Arvin's. We talked on the phone."

Grant reached out his right hand. I stepped forward and shook it. He invited me into his office, which was an unfortunate duplicate of the reception room in size and was blessed with no additional natural light.

He waved me to a chair and said, "I apologize for the facilities. We do most of our business elsewhere. As you can imagine, there's not a lot of class-A office space to be found in Gilpin County."

"Well, it makes no difference to me, Mr. Arnold. And, anyway, who am I to complain about appearances?" I invited his appraisal of my clothes. "I certainly apologize for mine. I was called up to Central City unexpectedly late last night, and I haven't—"

"Call me Grant. I bet you came up about the murder at the opera house, didn't you?"

Was that just a good guess? "Yes, I came up about the murder. I don't think I told you when we spoke before, but I'm a clinical psychologist in real life, and I've been consulting with the Boulder Police about Peter's death, about the possible psychological traits of the killer. They called me and asked me to come up here to take a look at what happened last night. And since I was here anyway, I thought I would take advantage of the opportunity and stop in and introduce myself to you before I headed back to Boulder."

"I'm glad you did. And I'm sorry about my tardiness in getting someone down to look at the cabinets. I'm having a hard time accepting that Pete's really dead, I guess. I did meet with that guy, the painter, his name is . . ."

"Tony Celli? Looks like a grunge Marine?"

"Yes. Mr. Celli. He said he'd call with a bid."

"Peter liked his work. He used him on all his important projects."

"That's nice to know, I'll keep that in mind when I get the bid. I hope you're not concerned that I haven't had a chance to send someone down to look at the work Pete did, there's been so much—"

I held up a hand and tried to stop him with a smile. "I understand. I didn't come by to bug you. I was out taking a walk earlier and was down by the highway and saw all the activity at your casino. There's obviously no great hurry for Peter's work, Grant. I mean, you guys are not exactly ready to install cabinetry, are you?"

He laughed. "No, we're not. We had foundation trouble, lost a few months right at the start. We couldn't find bedrock where the soil engineers told us we would. Hell of a lot of rock, but no bedrock. But it's okay, the city is way behind on the sewage-treatment upgrades they're doing, so the infrastructure isn't ready for us, anyway. You have my word, though, that I will get someone down to Boulder to inventory the work. Pete's widow doesn't have to worry about payment."

"She's not worried." Not about money, anyway, I thought.

In a more serious voice, he asked, "So what happened last night at the opera house? Can you tell me anything?"

I tried to determine whether his question was generated by some motive other than morbid curiosity. "I take it you saw the papers?"

He said he had, and told me what he had read. I confirmed what I could.

"Is it the same guy who killed Pete?"

"The cops don't exactly tell me what they're thinking, but I think it's safe to assume that concern about a serial killer is one of their working hypotheses."

He asked me a couple more questions, probing for details that I couldn't provide, and even if I could have provided, I wouldn't have provided.

My impression after sitting with Grant Arnold for ten minutes was that he was less lawyerly than I had expected. He was likable and nowhere near as pretentious in person as he had been on the phone.

"You lived here long?" I asked.

"I'm renting a place in Coal Creek. But I don't live anywhere long. I manage these development projects for Grubstake. In the last eight years, I've been in Atlantic City, Tahoe, Reno, two different places on the Mississippi. I'm a gypsy. But I've been to Colorado a lot. I still try to rock-climb as much as I can, so I try to get here at least once a year for the mountains."

"You climbed with Peter?"

"Not since college. He preferred to climb alone and started free-soloing."

"Yeah, I know. His wife didn't like it."

"I can imagine. I'm real comfortable on rocks, and I don't like it."

"The free-soloing—that started after the fire, right?"

Grant looked away from me and pressed his tongue against his closed lips before he spoke. "Yeah. That's when things changed. After the fire."

"A forest fire, right? He didn't talk about it much. What happened exactly?"

Grant Arnold gazed out the room's one tiny window. "That was a long time ago, Alan." The pause that followed was poignant; it felt to me like a pregnant silence at the beginning of a therapy session.

Lisa's sweet voice filled my head. The memory echoed with caution for me.

Peter didn't trust him.

I thought, *Why not? Peter, talk to me now, why didn't you trust Grant Arnold?*

Peter was silent.

Grant and I exchanged business cards. He offered me a ride up to my hotel, which I declined. I said goodbye to the receptionist, who had moved a big oscillating fan close to her desk. She waved at me, just a little trill of her pink-tipped fingers, and I left.

Lauren was looking lovelier than she had any right to when I tracked her down in the hotel coffee shop, where she was having what appeared to be a leisurely breakfast with Sam Purdy and Dale Hunter. My wife, smelling robustly of Binaca, kissed me lushly on the lips as I pulled a chair to the table.

I guessed from a quick appraisal of Sam's appearance that he had not seen a bed all night, or if he had found one, he hadn't slept in it. His face showed evidence of having received rapid attention from an electric shaver, but his eyes were rheumy.

Dale Hunter, on the other hand, was animated and fresh-looking. Her clothes, like Lauren's, were in much better shape than mine or Sam's. I guessed that observers of our table in the restaurant would wonder what the hell these two fine-looking women were doing with these two sloths.

"Where have you been?" The question was Sam's.

"Reading the papers, looking for coffee, out for a walk in town."

Sam didn't really wait for my answer. His attention was already turned to the dining room and an effort to flag down a waitress to bring him more of something he was eating or drinking.

Lauren guessed what I had been up to. She asked, "Did you go see that guy, the casino guy? Peter's friend?"

"Yes, as a matter of fact, I did, just now. I walked down to see the construction they're doing on the casino where Peter's bar is going and then stopped by the development company offices and introduced myself to Grant. He insists that Adrienne has nothing to worry about."

Lauren asked, "Then you don't agree with Lisa? Didn't she say that this Grant shouldn't be trusted?"

"I still don't understand why she thinks that. Grant seems like a nice enough guy. I think he's genuinely distressed by Peter's death and wants to do the right thing for Adrienne and Jonas. I got the impression he's still perplexed about why their college friendship didn't last. But maybe this wasn't the best day to visit him—you know, the whole town is just buzzed by the murder last night."

"Yeah, tell me about it," Dale Hunter muttered. "I'm not telling anybody else up here that I'm a cop. I could barely get the room-service guy to leave last night. So who's this man you went to see?"

"An old friend of my friend Peter. The guy had hired Peter to build the cabinetry for a saloon in a new casino up here. A place called the Silver Streak. Adrienne, Peter's widow, asked me to make sure everything he had built got delivered and she got paid."

"Who's the guy?"

"His name is Grant Arnold. He works for an outfit called Grubstakes Development."

Dale raised her cup. "And who was it who said you shouldn't trust him?"

"Lisa, Peter and Adrienne's nanny. She overheard Peter and Grant talking on the phone once."

Dale pondered this for a moment. "But it's not related to the case?"

"No. It's just carpentry business, as far as I can tell. Should be all taken care of in a few days, as soon as Grant can get someone to Boulder to inventory the cabinetry." Her curiosity had piqued my interest. "Do you see any connection to Lonnie Aarons and the Denver murder?"

Dale Hunter thought about it through a long swallow of tea. "No. But I'm always looking."

The waitress came by. I ordered waffles and juice.

Sam had returned his attention to the conversation at the table, and I couldn't help wondering whether he and Dale Hunter had spent the wee hours in anywhere near the proximity and state of undress that Lauren and I had enjoyed. Dale's attention, although not intrusive, was never far from him. Sam's own demeanor was sour, but the acid seemed directed more at me than at Dale.

"Sam, have you talked with anyone about Kenny Holden's death?"

"You mean Kenny Holden's murder."

"They've decided that already?" I was surprised, based on what I had read in the morning paper.

"No, *they* haven't. But Sam has," Dale said.

Sam's tone was impatient. "Kenny saw something that night in Boulder. Or the murderer saw him and thought he saw something. So Kenny was kidnapped. Then he was killed. And we're never going to be able to fucking prove it unless a witness saw somebody marching him through the park with a gun at his back."

A cloud of frustration quieted the table. I broke the silence. "Anything new from the opera house?" I asked.

Dale answered. "Not really. Unless a witness comes forward, anything new is probably going to come from the lab. But I can tell you that after seeing what I saw last night, I like your wife's theory about multiple killers a whole lot more than I did the last time we all ate together."

Lauren raised her eyebrows a millimeter or two.

"Same troupe," Sam said, his elbows on the table. "Goddamn bunch of gypsy fucking actors from hell."

Dale flashed a look at him and then turned back to me. "Can you work up a new profile based on the ensemble theory?"

"I've already given it a lot of thought. It won't take me long."

She reached into her blazer pocket, pulled out a business card, and handed it to me. "Copy me on the report, okay?"

Sam was staring at me. Sarcastically, I said, "I do whatever Sam tells me to do."

Dale looked down at her breakfast plate and said, "Yeah, me too."

Sam pretended not to have heard either my provocation or Dale's retort.

I was wondering, too, how Lauren's theory about a traveling troupe of murderers was going to play in the press when this new hypothesis become public, which it most certainly would.

The "Gypsy Fucking Actors from Hell" Murders.

It had a certain honesty and authenticity to it, I had to give Sam that.

I paid the breakfast tab and walked out of the restaurant with Sam. Lauren and Dale were a dozen feet ahead of us.

I leaned toward him and asked, "So what time did you guys get out of there last night?"

He said, "Fuck you."

V

Old Flames

The plane ride from Denver to Jackson, Wyoming, took about the same amount of time as the drive from Central City to Boulder. Although this trip to northwest Wyoming was my first, Lauren had been to Jackson Hole before, but only in the winter to ski, never in the spring. Her ex-husband was a profanely rich man, and in his company she had been, it seemed to me, almost everywhere amusing anyone would ever choose to go. Since she had gone to most of these delightful places in a context of romance and love that had nothing to do with me, or us, we had learned to talk about these prior visits in travel-agent terms. She invited me to share the wealth of her experience while she voluntarily excluded evidence of her traveling companion. The exclusion, we both knew, was a contrivance, but the artifice worked for us—another in a series of successful marital accommodations at which I marveled every day.

As the plane began its steep descent into the airport at Jackson Hole, she touched me high on my thigh to get my attention and said, wide-eyed, "Just wait."

She was talking, it turned out, only about the scenery at the airport.

The Jackson Hole Airport is in Grand Teton National Park, the only commercial airfield in any of

the nation's park preserves. But the Grand Tetons—
literally, in French slang, the big tits—are anything but
soft and round and inviting. If these peaks are indeed
mammaries, these aren't the round, welcoming
breasts of male fantasy, these mountains are young
and hard and jagged and scream for caution. These
are Madonna's on-tour breasts, granite-coned and
forbidding.

The French trappers who named these mountains, I
think, had been on the road too long.

Our noisy commuter plane descended into the
valley. The grandeur of the surrounding mountain
ranges was somehow magnified as we dropped deeper
and deeper into Jackson Hole—a long, narrow island
of relatively flat land in an otherwise all-encompassing
sea of peaks. I was reminded a little of the Uncom-
pahgre in Colorado's San Juans. I remembered, too, a
brief train trip through the Alps in Switzerland. But the
Grand Tetons were something else, something novel,
mountains that were more dominating, more fright-
ening than any I had seen before.

The plane touched the ground and taxied briefly.
Late spring in Denver meant the dropping of the
purple lilac blossoms and the parching of the grasses,
but May here in the Wyoming high country meant the
onset of spring. The snowmelt-fed mud season had
ended early, and the Jackson Valley was green and
lush with new growth fed by the abundant moisture
left behind by the winter snows. The days were still
too short for the inevitable bonanza of wildflowers
that would bloom in summer, but the valley's trees

were leafed out and the sky above was so blue it seemed to be lit with neon.

We picked up our rented car around three-thirty in the afternoon, the floor of the valley already shadowed by the mountains to the west, and drove south a dozen miles from the national park toward town.

The compact village of Jackson sits at the southern tip of Jackson Hole, where it is crowded into place by the Gros Ventre Mountains, the Gros Ventre Butte, and Snow King Mountain. We entered the outskirts of Jackson from the north, crossing over the brisk flow of Flat Creek, and drove a few hundred yards through a nondescript commercial district before arriving in the center of town. A minute of examination made it clear to me that Jackson has about as much in common with the rest of Wyoming as Utah has in common with the rest of the United States.

Lauren had booked us a room at the Teton Treehouse, a bed and breakfast clinging to a forested hillside on the west side of town. We found the place after a couple of false starts and checked in. Since Peter's mother was expecting us for supper at six-thirty, Lauren lost no time in stripping to a T-shirt and falling into bed for her afternoon nap, a sometimes futile attempt to rekindle the energy that has almost always betrayed her by midday.

While she slept, I walked. The center of Jackson is blessedly compact, maybe six blocks by five. One whole city block in the center of the village is consumed by a gracious town square, and another, on the perimeter, by a pretty park. The town in its current form obliges tourists. I suspected that I strolled past more restaurants on my tour of downtown than I had flown over in the entire time I had been in Wyoming airspace.

I stopped into a tavern and ordered a local beer, took my mug to an outside table, downing almost the entire glass in two long draws. In the space of an exhale I was wondering where Peter had fit into this gorgeous place and how he had ever managed to leave it.

For a split second, before I could shoo away the notion, I recalled the spate of murders in Colorado and how far from them I had managed to run in two short hours. The frozen image of Mark Literno impaled and inverted on the stage of the Central City Opera flashed in a corner of my consciousness like distant heat lightning.

I extinguished most of the residue of the image with my will, the remainder with the last of my beer, and the mental snapshot was gone, I hoped, for a while.

The mountain valley light that late afternoon was peculiar and sedating, subdued; the color was the palest smoky gray. It wasn't yet dusk; the sun was still high enough to brighten the clouds, and the blue of the sky hadn't begun to fracture into the colors of sunset. But the pre-dusk light was bridled and softened by the looming western mountains, and, in turn, the pace of life seemed to have slackened. It was a glorious time for a table with a view on a beat-up cedar deck, and for a cold beer and a kind smile from a pretty waitress with a café-au-lait spot on her neck who didn't even look old enough to drink.

I reminded myself to think about Peter, whom I knew I had been avoiding, as if he were still alive and the tension between us was ripe.

Peter.

Peter had moved away from this mountain hole when he was eighteen, and given that he chose to attend college in Las Vegas, I couldn't give much credence to the easy argument that he left Jackson because he was offended by the way the town had begun to curtsy to tourists. I assumed that he had left for the reason most kids leave, just to get away and to discover something about himself in the world away from home. Apparently, he had come back during the summers to work for the Outward Bound–type camp, so the schism between him and his hometown, and his family, hadn't been complete.

I pondered all this and ordered a second ale and—sure, why not?—this time, at the waitress's urging, a side of beer-batter onion rings. New questions about Peter were forming rapidly in my head, like summer thunderheads, and I knew as I took that wonderful first long pull of my second beer, that the quest to find him was no longer Adrienne's, but was, instead, my own. I would share the results with her gladly, but I was in Jackson, Wyoming, drinking local beer because I wanted to know this friend whom I had, regretfully, never bothered to know well enough before. I wanted to find Peter in order to bury him. To bury my guilt about not knowing him. To finally know him.

Lauren was in the shower when I returned to the B&B. I joined her with the best of intentions—of washing away the film of filth that travel always leaves—but soon we were running late.

The directions that Miriam Arvin, Peter's mother, had given me over the phone before I left Boulder took us south out of town along the banks of Flat Creek. "Follow the signs to Hoback Junction," she had said, "but if you get there, you missed our road."

Their road, which we didn't miss, was a rutted trail meandering west toward the Snake Mountains, which straddled the border between northwest Wyoming and Idaho. With Miriam's good directions in hand, the Arvin house was easy to find. It seemed to be nothing more than a big cedar box on a ridge, a gable on a shoebox, every second-grader's crayon vision of "home." A shiny new metal roof the color of old pennies capped Peter's family abode—homage, I assumed, to the gods who control wildfire.

As we drove up their steep driveway, I quickly decided that the location of the house seemed particularly uninspired; without even straining, I picked a half-dozen better locations on which they could have built.

Not too much remained of the day's ration of light. So when Miriam opened the front door to greet us, I didn't immediately notice the pale glow behind her.

My memory of Miriam from the funeral was of a stoic and reserved, almost distant woman. Her eyes were luminous—blue irises set in whites the color of glacier snow. I had waited for tears to flow from those eyes during Peter's requiem, for those eyes to redden, but had never seen the tears develop. I remembered wondering at the time whether I was witnessing part of Miriam's personality or merely viewing her adaptation to the most trying of circumstances—her child's funeral—an event, by necessity, being shared that day mostly with strangers.

She greeted Lauren and me with caution in her eyes and the faintest of smiles, and welcomed us by our first names into her home. She stood taller than I remembered, and was slight, without appearing at all frail with age. After a gentle handshake, she took Lauren's coat and guided us through her entry hall to the back of the house. That's when I noticed the orange light that was carved above mountaintops to the west and the twinkling of a river far below that glimmered as if it flowed only with the nectar of diamonds.

I forgot to exhale.

"What a gorgeous view," Lauren finally stammered.

Miriam was silent for a moment.

"We moved up here when Peter was four," Miriam said. "His father towed an old Airstream up here. The four of us lived in that little silver can for two years until the cabin was ready. He built it." With pride, she pointed north out one of the grand picture windows at a small cabin, thirty yards from this house, and shook her head a little, marveling at the changes and, I guessed, at the decay of time. "We had an outhouse then, but it's gone now. I don't even remember what happened to it. That was thirty years ago, that we lived in that old Airstream. But yes, dear, the view, it's as glorious to me now as it was back then. The dreams we had then, oh my, they have faded, you know?"

We settled onto sofas that faced each other and she

offered us drinks. We each gladly accepted a glass of beer. Miriam was drinking vodka or gin with olives over ice. A tall glass, almost full.

"This is very kind of you," I said. "Inviting us for dinner. Actually, agreeing to meet with us is very kind. I hope we're not intruding on your grief."

She seemed to flinch as I said "grief" and took a long sip of her drink before she spoke. "My hospitality, I'm afraid, is selfish, and not particularly kind. I'm not a kind woman, not usually, not anymore. I think I used to be, though. Life has been bitter lately."

"You mean something besides Peter's death?" Lauren asked softly.

"Oh, yes." Miriam placed her drink on a pine side table and rubbed her eyes. Below us, moonlight shimmered on the meandering Snake.

I took Lauren's hand to encourage her to wait this out quietly with me, to let Miriam take us wherever it was she chose to go.

The front door opened with a weather-stripped *swooosh* and a deep voice called, "Mom, it's me."

"Hello, dear, we're in the living room." She picked up her drink. "I asked Peter's brother to join us. He wasn't at the funeral." The tone of the last phrase was at least mildly scolding.

"Hi, I'm Colter Arvin."

I pegged the man standing at the edge of the room to be a few years younger than Peter. He was at least three inches taller, his skin already bore a midsummer tan, and his eyes twinkled like the Snake River in moonlight. I thought immediately that if I looked hard enough I could find Peter somewhere in them.

Colter, we learned over a dinner of pot roast and baked potatoes, was named by his father for John Colter, one of the first nonnative explorers of the Tetons and Yellowstone. John Colter had spent the winter of 1807 on a meandering journey through the entire region, including trips to both Yellowstone Lake and Jackson Lake, two journeys across the Tetons, and at least one traverse up and down the length of Jackson Hole. Given northwest Wyoming geography and the nature of the local winters, my professional opinion was that John Colter was definitely a persistent man, and possibly a deranged one.

John Colter's twentieth-century namesake had been educated across the state line, at the University of Idaho, and had returned to Jackson to run the family business, a task firstborn Peter had apparently declined to accept. The family business was electrical supplies, and its fortunes ran a course parallel to the fate of Jackson Hole.

Colter, who preferred to be called Colt, was obviously the most loquacious member of the living Arvins. "I guess I take after my father," he'd maintained when his mother asked him to please take a breath between sentences, because his food was getting cold. Between infrequent mouthfuls he described a childhood on the edge of poverty, as his father scraped for enough work as an electrician, not only to support his family of four but also to build a cabin in the wilderness without going into debt.

Burgess Arvin didn't like borrowing money; Miriam and Colter agreed on that.

When Colter graduated from college and returned home, he correctly foresaw that the future of Jackson Hole was tourism. "Wasn't hard, just had to count the golf courses," he explained modestly. He guided his father's electrical business from focusing on service to entering the then small wholesale supply market, and when Jackson Hole's boom accelerated in the mid-eighties, the Arvin Electrical Supply Company was poised to take advantage of the construction frenzy in the valley.

And Colter had made certain that AES was the only game in town that *was* ready.

Burgess Arvin became rich but never got to enjoy his change of fortune. A wealthy man with a big new house, he suffered a fatal heart attack in 1985. He had slept in his big new house, it turned out, exactly three times before he died.

At the end of the meal, Colt helped his mother clear the dishes and get the coffee ready. As soon as they had disappeared into the kitchen, Lauren turned to me and said, "Neither of them is talking about Peter."

I'd had the same thought during dinner, and didn't know whether the Arvins were savoring the opportunity to reminisce about Peter, or whether they were avoiding it.

Dessert was rocky road ice cream and canned fruit. Colt poured coffee for everyone, sat down, and as though he had somehow managed to eavesdrop on our thoughts, said, "In case you're wondering, I inherited Peter's crown."

Miriam looked askance at her son without rebuke or surprise at his words.

Lauren spoke before I did. "That must be difficult for you, especially given the way he died."

Colt offered her a kind smile. "No, not recently, not when he was murdered. I'm not talking about when he was murdered. I got the crown shortly after the fire. When was that? 'Eighty-two—yes, the summer of 'eighty-two. That's when we lost Pete. Last month is only when Pete actually died. Wouldn't you say that's right, Mom?"

Miriam nodded. "He was never the same after that summer, never the same. It had always been Pete who was going to take over the business, not Colter. Pete was always saying he would take care of me and Burgess, let us relax and enjoy life a little. Colter always wanted to fly airplanes. You and your darn airplanes, Colter."

I asked, "Why do you say 'crown,' Colt? What did you mean when you said you inherited Peter's crown?"

"Being Pete's younger brother wasn't always easy. Hell, it was never easy." Colt glanced at his mother with a thrust of his chin that was almost apologetic.

"That's okay, dear. I know what you mean."

"When we were young, it seemed like he never got in trouble. Never."

"Now, Colter, *that* is an exaggeration."

Colt ignored his mother's rebuke. "Pete was a born leader. In high school he was the smartest student—a National Merit scholar—he was the fastest skier—fearless in the downhill—the best rock-climber, the best shot, always caught the biggest fish. He was student-body president. My big brother was a hell of a tough act to follow."

Peter a leader? My neighbor an A student? My friend a superstar? No, I thought, this can't be right.

While I tripped over my tongue, Lauren sipped once at her coffee and said, "Would you tell us about the fire?"

"Even better," Colter said. "I'm a pilot. I'll not only tell you the story tonight, I'll take you there tomorrow and show you what happened."

Lauren begged off. One of her MS symptoms was intermittent vertigo. A ride in a small plane would not be what her doctor ordered.

The next morning I met Colter at the airport.

After completing a smooth forward thrust of the throttle with the palm of his right hand, Colt Arvin tugged back on the W-shaped yoke with a curl of his fingertips. He did this gently, as though he were beckoning a hesitant lover. The old Cessna 172 responded by lifting off the runway and beginning the hard climb out of the confines of Jackson Hole. Quickly, as the little plane continued to ascend, Colt banked a steep turn to the south, the expanse between us and the floor of the valley increasing dramatically, the distance between us and the ominous faces of the Tetons decreasing just as dramatically. The engine roared in a constant, reassuring clamor. Still, I checked my seat belt. Twice.

Long before it seemed to me that we had achieved anywhere near sufficient altitude to climb out of the valley, Colt turned the plane to the east and began a course that I'm sure he thought would take us out of the narrows around Jackson Hole and over the Gros Ventre into the expansive wilderness of western Wyoming.

If, I thought, we managed to clear the tops of these mountains.

Colt Arvin looked over to the passenger seat and saw the expression of concern on my face. He tapped the altimeter with his index finger, and over the din of the engine, he shouted, "Don't worry, we've got 'em cleared by six hundred feet. It just doesn't look like it."

"You're right, it doesn't," I called back just as the first ridge disappeared below the plane's nose.

Colter reached behind his seat and pulled out a pair of headphone units with attached microphones. He plugged them both into jacks in the dash and flicked a couple of switches. He handed one my way, and we each put one on.

"Can you hear me better, now?"

"Much better."

"I don't mind the noise, I guess I'm used to it." He rotated a small wheel that was nestled between the seats, and said, "I'm adjusting the trim. We're crossing out of Grand Teton National Park across the Gros Ventre Mountains into the Gros Ventre Wilderness Area. In just a little while, we'll cross the Continental Divide, and I'll drop down so we can be close to the location where the fire was. Peter and his group were camped out in the Washakie Wilderness, just above the Shoshone National Forest, when the fire started."

Through the cockpit glass I saw long ridges of mountains with enough trees to rebuild every frame house in southern California, and I saw endless sky. The scenery and terrain were magnificent, but from my vantage point Colt could have been describing the geography of Kamchatka and I wouldn't have been any the wiser.

The night before, as he recounted the story of the Wapiti Valley fire, Colter's manner had reminded me of Charley Chandler, the manager of the Buell Theatre in Denver. Like Charley, Colt was a storyteller at heart, and related his tale with confidence and flair in a voice that commanded attention without being intimidating.

As a preamble to the story, Miriam had broken the seal on an ancient bottle of port and moved us all back into the living room, where we sat on the sofas over-looking the moonlit Snake River. She poured us healthy shots of sweet purple-black wine.

Although it felt oddly anticlimactic, it was in this bucolic setting that Lauren and I were finally going to learn about Peter's fire.

I watched Colter as he first sat forward, then back against the cushion of the couch, where he stayed. He raised his feet and put his Vibram-soled boots on the edge of his mother's coffee table. He has told this story before, I thought, and he knows how he wants to tell it now.

"They collected in Cody on the Fourth of July, 1982," Colter began.

"There were seventeen of them in all. Five counselors, twelve kids, the oldest of the kids was sixteen. The counselors, of course, weren't much older. Three of them were only twenty-one, twenty-two, like Pete. One was the boss; he was more senior, thirty maybe. A couple of the kids were wilderness nuts, in it for the outdoor experience, but the others were doing time. Their parents had sent them to Wyoming to find themselves, to find discipline, to get off drugs, to get them away from their flaky friends. Graystone is marketed as self-esteem in a backpack, a wilderness summer camp for delinquents in training. Funny thing is, for a lot of them this cure actually worked.

"Well, after a day of training and orientation and checking equipment and putting the fear of God into the kids, seventeen of them went out of Cody on the fifth of July." Colt finished his port in one long swig and set the glass on the table with an audible thud.

"Ten days later, sixteen of them came back alive.

"Pete didn't ever talk much about what happened out there, but he did tell me the story once, and I can tell you he believed that no one should have died. Me, I think that was regret and remorse talking. Because if you ever really understand wildfire and flash fire, if you ever get a chance to see the ridge they were on, you'll know any of them were lucky to have gotten out of that fire alive."

Colter wet his lips.

"The trails in the Wapiti Valley start off pretty easy, they break off Highway 14–16–20—that's the road that goes from Yellowstone to Cody. In the Wapiti, especially at the trailheads near the highway, there are a lot of well-marked horse routes, and in the summer, plenty of day hikers and tourists. But six, seven miles in, the terrain gets vertical and tough and only the dedicated backpackers keep going. Well, this Graystone group was motivated—at least the counselors were—and after two and a half days of pushing these kids, the bunch of them were almost twenty-five miles in, all the way to the foothills of the Absaroka Mountains. That's where they had planned all along to set up their base.

"Nineteen eighty-two was Pete's first summer as a full counselor with Graystone. He had been a junior counselor two summers before, knew the ropes, and he sure as hell knew the Washakie. Dad had taken us there a dozen times when we were kids."

"More like two dozen," muttered Miriam.

I couldn't tell whether the memories of the Washakie Wilderness were pleasant ones for her or not. But it did seem to me that she was a little too enthusiastic about correcting her son.

Colter chose not to argue the point with his mother.

"This was his second tour of the summer. Ten days in, a week off, ten days in—something like that. Four tours in all before school started. Pete made okay money, and he got to do what he loved to do, which was hike, hang out in the backcountry, and climb some rocks.

" 'Eighty-two wasn't a bad fire year, like 'eighty-eight was in Yellowstone, or 'ninety-four was in the Pacific Northwest or down in Colorado. But every year, good and bad, there's lightning, and every year there are fires. The Graystone counselors received training in reading fires, knowing how to avoid them, how to stay out of their path. But wildfires are like the lightning strikes that cause most of them—you never really expect to get hit by one, that's something that happens to someone else. Hell, in all my time in the wilderness in Wyoming, I don't think I've ever been within ten miles of a fire that I wasn't dropping water on."

Miriam broke into the story again. "Colter flies slurry bombers. He flew fire retardant over the Yellowstone fires for three weeks in 'eighty-eight."

He smiled at her. "It was only two weeks. And I don't do it anymore, Mom. I've promised Karly I'm done dropping water. You know that."

His mother looked injured by her son's correction. "We'll see. If the Tetons or the Snakes are on fire again, Colter, then we'll see about Karly's objections to your flying slurry." Miriam turned away and looked out the windows at the aforementioned Snake Mountains, a maneuver apparently intended to indicate to her son that any argument he was considering should be reconsidered.

Colt returned to his story. "Anyway, the group split up, according to plan. Two of the counselors, including the boss, took six kids to some nearby rock faces for rappelling. Pete and the other two counselors took the other six kids for a survival experience.

"Little did they know," Colt said. "Little did they know.

"The fire started midday. Heat lightning, I guess— Pete never remembered that there was any rain early that afternoon. The forest was as dry as old leaves, humidity was down to twenty percent or less, had been most of the summer. The fuel supply in the Washakie is spotty. There are stands of trees, mostly evergreen, some scrub oak, and some hillsides covered with brush, but there are also rock ridges that have almost no fuel on them.

"The group was strung out in single file at the foot of a ridge, cutting across the base to get to a series of switchbacks that mount a saddle at the far end, maybe three quarters of a mile away. Pete said the lightning that started the fire cracked like a face slap a quarter mile behind them."

—◈—

From the air, the setting was breathtaking.

After a gentle descent had brought the little Cessna to within a few hundred feet of the ridge tops, Colter pointed straight out the windshield of the cockpit and said, "There, at twelve o'clock, maybe a mile out, that's the ridge. Before the fire, that ridge had some thick stands of lodgepole pine and other trees, mostly fir, on it and a lot of brush, especially near the top. If you look out on your right, you'll see the saddle that Pete's group was climbing. And you can still make out how the first couple of switchbacks that lead to the top of the saddle come back first across the ridge face. At that time, when the fire started, the first two or three of the switchbacks were in the woods."

Now the ridge had no woods. Stumps and saplings, grasses and brush, all the indications of a recent wild-fire. But no woods, not so soon after a clean burn.

The plane cleared the top of the ridge, the backside of which was barren and rocky. "See, there's almost no growth on this side. The safe places during the fire would have been on the saddle, which is pretty barren, or on this side of the ridge. But remember, the group was in the gully, down below, when it started. They had a choice to make."

The geography Colter was describing wasn't at all perplexing, even to my untrained eye. The saddle was a wide, bald concave cutout in the side of a mountain that eventually reached up to a narrow causeway well above the ridge top. The mountain appeared similar to ones I had hiked in the Routt National Forest in Colorado, and I surmised that this one, like those, had been formed by glaciers. Almost no vegetation grew on the saddle's stony face. The trail up the steep saddle was, by necessity, a long series of switchbacks; from the air the route appeared like one end of a shoelace that had been threaded to the top, never crossing over itself.

Colter banked the plane on a steep turn a full 270 degrees, and we quickly approached, again, the site of

Peter's fire, this time tacking toward the saddle face directly, with the ridge on our left.

The geography so clear in front of me, I easily recalled the rest of Colt's story from the night before.

Colter explained that the group couldn't go back out the gully, since that's where the fire had started and there was still fuel there. That route was blocked. The hillside that was opposite the ridge, on the other side of the gully, was covered with thick trees and dry fuel; it was the last place the group would choose to go during a wildfire. For the first ten minutes or so, Peter had told his brother, they saw only smoke, no flames, and the smoke seemed to be rising at a constant rate, so whatever was burning seemed confined; the fire wasn't accelerating. Pete and one of the other two counselors debated alternative routes as they watched the wisp of smoke become a narrow plume, at first no bigger than the exhaust of a big campfire, then suddenly grow and engulf a few trees. All this was occurring only five or six hundred yards behind them.

"Pete thought it was a simple choice. Climb the saddle, get away from the trees and brush and fuel and let the fire do whatever it was going to do. The other counselors both agreed with him that the saddle was probably the safest place to be while they watched to see which way the fire was going to burn. Hell, they all probably wondered if it was going to burn at all. Most wildfires never really take off, you know—they just burn themselves out.

"What the counselors disagreed about was how to get to the saddle. Remember, the first few switchbacks on the trail up the saddle came back into the woods on the ridge face. Pete wanted to avoid the ridge face altogether because of the trees that were there, and instead he wanted everyone to make the tougher climb straight up the saddle, something they would have to accomplish without benefit of a trail. That meant scrambling a long way up a steep cliff—more than forty-five degrees in places—over loose rock, with sixty pounds on their backs. The other counselor argued that the fire was far enough away and small enough that making a climb like that wasn't necessary, that instead they could use the switchbacks on the ridge face, because they would only be in the woods for twenty minutes, tops, and they were sure there was no way the fire was going to cover that much ground that fast.

"One of the other counselors was senior to Pete and the two of them apparently wasted some valuable minutes arguing about which way the group should go. That's when the wind came up. Pete said the wind started suddenly, from the northwest, in advance of a weather front of some kind. But even before he could check the horizon for clouds, the fire seemed to pick up steam and sent huge gray-and-white towers of smoke into the sky."

Colter looked at his mother until she averted her eyes. He continued.

"I need to give you a little lesson here. Momma knows all this. Flash fires—we call them blowups— are ferocious. If you've ever been close to one, it's the last thing in the world you ever want to be close to again. You would rather meet a mother grizzly protecting her cubs on a dead-end trail.

"The heat is awful, unbelievably hot, even from hundreds of feet away. You feel like you're suddenly in the Sahara, but the temperature doesn't make you crazy, your mind expects the heat, and as long as it's in the distance you're not surprised by it. But you don't expect the noise and the darkness, and together they are so much of what make up the terror.

"Blowups roar like a thousand lions, and they crackle and explode like the Fourth of July; it's so loud you can't hear yourself think. Imagine being inside the engine of a 747. You can't talk to the person right next to you. And the smoke is so thick that the light of the sun is gone. Twelve noon and you're fighting a fire in the dark. The sun, it seems, is the *only* thing that's extinguished. When that blanket of smoke thick with sparkling cinders covers you, it's like a total eclipse full of soot and ash and fire.

"And the blowup consumes what you want to breathe. The air gets thin and hot; the oxygen you want is all being stolen by the flames. What air is left is cooked and full of toxic gases.

"I know more about weather than Pete did, because of the fact that I'm a pilot. I'm not sure that the wind he felt was the beginning of a front, I think it might've been what we call a microburst, a powerful vertical wind that spreads out when it hits the ground. Pilots hate them 'cause they seem to come out of nowhere and they suck you straight down. And when you're flying an airplane, that's almost always a direction that you don't want to go.

"When the wind erupted that day, the little lightning fire became a blowup in seconds, and panic set in. The group stopped arguing and split up. Four kids went with Peter, directly up the saddle, up those loose rocks to the trail, and safety. Two of the other kids followed the two counselors who insisted on going up the switchback trail, onto the ridge, into the woods."

—◦◦◦—

Lauren hugged her knees to her chest, absorbed in Colter's story.

"The fire exploded. Unless you've seen it happen, it's hard to believe how fast a wildfire can go from a confined burn to a conflagration. I've only seen it from the air, but let me tell you, it's something. It probably climbed that hill, a thousand feet in all, in minutes, flames one hundred and fifty to two hundred feet high. Plenty of fuel, plenty of oxygen, and the wind blowing in just the wrong direction.

"Pete and the kids with him were approaching the first crossing of the switchback trail on the saddle, the one that would lead them right back onto the ridge, when the blowup swept into the woods below the ridgeline. The other group had already disappeared into the trees. Pete couldn't see them from where he was standing on the saddle and guessed that they couldn't see the fire spreading toward them. But the smoke was already starting to blot out the sun, and the roar, I'm sure, was deafening where they were. In a few seconds they had a preview of hell."

I asked, "How hot was it, Colter?"

"In the middle? Maybe fifteen hundred, two thousand degrees. But you're dead, your lungs are cooked, or you're poisoned by the fumes long before you ever feel that kind of heat.

"Pete told the kids who were with him to stay put on the saddle, no matter what, dropped his pack, and began running up the switchback toward the forest. But by the time he got to the edge of the ridge he was forced to stop. The whole side of the ridge was aflame.

"Fires defy gravity. Almost everything about being close to a blowup is counterintuitive. Fire climbs a hill faster than it descends one. If you don't know that, you can get trapped real easily. This one climbed the side of that ridge, Pete said, like it had been launched. The damn thing just out and out ran. Bottom to top in minutes. The winds carried it to the fuel and it consumed the trees and brush and oxygen and plowed up that ridge side. He was terrified for his friends and the kids, sure that the rest of his group was trapped someplace between the fire and the ridgeline.

"Pete just watched, that's all he could do. For ten minutes he just watched, going crazy, waiting, praying, for his friends to clear the woods, to somehow appear on the switchback trail. Twice he had to back farther down the trail because of the heat and the smoke. Then he realized that the only safe place for the group would have been the ridge top, and he began climbing to the top of the ridge on the steepest part of the saddle. It was a crazy climb for him to make. He wasn't wearing rock shoes and he didn't have any gear. He never should have done it."

From the air, I could see clearly what the choices had been that day. I had to imagine what the woods looked like before the fire, of course, because the sticks and fallen trunks that dotted that hillside were only the skeleton of the forest that had once dotted the side of the ridge. It was as though I were trying to picture what a person once looked like by examining a jumble of their scorched bones.

The saddle face that Peter and the two kids had chosen to climb was daunting. I wouldn't have wanted to scale it even without a heavy pack. I imagined that with sixty pounds on my back it would have been an arduous and treacherous ascent.

The switchbacks were designed, of course, to take the sting out of the angle of the climb at the cost of greatly increasing the length of the hike. Still, the relatively gentle incline of the traverse was much more inviting than Peter's route would have been. Given what I could see from high up in the Cessna, and what I knew about the fire from Colter's story, I couldn't say for sure I would have been prudent enough to take Peter's advice that July day, either.

Colter froze the Cessna in a steep "turn around a point," holding us in place in a constant bank near the ridge and saddle. My wing was down and I had no trouble seeing the thin line made by the trail of the switchback as it streaked off the saddle into the residue and rebirth of the forest on the adjoining ridge. Peter would have had a clear view of the rapidly spreading fire from his position on the saddle.

"Right there—that's where Pete climbed to the top of the ridge," Colter said, pointing across my body. Gravity was pulling me hard against the door of the plane.

Following his direction, I spied the narrow joint where the ridgeline intersected the saddle. The steep incline from the trail of the switchback to the top of the ridge looked almost vertical.

This, I thought, *was Peter's first free-solo.*

Colter leveled the plane off and asked, "Seen enough?"

"I think so," I said. I felt us climb.

"How steep was the cliff?" The question was Lauren's.

"Too steep," Colter said. "Too steep. But he made it. It took Pete fifteen minutes, maybe twenty, to get to the ridgeline. By the time he got there, the blowup had mostly flamed out. In less than an hour it had consumed almost all its fuel. The other side of the ridge is barren, so there was nothing left to burn when the fire got to the top. Plenty of trees were still flaming on the ridge face below, but the smoke was clearing and the mountainside was becoming visible through the ash. Where there had once been a small forest of pine and fir and scrub oak was now just a jumble of smoldering sticks and cinders and black-and-gray ash.

"The roar had quieted and sunlight was beginning to filter back through the haze. Pete was screaming for his friends, scouring the burned ridge for signs of them. But it turned out he was looking in the wrong direction. Two of them—one of the other counselors and one of the kids—came up behind him, from the barren side of the ridge.

"They were in shock, black with soot, they had inhaled a lot of smoke. But they weren't burned. Pete started first aid for their shock while he pumped them for information on what had happened. They didn't know where the other two were. They had gotten separated on the trail, the smoke was so thick. The roar was so loud. These two had ditched their packs and run for their lives up the steep slope to the ridgeline, the fire closing on them the whole way up the hill.

"Pete left them and hiked the ridgeline, fearing the worst. Hope, he knew, lay on the barren side of the ridge, the only safe place during the fire. On the firestorm side, all that he expected to find were charred corpses. But, of course, the barren side of the ridge was easy to search. And his friends weren't there."

As Lauren and I sat entranced, listening to Colter's story, I didn't notice his mother leaving the room. She returned with a plate of dried apricots.

Colter grabbed a handful. I took two. Lauren passed the plate on without even glancing at it.

"Pete found the boy's body curled up like a baby's, maybe a hundred feet from the ridge. The kid had come that close"—Colter held his index finger and thumb an inch apart—"that close to making it to the ridgeline. But he didn't. In the smoke he had gotten disoriented, had climbed to the ridge at an angle and couldn't stay ahead of the flames. He was cooked beyond recognition.

"Pete left the body where it was and kept searching for the other counselor, the senior one. He had no luck at first. He had to dodge hot spots on the ridge, and he says he checked every small scorched pile of ash he came upon for evidence that maybe, just maybe, it had once been a human body.

"But just like before, with the first two, he didn't find the other counselors—the other counselor found him, walked up right behind him, and just stood there, saying, 'I'm sorry, I'm sorry.' Sooty and shocky, the same as the other two."

He picked up his empty port glass and lifted it to his lips as though it were still full, tilting it back. It seemed that Colter was done with his story. Just like that.

Lauren said, "It seems like a miracle that only one person died on that ridge."

Miriam responded to Lauren in the same reproachful tone that she'd employed earlier with Colter. "No, dear, two died on that ridge. The boy who burned. And my boy, Peter. He died on that ridge as surely as that other boy did. That boy's mother had the blessing of being able to bury her son right away. I had to wait a few years to bury mine."

She stood and picked up the dish of dried fruit. "Now Peter's died twice. What's the difference?"

------ ❦ ------

Miriam Arvin disappeared through the door to the kitchen. She must have taken the back stairs up to her bedroom, because she never rejoined us in the main room of the house.

Colter, who I thought had wearied of telling the story of Peter's fire, continued on for a while longer. He seemed to need to cast his brother not just as a sage, but as a hero. "It was a sheer act of will—his will was as big as the sky" is how he described Peter's efforts in getting the group off the mountain and reunited with the main party. Since the fire had consumed four backpacks and all that was in them, the group had about half the supplies and gear that they needed. And the three of them who had been inside the fire all had damaged lungs.

"My brother was transformed by what happened. Pete, to my knowledge, never again went back into the wilderness with another human being. He never again took a job where he worked for anyone. And he never again allowed himself to be responsible for someone else's well-being.

"Although he went back to school in Las Vegas that fall, he dropped out after a few weeks and transferred to Montana for second semester. Over Christmas of that year he told me the family business was mine if I wanted it, that he wasn't ever planning on settling in the Jackson Valley."

"And you're certain it was because of the fire?"

"Absolutely."

"What about Adrienne and Jonas? Didn't Peter choose to be responsible for them?" Lauren asked the same question that was echoing in my head.

It was apparent that Colter had previously considered the paradox presented by the presence of Adrienne and

Jonas. "Adrienne let Pete be. And Pete let Adrienne be. She leaned on him some, but she never relied on him. That was an important difference for Pete, believe me. And by marrying her, he knew he would never have to address the question of returning to Jackson Hole. Adrienne wouldn't have moved here. She was, ironically, Pete's safety valve."

"And Jonas?"

"Jonas? You got me there. A failure of birth control, maybe. Or some pact with Adrienne that I'll never understand. I just don't know—you could have knocked me over with a feather when I heard I was going to be an uncle."

"It changed him. Having Jonas," I said. I felt the futility of arguing, but I said it anyway.

Colter stared at me for a moment, then lifted his fists and rubbed his eyes with the backs of his hands. The act made him look twenty years younger. "I doubt that, Alan. I imagine what it did—I hope what it did—was resurrect him. Maybe that's what he really wanted, what he was looking for when he agreed to have a baby. Maybe he was finally willing to risk being vulnerable again, but only with someone who wasn't likely to defy his judgment, like those fools did on that damn mountain that day."

It was, I thought, a better explanation than any I had been able to construct.

Lauren was curled up on the corner of the sofa and had begun to doze off. Colter, too, seemed to be acting as though the evening had run its course. I wondered aloud if he minded answering just a couple more questions.

"Shoot," he said, but didn't seem to mean it.

I asked him if he knew anything about a coffin that Peter had built, one with an ornately carved lid.

Colt smiled, almost chuckled. "Sure, I remember it. That was the culmination of Pete's ' borrowed time' phase. Actually, he used to say, 'My death has merely been postponed.' He didn't like to be called a survivor of the fire, felt instead that death was right around the corner lurking, lying in wait for him. He showed me the casket once when I visited him, talked to me about his funeral, how, if he didn't die in another fire, he should be cremated, but not in a crematorium. He thought he should be burned on a pyre—you know, like the Buddhists."

"Or like the boy on the mountain?"

"Yes, like the boy on the mountain."

"You said it was a phase?"

"Yeah, it passed. He was trying so hard for a while to make sense of the fire, of the kid dying, of his friends being assholes. But life went on, a different life for Pete, but life went on."

"What do you mean, his friends being assholes?"

"I shouldn't say friends. Friend is more accurate. One of the other counselors on the ridge was a friend of his from school, from UNLV. Pete could never understand why the guy—"

"Grant Arnold?"

"Yeah, you know him?"

"No, not really. We actually met just once."

"Pete could never forgive Grant for taking the risk of going into the woods with those kids when that fire was so close. He thought about it constantly for a while."

"Do you know any of the others who were there that day?"

Colter sighed loudly and shook his head. "God, how Pete's life changed with that fire. Mom's too." He gazed over at Lauren. "I think it's time for you to wake up your wife, and it's time for me to get home to mine."

Packing up to leave Jackson Hole on Sunday, Lauren and I agreed that Colter's story left plenty of unanswered questions about Peter, but we also agreed that what we had learned would provide a good head start for Adrienne in her belated search for her husband's essence.

Lauren was already making plans for a return visit to Jackson, "a girl's trip this time, just me and Adrienne. Maybe in the fall," so that Adrienne could hear Colter's story for herself, and so that Adrienne and her mother-in-law could have an opportunity to confront whatever parts of Peter they were so reluctant to bury.

In the meantime, we agreed to invite Adrienne over for dinner the coming weekend to tell her what we had learned in Wyoming. I was especially moved by the irony of Peter's resurrection. He had apparently started his rebirth just in time to die again. I wondered—were Jonas to have had the time to completely catalyze his father's rejuvenation—what would have happened to Adrienne and Peter's marriage.

It was a question, I quickly decided, that I would leave to Adrienne.

* * *

Lauren seemed vexed that her vertigo had caused her to choose not to accompany Colter and me on the Saturday flight out to the site of Peter's fire in the Washakie Wilderness. On Sunday, as our turboprop bound for Denver climbed out of Jackson Hole, I tried to indicate to her out the plane's windows the general direction in which we had flown. But the wilderness in Wyoming seemed boundless, and it was impossible to figure out exactly where the whole drama had unfolded.

The banal reality, I knew, as I tried to discern which distant range was the Absaroka, and which faraway shadow was the Wapiti Valley, was that after the inferno flamed itself out, the only place that Peter's fire kept churning was in his own mind. And I wondered about Grant Arnold and the others who were on that ridge, and considered how the ashes of the fire had settled onto *their* lives.

But it was Peter I had been searching for in Jackson Hole and in the Washakie and on the slopes of the Absaroka, and I left Wyoming convinced that he had never totally extinguished all the hot spots.

It was what I had been sent to learn, and I felt good about knowing it.

VI

The
Devil's Alibi

Late on Monday afternoon, I was scheduled to testify in court as an expert witness on a domestic-abuse case involving one of my patients. I dreaded everything about testifying in court. I dreaded what the court's peculiar calendar did to my schedule; I dreaded sitting in the bleak hallway of the Justice Center waiting to be called to the stand; I dreaded watching the attorneys joust over my words; I dreaded being dismissed before I was finished saying what I thought needed to be said, simply because no one had thought to ask me the right question.

So I was thrilled when the case was continued and I had three hours to kill.

Bike ride, I thought. Something long and lonely and exhausting. I considered the possibilities: the Morgul Bismarck, Left Hand Canyon, Lyons . . .

But by the time I had rushed home to change clothes a steady, cold drizzle had blown down from the mountains and blanketed the Front Range in mist.

Reminding myself that there were many days in the not-so-distant past when a little spring shower would not have deterred me from a ride, I considered taking a nap, contemplated running some errands, and even thought about taking Emily for a walk in the rain. But there was something else I wanted to do, and this was probably going to be my only good opportunity in the near future to do it.

I phoned Lauren at work and left her a message that I was going up to Black Hawk to talk with Grant Arnold about the fire. Then I called Grubstakes to make sure Grant was in. Ms. New Jersey assured me he was, but that he was on the other line, and would I like to leave a message?

I declined. That Grant was there was all I wanted to know.

The drizzle had slickened the twisting roads of Coal Creek Canyon, and I drove up the mountain at a measured pace. Unlike the canyon road, though, the Peak to Peak Highway, which runs in the shadows of the Continental Divide, was steaming in the late-afternoon sun, the residue of the rain rising in silky clouds hanging only inches above the asphalt. The narrow little storm had apparently already slid downslope toward the plains.

The storm had never extended as far south as Black Hawk; the roads there were totally dry when I arrived at the offices of Grubstakes Development a few minutes before five. I feared that Grant might have packed it in for the day, but the receptionist was still at her desk when I entered.

"Hi, is Grant in?" I asked.

She looked at me as though she had never seen me before. I realized belatedly that the fact that I had showered and shaved that day and was wearing clean clothing might have interfered with her ability to recognize me from my last visit.

"I'm Alan Gregory, I was here last week."

"Oh yeah. Yeaaah. I remember. No, Grant's not here. Well, he is here, but he's down at the site. Had to meet somebody about something. A problem with a concrete pour. They were supposed to finish pouring the last deck today, but something got screwed up, something about the pumper truck. He might come back up here, he might not. I gotta lock up soon. You wanna wait outside?"

"I think I'll just go down to the casino and wait for him to finish up down the hill."

"That's fine, that's what I'd do," she said.

"What's Grant drive? So I'll know he's there."

"He's got a Jeep Cherokee. You know, it's kind of cute and kind of hunky." She smiled to herself, enjoying some private thought. "Just like Grant."

The big opening in the Cyclone fence that allowed truck access to the site of Silver Streak Casino had been closed, the lights in the construction trailer were dark, and the only vehicles on site were a cement truck parked inside the fence and Grant Arnold's green Grand Cherokee outside, behind the filthy trailer where Molly worked.

I parked my Land Cruiser near the entrance to the trailer and got out of the car. The air was moist from the storm that had passed nearby, and I grabbed a rain shell from the front seat as a precaution. After two steps, I turned back, unlocked the car, and searched the glove box for a flashlight.

The canyon that rises above Clear Creek runs north and south, and quickly darkens with shadows once the sun has disappeared behind the Continental Divide. The light was already dim when I arrived at the Silver Streak, and most of the traffic roaring down the highway was doing so with illuminated headlights.

I called out for Grant.

No reply.

I tried again. Still no reply.

Frustrated, I walked part of the perimeter of the Cyclone fence, looking for some sign that Grant was inside the site. I didn't see him and guessed that he was with the driver of the cement mixer, attending to whatever problem had occurred that day with the concrete pour.

Finally I heard scraping and clanging high up in the concrete shell. The sound was shrill and hollow, and I figured somebody had moved some rebar on the con crete deck.

"Grant," I yelled through cupped hands, but my voice was swallowed by a downshifting tractor-trailer on the adjacent highway.

In retrospect, I think that's when I should have gone home.

The purpose of the eight-foot-tall construction fence around the Silver Streak was, it seemed to me as I sought to breach it, not so much to deter access to the construction site as to inhibit theft of the many large, valuable things stored inside. Without too much effort I was able to find a slender gap between two sections of chain link that was wide enough to permit me to squeeze through.

With what was left of the day's light I wouldn't have needed a flashlight to casino-hop down the sidewalks in Black Hawk, but in a big, unlit area like this, where the ground was cluttered with construction equipment, supplies, and debris, I was glad for the little flashlight I had pulled from the glove box of my car.

I crossed from the yard to what appeared to be the main entrance to the casino structure, the whole time calling fruitlessly for Grant Arnold. To my surprise, as I entered the shell of the first floor of the Silver Streak, I saw that interior work had already begun. Shiny metal studwalls sprouted in various places inside, and electrical, plumbing, and ventilation rough-ins were being completed high up in the ceilings and in the studwalls. Massive window units had already been set in place on two of the exterior walls. Metal staircase shells dropped down from the first floor into what must have been the basement and climbed up in two different locations to the second floor.

Before I put my foot on the first tread of the staircase that would take me up, I seriously considered going back out the way I had just come in. A more prudent alternative to exploring an unfamiliar construction site in the dark—that is, sitting and waiting on the hood of Grant's green Grand Cherokee until he decided to come out of this place on his own—had its seductive merit. But because construction sites had fascinated me since I began producing testosterone, I continued with only mild trepidation up the long stairs that reached toward the second level.

The interior rough-ins of the second floor weren't as far advanced as those on the first. Stacks of band-wrapped metal studs had been lifted up onto this floor, but so far none had been air-hammered into place. Long piles of ducts and boxes of connectors were stacked neatly against one wall. The concrete deck was relatively uncluttered, as though it had been cleaned off in preparation for the assault of the carpenters, electricians, plumbers, and sheet-metal workers soon to come.

A slow study of the floor plan revealed an open atrium that dropped back down to the first floor and reached up to the third and fourth, an elevator core without any elevators, and at least a couple of other big holes in the concrete deck plenty large enough for a careless human being like myself to fall through. I shone my little flashlight into the depths of each of these caverns, finding nothing of interest.

The next level, the third, was accessible, it appeared, only by wooden ladder; the permanent staircases that would reach to the third floor had not yet been installed. I reconsidered the wisdom of what I was doing and again toyed with the idea of going back outside and just perching my butt on Grant's Jeep. I also seriously contemplated the likelihood that Grant was not in this structure at all but had instead left his car parked outside while he joined a girlfriend across the street for cocktails or dinner—which, given the cost of parking a car in Black Hawk, would make perfect sense. It would also make me a fool and a trespasser.

It was in the midst of these ruminations that I heard the dripping.

The pulse of the drips was slow, much slower than my own racing pulse. But the splatter sound was distinctive, especially during lulls in the drone of traffic from the highway. Logic said that there shouldn't be any water this high up in the structure. The storm that had misted the canyons farther north that day had apparently skirted Black Hawk. And the long copper tubes that someday soon would contain the water pressure in this building lay in neat, long rows not ten yards from my feet.

I began to walk gingerly toward the dripping.

In my mind, I heard a voice calling to me. The voice was Lisa's and was swollen with caution.

Peter didn't trust Grant.

The *splat splat* was coming from the opposite side of the atrium from where I stood. With careful steps I made my way around the spacious opening in the concrete deck, suddenly aware of the muted sound of my shoes as I stopped. The atrium was at least forty feet in diameter.

From a few yards away I saw a drop land on the gray cement. The splatters were dark. The splatters were red.

The splatters were blood.

I stepped back and swallowed my terror before I raised the flashlight and shone the beam straight up to locate the source of the dripping. The dead eyes of a man I had never seen before stared back at me.

I should say "eye," because this man had only one remaining orb. The other one had been blown away along with much of the right side of his blond head. The blood was dripping from the point of a goatee that graced his chin, then was shinnying down a ridge of concrete, and finally was falling in little red starbursts at my feet.

The horror above me was so complete that it felt unreal. I should have felt sickened and I should have felt terrified. I felt neither. Nor did I feel any ability to move.

Suddenly the whole skeleton of the building seemed to shake as an electrical motor started humming loudly to my right. My stupor ended. I half expected to see a forklift or mini-frontloader aimed at me. What the hell could be causing the noise?

Again my impulse was to call out for Grant, but instead I ducked behind a heavy wheeled cart that was plastered with the decals of the company doing the electrical rough-in on the Silver Streak.

A groaning elevator cage descended from the third level on the outside of the building shell. *Shit*, I thought, *of course this place has a construction lift. How else would they get supplies up here?* The elevator car was an enclosure of metal mesh that rose no higher than a man's waist, and I could see two distinct figures silhouetted against the last light in the northern end of the canyon, but I couldn't make out any details about them other than that one person was taller than the other. A flash burst from the middle of the smaller person's chest, and in the same instant I heard a whistling and a sharp crack behind my left ear. Apparently, one of the details I hadn't been able to make out in the dark was the fact that these two had guns. Since I hadn't heard a roar to go along with the shot, I quickly decided that the gun firing at me was silenced. I fell prone to the deck and hugged the concrete behind the metal cart, counting the ricochet of two more shots before the motor of the cage cranked up and it started to descend to the second level.

Terrified, I scurried toward the wooden ladder, wanting to be certain the two people from the elevator wouldn't try to return that way to ambush me from behind. But the second I dropped my left foot toward the top rung so that I could check the progress of the elevator, a slug slammed into my shoe. I screamed and pulled my leg back up. I also reconsidered the wisdom of my strategy, which so far seemed to consist of making an unarmed pursuit of two people with semiautomatic weapons and a proclivity for firing them at me.

The elevator motor creaked for ten or fifteen more seconds before it stopped. I strained to hear voices, but couldn't. The elevator cage, I guessed, had reached its destination on the ground floor. The shooters, I guessed, figured me for wounded.

They figured right.

With my little finger, I probed the hole in the bottom of my shoe. My finger slid into a hollow formed by the slug, which had entered on the left side of the rubber sole and exited the leather at the front of the shoe, apparently carrying with it a small piece of my baby toe. My finger came back from the groove red and wet. I was bleeding plenty.

So far, there wasn't a whole lot of pain, although I didn't anticipate being able to make that same assessment five minutes later.

I crawled on my hands and knees to the front of the casino and watched the two people from the elevator standing just inside the chain-link gate. One was gesturing toward a spot beyond the fence, the other's head was shaking back and forth. The wind from the canyon carried their voices away from me.

Finally, apparently in exasperation, the one who had been shaking his head—I had decided that it was Grant—wound his right arm up like Bob Gibson on the mound and launched something from his pocket on a long arc across the highway toward Clear Creek.

Instantly, a fight started between the two people below me, and I realized that they were, for the moment, paying no attention to me. I ran back to the top of the ladder and began to descend. I absolutely did not want to be trapped in this building should either of them decide to return with a weapon.

Blood had soaked my sock and filled my shoe, and each step I took was syncopated by a gruesome squishing sound. The onset of significant pain in my toe made walking graceless. I was hunched over, limping badly.

I hadn't actually laid eyes on the two people by the gate since I had left the third floor to go down the stairs. At first I thought I could hear them; then I was certain that I couldn't. On two distinct occasions, I heard some clanging sounds, metal on metal.

When I finally got down to the first floor, not at all eager to risk another confrontation with two people who had already killed someone else, I climbed out a window opening rather than exiting the building through one of the doorways.

I crossed the yard to the side, running perpendicular to the highway, to the same opening in the fence that I had originally used to enter the construction site. A door slammed loudly across the compound. I paused. A vehicle door? Grant's Jeep? I couldn't tell. I waited for the sound of a second door.

Nothing.

Close by, an engine started. The driver revved the engine and it roared. This wasn't the purr of a luxury Jeep motor or my Land Cruiser.

My short-term destination was Molly's office and a telephone. Staying outside the fence and lurking low, I circled back toward the construction trailer.

The headlights came on in the cement mixer. The light frightened me but the truck was parked facing the road. The engine revved again and was soon followed by the crunch of gears. I was crouched low behind a pile of boulders, and since the driver of the cement mixer was invisible to me, I figured that I was invisible to someone sitting in the driver's seat of the truck. But I could tell that if I risked a climb up the wooden stairs to the door of Molly's trailer, I would be terribly visible and vulnerable for whatever time it took me to crash down her door.

The big cylinder on the back of the truck began to

rotate, slowly at first, then faster and faster. In thirty seconds or so, it stopped. Back-up lights flashed on, a droning *beep beep beep* filled the canyon, then ceased.

The engine revved again, and once more the awful sound of the grating of gear teeth pierced the night. The driver was unfamiliar with the cement mixer, was trying to figure out the controls, and was making a racket.

I figured it was as good a time as any to try for the trailer. I made my move.

My first leap carried me up three of the four steps and left me with my weight on my right foot. Immediately I pushed off hard and made it all the way to the door with my next vault. I landed with a squishy thud on the side of my left foot and immediately crumpled in a ball from the inspiring pain. Tears in my eyes, my back to the truck, I could only hope that the driver had been too distracted by the confusing controls of the cement mixer to notice my leap to the stairs.

Within a second, I had my answer. I heard, and even felt, the sharp thud of a bullet piercing the aluminum skin of the trailer and had no difficulty at all imagining what that slug would have managed to do to my skin. I leaned all my weight into the door, praying that it was flimsy enough to give from the pressure. It wasn't.

I fell prone to the wood deck just as another shot impacted the trailer exactly where my chest had been one second before. With my left arm, desperate, I reached up and turned the doorknob.

The door swung open.

My relief at Molly's failure to lock up that night

could not have been more total. I scurried through the door, kicked it shut behind me, and crawled on all fours to get behind her desk. Slugs were piercing the shell of the trailer with terrifying frequency and the desk was the only substantial cover the office had to offer. One or two slugs penetrated the Pepsi machine and foaming cola rained through the air.

I pulled the rolling steno chair out of the way and crept between the desk and a credenza that sat behind it. As I did, my right hand slid into what my mind first identified as a pile of relatively fresh dogshit, but which I soon correctly surmised was a pretty good size glob of Molly's gray matter.

I screamed.

Molly had been shot in the face. She had been sitting at her desk, facing the door. Someone had walked into the trailer with his gun drawn, pointed the barrel at Molly's stupefied face, and, with a single squeeze of the trigger, executed her. Molly had fallen to her left, dead, I guessed, before she hit the floor. Much of her brain was splattered on the wall behind her desk, although a big chunk was oozing between my fingers.

The room, of course, smelled like blood and feces and urine, and after ten seconds of my violent retching, it also reeked of vomit. I shook my hand to get Molly's brain tissue from between my fingers and wiped the remaining muck on my jeans. With my left hand, the dry one, I reached up and pulled the phone down to the floor, lifted the receiver to my ear, and heard nothing, which was exactly what I expected.

Molly's killer was no fool. He had cut the phone line.

It took me a moment to realize that the bullets from

outside had stopped piercing the trailer. I listened as
the engine of the cement mixer roared anew. Feeling
that destiny had either spared me, or already chosen
for me to die, I stood and walked at a measured pace
to a small window at the end of the trailer just in time
to watch the cement mixer drive through the gate and
edge Grant's Grand Cherokee out of its path. When
the truck reached the road, it turned left and headed
down Highway 119 in the direction of Interstate 70.

I watched the truck get a green at the traffic light in
front of Bullwhackers Casino, where it eased into the
flow of traffic, its taillights disappearing south into
the night.

The inside of the trailer was dark; the only light fil-
tering through the filmy windows came from the
moon. My eyes wanted to sweep the room and lock
onto Molly's corpse and make a close-up examination
of the damage that the slug had done to her cranium. I
inhaled deeply and swallowed twice trying to restrain
the urge, and sat down close to the window on an old
metal folding chair next to the fax machine.

My head was spinning.

I wanted to talk to Lauren. I wanted to talk to Sam.
And I was still fighting an impulse to look over at
Molly, who was sprawled, fortunately, on the oppo-
site side of the desk.

The fax machine.

The fax machine had its own phone line.

Absently, I lifted the receiver and called home, but
our line was busy.

I punched in Sam Purdy's number in Boulder.
Madeleine answered Sam's line and told me Sam

wasn't in, so I filled her in on the carnage all around me in Black Hawk and told her about Molly and her brains between my fingers and the *drip-drip-drip* on the third floor of the casino from the guy with only one eye and that I had been shot at over and over and over. Despite the fact that I was blithering like a moron she asked me if I was okay and I said yes, honestly forgetting for that second about my toe, and she told me she would immediately relay my predicament, but that I should stay right where I was and call 911.

So I did. I dialed 911 and in a flat tone reported that there were two murder victims at the construction site of the Silver Streak Casino in Black Hawk.

The person who answered my call had lots of questions for me to answer. My identity seemed to be the number-one item on her wish list. I declined to supply it—politely, I thought—but her curiosity shook me from my stupor.

Covered in Molly's blood and brains, and my own blood and sweat, my fingerprints and DNA everywhere that they shouldn't be in this mess, I quickly mobilized enough sense to realize I was facing a terribly unpleasant inquisition by the local authorities if I didn't get the hell out of the trailer. Fast. My judgment obviously wasn't what it should have been, but I figured that even if justice ultimately prevailed, I was going to get seriously inconvenienced by the course it would take.

The other factor I was juggling in my head was the enigma of Grant Arnold. Had he been shooting at me?

Or was he being held hostage by whoever *had* been shooting at me?

I certainly wasn't going to get any insight into that quandary by submitting to a night-long interrogation by the Gilpin County sheriff.

Leaving a nice clear trail of my bloody footprints behind, I ran out the door of the trailer, hopped into the Land Cruiser, and took off south on 119. In less than a block, I was stopped at the Black Hawk traffic light, where I watched a police department vehicle, lights on, weaving downhill from town through the congested casino traffic. The police officer pulsed his siren twice, freezing the oncoming cars; then he turned left, screaming through the intersection in the direction of the nearby Silver Streak Casino.

A moment later, I was the second car through the same intersection. At the first available break in the oncoming traffic, I pulled over into the northbound lane and passed the car in front of me, an old Plymouth driven by a gray-haired woman apparently confused about the speed limit.

I was, it seemed, chasing after the cement truck.

—————※☙☙※—————

The chase was leisurely—not deliberately slow, like the California Highway Patrol and O.J., but not frenzied like Steve McQueen in *Bullitt*, either.

My wits were returning in small increments after the terror in the trailer, but already I had come to the conclusion that dying in a flaming car crash only minutes after I had barely escaped being shot to death by semiautomatic weapons would be an irony that no one who cared about me would be able to fully appreciate.

The odds of catching the truck weren't great. I had a chance, something maybe a little better than the customers enjoyed at the casinos down the road. Although the cement mixer was blessed with the advantage of a five-minute head start, it was also burdened with the disadvantage of being large enough to be spotted over the rest of the canyon traffic. I also busily consoled myself with the knowledge that the driver of the truck was inexperienced at handling a rig that large and complex. The lack of familiarity should slow him down measurably.

I was in need of the additional consolation because by then I was aware that in my cognitive stupor immediately after the shooting, I had failed to mention to either Madeleine or the 911 dispatcher that the getaway car had been a cement mixer.

Maybe I would catch it, and maybe I wouldn't. With luck, though, I could keep it in sight until the police put the pieces together. Highway 119 between Black Hawk and Interstate 70 offers few options for turnoffs, and unless the driver of the cement truck was familiar with where the few side roads went, odds were great that pulling off on the dirt lanes would lead to his getting hopelessly lost. So in the fifteen or so miles between Black Hawk and the freeway, I was going to have to get close enough to see whether the rig was planning on taking Highway 6 east into Denver or proceeding up to I-70, where the driver could choose to head either east or west.

Fate felt like it had been a fickle companion that day, but I was still alive, and considering the alternatives that I had witnessed over the past hour, alive was something to celebrate. If Peter had been riding shotgun, he would have said something to me about destiny and death that I'm sure I wouldn't have been able to comprehend.

The tide of my afternoon adrenaline rush was receding and I fought the undertow of malaise left behind. The searing pain in my foot was pounding my consciousness to a degree of distraction that was greatly out of proportion to the size of my toe or the size of the wound. My baby toe felt as though I had first stubbed it into a brick, then ripped off the nail with pliers, and finally pounded it repeatedly with a small sledgehammer.

But the agony was keeping me alert.

For months, Lauren had been urging me to get a car phone, mostly because she needed one occasionally when she was driving my car. My usual commute to work was brief, though, and I had never felt that I could rationalize either the expense or the pretense. Right then I would have paid a thousand dollars for a rapid installation and immediately called my wife and told her she had been right all along. Then I would have called the police and told them that, by the way, I had forgotten to mention that the murderer's getaway

car was a cement mixer that was heading south on
Highway 119.

In front of me triangles of red brake lights began
flaring on, one after another. When I pulled to a stop I
had just rounded a curve on the two-lane highway
and could see maybe two dozen cars stopped on my
side of the bend. Traffic in the other lane was apparently blocked totally, too; for those few seconds no
northbound traffic rounded the curve at all.

Two or three minutes later I had covered the hundred yards or so that took me around the bend in the
road and could finally identify the problem up ahead.
A rollover accident in the northbound lane had
blocked off traffic completely in that direction. A
gaper's crawl in our lane, coupled with vehicles from
the other lane trying to squeeze by the wreck on the
narrow road, had stalled southbound progress almost
to a standstill. No emergency vehicles had arrived on
the scene to direct traffic or help the injured.

With my peripheral vision, I saw the truck. Stopped
halfway between my Land Cruiser and the rollover
was a solitary cement mixer.

I had made up my five minutes, and it was going to
do me absolutely no good.

I considered pulling onto the shoulder of the road
and trying to sneak up on the cement truck. On this
narrow stretch of road the Peak to Peak Highway
squeezes between the waters of Clear Creek and the
steep cliffs of the canyon wall. The gravel shoulder of
the road is not reliably wide enough to handle a
vehicle the size and weight of my Land Cruiser, and
anyway, if the driver of the cement mixer looked in his

mirror, he would certainly see me approaching. And that driver, I reminded myself, was armed and dangerous and desperate and surrounded by innocent people.

So I waited, pulling forward twenty or thirty feet at a time, hoping that a sheriff's vehicle or State Patrol car would soon show up to help. My plan was to block the progress of the troopers until I could tell them about the murderer who was up ahead driving the cement truck.

But a few minutes later, by the time the truck inched past the rollover, I still hadn't spotted any emergency vehicles arriving.

I'm going to lose him now for sure.

Neither hesitating nor thinking, I pulled the lever that switched the Land Cruiser's differential into the "low" four-wheel drive option—which in the past had given me enough traction to climb trees—pulled off the highway, and turned straight down a steep, rocky incline toward the creek bed. A few feet from the waters of the creek, I yanked hard to my left and began to parallel the creek and the highway, two wheels in the water.

Stealing my eyes from the path in front of me, I watched in the distance as the cement mixer rounded the far curve and disappeared from view. My response was to race faster down the banks of Clear Creek, sending up huge fan sprays of water. I dodged boulders and fallen tree limbs and discarded debris, and in less than a minute had cleared the bottleneck on the highway caused by the wreck. Far behind me I could hear the sirens of approaching rescue vehicles echoing off the canyon walls, and for a moment I considered waiting for the authorities to arrive at the crash so I could explain my situation.

The problem was, explaining would take too long, and the cement truck would be on the interstate within minutes. *And* the cops at the scene probably wouldn't believe me right away. *And* they would already have their hands full coping with the rollover on the highway. Far too many potential complications.

I slowed the Land Cruiser and pulled it perpendicular to the creek bank and began to climb the incline back up to the highway. The bank in this stretch was so steep that if the car had been equipped with an incline gauge, I would have been too frightened at what it would tell me to even glance at it. But the big Land Cruiser mounted the slope without hesitation and cleared the rim back to the highway with a heavy clunk as its undercarriage scraped rock. In seconds, I had turned south onto the highway in pursuit of the cement truck, no more than a minute behind him.

I levered the differential out of its locked position, freeing the big car to fly down the road. Before long I was doing sixty, far too fast in this canyon, just trying to stay on the damn road.

My foot hurt like hell.

I assumed that the driver of the cement mixer was concerned about being followed and that he was eager to ditch the vehicle and get into something less obvious. If I were in those circumstances, I would drive to Interstate 70 as fast as I could and then speed east to Genesee or Evergreen or west to Idaho Springs, find someplace to stash the truck, and then steal or commandeer a car.

So my surprise was almost complete when I watched the cement truck veer left onto the access road to Highway 6, a heavily traveled, mostly two-lane road that twists and turns through the canyons above Clear Creek before arriving in Golden, at the foot of the Front Range west of Denver.

At many places on Highway 6 between 119 and the town of Golden the canyon is too narrow to accommodate both a highway and a creek, and in each of these locations tunnels carved through the rock walls of the canyon carry the roadway. This stretch was considered one of the most treacherous highways on the Front Range.

Because I was not at all eager to close on the cement mixer, I was keeping a pace that would freeze me about a quarter mile back. My plan was simply to keep the truck in sight and flush it into the roadblock that I prayed the authorities would have set up around the next curve. Or the one after that.

Surely the murder victims at the Silver Streak had been discovered by now. How long would it take to put the word out to block the highways leaving the gambling meccas of Gilpin County?

The cement mixer wasn't speeding but was handling the canyon curves nicely at about five to ten miles an hour above the posted speed. I couldn't make any sense of that strategy unless the driver figured that I had died in the hailstorm of bullets that had pierced the trailer. Otherwise the guy would have been concerned that I had seen the big truck pull out of the construction site of the Silver Streak, and that I had notified the police.

But the driver of the rig was taking his time getting down the canyon, apparently not at all concerned about either roadblocks or pursuit.

At a short tunnel about halfway to Golden, the driver made his first serious error. He entered the tunnel far too close to the right side, not adequately compensating for either the height of the rig or the curve of the tunnel walls.

Sparks flew as the tall mixing barrel scraped the rough stone walls. Immediately the rig swerved hard into the westbound lane to escape the protruding rock. I said a silent prayer that there was no oncoming traffic.

The driver again overcompensated and pulled the truck back into his own lane just as a pair of headlights cleared the truck's path. The barrel of the cement mixer crashed hard into the rocks this time, and bright sparks filled the night like stars.

I was entering the tunnel just as the cement mixer cleared the east end. My headlights illuminated the faces of the passengers of a station wagon packed full of gamblers. They looked as if they realized that they had just beaten the toughest odds they would face all night.

The truck slowed considerably before entering the next tunnel, and in order to keep my distance I had to brake hard. We cleared that tunnel without incident.

I kept wondering where the roadblocks were.

The next tunnel curved about thirty degrees to the

left over the course of a couple of hundred yards. Again, the cement mixer entered the tunnel cautiously, its tires straddling the yellow paint stripes that divided the lanes.

I slowed.

Suddenly the truck lurched to the right, slamming the rock walls at a sharp angle, sparks again shimmering in the dark. The blunt face of a big tour bus filled the oncoming lane, the bus's horn blaring. The cement mixer bounced off the right tunnel wall and ricocheted out to clip the back end of the bus, which immediately veered into the eastbound lane as it began to clear the west end of the tunnel.

The damn bus was pointed straight at me. Acting on pure reflex, I yanked the wheel hard to the left and pulled into the lane that the bus had just vacated.

A bleating horn filled the night air as another pair of headlights bore down on me from the tunnel.

Up ahead, the cement truck was swerving wildly and the headlights of another vehicle squeezed past it just as it crashed back into the tunnel wall. I yanked the Land Cruiser into the eastbound lane just as the driver of the cement truck pulled the cab away from the wall, finally lost control, and crashed head-on into the opposing tunnel wall.

The screech and crunch were deafening, and dust and smoke filled the tunnel.

I skidded to a stop just west of the tunnel entrance and flicked on my emergency flashers. The last set of headlights I had seen exit the tunnel belonged to another tour bus full of gamblers. The driver had stopped his rig just opposite my car.

When I got out of the car, the bus driver was already speaking on his cellular phone, reporting the wreck. I walked toward the bus. He opened the door and gestured for me to come on board. When he finished his call, I asked him if I could use the phone.

He handed it to me and told me he had just called 911. He grabbed a fire extinguisher and said he was going to go help.

I said, "You can't. The driver of the truck—it's just not as simple as it looks. There's been a murder, too. The guy in the truck has a gun." I wasn't looking at him as I spoke. Rather, my eyes were frozen on the tunnel entrance. I was waiting to see if someone would try to escape the tunnel on foot.

I phoned Sam, and got Madeleine again; I told her what had just happened. She listened carefully and said she would make all the necessary calls. I asked her to phone Lauren as well and tell her I was okay.

She said she would.

I thanked the driver and gave him back his phone, suggesting that he move his passengers farther up the canyon, just in case, and took the fire extinguisher from his hand. I hopped off the bus and walked back in the direction of my Land Cruiser.

I hoped no one was trying to enter the tunnel from the east portal. Any second, I feared, I would begin hearing the *thwtt, thwtt* of more silenced gunfire.

Just then, a thunderous shock wave and a huge roar blew out of the tunnel as the cab of the truck burst into flames. The concussion stunned me and threw me on my ass, which was probably the safest position I had been in all night.

---◆◆◆---

The fire that exploded in the tunnel engulfed only the engine and cab of the truck, and an engine company arriving from Golden extinguished the flames within ten minutes.

After water from the hoses of the pumper had cooled down the wreck, cops with drawn guns approached the vehicle to search the cab of the truck. It was empty.

The area immediately surrounding the east portal of the tunnel was soon the focus of a hornet's nest of attention. Two different helicopters crisscrossed the terrain around and above the creek, flitting from dark canyon to dark canyon, their brilliant lights illuminating every escape route that might have been available to the driver of the cement mixer. A dozen Jefferson County sheriff's deputies spread out and paced the creek bed—both sides, in both directions—searching the banks of Clear Creek with flashlights, looking for fresh tracks.

News crews in satellite trucks arrived from the Denver network affiliates. Paramedics and more law enforcement authorities arrived from Jefferson County. Cops came down the hill from Gilpin County and Black Hawk, too. And everyone with a badge, it seemed, wanted to talk with me.

To say that my personal situation was complicated

was an understatement. I had been on the scene of two murders in the town of Black Hawk in Gilpin County and had vacated the crime scene to chase the potential murderer into Jefferson County, where I had witnessed the tunnel crash.

The Gilpin County sheriff and the Black Hawk police would want to know what I had been doing at the Silver Streak Casino, what I had seen, and, mostly, why I had left. The Jefferson County sheriff, on the other hand, would be primarily concerned about my contention that the driver of the cement truck might be a multiple murderer who apparently had just escaped into their jurisdiction.

In order to postpone the inevitable interrogations until my reinforcements arrived, I begged for medical attention for my toe. Upon removing my shoe, the emergency medical techs immediately recognized that a small part of my toe was history and wanted to transport me down the hill to the hospital for treatment, but I protested and refused to go. Lauren was on her way from Boulder, and if my calculations were correct, she should have almost completed the forty-minute drive.

She was my wife, she was a lawyer, and she was a deputy DA, which meant she cared about me, she knew my rights, and she could speak cop-talk. No matter what kind of pressure the police mounted, I planned to try to procrastinate until she arrived. She would be my guide through the sticky ordeal ahead. I was not at all convinced that I hadn't broken a few minor laws in the past couple of hours and didn't want to incriminate myself inadvertently.

But I hadn't murdered anybody, and with any luck

at all, I figured, I would get to spend whatever remained of this night in bed with Lauren, and not triple-bunked with some scumbags in the Jefferson County Jail.

Lauren was led to the west side of the tunnel by a detective from Black Hawk. She hugged me the way parents hug children who have just darted out into the street and have managed not to be flattened by a car.

The Black Hawk cop and I developed a quick initial camaraderie, primarily because he shared my acute interest not only in the missing driver of the cement truck but also in the other person I had last seen in the yard of the Silver Streak Casino and Gaming Club up the hill.

To my surprise the cop told me that an exhaustive search of the building site in Black Hawk had yielded only two corpses: the guy on the fourth floor whose blood had been dripping into the atrium, and Molly in the construction trailer, whose brains were all over my jeans. All along I had been assuming the existence of a third victim, having voiced my prediction that the other person I had seen exit the elevator had been killed, too.

"When is the last time you saw the second guy?" The Black Hawk cop was young and had a goatee. His hair was short and his build was buff from serious gym time.

Lauren's hand rested on my knee. My bullet-damaged shoe was off and my foot was wrapped in gauze and elastic bandages. The pace of the throbbing indicated that my pulse was finally slowing. She and I were sitting with the Black Hawk detective about thirty feet inside the west portal of the tunnel, out of view of the local news crews, who were still confined to the east side.

The stench of burned plastic and fried rubber clung to everything inside the tunnel. Every noise seemed to echo once in the cavern, then die.

I thought about the question posed by the cop. "It was when I was still inside the building, on the third floor. They were down by the gate. I saw them start to fight after the second guy threw something across the road. That's when I made my move to get out of the building. I was feeling trapped up there; I was afraid they would come back for me. But when the fight between the two of them started, I made my move, and that's actually the last time I saw the second guy."

"Well, at least that explains the keys. We found a set of keys on the other side of the road."

"Keys to the Jeep?" I asked.

"Yeah."

"Grant's Jeep."

The cop didn't respond. I was sure that they had checked the registration of the demolished Grand Cherokee and knew exactly whom they were looking for.

Did Grant throw his own keys away? Did the other person throw Grant's keys away? Was Grant shooting at me?

What happened to the second person?

"You're sure that only one person was in the truck when it left the yard?"

"No, I'm not sure at all. I never saw the front of the truck clearly. There could have been two people in there, I guess. Especially if one was crouched down and didn't want to be seen. I just assumed—"

"Ah. You assumed," he said. Our rapport seemed to be evaporating.

Lauren was looking down the tunnel at the wrecked truck. I followed her gaze and recalled the noises I had heard as I was escaping the casino building.

First the fight, then the metal noises. Clanging, banging, scraping noises, the whole time that I was trying to stanch the bleeding on my foot.

"Has anybody checked the back of the truck?" I asked. "The cement-mixer part?"

The detective stared at me, then glanced down the length of the tunnel at the cement mixer. He stood, hesitated for a moment, then walked away and began to speak with a Jefferson County deputy and the Gilpin County sheriff, who were just outside the tunnel, waiting their turns with me.

A moment later, the three cops marched back into the tunnel together and proceeded past Lauren and me toward the cement mixer. Lauren helped me up. With her assistance, I hobbled down the eastbound lane after the three cops.

The Black Hawk cop hopped up on the raised platform at the back of the mixer, scrambled up to a high perch on the rig, and shone his flashlight into the wide neck of the top barrel, at least five feet above the narrow chute that was used to guide the mixed concrete out of the truck.

He peered in for fifteen or twenty seconds, squirming his body around, before he tossed his long black flashlight to one of his compatriots on the ground, hoisted himself up to the big opening, and began to crawl head-first into the neck of the chute, extending his arms as far into the big metal drum as he could reach.

When he edged, wriggling, back out of the truck, it looked as though the cement mixer was delivering him breech. He stood high above us on the platform of the truck.

The ends of his fingers were coated with gravel and blood.

The sheriff's deputy standing in front of Lauren squared his shoulders and raised his chin an inch. He lifted his Motorola radio to his lips, then apparently thought better of the idea. Instead he marched down the tunnel to relay the gruesome news.

Soon after the body was discovered in the mixer drum, I was transported down the hill by paramedics and a deputy and spent an hour in the ER at Lutheran Medical Center. Lauren, melting from fatigue, met us at the hospital. The deputy then drove me to the new Justice Center in Golden, where someone else had already delivered my car. I gave a statement for all the anxious law enforcement types and then, to my relief, was cleared to go home. I followed Lauren down Highway 72 to Boulder.

I had half expected to see Sam Purdy before the night was out, but he didn't show his face until the next morning.

My toe ached viciously, I hadn't slept well, and I was already awake and out of bed when he pulled his car down the lane to our house. Emily and I greeted him at the front door so he wouldn't knock and wake Lauren.

I was reminded of the day he arrived to tell me that Peter had died.

"It's purely preliminary, but the medical examiner thinks the guy was dead before the mixer was turned on. He had one bullet wound, high in what was left of his neck. The pathologist thought he had seen every inventive way that motor vehicles can possibly mangle human bodies, but he says that after the guy got tossed around on the blades inside the drum of that cement mixer, it was like trying to autopsy a body that had been in a Cuisinart. How well did you know him—the guy in the mixer?"

"I spoke with him twice, Sam, that's it. Once in person, once on the phone."

"So why were you going up there to see him?"

Although I was pretty sure that Sam had already read a faxed copy of the statement I had provided to the Jefferson and Gilpin County authorities the night before, I explained as succinctly as I could about the trip Lauren and I made to Wyoming, and about Peter's fire and Grant Arnold's poor judgment and Peter's apparent inability to forgive him for what had happened in the Washakie that day thirteen years ago.

"I wanted to hear from Grant what had actually happened on that ridge. To try and understand better why Peter was still so angry, so I could tell Adrienne."

"But you never actually saw him?"

"I never spoke with him yesterday. I assumed that he was one of the people I saw at the job site. His car was there. His secretary said he was there. I think he's the one who threw the keys away."

"Why? Why do you think he would do that?"

"Do you want a guess? It's all I've got. I'm guessing to slow the other one down. If the other guy had the gun and had killed these people, maybe Grant didn't want him to get away. Figured, I guess, that he was denying the guy a getaway car."

"You saying you think the guy who got pureed in the back of the truck was a hero?"

"A hero? Maybe. Maybe an act of contrition on his part. I think maybe this was undoing."

"Huh?"

"Psychologically speaking, acts that create internal anxiety—shame, remorse, whatever—are sometimes followed by acts intended to wipe the slate clean—you know, even the score. It's called doing-undoing."

"This guy was guilty about your friend Peter's fire? That was the doing. Last night's futile heroics were the undoing?"

"It's just a theory. Where were you last night, anyway? I expected you to show up and help slam a cell door in my face."

"You know I wouldn't have missed that for the world, but I've been busy following some leads. Been out of town a lot. The Kenny Holden thing."

"Promising?"

"Yeah, promising."

"Want to talk about it?"

Sam just smiled his reply.

"So, is this a coincidence? This slaughter in Gilpin County? Or do you think it's part of the 'gypsy-fucking-actors-from-hell' murders?"

"MO is a little different, don't you think? Where's

the signature? Nothing ties these new killings in with the others."

"Except Peter and Grant."

"Which is what? One of the guys who was killed yesterday knew Peter. But Peter didn't know Lonnie Aarons, did he? And he didn't know the kid who was slaughtered at the opera house, did he? And he didn't know the construction secretary or the cement-truck driver who got their heads blown away. Shit, you knew one of the people killed yesterday, too. So what?"

"Then what's the motive for the murders yesterday?"

"Not my problem, is it? There's big money involved in that casino they're building. I'm sure there'll be plenty of motive to go around once the politicians and accountants and lawyers and building inspectors all get brought in and interviewed. All I know so far is that these latest murders didn't look too damn theatrical. The hits all look professional to me. The most interesting puzzle to me is how the damn cement-mixer driver disappeared into thin air."

Sam seemed uncomfortable with my line of inquiry, and his answers were uncharacteristically lacking in reflection. I didn't know what to make of it.

"It's not like you to be so comfortable with coincidence."

"Fuck, Alan, my hands are so full there're already leads slipping through my fingers every few minutes. If the Gilpin County cops find something that will allow them to dump this new problem in my lap, so be it. In the meantime, I don't have any extra hours to spend turning over rocks up in Black Hawk looking for new worries. Anyway, I don't have any jurisdiction.

And I keep getting reminded of that fact by my sergeant." He stared at my bandages.

"How's the gunshot?"

"It's just my toe, it's okay. The nail is history. It hurts."

"Bet it's fucking ugly."

I smiled. "That, too."

"What are you going to tell your patients when they ask about your foot?"

"Half of them won't mention it. I'll tell the other half that I hurt my toe." The news media had reported that a bystander had been injured during the shootout in Black Hawk, but since I was a witness, they had been gracious enough not to print my name.

"And when they ask how? What, you going to tell them you got shot?"

"They won't ask."

He scoffed.

I was absolutely right about my patients; they didn't ask.

Diane Estevez, my partner, asked, of course. Her response was about what I had come to expect from her. After she "Oh my God"-ed me and comforted me and assured herself that I was in no danger of passing away from my injury, she wanted to garner as much gossip about what was going on as was possible.

She was a sweetheart.

The Boulder Public Library is only a block and a half from my office. With the aid of one of Lauren's canes, I hobbled over there in about fifteen minutes during my lunch hour. An incredibly solicitous person in the reference department helped me get set up on a microfiche reader and began to deliver the little plastic sheets that stored the archival records of old newspapers, specifically, the *Denver Post*, the *Rocky Mountain News*, the *Wyoming Tribune-Eagle* for July 1982.

Not surprisingly, I discovered that I knew more from speaking with Colter than the reporters had found out in the first few days after word of the fire had become public, which wasn't until almost a week after the boy had died in the flames.

From my research, I learned the identity of the victim, a young man with the name of Trey Crandall. And I learned that the reading public was left with the impression that Trey and his three companions were caught off guard by a flash fire. The newspapers didn't even hint at any misjudgment by the counselors. Yes, one young camper died, but the news accounts portrayed the event as though it were a miracle and a tribute to the counselors that anyone on that trail had survived.

The owner of Graystone acted as spokesman for the company. The counselors all declined to speak with the press. I guessed a lawyer or two had something to do with their decisions.

I frittered away the rest of my lunch break learning how to make paper copies of the miniature plastic articles I had read and hobbled back into my office just in time for my one-fifteen patient.

The words of the owner of Graystone kept reverberating in my head. He had called Peter's fire "an unavoidable natural tragedy."

Maybe, maybe not, is what I was beginning to think.

I placed a call to Cody information and got a number for Graystone. The phone was answered by a machine. I didn't leave a message.

———⁂———

Lauren walked over to my office after she finished her day's work at the nearby Justice Center and seemed to find some amusement in the fact that for once it was I, not she, who was relying on a walking stick for support. I begged her to make our stroll to find a place for dinner a short one, and in a few minutes we were settled at a tiny table in a Nepalese restaurant on Pearl Street.

We hadn't spoken since breakfast, when shortly after Sam's visit ended she had reprimanded me for my judgment the night before, not only about chasing the cement mixer down Highway 6, but also about even considering entering the construction site without an invitation or a hard hat.

I told her I was pretty sure a hard hat would not have been of much help.

Then I apologized. Given what had happened, who could argue with her criticism? I tried to explain that I didn't think I was being particularly reckless because I hadn't been anticipating any danger when I went up to Black Hawk looking for Grant Arnold. It had never crossed my mind that I might end up being the target of semiautomatic weapons fire.

The stress of the few weeks since Peter's murder was taking a physical toll on Lauren, I could tell. I'd noticed that for the last few days she had been absently rubbing a place on the outside of her arm, halfway between her wrist and elbow, and was occasionally allowing her fingertips to examine an area on the left side of her abdomen below her ribs, as though the spot were quite tender. Her gait, which had steadied over the past few months, had once again regressed to show the unbalancing effects of vertigo, one of her old MS symptoms.

I was responsible for much of her recent stress and I felt awful. The late nights that she had been suffering were my responsibility. I hoped that her increased fatigue and the paresthesias on her left side and the return of her old symptoms didn't signify the imminent arrival of an exacerbation, a novel symptom constellation caused by some new area of demyelinization in her brain.

"What does Elliot think about the new murders? Does he think it's coincidence, too?" I asked as we picked at a delicious appetizer Lauren had ordered. I was almost certain that what I was eating was made from legumes and other vegetables.

"It's funny, I don't know what Elliot thinks. But something is going on at work. You told me Sam implied this morning that he has a new lead about the Kenny Holden thing. Well, Elliot and Royal have become absolutely tight-lipped about this whole case, a major change from last week, before we left for

Jackson Hole. Peter's murder wasn't discussed in the case review yesterday morning, and Elliot was away from the office all day today for something. Elliot and I share a secretary, and she told me that Roy wanted all calls about Peter's murder directed his way while Elliot was gone."

"Something's cooking."

"Yes, something, but what?"

"The phone lines at the office haven't been buzzing with new activity after the shootings at the Silver Streak?"

"Don't think so, but it's possible I didn't notice. If those calls came in, Roy took them."

"You're not feeling well, are you?" My goal in abruptly changing topics had been to catch Lauren, usually reluctant to talk about her illness, off guard.

She shot a reflexive "back off" glance my way; then I watched her face soften; she was going to grant me some latitude. She said, "Just some paresthesias, so far," carefully examining my face.

"New ones or old ones?" Paresthesias—sensory anomalies—in previously unaffected locations might indicate new lesions in her central nervous system, and thus were much more significant than sensory flare-ups associated with inflammation of old lesions.

"Just old ones."

"The vertigo's back, too. I can feel it when we walk; you're using me for balance again."

"It's just the heat. It'll pass, it always does."

"Can you manage to take it easy for a few days? Get some extra rest?"

"Can you manage to avoid being shot at for a few days?"

I smiled. She smiled. For us it was a good conversation about multiple sclerosis, still the most difficult topic we ever tried to talk about.

I recounted my efforts at the library that afternoon checking on the old press accounts of Peter's fire and shared my suspicion that Peter and his friends may have been harboring a secret about what had really happened that day in the Washakie Wilderness.

"Something that Colter didn't tell us?"

"Maybe something that Peter never even told his brother. Never told anyone."

"Are you suggesting that Peter's death and Grant's death are linked in some way?"

"I don't know. I guess I'm raising, once again, the possibility that Peter's murder wasn't random. That somebody wanted him dead. From there it's not a big leap to conclude that someone wanted Grant dead, too. Maybe because of something we don't know about the fire."

"What? Revenge? For the kid's death?"

"As a motive, that would be at the top of my list. Especially if the fire didn't come down the way that Colter thinks it came down."

"Someone would have been showing tremendous patience. They waited an awfully long time to exact their pound of flesh. What is it, now, twelve years since the fire?"

"More like thirteen. But how does that saying go? 'Revenge is a meal best eaten cold.' Isn't that it?"

"You know anything about the kid, the one who died in the fire?"

I told her what little information the news articles had reported about the sixteen-year-old Trey Crandall. Reading between the lines, I was guessing that he was one of the kids who had been enrolled in the Graystone expedition not because of any love of the wilderness, but because his parents were hoping for an early redemption from their son's adolescence.

"Did the articles have the names of the other people who were there?"

"Last names, initials, and hometowns."

"I'll check it out tomorrow. Maybe something interesting will pop up on the computers."

"And I'll talk to Adrienne, see if she remembers anything else that Peter might have said about the fire. It's hard to believe they didn't talk about it."

She laughed. "As incompetent as I am with computers, I think I've got the easier job," she said.

By eight-thirty Lauren had fallen asleep in bed with a magazine in her lap. I slid out from under the covers, tugged on a sweatshirt and jeans, turned off the bedroom lights, and called quietly for Emily to join me upstairs. She ignored me until I said, "Walk."

After watching a dog I loved get hit by a car, I had become a fanatic about leashes. Late in the evening in Spanish Hills the traffic ranges from sparse to nonexistent, but still I buckled a long, retractable leash to the hook on Emily's collar and we took off on as much of a stroll through the country lanes of my neighborhood as my aching toe was going to permit. Although

Lauren and I seemed to be doing our best to cure Emily of all her good habits, the truth remained that she was a show dog and still recalled most of her training when she was around a human who knew what to say and do. She sat when I said "Sit!" and heeled when I said "Heel!" So I said "Heel!" occasionally, just to feel that wonderful sense of effectiveness. Then I would say "Okay," releasing her, and she would do what came most naturally, which seemed to involve either running around aimlessly sniffing the ground or staring straight up toward the sky tracking jetliners cruising at thirty thousand feet.

Occasionally she jumped up to nip at them.

I found her behavior to be a little bit demented but generally quite appealing.

While Emily squatted to pee, I checked to see if Adrienne's minivan was in her garage. It wasn't, so Emily and I started down the lane.

Within a couple of hundred yards of the house, my dog and I ran into a trio of late-night joggers and an elderly couple who were into power-walking. They remembered my dear old landlord and paused a few moments to reminisce about her.

We also ran into Lisa, pushing Jonas in a stroller.

Both Lisa and Jonas seemed thrilled to see Emily. I was thrilled to see Lisa. There were delicate things I needed to ask her and this seemed like a great time to do it.

So, disarmingly, I said, "You already knew about the coffin, didn't you, that night. I saw it in your eyes."

"Yes," she replied, fussing with the blanket that Emily seemed eager to remove from Jonas's lap.

"And the fire, too. I bet Peter talked with you about the fire, didn't he?"

She stood up and faced me, her lips only inches from mine. "The stupid fire had ceased to exist for Peter. Those flames were out. What on earth did you do to your foot?"

"I hurt my toe."

I stayed silent for a moment, hoping she would continue to talk about Peter and the fire. She didn't. "Then do you know why he kept the coffin all these years? And why did he keep it a secret?"

"Who says it was a secret? Just because you and Adrienne didn't know about something doesn't mean it was a secret."

I weighed these words for hostility and thought I detected a distinguishable mass. The discovery surprised me.

"It's important, Lisa. There are things going on about Peter's murder that might have to do with that damn fire. It could be really helpful if he spoke with you about it, told you something we don't know." She was so close I could taste her sweet breath and smell her bath soap.

But Lisa, for the very first time, suddenly felt like an adversary. The reactions she was displaying as I queried her about Peter seemed maternal, as though she were protecting someone with her defiance.

"I knew about it."

"You know that a boy died?"

"I knew what Peter wanted me to know. That was enough for me. It should be for you, too."

"Peter's old friend Grant Arnold was shot to death last night at the new casino in Black Hawk."

"I know, I heard. It's awful and I'm sorry." She shook her head a little. "But Peter didn't trust Grant."

"You've said that before; I still don't understand why."

She edged even closer to me, and for a moment I felt, incongruously, that I was about to be kissed. I could sense her heat. She said, " 'Why?' is not as simple a question as you might think. 'Why' is complicated. 'Why' is an onion."

I waited. The philosophy of inquiry was a sinkhole in which I was certain I would have no trouble getting trapped. I hoped that if I remained quiet, which was easy since I was absolutely befuddled, Lisa would take this conversation someplace else. My heart was pounding from her physical proximity and her overt challenge.

I said, "Grant was at the fire, too. He was caught in the forest when it blew up. He was almost killed."

"My understanding is that Grant waltzed into the path of a wildfire and got somebody else killed."

"Is that what Peter said?"

She hesitated. "It's what I understand."

"Two of the counselors who were on the mountain that day have now been murdered. That could be important, don't you think?"

With tears in her eyes she said, "The fire was out."

Emily started to clean the residue of whatever Jonas had enjoyed for dinner from his face. The baby cried from the dog's attention. Lisa stepped back from me and tended to him. As Lisa bent down, Emily licked her, too.

I told Emily to heel. She obeyed me.

I was one for two in getting cooperation that night. Pretty good in almost any league except this one.

―◦◦◦―

Lauren and I had only a few minutes together before work the next morning. I was going in early to see a patient who was trying to recover from a difficult divorce. Lauren had a breakfast meeting with a defense attorney who wanted to try to reach a plea bargain on a vehicular-homicide charge against his client.

Before falling asleep the previous night I had reached another conclusion about Peter's murder. This new insight seemed tangential, even to me, so I decided to run it by my wife, whose objectivity I usually considered more reliable than my own. She and I were standing in the kitchen drinking coffee and eating a plate of cut fruit.

I said, "You know, I think Peter and Lisa might have been having an affair."

Lauren pulled the coffee mug down from her lips and smiled mischievously. "Well, Peter might have been having an affair. But technically, had they indeed been screwing, Lisa would have only been having a fling."

"I'm serious, sweets."

"You are, aren't you?" She laughed a little.

"Why not? They were alone here together for a year. Lisa hung out at Peter's studio all the time. She's attractive. He was an intriguing guy."

"And so that means they were lovers?" Lauren's tone said, *Men*, even though she was wise enough not to verbalize her thoughts.

I recounted the conversation I'd had with Lisa the previous evening and my sense of how protective she was of Peter. "That has to mean something."

"You're not just trying to rationalize your once-removed little fantasy of boffing the nanny?"

I forced a smile. "Lauren, I'm serious. If they were having an affair, it would explain a lot."

"Such as?"

"Why they were so close, why she knew about the coffin, why she knows more about the fire than anybody else, why—"

"Do you actually know that? That she knows more about the fire than anybody else?"

"No, but she seems to. I'm sure she does; there's something else about the fire she doesn't want to talk about."

Lauren raised her eyebrows. Although she was certainly able to luxuriate in intuitive moods at times, generally, where evidence was concerned, Lauren was a prosecutor. "Seems to" didn't cut it with her.

"But there are other ways of explaining every one of

those things. Simple ways. Friendship, for example, comes readily to mind. It didn't have to be sex."

"No. I'm not saying just sex, I'm saying love. Lisa's reaction isn't that of a mere friend. There was something special between them, I'm sure of it."

"Maybe, but I've got to run. How are you going to handle this little suspicion of yours with Adrienne?"

It was my turn to equivocate. "I think maybe I'll jump off that bridge when I get to it. Maybe I should gather a little more data first."

Lauren pulled out of our lane a few minutes before I was ready to head to town. When I finally hobbled out to my car, I caught Adrienne just as she was backing her minivan from the garage.

I limped over. "Got a second?"

"Literally, yes," she said, peeking at her watch. "Morning Edition" was blaring from her radio. She didn't even bother to turn Bob Edwards down.

I needed her undivided attention, so I decided to employ the most effective of weapons, guilt. With Adrienne as a target, it was as reliable as firing a smart bomb.

"I got shot in the foot while I was trying to track down some things about Peter and the fire."

"You *what?*" She turned off the ignition.

She had, of course, heard about the multiple murders in Black Hawk and the body in the cement mixer. I explained my role in some detail.

"Oh, my God, I'm so sorry."

"I'll be okay. It was only my little toe."

Now that I had captured her attention, I had to

work vigorously to refocus it. She kept saying, "Oh my God," and asking questions about my well-being.

Finally I said, "I need to talk with you about the fire, Ren. The one Peter was in. The one in Wyoming. Now that Peter's friend was killed in Black Hawk, I think whatever happened during that fire may be related to all the murders."

Adrienne glanced at me, then at her watch, then at me again. She sighed, started the car, and said, "Come by tonight, honey. I don't know much, but I'll tell you what I know. I'm not on call. And I'm so sorry about your foot."

She drove away.

I arrived at my office under a splintered canopy of high clouds that feathered away at each horizon to reveal a ribbon of sky. The horizontal streak of blue stretched above the Flatirons glowed like a backlit screen.

Sam's assistant, Madeleine, had left a message on my voice mail asking me to call. I did. Sam wanted to see me sometime around midday and asked when I would be free. Being invited to a rendezvous with Sam was a novel experience; usually when he wanted to see me at a time that was inconvenient for me he just drafted or hijacked me. I told Madeleine that one o'clock worked that day. She said great, he would pick me up.

My morning schedule was busy; I would see patients virtually nonstop until Sam dropped by at one. Although the pain in my foot had moderated to the point where I could wear Tevas and walk without the support of Lauren's cane, I nevertheless hoped that whatever Sam had in mind wouldn't require a great deal of ambulation.

Lauren called in the late morning and left a long message on my voice mail informing me that the National Crime Information Center computer pulled up records on two of the kids from the Graystone group. One was currently in federal prison in Florida on embezzlement charges, and the other was a parolee working as a laborer in an oil field outside Anchorage.

She said that with better data, like birthdays or social security numbers, she might be able to learn more about the members of the group. I made a mental note to begin to assemble as much mundane information on the Graystone counselors and students as I could.

Sam picked me up at one exactly and drove east down Walnut. He parked his car in one of the reserved spots at the police department annex next to the post office on Fourteenth Street and bought us both lunch at a taquería cart set up on the thirteen-hundred block of the Mall. We ate our burritos under the shade of the big maple tree on the old courthouse lawn. About a dozen of what Sam called "my favorite clients" loitered loudly close by, occasionally pan-handling as though their hearts weren't really in it.

I was still trying to figure out the purpose of our rendezvous. The day was warm but not hot, the people were pleasing, the flowers were gorgeous, and the burrito was just fine. I wasn't complaining. My best guess was that Sam wanted to use me to preview his current thinking about Peter's murder before running it by somebody who really mattered, like his sergeant in the police department, Dale Hunter in Denver, or Elliot Bellhaven in the DA's office.

Sam devoured his burrito before he began revealing his homicide musings. I stopped eating at about the same time.

"Kenny Holden was murdered. I'm sure of it now. I've been spending a lot of time the last few days with the feds who've been investigating his death in Rocky Mountain National Park. They wanted this to be a suicide real bad, but I ruined their week and tracked down a witness who said that he saw two people setting up that bogus campsite that night. It was dark, and the witness can't ID anybody, but he's absolutely one hundred percent fucking certain that Kenny Holden was not alone the night he disappeared.

"So, you with me? You've got that witness, you've got the fact that he doesn't even bring his goddamn Instamatic along on his little wilderness excursion, and you've got the fact that he was a possible witness to Peter's murder, whether he knew he was or not."

"How do you figure the last part, Sam? I still don't see how the kid could have seen anything. He showed up after the fact, didn't he?"

Sam flipped open a notebook that he pulled from his pocket and began to draw with a mechanical pencil. "Sometimes—not real often—I'm just stupid. The kid's statement is that he walked down Fourteenth Street past the front of the theatre, then turned right on Spruce. A few more blocks and he would have been home. Right?"

Sam's diagram showed the Boulder Theatre, Four-teenth Street, Spruce Street, and the alley and parking lot behind the theatre. From our picnic spot on the courthouse lawn we could clearly see the marquee of the theatre. On his drawing, Sam put X's at the front entrance to the theatre and at the alley exits on either side of the stage at the rear.

"The janitor who found Peter runs out the back door of the theatre—here—and sees the kid on Spruce. He literally pulls Kenny inside the theatre to help, and together they carry Peter out the front door to the janitor's El Camino, which is parked in the loading zone on Fourteenth Street."

Sam's face was enthusiastic.

I said, "I still don't see a witness lurking anywhere in this scenario."

Sam was hunched over, his forearms temporarily obscuring his diagram. "I'm not done explaining. See, here's how it came down. The killer is in the theatre, on the stage, with your friend, doing whatever he was doing with that goddamn knife. The janitor shows up outside and lets himself in the front door of the the-atre. That's his routine; and that's what he says he did that night. The killer hears all this commotion and knows he's got to split to keep from getting caught. He runs to this door"—Sam stabbed at the X nearest to Spruce Street—"because it's closer than the other one, and he makes his getaway, either on foot, or he's got a car waiting close by or something."

He sat back on his chair and grinned. "Now here's the good part, the part I was stupid about. The first detective to interview Kenny at the ER noted in his report that Kenny Holden is intoxicated and that he smells of vomit. No big deal, right?"

"Everybody, including Kenny, agrees Kenny was really drunk that night. He puked, so what?"

"Right. But do you know where he puked? Kenny puked right fucking *here*." Sam circled a spot on his diagram between the theatre exit door and Spruce Street. "It was part of the crime-scene survey. 'Fresh emesis, approximately 500 milliliters' is what Kenny's little prize was called by the CSIs. None of us paid any attention. I mean, finding a puddle of vomit in downtown Boulder on weekends after the bars close usually ain't exactly revelatory."

"Shit, Sam, if that's where Kenny puked, then the killer may have run right by him," I said, suddenly grasping the importance of what Sam was proposing.

"And maybe the killer didn't even know it. We don't know that. I'm not even sure that Kenny knew it. He didn't remember any of it during the interviews we did. Or if he did remember, he didn't tell us."

"But the killer was afraid he *would* remember. He was afraid Kenny was going to be able to identify him."

"Yeah. So he kills him. Does it real well. Makes it look like suicide. Almost."

Something wasn't fitting for me. It was as though I were trying on the wrong-size clothing. "We're talking here, Sam, as though there were only one killer with Peter, not an ensemble, not an audience."

"Yeah, we are talking that way."

"So now you've rejected Lauren's theory?"

"It's a great theory. But, uh-uh, I no longer think

that we're going to be arresting a theatre troupe," he said. "On the contrary, I think that we've all been getting pimped by a fucking genius."

Sam was ignoring something crucial. "Wait, what about the semen? If there was only one of them, when did this guy have time to jack off in the audience? Twice, yet."

"Bingo, there you go. You're thinking like a detective now. The fucker didn't beat off. He couldn't have. Hell, he wouldn't even have had time to get it up."

I was tempted to give Sam a lesson on Kinsey's reports of the rapidity with which some men could go from flaccidity to ejaculation. I didn't. "What do you mean? Then where did the semen come from?"

"I have no idea. Remember when Lucy said, 'Follow the semen.' I think maybe she was right, and I'm going to ask her to do just that."

I had been home from work for less than five minutes when Adrienne phoned me from Peter's studio and asked me in a tired voice if I would mind joining her there so we could chat about Peter's fire. I had some things to do first but told her I could be over in a few minutes. Emily's water dish was empty, and the ficus in the dining room had dropped about twenty or thirty of its long leaves since morning. I attended to the fresh-water needs of both dog and tree, then went downstairs to change into some jeans.

Before heading out the door, I scribbled a note to Lauren to let her know where her family was going. A stiff downslope had begun rushing off the Divide and Emily and I had to fight the crosswind as we hurried over toward Peter's old tackhouse. The big dog's beard dripped water the entire way across the yard. I think it is a zoological fact that Bouvier beards store more water than a dromedary's hump.

The tops of the east-facing double doors to the studio were open. White shrouds still hung limply over the cabinetry for the Silver Streak Casino and Gaming Club, but nothing obscured Peter's pine coffin. I thought there might be a metaphor there, but I couldn't quite put my finger on it. Adrienne sat cross-legged at her dead husband's desk, the surface of which was littered with piles of receipts, canceled checks, account statements, and invoices—all the financial records of Peter's once-lucrative business.

Adrienne didn't say hello. I did, though, then walked over and kissed the top of her head.

Absently she began scratching Emily's ears with her left hand. Emily responded by sniffing Adrienne's crotch, the little nub of a dog tail doing its best impersonation of a wag the whole time. "You're walking better. How's the toe? You got a good doc?"

"Better, thanks. I think it will be fine. Considering how stupid I was, I'm pretty lucky."

"Yeah, I talked to Lauren, she gave me the scoop. You *were* stupid, but lucky's good. Nothing wrong with lucky. Ask Peter, I bet he would have settled for lucky."

I smiled ruefully, my gaze having moved to the papers on the desktop. "What are you doing?"

"Harold, our accountant, needs more information to get me an income-tax extension for last year. I'm trying to make some sense of this mess. I don't even do my own books, and I sure as hell don't have a clue how to do Peter's."

"What does the accountant want?"

"He just wants everything organized. He says he can make sense of it once I get it in the right piles and in something resembling chronological order."

"Want some help?"

"Actually, believe it or not, I think I'm almost done. I took a few hours off this afternoon, and it wasn't as bad as I thought it would be." She stretched her neck and cracked the knuckles on her right hand.

I moved over to the machinery side of the studio and plucked a nonalcoholic beer out of Peter's little refrigerator. I would have preferred a real beer, but Peter had never permitted alcohol in the shop.

"Want one?"

"Any Scotch over there?"

"No. But it looks like there's an old can of Similac, if you want that."

"Ah, it's so tempting, but thanks, I've been trying to cut down."

I pulled a stool up close to the desk and sat.

She looked me in the eyes. "You know, Alan, it looks like I'm a rich fucking widow."

I smiled. "I'm glad to hear that, Ren. It's one less thing for you to worry about."

"Most of it is in retirement funds. I haven't added it all up, but it looks like the total might exceed the gross national product of Guatemala. Peter has apparently been socking away twenty-five percent of what he made since forever."

"That's great."

"I guess."

"You guess?"

She shrugged. "Most people would argue that rich is better than poor. So I guess it's great. The thing is, I really don't need more money. I have plenty. I needed my husband, though. And I still do. And Jonas needed his daddy. And he will for a long, long time. I know I'll never find another man who'll treat me so well and put up with my act. I'm way too much of a bitch."

Adrienne's little speech was complicated. She had been vulnerable—a rare event—and in return I wanted to be comforting and receptive. She had also been self-deprecating in a way that I thought was far too swollen with hopelessness.

I probably made the wrong choice, but I said, "You're not a bitch. At times you're, um, disagreeable . . . you know, cantankerous."

She cracked a smile. "Thanks. I'll remember that when I put my personal ad in *Westword.* 'Vertically impaired, cantankerous, widowed Jewish female seeks sensitive spiritual Gentile New Age carpenter husband to replace recently murdered same.' That should draw them like flies on horseshit, don't you think? Maybe I should also include the fact that—

although I'm still adding up the figures—it appears that I may be richer than the Sultan of Brunei."

"Adrienne, I'm sure—"

"You know, I like it here in the studio now. It's quiet, peaceful. It was always so noisy here when Peter was alive. Those damn power tools of his and the goddamn Almond Brothers blaring away, but—"

"It's Allman Brothers, Ren."

"Think I care? But now, when I come here, it's just a place I can be with him. I'm not sure I ever want these cabinets to go to that casino. I might just keep them, install them on that wall, invite in his friends, serve drinks. Right now, the place is full of Peter. That feels good."

"Yes," I said, looking around, "it does."

She leaned over and kissed Emily on her little dog lips.

"Have you ever had moments when you wonder whether you are ever going to have sex again? I mean, like, *ever*?"

What? "No, I—"

"Well, I've been thinking about that lately—that this could be curtains for me, fucking-wise. It's a weird thought; I mean, imagine thinking you weren't going to eat ever again or shit anymore. You know that if those things turned out to be true, hell, the next visitor you're gonna get is gonna be some nurse from a hospice. But screwing? My lord, I'm only thirty-seven damn years old and my fucking-life could be history. I could be hanging up my vagina for good, recreationally speaking. It's bizarre. And you'll love this, what's really tragic, what's really ironic, is that I was just get-ting good at it. Screwing, I mean."

The moment was both poignant and indescribably word-sucking. Fortunately, Adrienne seemed to notice how boggled I seemed.

"Peter used to tell me that sometimes I would say things that were kind of hard to respond to. That my mouth was the only force on this planet that was capable of leaving Jesse Jackson speechless. This is one of those times, I guess, huh?"

I nodded.

"So what do you want to know about the fire?"

Stumped by the segue, I recovered and said, "Lauren and I found out a lot about the fire when we were up in Jackson last weekend. When we get together on Saturday, we'll fill you in on all the details, but, to cut to the chase, it appears that Peter harbored a grudge against one of the other counselors who was on the same trip. The guy apparently showed bad judgment during the fire and Peter held him responsible for the kid who died. Anyway, it turns out that the guy Peter was angry at is the same guy who ordered all these cabinets from him"—I ges-tured at the white shrouds all around us—"and he's one of the people who were murdered up in Black Hawk two days ago. So I'm left wondering whether maybe all this has something to do with the fire."

"Peter's death, too?" Adrienne's voice was sud-denly soft and tentative, as though she didn't want what I was saying to be true. Perhaps random, sense-less violence was an easier atrocity for Adrienne to swallow than the possibility that someone had wished her husband dead.

"Maybe. I'm just stabbing in the dark here. I really don't know."

She flinched at my words and her eyes filled with tears. "Bad image, Alan."

Oh God. "Shit, I'm sorry." I stood to hug her but she flitted her hand as a sign for me to stay away.

"It's nothing."

"I'm so sorry. That was thoughtless."

She swallowed. "Listen, I don't think I even know as much about the fire as you do. Peter avoided the subject. You know how there're certain things married people don't talk about?" Impishly, she continued, "You don't think Lauren really wants to know about the Fourth of July when you and Merideth did the wild thing on a blanket on your roof during the fire-works show at Folsom Field, do you?" She smiled an evil smile. "Me and Geppetto were home. And I have videotape, *dear*. I'll tell you, it gave 'O'er the ramparts we watched' a whole new meaning for me."

"Ren—"

"Peter's fire was like that. I knew it had been a monumental thing for him, but I also knew he didn't want to talk about it. I left it alone." She stared at me for a second, mistaking my consternation for argument. "Don't give me that shit. You left stuff alone with Peter, too. It was part of being his friend. You only went where Peter wanted. Those were the rules. You and Lauren have rules. You and Peter had rules. Me and Geppetto had rules. And as far as Peter's rules went, the fire was like a commandment."

She was right about Peter, of course.

She was also right that she knew nothing else of any consequence about the fire. I asked her a dozen questions trying to trigger a memory fragment. But she knew much less about what happened in Wyoming than I did.

"Things had been getting better for us, you know. We had some bad times right after Jonas was born. I doubt if you knew that. But the last few months, things were better. That makes it harder for me, his dying."

I wanted to reply, but my mind kept wandering back to Peter. I wondered if he had been sleeping with Lisa. And whether it mattered anymore. Time causes the relevance of certain things to decompose.

Adrienne slid her carefully straightened piles of financial records into individual manila envelopes that I was certain she had usurped from the supply closet at her office.

"Yo. Earth to Alan? You know what I *didn't* find here? I didn't find any record of the money that Peter supposedly got from the casino for all his work. How much was it? Forty, fifty thousand?"

"Something like that."

"Well, it isn't here." She stuffed the manila envelopes into a plastic grocery bag. "Maybe Harold will find the money. God knows, I'm sure as hell gonna end up paying him a big enough chunk of it for his efforts."

Lauren ferreted out the implications of the day's revelations before I did, which wasn't at all surprising to me. In the few hours since Adrienne and I had departed Peter's studio, my mind had managed to get stuck a half-dozen times on a clear, Annie Leibovitz–quality picture of Peter and Lisa in passionate coitus—Lisa on top—an image that caused some significant interference with my usually sharp deductive powers.

I was getting ready for bed, brushing my teeth, when Lauren called out her thoughts about the day's news from our bedroom. She raised her voice to be heard over the whining bathroom faucet. "Sam's new evidence leads me to believe that the semen in the theatre might be a red herring. In fact, it has to be, if he's right."

Visualizing sperm as little fishes was, of course, familiar territory, but the metaphorical leap from brine shrimp to red herrings gave me pause.

I spit out a gob of toothpaste foam. "Explain, please."

"Sam is saying that he thinks the semen at the first two crime scenes was left behind with one intended purpose, to screw up the forensics. If he's right, then the hair discovered in the theatres may have been left for the same reason. And at the Boulder Theatre, at Peter's murder, Sam thinks he can make a good argument that the seminal fluid was deposited even before the murder was completed."

Sam's argument about the semen still gave me trouble. "It's not the most efficient theory, sweets. Couldn't the guy have taken breaks from what he was doing? He starts cutting on Peter, gets excited, then he goes into the audience and jacks off before he comes back onto the stage to finish up."

"That scenario is more efficient, and of course it's possible, but does it really fit the facts? That would mean the murderer does this hit-and-run murder-masturbation thing twice? I don't think so. You and Sam told me that the first murder, the one at the Buell, got frenzied, right?"

"Yes, in Charley's rendition, at the end, it got pretty nuts, free-form even."

"Well, if the perpetrator started off in control and was indeed getting progressively manic, *and* he was going to jack off during his rave—assuming the frenzy was sexual—wouldn't he have ejaculated on the body, or at least near the body? Why pack up and go masturbate in the audience? It doesn't make sense, does it?"

Lauren's point was valid, if I accepted the underlying assumption that sexual homicide should, at an objective level, make sense. The sexual-homicide literature included many examples of murderers ejaculating on, into, or near their murder victims. However, I couldn't recall any accounts of the killers I read about moving dozens, even hundreds of feet away from their victims and their crime scenes before expressing themselves sexually.

"Keep going," I said.

"Peter's murder was much more methodical than the one in Denver, right? No frenzy during the act?"

I nodded at myself in the bathroom mirror as I cleaned wax out of my ears with a swab. For Lauren, who hadn't witnessed my nod, I said, "Right."

"The killer used short, clean knife strokes. Lots of them, without variation. So where was the sexual passion that's going to lead to repetitive masturbation? It's not there. Peter's murderer was too clinical, too detached, for the behavior you're proposing. It would have been like an accountant masturbating on a 1040."

I was wearing only sweatpants when I walked from the bathroom to the bedroom and perched myself on the end of the bed. My wife was dressed in a long chenille robe that accentuated her bust and hips. Her legs were crossed at the knee and the slit of the robe revealed Lauren's pale flesh all the way to mid-thigh.

The conversation we were having was making me uncomfortable in at least a couple of ways.

"So where did the two globs of semen come from?" I asked. Since my question was largely rhetorical, I pressed my argument before she had a chance to respond. "Personally, I still like your ensemble theory, the idea of somebody being in the audience during the murder. It fits all the facts."

"That's sweet of you, thanks, but my theory doesn't fit all the facts, love. The escape from the Boulder Theatre is too problematic. I can see one person getting out of there unseen by the janitor, maybe. Even that is tight. But from the time the cleaning guy opens the Fourteenth Street door and turns on the houselights to the time that he has a clear view of the orchestra and the stage is no more than ten or fifteen seconds, maybe as few as five. I don't think that's enough time for two or three people to make sense of what's happening behind them and get from distant parts of the theatre out the back door without the custodian seeing them."

My wife usually made sense. She was making sense then, too. "So back to the semen," I said. "Where did it come from?"

She opened her robe, never taking her eyes off my own.

"Come here, I'll show you how it works."

da da da da da da DA

At four o'clock in the morning I was sitting, wide-awake, on the living-room sofa scouring the pages of a souvenir book that Lauren had picked up weeks before in the lobby of the Buell Theatre during the intermission of the performance of *Miss Saigon* that we had attended in Denver.

The book was *The Story of Miss Saigon*.

At three forty-five I had awakened as fresh and alert as if I had enjoyed fourteen, and not just four, hours of sleep. A simple thought had buffeted me awake, a thought that was conceived with greater clarity and firmer flesh than a middle-of-the-night revelation deserved. The thought was born full-grown from a dream, as a gray whale delivers its offspring, already big and squirming and ready to swim on its own.

Charley Chandler had said that everything started with the play.

The play.

Charley said that *Miss Saigon* mesmerized the killer. Charley said that *Miss Saigon* imprisoned the killer and wouldn't let him out on parole.

Charley said it was *the play.* Not the theatre, but *the play.*

The house was full of the thick chill that always seems to blanket lonely living rooms during the hours called the-middle-of-the-night. I was wearing an old T-shirt and frayed sweatpants and a thick pair of white socks. On top of my uncombed hair, as prominently as the Mad Hatter's top hat or Daniel Boone's coonskin, I was also wearing my psychologist's cap.

Although I had enjoyed occasional brief moments of clarity in the weeks since Sam had first announced to me the fact that my friend had been murdered, after reflection, each of those winks of lucidity had turned out to be illusory, only a prank hologram of enlightenment. But now my insight felt settled and my confusion had vanished. And suddenly I knew exactly what I was looking for.

I was looking for *bui doi.*

The dust of life.

Miss Saigon is the story of the tragedy of Vietnam, of the failure of a policy, of the obscenity of war. More, it is the story of Kim, robbed of her Vietnamese family and her future. And of a GI, Chris, who found and lost love in Saigon.

But mostly, *Miss Saigon* is the story of Tam, a fragile little boy who is not only the product of Kim's and

Chris's love; he is also the product of the war, and, ultimately, the recipient of a gift from his mother as grand as Asia itself and as ironic as O. Henry at his darkest.

In Southeast Asia after the war, along with thousands of other children, Tam was a mixed-race bastard, *bui doi*, the dust of life.

What I knew at four o'clock that morning, as a black sky glimmered above Boulder's quiet luster, was that the murder in the Buell was about Tam and Kim and Chris. It wasn't about sexual frenzy. It wasn't about politics. It was about the rage of a little wounded boy who suffered because of monumental injustice, because someone couldn't give him the gift. It was about *bui doi*.

I knew then, sitting in the dark, that Lonnie Aarons died not for sex but for love.

da da da da da da DA.

The heat is on in Saigon.

Lauren crawled out of bed and into the shower at six-thirty the next morning. By then I had already rewritten my psychological profile of Lonnie Aarons's killer, pecking it out inefficiently on the keyboard of my computer. After being diverted at least twice by the wiles of a beguiling killer, I was finally back to the place where I had started, back to the conclusion I had originally reached after my first visit to the Buell to speak with Charley Chandler.

The man who killed Lonnie Aarons was not the same one who killed my friend Peter.

I didn't know the identity of the man who murdered

Lonnie Aarons, but for the first time I was confident that I knew, psychologically speaking, who the man was.

The trouble was, this sunbeam of insight didn't tell me anything about whoever had killed my buddy.

———•∞•———

"Other than that night we were at the Buell, I haven't seen the play, and I don't know what the hell you're talking about."

"I thought you had seen the play."

"Well, I haven't."

Although this conversation with Sam Purdy was taking place on the phone, previous experience helped me imagine his posture. His big shoulders would be sagged forward, his eyes focused vaguely somewhere beyond the horizon.

His voice radiated irritation.

I asked, "Do you at least know the story of the play, do you know how it ends?"

For a moment I wasn't even sure he was planning on answering me. Finally, he said, "It ends when the curtain comes down. What's your point, Alan, assuming you have one?"

"I've gotten lost, Sam, in my thinking about all of this. You know how you said that occasionally you're stupid. Me, too. We've both gotten lost. We have to go back to the beginning and remember that this didn't start off being about the theatre, it started off being about a single play. *Miss Saigon.* The guy who killed Lonnie Aarons was entranced by that specific play, it was a drug for him, he consumed it. That's what Charley Chandler said, remember? And that's what the murder at the Buell was about. It was about the play. And I think that since Peter's murder somebody has been deliberately misleading us, to take us away from that reality."

Impatience isn't always palpable over the phone. This morning, as I talked with Sam, it was. The mass of irascibility I could detect over the line was big and necrotic, and I guessed that I didn't have much time to make a point that he would consider salient.

"Tam—he's the little boy in the play—his story was, I think, the killer's story. More likely, Tam's story was the killer's fantasy story. He identified with Tam. I'm guessing that when you find Lonnie Aarons's murderer, Sam, you're going to find a boy who was deserted first by one parent, and then voluntarily by the other. The child's rage at his parents' unwillingness to sacrifice for him, as Kim did for Tam, was overwhelming. And, ultimately, he acted out his story, his fantasy, on the stage of the Buell."

Sam was silent for at least ten seconds. Crisply he said, "Continue, I'm listening."

"I'm guessing multiple foster homes, maybe abuse, certainly neglect. The real blow, though, was before that when this kid was deserted by his remaining parent. Lonnie's killer was old enough when that happened to remember it clearly, or to think he remembers it clearly.

"The rest of the profile that I originally developed about the guy still fits, except for the sexual part. Age is right, the fact that the guy's a loner, that he perceives himself to be judged unfairly, that his life is a series of mistreatments and squandered opportunities. Bright guy, but he changes jobs a lot. May not have a criminal history; if he does, it'll be mostly minor stuff, impulse things, maybe an assault or a disturbing-the-peace charge. I still think that he's knowledgeable about computers and theatres. All that still fits.

"But the crime at the Buell wasn't sexual. I was wrong about that. The murder of Lonnie Aarons was about shame and degradation and humiliation and revenge and rage. It was never about pathological lust."

"What about the semen?" Sam's voice had covered the uneven terrain that lay between irritation and interest. He was challenging me now.

"A red herring." I decided to let Sam struggle with that image, too. "I'm beginning to think it's not even the killer's sperm. I'll be surprised if it is."

"Then where did he get it?"

"I don't know. Maybe he's gay and he collected it that way."

"What way?"

I was being dissed—a good sign, given Sam's mood. "Use your imagination."

"But why? Why leave somebody else's semen behind?"

Sam already knew the answer to his question; what

he was doing was assessing the quality of the logic I was employing in this new rendition of the truth.

"For the obvious reason. Remember, the whole crime at the Buell was elaborately planned. This production was rehearsed and refined for weeks. The guy figured that if the cops ever managed to track him down, he couldn't be blamed for the murder if his semen didn't match the crime-scene semen. The semen was his get-out-of-jail-free card."

"Why leave it up in the audience then, and not onstage? Wouldn't it make more sense to leave it onstage?"

"Because the stage belonged to him that night. He didn't want to contaminate his scene, his stage, his production."

"And Peter's death?"

"Different guy, Sam. Different murder."

"No doubt?"

"None."

"Copycat?"

"I don't know. If it's a copycat, it's someone who didn't truly understand what the first killer was up to. Who he really was. The characteristics of Peter's murder only duplicate the gross details of the Buell murder. What happened at the Boulder Theatre may look like the guy's signature, but it isn't really his handwriting. It doesn't have the nuance, it doesn't have the affect, and it totally distorts the motive. Hell, we've felt all along that it was like a bad counterfeit bill; it's always only looked real from a distance."

"But we're talking about somebody close to the

Denver investigation? It had to be somebody who knew those gross details."

"Sure, though I imagine, on a high-profile case like the Buell murder, a lot of people would know enough to pull this off."

"Way too many, but at least manageable. Less than a hundred." I heard someone, maybe Madeleine, walk close to Sam and say something to him. He said, "I'll get to it," then back to me, "A moment ago, you said 'who the killer was'? Why did you say *was*?"

"I'm sorry, Sam, I'm leaving something important out. I think the guy may be dead. I suspect that Lonnie Aarons's murderer may have killed himself, right away, in the first few days after the murder. Maybe even the first few hours. It has to do with the play, the way it ends. And if I'm right about the suicide, I'll give you odds on a gunshot wound to the head."

"Well, you've finally said something that I can actually check out without visiting a psychic. What about the kid who was killed at the Central City Opera House, where does he fit into your scenario?"

"Sorry, I haven't been able to squeeze that one in yet."

"That's reassuring; welcome to the club. I want you to keep this new theory to yourself. You tell nobody, you understand? Nobody means nobody. Not Elliot, not Lucy, not Dale Hunter, not your friend Peter's wife. Nobody."

"Lauren knows already."

"Well, tell her the same thing. Woman has enough discretion for all of us."

"You want to see my new profile? It's all ready, I can fax it to Madeleine."

"No, I'm on my way over to see Sherry. Fax it to her flower shop. I'll pick it up there in ten minutes." He gave me the number.

So that it wouldn't start ringing and whirring and interrupt while she was seeing a patient, Diane kept her fax machine in the tiny kitchen of our office suite. After I hung up with Sam, I ventured in and stared at all the unfamiliar buttons for about thirty seconds while I was trying to figure out what I had to do to get the machine to work. The clock of the adjacent microwave flashed "00:00," mocking my characterological lack of technological acumen.

Diane walked into the kitchen to pour herself a cup of coffee, and without asking if I required assistance, took the report from my hand, fed the two pages into the slot, asked me for the number of the receiving fax machine, and seconds later the newest edition of my psychological profile was on its way all of three blocks to Sam's wife's flower shop. In order to be certain that I clearly registered her derision at my ineptitude, Diane smiled sweetly at me and shook her head an infinitesimal amount.

I waited for an eye roll that never materialized.

I had discovered long ago that if I stay humble, keeping pace with the advance of technology is really not much of a problem.

I phoned Lauren before I started with my next patient, mostly to tell her that Sam Purdy wanted her to keep the latest theory to herself. She was silent while she

considered whether she could withhold the hypothesis from Elliot Bellhaven, the deputy DA who was
responsible for the prosecution of Peter's murder. The
ethical quandary was an awkward one that, knowing
my wife, wouldn't be resolved in Sam's favor. She
finally decided she would ponder Sam's directive for a
few more hours before deciding what to do.

"Which means that I should tell Sam that his ability
to investigate this new theory under the cloak of darkness will expire sometime this afternoon?"

"Good translation, honey. *Very* good. Yeah, something just like that."

"Done. It's generous of you."

Her words picked up speed. "Listen, I need to run,
but I just realized something that's kind of interesting.
Trey Crandall—you know, the kid who died in Peter's
fire in Wyoming?—the articles you gave me say that
he was the son of Truman Crandall of Arizona."

"Truman Crandall—why do I know his name? What
is he, the president's new drug czar or something?"

"Almost. Bridesmaid, not a bride. But he's still
second in command of the Justice Department. Back in
1982, during the fire, he was just a Phoenix DA, but
yes, one and the same."

"It is interesting."

"I thought so. Got to run. Remember, I'm out late
tonight, and I won't be home for dinner."

———∞∞∞———

After relaying to Madeleine the gist of Lauren's response to Sam's entreaty, I decided to walk over to the Mall, get a burrito and a lemonade for lunch, and people-watch.

I was halfway down the front walk that led to the street when Sam drove up, threw open the passenger door of his car, and told me to get in. He said this with an irascible manner that I found instantly irritating. It was as though I had asked him for the ride and had arrived twenty minutes late.

Continuing to walk, and resolved not to be bullied, I said, "I'm on my way to get some lunch, you're welcome to join me."

He drove alongside me. *"Get in, Alan."*

"Not today, Sam."

"Do you want me to say 'please'?"

"That would be nice."

"Would you fucking *please* get in?" He had to stop his car abruptly to keep his open door from being severed by a parking-meter post.

I stopped walking and leaned down so I could look at his face through the windshield. "What's so damn important?"

"You might be right about the killer at the Buell. Your new theory, it may be right."

What? "You found him?" I was incredulous.

"No, but I think I may have identified him. Come on, get in, I don't think it's particularly prudent of me to be screaming this out the window."

I got into the car. My mouth was dry. "I've got a patient in forty-five minutes."

"This is more important than that."

"That's not a decision you get to make."

He ignored me. "After I got your fax this morning I called the coroner's office in Denver and asked them to pull all their suspicious deaths, murders, suicides, and any gunshot deaths since the day before the murder at the Buell." He waved a manila envelope at me. "A shitload of them. God, I'm glad I don't work in a city where so many people die. Can you imagine? I have to do one or two of these a year and I'm not very pleasant when I'm doing them."

"That's true, you're not," I agreed.

"Then I called Dale Hunter, but she was out someplace interviewing. Apparently she's gotten smart and is looking at some job with the feds."

I told him I heard that she was up for a job with the Justice Department, something in community policing.

He ignored me. "Anyway, I got her partner, a Hispanic guy named Granger—the guy's all right, I've met him a couple of times—and asked him for any lists of potential suspects they had put together. You know, people who worked at the theatres or at the convention center. People who traveled with the road show. Whatever—all their goddamn lists. I don't tell Granger what I'm thinking, of course. Hey, is Granger an Hispanic name, am I missing something? Anyway, I tell him I want to do some cross-checking with the lists we have for the Boulder Theatre murder. Granger told me it was a waste of time, that he had already done it himself—by computer, no less. I said fine, Granger, I believe you, but I'm getting my nuts squeezed by my sergeant here, humor me.

"He faxes me his lists—like I said, he's okay." Sam waved another manila envelope at me.

"Well, guess what? Using your little treasure map, I struck gold. I found a guy who shows up on a list of people who local ticket brokers say bought tickets to *Miss Saigon*. And the same guy, turns out, is on the coroner's list of suspicious deaths. And, just as my genius psychologist friend predicted, the guy killed himself with a gunshot to his head."

"When?"

"His body was found six days before Peter was killed. But it was ripe; he probably killed himself days prior to that. His name was Martin Scott. Wouldn't you know the guy would have two first names, like you?"

Sam thought that people with interchangeable first and last names were an unnecessary irritation in life.

"Coincidence?" I asked.

"Maybe. But, see, it seems Mr. Scott not only bought *Miss Saigon* tickets from a broker but he also got a pair from a man who sold some subscription seats with a want ad in the newspaper."

"How do the Denver cops know that?"

" 'Cause cops are smart, asshole. Dale and Granger got somebody to go through back issues of the paper and comb the want ads. They tracked down ticket transactions for the play, then they interviewed the sellers and the buyers."

I was impressed, but still skeptical. "Odds are pretty good that one or two of the tens of thousands or so people who saw *Miss Saigon* while it was in Denver are going to end up on that list," I said, pointing at the envelope that contained the coroner's information.

Sam said, "Yes, that's true. But how many of them are also going to have been employed as computer-research specialists."

"So our guy knew computers?"

"Yep. At the medical school. He did data analysis for at least three different labs."

He stuffed his hands in his pockets, not an easy accomplishment for someone of Sam's size in the front seat of a car. "One of them was an andrology lab."

"What's andrology?"

"You really don't know?"

"No."

"Sperm bank. Semen samples. Male fertility." He was beaming.

"No shit?"

"No shit. The asshole worked in a big research laboratory at the Health Sciences Center, surrounded by frozen sperm."

"So do you know who interviewed him before he died? What did he say when the cops talked to him?"

"I don't have copies of the interview reports from the murder investigation, but I'm guessing that nobody *ever* talked to him. According to the coroner's report, the cop who found Martin's body was investigating the Buell murder. And Martin, of course, wasn't particularly talkative by then. Some detective was probably on his way to interview Martin Scott when he literally smells something funny and trips over the corpse."

"Any question about the death?" In my brief stint as a consultant to the Boulder coroner investigating suspicious deaths I had learned that the way people died was not always uncomplicated.

"Nothing pending. Denver coroner gave cause and manner—suicide by gunshot wound of head."

"But you haven't spoken with anybody who might have, you know, examined the scene, to see if there was anything suspicious?"

"I haven't, but I will. I got a call in to the guy who found him."

"But you haven't reached Dale?"

"No. Like I said, Granger says she's taking a personal day. He thinks it has to do with that job she wants, says I can probably catch her tomorrow. I may try her at home tonight."

"Sam, this is really something. How do you think it adds up?"

Just then a loud *squaack* bleated from the police radio. Sam squelched the noise and faced me. "I think somebody wanted Peter Arvin dead. I think it was somebody who knew him well enough to know he hung around theatres, who knew they could kill him on a stage and make it look like the Buell murder. I also think it was somebody who knew that the real murderer from the Buell wasn't ever going to get caught, because he was already dead. And I think it all has to do with that damn casino where you got shot."

I stated the obvious. "But not Martin Scott?"

"No. At least for murders two and three, Martin's got himself the devil's alibi."

"Then who are you thinking?"

"My hunch right now is somebody at the medical school. Somebody who knew Martin and who knew Martin's fantasy. We've got enough dots, it's time to connect them."

———❦———

If I conveniently ignored Lonnie Aarons's murder in the Buell Theatre in Denver and Mark Literno's murder on the stage of the Central City Opera House, everything else, all the other unwieldy strands, could be linked together.

Peter's fire. The coffin. Peter's death. Kenny Holden's death. The massacre at the Silver Streak Casino. Grant Arnold's death. The cement mixer.

I wasn't imaginative enough to get the links to arrange themselves neatly, like the symmetrical diamond weaves of a hammock, but instead, the strands lay jumbled, like a pile of loose shoelaces that have wormed together in a drawer.

Say I was right about *Miss Saigon* and Tam and *bui doi*. And let's say Sam was right and that Martin Scott had killed Lonnie Aarons. If we're both right, then Martin Scott was Tam, a deserted and neglected little boy, and Lonnie Aarons didn't die merely as the first domino to fall in a serial killer's spree of sexual homicide. Lonnie Aarons died to serve Martin Scott's primitive rage.

Say all those things, and let them be true, and by the time Peter was flayed and left to die on the baby grand piano on the stage of the Boulder Theatre, Martin Scott was already dead by his own hand and decomposing in a carriage house on Denver's Capitol Hill.

As alibis go, I had to admit, it was platinum.

So Peter's killer wasn't Lonnie Aarons's killer. And Mark Literno's killer wasn't Lonnie Aarons's killer.

But Peter's killer knew about Lonnie Aarons's killer, had to. Peter's killer had the correct kind of knife and knew exactly where in the theatre to leave the tell-tale semen. So Martin Scott had told someone the details, right? And that someone followed in Martin's footsteps?

No. Sorry. Where's the motive?

What about Mark Literno's impaled naked body in Central City? Lots of pieces of that tragedy fit the pattern, too. The signature stage set, the victim's build and coloring, the knife. But no semen in the theatre. Why no semen that time?

Different killer, part of a troupe? Everyone seemed to be discounting that theory.

Not enough time for the luxury of masturbation? Too risky? Was the killer becoming impotent?

Or . . . *maybe the killer didn't have any more semen.*

God. Sam was wrong about the killer's being from

the medical center. A coworker of Martin Scott's in the andrology lab wouldn't be suffering from a sperm shortage.

Of course. The first two murders had used up all the available semen that Martin Scott had secreted from the sperm bank. Which means that the third murder was never really part of the plan. If it had been, the second killer would have saved some semen to complete the pattern, right?

So why was Mark Literno killed?

Back to the beginning. Lonnie Aarons was killed because of Martin Scott's damaged soul.

Peter was murdered for a motive about the casino or *something*.

Mark Literno must have been an afterthought, an ad-lib. He was killed because someone wanted the authorities to believe a serial killer was still on the loose. Mark Literno was killed for distraction and deception.

But by whom?

Let's face it, Martin Scott wasn't requiring any distraction by then.

Everything pointed to the fact that Mark Literno was murdered in Central City by the same person who murdered my friend Peter. That person needed distraction. Which meant that one of us—Sam, Dale, Lucy, Elliot, me—had been breathing down his neck.

I wondered which one of us, and I wondered whose neck.

Between patients, I started making some calls.

Lisa wasn't at Adrienne's house. I got the machine but didn't leave a message.

After a telephonic dance with Adrienne's receptionist, who was again intent on not permitting me to speak with "Doctor," I finally prevailed by saying I was with the police department.

An irascible Adrienne came on the line saying, "Yeah. How can I help you?"

"Hi, Ren."

"Alan, I should have known. What's the penalty for impersonating a police officer? Maybe if I get you thrown in jail you'll stop bothering me at work." Her voice was playful.

"I need some information. It's important. It's about sperm, actually semen, and it can't wait."

"Your little query can't wait, but the guy who's bent over my examining table with his shorts around his ankles dying for my gentle finger to massage his prostrate, he can wait?"

"How are semen samples frozen?"

Deep inhale. "First you get a copy of *Penthouse*, then—"

"Ren—"

"Liquid nitrogen."

"In what, like test tubes?"

"Depends on the lab. I've seen vials, ampules, little pipettes that look like straws. They're even *called* 'straws.' "

"How much semen in a sample?"

"How much does an elephant weigh? Depends on the guy. Depends on how long since he's done the deed—either into a cooperating partner or into an unsuspecting handkerchief. Medically speaking, depends on a myriad of factors, including the frequency of wet dreams."

She was enjoying this. I made a clinical assessment that Adrienne's grief was abating. "Stay with me here, okay? For a semen sample to end up being typical, in terms of quantity, how many of these vials or straws would it take?"

"Ask Lauren. She'll tell you that there's no such thing as a typical ejaculation. Sometimes the stuff seems to just disappear, sometimes it drips down your thighs the whole next day."

"Ren, *please*."

"It's hard to say. There isn't only one way to do this. Sometimes the semen is spun down in a centrifuge first, sometimes not. I think the sample is mixed with some sort of freezing medium, a nutrient of some kind, glycerol and egg yolks—"

"If a frozen sample were defrosted and you looked at it under a microscope, could you tell any difference between the defrosted sample and a fresh sample? Could you visually identify the presence of the freezing medium, for instance?"

"Don't believe I could, no, but then again, maybe. The sperm would look the same. The fluid might look a little more yellow in the defrosted sample."

"How long do sperm stay alive, once, you know, the, um, they—"

"Once the guy comes?"

"Yes."

"Unfrozen, in the right environment, sperm are

motile for up to seventy-two hours. Four or five days in the fridge. Indefinitely in a tank of liquid nitrogen." Pause of two heartbeats, her voice breathy when she continued. "God, this is about Peter, isn't it?"

"Yes."

"You got something?"

"Close. Maybe. Shit, I don't know."

"You think the samples they found in the theatre might have been frozen, not fresh?"

"That's what I'm wondering."

"It wouldn't be hard to do. If the serologist didn't specifically look for the components of the nutrient medium—if you had access to a sperm bank, shit, you could do it, you could leave somebody else's genetic signature wherever you wanted. You'll tell me as soon as you know something?"

"Absolutely, if you'll take my call."

"Cute."

"One last thing. Do you know where Lisa is? She's not at your house. I want to ask her something."

Alarm reverberated in Adrienne's voice. "You don't think she's involved in any of this, do you? My God, my baby is with her."

"No, Ren, I don't think she's involved. At all. I just wonder if she saw something, might remember something, some visitors to the studio, anything that might add another piece to this puzzle."

"She and Jonas are at her place today. She has some disgusting sewer problem, had to be home to wait for the plumber to show up. I told her she could take Jonas over there and spend the day."

"Where does she live?"

"One of those vacation shacks in Eldorado Canyon. You know, down below the Eldorado Springs pool?"

I knew. "Do you have a phone number for her?"

She rattled it off from memory, then said, "I mean it, if you've got something, Alan, I want to know. Even if I won't like it. Promise?"

"Promise."

"Good. But first there's a half-naked man bent over a table waiting for me, and in my hand there's a tube of K-Y Jelly with his name on it."

"I can't believe what you do for a living."

"And I can't believe I get paid for this."

My next call was to the New Jersey–bred receptionist at Grubstakes Development in Black Hawk.

She remembered me from my earlier visit, seemed lonely and displaced—I guessed by Grant's death—and was eager to talk. But she wasn't of any actual assistance; she didn't know anything about Peter's fire, and she had never met Grant Arnold's family or friends.

"He dated a lot. Was always with different women around town. Grant had something to prove with women. It's why he and I never, you know, made it together. He hit on me, of course, but I'm a girl who prefers to be with confident guys."

I was silent, contemplating this new dead end, and debating what I should do next. I wondered whether I should try to track down Lisa and Jonas at the end of the day.

Ms. New Jersey interrupted my musing by asking, "You married?" with pronounced nonchalance.

"Yes," I said, "joyfully."

Her voice swelled with bewilderment. She said, "I hear that happens sometimes."

VII

Show Time

Boulder is surrounded, for miles in some directions, by publicly owned, undeveloped land purchased with tax revenues volunteered by the local citizenry. The dollars have bought mile after mile of beautiful buttes, wild mountainsides, bucolic plains, and lush pastures, any of which would be absolutely perfect for a Wal-Mart or a cul-de-sac or two. The city owns thousands of acres of virgin turf so ripe for housing and clean industry that insomniac developers, hungry for land, probably use the image of Boulder's pristine greenbelt as a way to cry themselves to sleep.

As I drove south out of the city on Broadway to see Lisa that afternoon, the last apartments and single-story office buildings of Table Mesa disappeared in my rearview mirror and the open space of the Mesa Trail beneath the Flatirons began to dominate the landscape. After another half mile, all evidence of Boulder had totally disappeared behind a high green-belt butte. Only a couple of minutes later, the two-lane road to Eldorado Canyon broke off to the west.

Eldorado Canyon Road is lined with a motley assortment of housing. Log cabins, pine shacks, fifties ranches, and modern architectural palaces all share the horse country along the road, the only commonality between the dwellings being a frontierlike adherence to belief in the value of tightly strung barbed wire.

Before the advent of the automobile, Eldorado Canyon was a booming Front Range resort. Because of its abundant warm springs, the area had long been in use as a wintering site by Plains Indians but wasn't settled by white men, who came mostly to harvest timber, until 1860. A huge spring-fed pool was constructed at the mouth of the canyon at the turn of the century, a luxury hotel soon followed, and a train line from Denver provided easy access for city dwellers eager for the wonders of the steep rock canyon and the soothing waters of the warm springs.

After a few decades the hotel burned to the ground, and good roads were built to carry tourists much farther into the Rockies. By the end of World War II, Eldorado Canyon had reverted from famed resort to its current status of sleepiness and eccentricity.

It was, I thought, a perfect place for Lisa.

The mouth of the canyon loomed ahead of me as the pavement ended on the two-lane road into residential Eldorado. I slowed my car and looked for the bridge that Lisa had told me on the phone would take me over Eldorado Creek to a cluster of cabins that included her home.

The bridge was narrow and the lane across it was dirt. The cabins along the creek dated back to Eldorado's resort days, and most had suffered neglect. Too many residences seemed crammed in together beneath the thick canopy of overgrown hackberries and elms that thrived close to the creek. Spring leaves had matured on the high branches of the trees, and the shade they cast combined with the deep shadows from the mountains looming a hundred yards to the west to engulf the neighborhood in an afternoon darkness that was primordial and eerie.

"Turn left, three down, two up," Lisa had said. "The house is stone, the one below it has yellow siding. You should park down below and walk up the hill. It's easier to get back out."

Lisa hadn't been happy to hear that I wanted to speak with her again about Peter's fire. When I asked if I could come over, she initially said no. Then, seconds later, as though the idea had been hers all along, she changed her mind and invited me to come.

"It's time," she said.

Although I didn't know what that meant, I didn't argue.

I left my car in a cutout by the creek and hiked up a steep incline, past the house with the peeling yellow siding. The cabin's downhill foundation had apparently not been dug deep enough and the yellow house showed signs of moving inexorably in gravity's favorite direction.

Lisa's house was faced with river stones, round and polished, and the structure stood secure and proud on a piece of flat ground no bigger than a suburban three-car garage. The front door opened to the west, the narrow walkway leading to it lined on both sides with newly turned dirt awaiting a border of annuals. To the east, behind the house, the sky retained a glimmer of the day's brightness, and I could tell that at least part of the cabin would enjoy great morning light.

I was five feet from the house when the door

opened. Lisa greeted me with a warm smile, and some of the tension I was feeling about the visit ebbed. Jonas was in her arms. He waved maniacally at me and I stopped walking and waved back. We played this game for at least thirty seconds; I tired of it long before Jonas did. I was beginning to see a lot of his mother emerging in him.

Jonas's weight rested on Lisa's hip. Done waving at me, he used his free left hand to tug on the neckline of her shirt, exposing her right breast all the way down to the nipple, a dark crescent of which was visible.

Lisa made no motion to cover herself. The moment was awkward; I didn't know if she knew her breast was uncovered. I wondered if this is how women felt in open-zipper situations.

"Peter said I could trust you. I've decided it's time to do that. Come into our house, please."

The outside was stone. The inside was wood.

Peter's wood.

Our house?

The cabin was tiny, maybe six hundred square feet total, but Peter had made wonderful use of the space. A wall of bookcases seemed to recede into the stone in the main room. A desk with a curved façade hung suspended from a corner beam. Futon frames filled with cushions fronted a big low coffee table that was covered with Jonas's toys and picture books. A tiny kitchen alcove was lined floor to ceiling with gleaming cherry cabinets adorned with inlays of some light, fanciful wood. A dining table folded down from the wall, and benches swung out below it in an ingenious use of space.

Lisa stood in the only open doorway in the room. She beckoned with a finger and I followed her through the door, into the bedroom. This room faced east. Peter had lined the back wall with knotty-pine cabinets and a Murphy bed, which was folded up into the wall. He had enlarged and extended the only window, and below it created a tempting seat above a set of neat drawers. A sisal rug covered the scratched oak floor.

"We were lovers." Lisa's voice was bruised with sadness and loss, but it carried neither an offering of guilt nor any note of apology.

I thought, *apparently*, and looked into her young face for guidance on how to respond to her pronouncement.

"He did this for us, not for me." She meant the cabinetry and the furniture and the remodeling, of course. "He said he was going to leave her. Adrienne. He loved it here with me. He loved it here, in the canyon, with the water and the rocks. Peter was joyful up here, a little boy."

Joyful. Peter? There's that word again. Hadn't I just used it with the receptionist from Grubstakes? What had she said in reply?

I hear that happens sometimes.

"Lisa, I'm sorry for your loss. Now I know it's even greater than I imagined." How, I wondered, would Miss Manners recommend I express sympathy to the mistress of my dear friend's dead husband? Does Hallmark have a card that conveys both sympathy and rebuke?

"My love allowed Peter to extinguish, finally, the

fire you are so curious about. My touch"—she paused, and slid the fingers of her free hand slowly down to tug her neckline back into place—"made him alive again."

I could only imagine.

"Everyone thought it was Jonas who changed Peter. It wasn't, it was me."

I didn't want Jonas to listen to this.

I didn't want to have to listen to this myself, and I didn't want to get lost considering how much of it was true. Selfishly, I considered my responsibility to Adrienne. I wasn't sure of much at that moment, but I was certain that I didn't want to be the one to tell Adrienne about Peter and Lisa.

Recalling my conversation with Adrienne in Peter's shop, I wondered if she already knew about Peter and Lisa.

Lisa followed me as I stepped out of the bedroom. I sat down in the front room as she laid Jonas, who was now sleeping, on the cushions of one of the futons. She squeezed in beside me on the other. Our knees touched. Hers was cool.

"I'll tell you about Peter's fire. Everything I know. It won't help you understand anything about his murder, but I will tell you, anyway. For me, it's about trusting you to know him well. It's important that you know him well."

I tried to swallow, but the act was stymied by my dry throat. "May I please have a glass of water?" I said.

"Back when Eldorado was a resort, before the Depression, a man named Ivy Baldwin used to do a high-wire act almost six hundred feet above the canyon floor. Without a net. Did you know that?"

I said I didn't know that.

"It was apparently pretty spectacular for the tourists. I mean, think about it, with the winds that knife through this canyon and everything? But Peter used to say that as far as death-defying acts go, it was nothing compared to what he and I had pulled off over the last year." Lisa said this with marked pride.

She meant their affair. Peter had apparently also meant their affair.

Peter? Are we talking about my friend here? Peter?

"We met up here, Peter and I. I was living in this house with a roommate during my senior year. We met in the fall, in late September. One day I just started talking with him. It was magical."

I calculated quickly. That would be almost two years ago. Adrienne was either just pregnant with Jonas or almost pregnant with Jonas.

"My roommate and I used to hike a lot, and sometimes we would go into the canyon and watch the rock climbers. The days that Peter came to climb, he was the only one I watched. And on the days when Peter went up without gear—on those days, it wasn't just me; *everyone* would stop what they were doing just so they could see him climb. Word would spread and other climbers would come off the rocks just so they could watch him free-solo. Did you ever see it?"

"No," I said, "but now I wish that I had." I had never gone to see him because I was afraid that I would be going to watch him die. Now that I knew how the story really ended, I wished I could have seen him on the Diving Board with nothing to rely on but his bravado and his grip.

Lisa smiled, trusting my words. Then she giggled, and for a solitary moment she appeared as young as she actually was.

"He was amazing. I already had such a thing for him that I started skipping classes just so I could watch him climb. Just so I could watch him . . ."

Jonas murmured then, and rolled close to the edge of the futon. Lisa's hand was in place scooting him back to safety even before I could raise my voice in warning.

A pair of cats I hadn't previously noticed began playing in the corner, below the suspended desk. The room was growing dark but Lisa didn't move to illuminate it.

"He did the bedroom first. He built the cabinets without ever asking me if I wanted them, just showed up with them one day. He said he thought the pine was right for this house. It was from an old barn that fell down near Gold Hill, and he felt the wood belonged here with the river stones."

Lisa's eyes traveled the room, before she settled her

gaze on the bookshelves. "It was Peter's idea that I be Jonas's nanny. Did you know that? He didn't want me to leave town after I graduated. But he really didn't know what we had."

"Didn't Adrienne hire you?" I asked, puzzled at what she was telling me. I remembered the protracted nanny interviews, the painful second-guessing that Adrienne had endured.

"Sure she did. I'm a great find. Wouldn't you have hired me?"

In a second. Irony abounded.

"A few days after he was born, I took Jonas down to the shop to see his daddy and while they were playing I was snooping around and I lifted a sheet off one of the finished pieces and I saw the coffin. I asked Peter about it and he wouldn't say who it was for or why he had built it. He wouldn't talk about it at all. But I couldn't get it out of my mind.

"That night Peter worked late, and the baby and I went back down to the shop. Adrienne had gone somewhere, I don't remember where. Jonas was asleep in his buggy." Lisa inhaled, her eyes widened, and her tongue moistened her lips. Her teeth sparkled in the dark room. "I lit candles in the shop, which freaked him out. He used to hate fire. He followed me around, blowing them out, but the whole time I'm pulling off my clothes and running back and re-lighting the candles.

"Before long I was naked. I wasn't thinking. It was, like, I had this play to perform and I already knew all the lines. I turned off the lights in the studio and I put on some music and I opened up the casket and I climbed up and stood inside it and I began to dance. I still remember the music that was playing; it was the first album by Cream. I begged Peter to join me in the casket. He wouldn't. I pleaded."

Lisa pulled her knees to her chest and I realized I was holding my breath.

"Finally he did. He reached up high and took my hand and I swear I lifted him up with only my fingertips. At first, as he stood inside the coffin with me, he shook like a frightened dog. He seemed terrified, as though he were going to die. I held him for a while, and then I undressed him slowly and I kissed him—I kissed him everywhere—and he finally started to relax and we began to make love, but I kept stopping and starting and I wouldn't let him come until he told me his secrets."

Her stare froze me in place. "Until he told me about the coffin."

Lisa's eyes were as wide as I'd ever seen them, her smile as crooked as it got. "So the story I'm about to tell you is a story that I heard as I lay naked in that coffin with Peter inside me. If you ever go back to the shop and you look closely at that box you'll see the stains and you'll see black specks of blood from the splinters in my butt."

I wanted her to be kidding. I knew she wasn't.

"We used the coffin to bury the fire that night. Jonas was a week old. And Peter was reborn. The entire experience was a miracle. I felt a breeze passing over me that whole night, from the very moment I climbed into the box. Long, gentle pulses of air as warm as Jonas's breath. Even then I knew that the wind was fluttering off the wings of angels."

It was as though I were listening to *him*. My old friend. Lisa had mastered his inflection and digested his cynicism. And she was, I was sure, the only one left on this planet who could tell his story.

I knew that I was as close to Peter just then as I would ever be again.

Now the room where we sat was dark, the cats were quiet, and Jonas's breathing was as regular and soothing as a metronome.

The story Lisa began telling was within ten degrees or so of the one that Colter had captivated Lauren and me with in Wyoming. Nothing new emerged that seemed particularly important until Lisa got to the part about the blowup on the ridge.

Peter apparently felt that everything had already been determined long before they reached the switchback that traversed the saddle, even before the lightning ignited the tree. Who would go where on that ridge, who would align with whom—all those things had been carved out in the previous few days in the backcountry.

The kid who died in the fire, Trey Crandall, had been absolutely unprepared for the wilderness when he arrived in Wyoming; he was a city kid who thought camping was something done in his dad's fifth wheel. Out of fear for his life, he had aligned himself with Grant Arnold from the first day away from base camp; a few days in and he thought that Grant walked on water. Graystone encouraged that kind of attachment, felt that if the kids could identify with a positive role model, then the experience in the backcountry would be that much richer and more rewarding. So, long before the lightning struck, Trey was tethered to Grant. If Grant was going to traipse unsuspecting into an inferno, Peter knew that Trey was going to be only so much more kindling.

Lisa said that the truth was that Grant wasn't really a party to the argument about whether to traverse the switchback into the woods or climb straight up the barren saddle to the ridgeline. That battle was fought solely between the group leader and Peter. Peter knew Grant well enough to know that he wasn't going to defy the group leader. Peter also knew that if he wasn't persuasive and didn't win the argument about climbing the saddle, Grant was going to go into those woods with the kid from Arizona leashed to him like a lost puppy.

As Peter's arguments became more heated, the group leader grew more frustrated and ultimately walked away from Peter and called everyone together, spelled out the dilemma, and permitted the kids to make their own decision. That was a big part of the Graystone philosophy, personal responsibility. If the counselors thought the choices were safe and prudent, then the kids were encouraged to make their own decisions about how to accomplish a task or meet a goal.

The breakdown of who went with whom turned out as badly as Peter had feared. Only four of the kids chose to accompany him on the tough climb up the saddle face. The other two, Trey and one other, who was attached to the group leader almost as symbiotically as Trey was attached to Grant, chose to follow the switchback trail that the lead counselor and Grant Arnold were taking back into the woods.

"Why was Peter so sure that Grant would follow the other counselor on the switchback, toward the fire? I thought Peter and Grant had been friends at school. It seems to me they would stick together."

Lisa said, "I'm getting to that."

Colter had understood the blowup well.

Peter and the kids who had joined him had been on the saddle face when the wind came up and the fire started its march into the woods, at a sharp diagonal up the ridge face. Peter heard the roar of the blowup and ordered his companions to stay where they were while he raced down the switchback to the edge of the woods to help. Thwarted by cinders and darkness and flames and heat, he quickly abandoned that route and instead climbed the almost vertical face of the saddle in order to get to the ridgeline to search for survivors.

His first free-solo.

"Lisa, I still don't understand. Why did Grant go into the woods with the group leader? Why didn't he stay with Peter?"

"Because Grant was *fucking* the group leader. And

he apparently wanted to continue fucking the group leader. That's why."

"Man or woman?"

"I don't know."

"You don't know who it was?"

"Peter never said."

"Why not?"

"I'm getting to that part, too."

When Peter arrived at the top of the ridge, he was searching for survivors and was examining the charred ridge face below him for evidence of victims. The first people he came across were Grant and the other kid.

Not Trey.

Peter was joyous that anyone had survived the firestorm. He was also angry enough at Grant to kill him on the spot for his stupidity. Eventually, Grant told Peter what had happened, and said that he feared the worst. Peter treated both of the survivors for shock, and moved on down the ridgeline looking for the other two members of the party.

"Wait, Lisa, what had happened? Why didn't all four get off the ridge face together?"

Lisa eyed me as though she were deciding whether to trust me with this truth. She closed her eyes for a few seconds and opened them when she'd made the decision.

Grant had told Peter that once they were in the shadow of the woods the proximity of the fire terrified

Trey. By then, Grant said, he realized Peter had been right about staying off the ridge, and he suspected that the other counselor knew it, too. The group leader was tense. The sky was beginning to darken. The fire was loud and they could smell it but they couldn't feel the heat yet. By then they were all scared, but Trey was frantic.

Loudly, he announced that he had changed his mind, that he was going back down the switchback trail to the saddle, to join Peter and the others. The group leader's false calm snapped at Trey's defiance. The leader yelled at him, wouldn't let him leave. Grant thought that letting him go would have been like admitting an error in judgment and the leader couldn't do that.

Trey tried to drink from his canteen. Most of the water went down his shirt. He kept looking at the sky, at the smoke. The leader teased him about drooling. When Trey tried to clip the canteen back on his pack, he dropped it, and it rolled ten or fifteen feet off the trail, down the ridge. The leader continued to berate him, and told the other two—Grant and the other boy—to keep going. The other boy ran up the trail like a sprinter. Grant had just started after him when the group leader ordered Trey to go back down and retrieve his canteen. Over his shoulder Grant watched Trey begin to edge down the ridge with his pack still on. The kid was crying.

That's when the blowup exploded. A hundred yards away, it burst through the wall of trees like a fire-breathing dragon. Grant stood stunned by the monster for a moment, then he dropped his pack and ran up the hill after the other kid—screaming for him to ditch his equipment and run. They never saw Trey again.

"So, in a way, this group leader killed him."

Lisa said, "Peter was forgiving. You know that. At first he called it negligence. Later, when he spoke about it, he called the whole thing 'a malicious accident.' "

Peter was the next person to find Trey, or at least Trey's remains. Somberly, crying, he went searching for the group leader's body, expecting it to be close by.

It wasn't.

Within minutes, though, the group leader found Peter. The leader wasn't in shock, as Grant and the kid with him had been.

The group leader's greeting stunned Peter. "You fucker, if you hadn't argued with me, we would have had enough time to make it out."

Peter asked if the leader was okay.

Over Peter's shoulder, the leader spied the smoldering remains of Trey Crandall and asked who it was.

Peter said it was Trey.

The leader said, "Oh God," and asked about the others.

Peter said that Grant and the other kid had barely gotten off the ridge in time, and that the kids who had stayed on the saddle with him were fine.

The leader asked if he had talked to Grant.

Peter said, yes, he knew what had happened on the trail. They both knew that he meant he knew about Trey and the canteen.

Spitting out ash, the leader said, "This is all your fault, you little fuck. I spent fifteen minutes listening to your bullshit about what to do, and now a kid is dead. Goddamn you. Give me back that fifteen minutes and we're all out of the woods and everybody is fine. *Fine*."

"Peter kept his mouth shut about what happened?"

"Yes, I guess. He said that after they got off the mountain, the leader got treated like a hero. But Peter walked away feeling as though he had killed the kid himself."

"I don't get it. Why did Peter feel guilty? Why didn't he just tell everyone what happened?"

"He never said exactly why he went along with the story. Grant was begging him to keep his mouth shut—that was part of it. But I think Peter stayed quiet mostly because, in his heart, he felt that he had killed that kid."

"His name was Trey. The boy who died, his name was Trey."

"Okay, okay. After a while, though, maybe even by the time they all got back to Cody, I think what had really happened on that ridge didn't matter to Peter anymore. All that mattered to him was that by being right, he had ended up killing the kid—Trey, okay? Standing up to the group leader afterward would have been just hot air."

What was she talking about? "You keep saying he killed Trey? How did Peter kill Trey?"

"Don't you see? It turned out that the group leader was absolutely right. Give back the fifteen minutes

Peter wasted arguing about this route and that, and the whole group escapes the blowup, no matter which trail they take. Yes, Peter was right about the fire. And by debating the point, he wasted the minutes everyone needed to get to safety. Peter lost faith that day. In himself. In the universe. In being right. He called it being 'dead right.' "

"Everything after that, all the changes in his life, that was just guilt?"

"Shame. Remorse. Confusion about God. Whatever. You choose, you're the shrink."

"Whatever happened to the group leader?"

"He never said. I don't think he knew. See, it didn't matter to Peter. He didn't blame the others. He blamed himself."

Lisa got up from the futon and pulled the chain on a nearby lamp. Jonas squinted in response to the wash of light.

Who was this person? If Peter's knowledge of the incident with the canteen was the motive and the group leader killed Peter to silence him, it had to be someone who was close enough to the Buell murder to take advantage of the opportunity it provided to kill Peter. But what about the opera house murder? Who did that? Did that victim have something to do with the damn fire, too?

"Lisa, this is really important. I think it's possible that this group leader may have been involved in Peter's death. Do you have any idea who it might be? Any clues at all?"

She gazed on me in a patronizing way. "You really don't understand, do you, Alan? Peter said you

would, but you don't. It was over. Don't you see? All
that was left of the fire was inside him. I saved him
from that. *The night in the coffin.* He was cleansed.
Everything else was unimportant. The fire didn't kill
Peter. The fire was out."

She had prevaricated about what she knew and
what she didn't know so many times already that I
wasn't confident I could believe her now. I prodded
for a name—the group leader's name. Who was this
person who had threatened Peter after the fire in
Wyoming?

Once more, she said she didn't know. I asked the
same question a different way, and then another. She
adopted a weary, disdainful tone, incredulous that I
didn't comprehend that the person's identity never
really mattered.

I watched Lisa as she reached to untangle Jonas's
feet from a cushion. Something about this woman had
captivated my dear friend. The more I got to know
her, the more difficult it was to understand what it
could have been.

⟨∞⟩

Frustrated, I stood to leave, every bit of flirtatious
tension I had ever felt with this woman absent,
evaporated.

Lisa, though, apparently wasn't done with me. She said, "I'm going to see them tonight."

I was already at the door. Politely, I turned back toward the room. "Excuse me, you are going to see *who* tonight?"

"George Paper and Peter."

"Who?" I knew I had heard George Paper's name before, but I couldn't recall when or where.

"Peter wasn't the first person to die at the Boulder Theatre; George Paper was. And he's still there, people see him all the time. People with vision see him. When Peter was at the theatre late at night he used to see George in the wings or in the balcony. He said George is an old, old man, very proper and proud, but that his face is full of pain. Peter felt that George approved of him. Peter used that word, 'approved.'

"I've been bugging the theatre manager to let me spend some time there alone with them. There's nothing happening at the theatre tonight, no shows scheduled, so this is it. This is my chance, tonight's my night to see them. George Paper and Peter. They're together now, forever. I'm hoping that Peter's face is more peaceful than George's."

I recalled Sam Purdy's story about George Paper's death in the early days of the theatre. The projectionist had, I recalled, hanged under suspicious circumstances. Whether George's hanging had been the result of suicide, homicide, or accident had apparently never been resolved.

My patience gone, my eyes scrunched in disbelief, I said, "You believe in ghosts?"

The expression on Lisa's face was one of peculiar amusement at my ignorance. "Ghosts? Nooooo, don't be silly. I'm going to spend my night with angels."

"That's nice," I said, defeated, retreating.

"Alan," she said.

I stopped and faced her. She was staring at the floor.

"The truth. Peter was already fading on me. You should know that, too. The day he died, he hadn't been inside this house for ninety-two days.

"I've stopped counting now."

I had left my pager behind in the car. The little screen on top informed me that I had received three calls while I was inside the stone house with Lisa musing about adultery and the netherworld. All three numbers in the pager's memory were Sam Purdy's, which was fine with me, since I had planned to call him, anyway. My day had not been uneventful; I had a lot to tell him. After once again rebuking myself for not having gotten around to purchasing a car phone, I stopped at a convenience store at the end of Eldorado Canyon Road, bought a bag of pretzels, and dropped the change from a dollar into a grimy pay phone.

Sam answered. He said, "Purdy."

"I think I have a motive worth checking out, Sam. May at least give us a place to start."

"Great. I got a new theory myself."

"You know who did it?"

"I don't exactly *know*. I'm being deductive. It's one of the things I do best."

"This is just supposition, right?"

"No. It's *deduction*. And it works. It's what Lucy

Tanner would call efficient. Where the hell are you? I've been paging you all afternoon."

"I'm at the Dynomart in Eldorado Springs. Never actually been here before. It's like a déclassé 7-Eleven. Not bad, but the pretzels are a little stale."

"Then you can be here in five minutes. See ya."

"If I make every light and ignore the tired sirens of your colleagues."

He hung up the phone. I went back inside the Dynomart, where I bought a plastic bottle of lemonade from the clerk, who was dressed like a biker. As I was climbing into my Land Cruiser, I spied Lisa's little car rounding the bend in front of the store and turning north toward Boulder. The top of Jonas's carseat was visible through a side rear window.

I guessed that Lisa was heading to Spanish Hills to drop Jonas home with Adrienne before continuing on to Boulder to commune with the Boulder Theatre's two resident angels.

I was thrilled that I wasn't accompanying her.

And I was thrilled that the ash of Peter's fire was finally starting to deliver its secrets.

─────◆◆◆─────

When the day had started I knew no one with a motive to murder Peter. Suddenly, I could identify three: The group leader from Graystone. Adrienne, whom Peter was cheating on. And his young mistress, whom, apparently, he was planning on leaving.

Despite my discomfort with the fact that I was impugning Adrienne by assigning her a motive to kill her husband, I still called that a productive day.

Sam had cleared my entry to the detective bureau of the police department. He was at his desk, wearing jeans and a polo shirt and, I swear, cowboy boots. I couldn't get over the sight of him. The boots didn't look particularly new, which meant that this probably wasn't a recent fashion epiphany for him. I thought he looked like Garth Brooks on steroids.

He guessed that I was about to say something I would regret and headed me off at the pass. "I'm off duty."

"Apparently," I said.

Sam was eager to get his story told.

"Martin Scott was the killer at the theatre in Denver. If there's any truth at all in your latest profile of the murderer at the Buell, Martin Scott was definitely the guy. I spoke with his supervisor at work, I spoke with his only friend in the lab, and I spoke with the stage manager at the Civic Theatre in Denver, where Martin has volunteered during almost every production. That's right, almost every damn production. He was a theatre *nut*.

"Martin had the theatre knowledge, he had the computer know-how, he had easy access to more seminal fluid than a hooker—fresh, preprocessed, processed, frozen, whatever. The physical security in the lab, turns out, is good, but once the semen samples are counted and dropped into the tank and frozen, there's really no ongoing inventory control. With his computer skills he probably could have adjusted the inventory records, anyway. And this friend of his says Martin was fascinated by *Miss Saigon*. The guy doesn't know all the details but thinks that Martin had a tough childhood. Knows he was in foster homes, but didn't know for how long or when. Thinks Martin grew up in Delaware. I've got calls out to try and track down social-service records, see if they can find any history.

"One down, two to go. And the murder we've nailed down isn't either of the ones I'm most concerned with. Now, tell me about your motive."

I relayed the new information I had learned from Lisa about Peter's fire and that I guessed a phone call to Graystone would identify the group leader who had argued with Peter before leading three people, including Grant Arnold and Trey Crandall, into the face of a flash fire.

Sam's face told me he was hoping for something better. "It's an interesting story. But where's the motive? Why does this guy suddenly start killing these people after all these years? And what about the other kids who were with them in the wilderness? One of the two kids who went into the fire lived. The four that went up the other way with Peter, they lived. Wouldn't they be witnesses, too?"

"I don't know, maybe, but I don't think so. Remember, Lisa's version of Peter's story is that the counselors argued about strategy away from the kids, not in front of them. All the kids ever knew was the outcome, which was that they were given a choice about what route to take. And Grant apparently told

Peter that the other kid who went into the fire may not even have seen the group leader order Trey Crandall down the slope after his canteen. So the leader wouldn't have to worry about the kids ever coming forward, because they didn't hear anything and they weren't witnesses to the stupidity on the ridge."

"Listen, I'm sorry, but it's lame. Though at least it's a motive, which is more than I've got. Shouldn't be hard to check who this person was. I'll track down the Graystone folks in Wyoming and see—"

My pager chirped and Sam paused as I checked the number on the screen. It was Adrienne's home phone.

I walked over to an unoccupied desk and called her.

"It's Alan, what's up?"

"Hi. Do you know where Lisa is? I was late getting home, and she left me a note saying that she couldn't wait for me any longer and she was taking Jonas to see his daddy. Did you ever find her today? Has she gone batshit or something? Please don't tell me she took my baby out to the cemetery in the dark."

I sighed. "I think I know where they are, Ren. I'll go get him and bring him home. I'm sure they're fine."

"Are they at the cemetery?"

"No. I think they're at the Boulder Theatre. Lisa said something about going there tonight to find Peter— you know, in a metaphysical sense."

"You mean like ghosts?"

"I think Lisa's more comfortable with the concept of angels."

"Oh God, save me."

"Let me go get him for you, okay? I'm much closer

to downtown than you are. I'll get the carseat from Lisa's car."

She was silent a moment, considering my offer. "Call me the second you get there. Please?"

"Sure." I hung up.

Sam appeared curious about my conversation with Adrienne.

"It seems I need to go downtown to the Boulder Theatre and rescue Adrienne and Peter's baby from the ghost of George Paper. Want to come along and continue this conversation?"

———◦◦◦———

To my surprise, Sam jumped at the chance to run my errand with me. Once in the car, though, he seemed distracted.

Whatever was going on with him was contagious; my bowels began to feel as tight as a garden hose.

"What does Dale think about the Martin Scott theory, Sam?"

"Don't know. I told you earlier—she's taking a personal day today. There's no hurry, I'll talk to her about it tomorrow. That's the one good thing about a dead suspect, he's extremely unlikely to go on the lam."

We were approaching the Downtown Boulder Mall. The mountains were ragged shadows against the western sky, still bright from the setting sun. The peaks were so close I felt I could spit on them.

Sam asked, "Who did you say is with this baby we're going to get?"

"Lisa. Jonas's nanny. You met her. She's the one who told me what Peter said happened in Wyoming. You know, Peter's fire."

"Yeah. The blonde. So now she's the goddess of hearsay. I adore hearsay. And you're sure she's at the theatre?"

"No, I think she's at the theatre. I know she had the baby an hour ago. And she left Adrienne a note that she was heading to the theatre with him."

"She was all right when you saw her, though? How long ago?"

Why was Sam asking me if Lisa was all right? "Yeah, she was fine, not long ago. When I was on the phone with you from Eldorado Springs, I saw her drive by. Why? What do you think is going on?"

"Nothing, just keep driving."

While we were stopped at a light, Sam used his portable radio to call dispatch and check for messages.

Thirty seconds later the reply was "Negative."

He signed off. I thought I detected a sigh.

It didn't take my clinical skills to tell he was concerned about something. But I couldn't guess *what* was needling him.

"Sam, are you worried about Lisa and the baby?"

"I'm sure they're fine," he said, compressing reassurance into his words in a manner that I found particularly alarming, "but why don't you speed up just a little. Don't worry about cops—you know that they're never around when you need them."

He touched the outside of his boot and pressed.

"You have a weapon, Sam?"

"Yeah."

"Where, in one of your boots?"

He laughed.

———⁂———

Although the front doors to the theatre were locked, the door to the adjacent box office was not. Sam ushered me into the building as though it never crossed his mind that we might be trespassing. Inside, the box office opened onto the lobby. Light from Fourteenth Street washed in through the glass doors, casting a pastiche of shadows on the clutter of the snack bar. The hum of refrigeration compressors provided an annoying soundtrack. The pungent aroma of old popcorn oil and fake butter mingled with the must of yesterday's spilled beer.

I listened for sounds of Lisa or, more likely, Jonas. But I heard nothing except the background drone—no voices, no Peter, no George Paper. Sam had buried whatever was bothering him and swaggered away from me toward the theatre proper, the heels of his cowboy boots clicking quietly on the tile. Despite his ample weight, the man could float like a cloud when circumstances demanded. I was glad he had come along.

I joined him as he stood beneath the overhang of the balcony.

The lights in the theatre were set low. The effect was moody, as sconces high on the walls left oblique triangles of muted illumination on the walls above them and vague stains of straw-colored light below. The stage area was dark—no footlights, no spotlights. No bodies.

The "no bodies" part was a reflexive assessment on my part these days. I had checked the stage carefully the moment I could see it.

Sam shrugged his shoulders at the empty room and marched down the aisle. For some reason I felt dread, my heart full and tight and straining against my chest wall. Sam had a weapon, and I thought that was good. His demeanor earlier had left me anxious and I wanted to stay at his side.

As though he could read my thoughts he whispered, "I'll check the stage, you look up in the balcony."

"We're looking for Lisa and the baby, right? Maybe they stopped someplace for dinner."

"Check upstairs, okay?"

With feigned nonchalance I nodded, shoved my hands into my pockets, and began to climb the carpeted stairs. Below me, I heard Sam as he *click-clacked* across the parquet dance floor toward the stage. I stopped at the top of the steps and watched him disappear into the wing stage left. Distinctly, I heard a scraping sound, and tried to place its origin. I couldn't. I decided that Sam had generated the noise, mostly because the alternatives were too disconcerting to me.

The balcony itself was easy to check. The seats were all unoccupied and the shadowed, dark narrows between each row were empty. One of two doors at the top of the balcony was open and led to a projection booth. The room was cluttered and seemed to have been relegated to storage-room status. On another day, with a different agenda, I would have been tempted to stop and examine the various projectors still in the room. One looked old enough to be the original one that George Paper had been responsible for early in the century. Another seemed high-tech enough to launch holograms across the orchestra.

But no Lisa up here. No Jonas.

The second door from the rear of the balcony led to a series of windowless rooms that lined an L-shaped hall. The air in these back spaces, high behind the theatre marquee, was stale. Brackish water filled a toilet and a sink in a tiny bathroom. Dust covered a few pieces of ancient furniture. A closet door screamed in rusted protest as I yanked it open. Inexplicably, the closet held nothing but a green canvas duffel bag that contained a dozen or so metal softball bats that had seen plenty of use. I grabbed one and moved on to join Sam at the stage.

By then, I was more concerned about traipsing through a spooky old theatre with George Paper and Peter than I was about finding Lisa and Jonas, who I figured weren't actually in the theatre at all but were probably down the mall at Häagen-Dazs, where Jonas was painting himself with a scoop of chocolate chocolate chip.

As I approached the stage a door slammed shut somewhere in the building. My ability to exhale was immediately compromised.

"Sam," I called in a loud whisper. I heard no reply.

From where I was standing I couldn't see the wings, but the stage was vacant and the orchestra wasn't occupied. Sam was either in one of the wings or in one of the many basement dressing rooms below the stage. Again, I said, "Sam."

A voice emitted an annoyed "Shhhhhhhh."

I thought it came from the area stage right beyond the curtain.

On tiptoes, I climbed the stairs to the stage and said, "Lisa?"

"Shhhhhh. They're here."

Fuck this, I thought, *I've had enough.* "Where's Jonas? Where's the baby? Adrienne wants me to bring him home."

I could see her now. She was on a narrow platform ten feet or so above the stage, a rough equivalent of the fly floor at the Buell Theatre in Denver. The ropes and cables that controlled the battens snaked up and down from cleats on the wall behind her.

"Where's Jonas, Lisa?" My tone was crisp and mildly rebuking. I needed to orient her, to bring her down from her angelic perch. "Adrienne wants me to bring him home."

She didn't look my way as she spoke. "George Paper died up here. This is where he was hanged. Did you know that? I think I'll find him if I stay up here. Don't you think he'll come to see me?"

"Where is Jonas?"

Hell! For that matter, where is Sam?

"He's looking for his daddy. Peter will come to Jonas first, I think. That makes sense. I'll wait for George and Jonas will wait for his daddy."

"Lisa, did you see a big guy with cowboy boots a couple of minutes ago?"

"George is old and has white hair. He's not happy."

This was getting frustrating.

Sharply, I said, "Lisa, look at me."

She did.

"Where-is-the-baby? Adrienne wants me to bring Jonas home."

Just then, I felt, as much as heard, a deep thumping from below the stage. Seconds later, another. The scarred wood floor beneath my feet vibrated from the repetitive impact, which sounded metallic. Eager to find Jonas and Sam and tired of this charade with Lisa, I turned and sprinted towards the stairs that led to the dressing rooms.

The light switches were not where I expected to find them, and since I didn't have the advantage of either a flashlight or a lighter, my search of the basement dressing rooms was done by Braille.

The pounding continued unabated in ten- to fifteen-second intervals. Each concussion reverberated powerfully, lingering like the vibrations of a tuning fork.

Moving toward the sound through a maze of narrow corridors, I kicked something on the floor and it skittered away from me against a wall. Tracking its path with my toe, I nudged it again to determine that it wasn't alive and wasn't about to bite me. I bent down and picked it up.

Sam's radio had been crushed. Deliberately, I guessed.

Quickly I surmised that the perpetrator had not been Sam. Nor had it been Lisa up in the wings.

Just as I was considering that Lisa would have insisted that I rule Peter and George Paper out as radio mutilators, above me I heard the soft clip-clop of footsteps moving across the stage, from stage left to stage right. The sounds were moving toward Lisa.

Sam?

I turned a corner and felt the wall vibrate from the thunder of another crash.

"Sam?" I called.

The crashing stopped and was replaced by a sharp rap.

I felt along the wall trying to find a door. Finally I crossed through an open doorway into a small anteroom and discovered a closed door. I opened it and moved carefully into what turned out to be a boiler room. In seconds I located Sam, who had been locked inside an abandoned coal bin, a simple metal pin inserted into the latch to prevent his exit.

A sharp scream vibrated through the darkness. The sound came from upstairs, from the stage.

Anxiously I said, "Are you okay? I've got to get back upstairs. Do you know who did this to you?" His reply left me little doubt that his mouth was gagged. I felt for him in the darkness and stripped duct tape off his face.

"Ouch. Head. Go," he said. "I can't think. My gun's gone."

"I'll be back. You don't know who it was?"

He reached out in the dark and grabbed my arm. He shoved his badge wallet into my hand and said, "Perfume. Smell . . . perfume."

Louisville Slugger in hand, trying to remember the pattern of the hallways, I began to run back upstairs.

Sam had just handed me the two elusive corner pieces to the jigsaw puzzle.

=∞∞∞=

I weaved back through the maze of dressing rooms and hallways. With each step I felt more certain whom I would find above me.

Sam had smelled perfume.

Sam had handed me his badge.

The casting for the show was complete. And as I arrived at the top of the stairs, I saw that all the players had reached their marks.

Her back to me, Dale Hunter stood center stage, inches from where Peter had been stabbed to death. Across the stage, Lisa remained on the catwalk above the right wing, but she had started to climb the stone wall, using the cables and the cleats for leverage. I assumed she had been seeking a better vantage from which to spy on George Paper. From her eyes, I could tell that Lisa saw me enter the wing on the opposite side of the stage.

I hadn't found Jonas. *Please be okay*, I prayed silently. *Please.*

To my left, at the top of the orchestra, silhouetted against the windows of Fourteenth Street, stood Adrienne. As I suspected she might, she had come downtown to rescue her baby from spirit daycare.

Lisa, Adrienne, Dale.

My recent homework had revealed that each might have had a motive to kill Peter.

My experience chasing the cement mixer down Clear Creek Canyon told me that only one of the three could have escaped that canyon search.

Only one of the three should have known how to mimic Lonnie Aarons's murder.

Only one of them actually could have killed my friend.

Sam's clues cinched it.

A badge. *A cop.*

Perfume. *A woman.*

Perfume and a badge. A woman cop.

Dale.

Though she had weapons, both her own and probably Sam's, I figured that Dale would be reluctant to use a gun to kill Lisa for reasons having to do with ballistic evidence and an understandable eagerness not to be apprehended. And Adrienne was way too far off to be reliably picked off with a handgun. If Dale missed a quick shot, Adrienne could be out the door to safety in three seconds.

But I also assumed that when Dale discovered that I

was behind her with a baseball bat, her reluctance to use firearms would rapidly evaporate.

Without overture or preamble, Dale turned toward the audience, toward Adrienne, and ordered her to join the party onstage. "Come on down and I won't hurt your baby."

Behind Dale, I shook my head to Adrienne in a wide, slow arc, and mouthed the word "no." Adrienne's distance from Dale was her only protection.

Lisa stopped her ascent on the wall, her hands on the ropes, her feet on the cleats that held the batten cables in place. She hung there, frozen. Apparently unable to see Adrienne, she had thought Dale was talking to her.

Lisa's posture on the wall, her feet resting on the cleats, inspired me. I looked up into the vault above the stage and saw dozens of long, heavy metal pipes running horizontally across the dark space. Each pipe, I knew from my lessons with Charley Chandler, weighed hundreds of pounds. Each pipe, I knew, corresponded to a single cable and could be released by a single cleat on the wall below Lisa's feet. In a theatrical production, scenery would be hung from those pipes. That day, though, the heavy battens all hung naked.

Dale's attention was on Adrienne. "Come on," she called. "Trust me. I won't hurt your baby."

After a silent prayer that Jonas was nowhere in the vicinity, I pantomimed for Lisa what she needed to do. I mouthed the words "Release the cleats," and flicked my right toe in the air to demonstrate the motion.

She looked at me curiously. I repeated the foot kick.

She looked down, then back at me, then up to heaven. She raised one foot. I prayed that she was getting it.

She kicked an iron cleat swiftly with the instep of her right foot.

The sound of the first bar falling from the vault reminded me of a Roman candle on the Fourth of July, a sharp, clear whistle that accelerated as the narrow metal pipe pierced the still air, and the cable flew, unimpeded by counterweight, up the stone wall. The screeching sound was everywhere at once, not just above us, and Dale looked all around her, everywhere but up, as the pipe bore down on her.

It crashed to the stage only eighteen inches from Dale's left shoulder, the whole wooden platform thundering from the impact. Dale raised her gun to fire as Lisa released another cleat. A whistle pierced the air.

Dale looked up and hopped to her left, firing her gun wildly, jumping left again, then right, finally falling to the stage floor, not knowing where this batten or the next one would be falling.

Lisa released another cleat and another.

Just then, Jonas cried. And as the fourth or fifth batten crashed to the stage he emerged from behind the curtain near the fly floor, standing, his eyes heavy from sleep but each orb as wide and bright as a watch face.

Dale rolled to her side and prepared to fire at Lisa.

Adrienne screamed at the sight of her baby.

Lisa jumped down to the catwalk and turned her back, rapidly releasing another cleat and then one more and one more and one more.

Jonas chose that moment, for the first time in his

young life, to begin to walk more than a step or two. His eyes were fixed on a spot in the center of the stage. And his little feet carried him toward that spot with the unbending force of gravity.

Adrienne began a sprint down the left aisle.

I leaped forward from my hiding place as everything slowed in front of me. The whistles from the falling bars became muted. The thuds they made as they fell to the stage stopped roaring. The gunshots sounded now like caps, not cannons.

I screamed to Lisa to stop releasing the cleats, but her back was to me and she couldn't see that Jonas was in danger.

One bar crashed a foot behind Jonas, then another a yard in front of him. He stumbled forward like a drunk, his arms outstretched. From the corner of her eye, Dale finally saw him. The baby's presence momentarily distracted her from the dance she was doing through the minefield of falling battens. She reached for Jonas—as rescuer or hostage-taker, to this day, I do not know—and the second she did, her welcoming arms were ravaged by a falling pipe, the heavy iron bar missing Jonas's face by inches. I lunged for him and buried his body below mine as the last two battens crashed to the stage.

Next to me, Dale screamed in agony.

The whistling stopped. The crashing stopped.

Lisa turned and with an enthusiastic voice said, "George Paper showed me how to do it."

Jonas never cried.

He squirmed out from under me, stood up proudly,

took two more steps to the center of the stage, pointed, and said, "Da."

———◦◦◦———

Two injured cops. Two ambulances on the way.

I chose to pass the time waiting for the paramedics to arrive by sitting in the dark with Sam in the boiler room. Adrienne took Jonas. Lisa, comfortable with guns, promised to keep one pointed at Dale Hunter, whose agony continued to fill the theatre like a toxic fume.

The boiler room was stuffy and as black as a stage with the blue lights off.

Sam listened while I told him what had happened upstairs.

He started and stopped a couple of sentences, then was silent.

"You knew, didn't you?" I said.

I heard him shift his weight in the cramped space of the coal bin. "I figured it might be a cop, but I didn't want it to be. Shit, it had to be a cop, Alan. Who else could have gotten out of that canyon after the cement mixer crashed? A cop would have just left the truck behind, flashed a badge, and asked a citizen for a lift down to Golden before the fire trucks arrived. Anyone else but the Invisible Man would have been spotted in that search."

"I had the same thought about the canyon, that a cop could have gotten out easier than anyone else."

"It makes me sick to admit it, but I've been afraid since then that it might be Lucy. I've been tracking her movements the last week everywhere she went. When you came up with a motive that matched somebody her age tonight, it really worried me. I was afraid we might find Lucy here."

"That's why you were so uptight on the way over here?"

"No. It was on the way over here that I *stopped* worrying about Lucy. When you mentioned Lisa and the baby, I remembered that breakfast we all had in Central City. You know, Dale, Lauren, you, and me? God, you were gabby that morning. But that's when you talked about Lisa. Dale was real curious about her. Don't you remember?"

Oh God, yes. After my first meeting with Grant, Lauren had asked me if I had agreed with Lisa that he shouldn't be trusted. "You think I set Lisa up?"

"After you set Grant up, yeah. I bet that Dale didn't even know about Grant being in Colorado until you told her about him that morning. A few days later, she kills him. I'm sorry, Alan, there's no way you could have known."

I shivered at my unwitting stupidity.

Sam kept talking. "But Dale makes great sense, too. She's the one who finds Martin Scott's corpse in Denver. She's been wanting Peter dead since she discovers he's living in Colorado. I mean, shit, she's about to take a job basically working for the father of the kid she killed in Wyoming. She sees her opportunity. Borrows Martin's sperm stash. Stalks Peter, waits till he's alone in the theatre . . ."

We could hear the sirens approaching.

"Alan?"

"Yeah?"

"If Lucy ever hears that I suspected her, I think I might kill whoever told her."

"I'm good with secrets, Sam."

"Dale being the killer—it explains something else that I've been wondering about, too."

"What's that, Sam?"

"It explains why she's been coming on to me like I'm Brad fucking Pitt."

≈≈≈

Lauren knew that sleep would visit me only fitfully that night, and she shaped her naked body next to mine in comfort. It was the time of the month where she couldn't cuddle comfortably without sculpting her breasts just so. That task complete, she spoke to me in calming tones, encouraging me to talk it out.

"Sam's okay, right?"

"Just a concussion, he should be all right, they might keep him in the hospital till tomorrow. I talked to Sherry, she seems pretty level, considering she's been in cop-wife hell for a few hours."

"Do you think Sam ever slept with that Denver cop?"

"All I'm sure of is that he was tempted. But I don't know. Sam is cynical enough to have suspected Dale of coming on to him just to stay close to his investigation. Which, in a perverted way, makes some sense. But I doubt that I'll ever know the rest."

"How is Dale?"

"She was moved to the jail unit at Denver General while they contemplate charges. It's more secure than trying to keep her at Community, where I think they feel that Adrienne would have too good a chance to gouge out her eyes. Dale's arms are an unbelievable mess, multiple fractures, crushed bones. She looked like a rag doll when they put her on the stretcher. She's facing some serious rehab time."

Lauren cautioned, "Maybe more rehab time than jail time. You know, despite Lisa's testimony—a lot of which will never be allowed in court—there's not much evidence against Dale. Even what happened at the theatre can be construed as self-defense. And Sam apparently never saw who hit him."

"I know, I'm glad it's the cops' problem."

"Why do you think she did it? Why did she kill Peter after all these years?"

I turned my head to face her. "Dale became afraid of her past. The irony is that this thing on the mountain was a tiny tumor. If she had excised it when it was small, a dozen years ago, I'm not sure how much the truth would have hurt her. But she buried it, lived with it, denied it. Now, with that job on the line, had Peter or Grant decided to tell their story, even if they couldn't prove anything, the damn tumor had grown big enough to kill her career. By killing them, she was killing her past. Psychologically, it's a great motive. Legally, it's awkward and probably hard to prove; it's going to cause Elliot a problem."

She fingered my chest hair and slid her hand low on my abdomen. "And what about you, what is your problem?"

"I have three. Adrienne, Jonas, Lisa."

"Ahhh."

"I couldn't believe Jonas walking tonight. What a time for him to take his first stroll."

"You think he was looking for Peter?" I'd told Lauren about Jonas calling out "Da" as he moved across the stage.

"You know me—I'm a natural-born skeptic—but even I have trouble ruling it out. Lisa says they were both there, she saw them, George Paper and Peter. She says that the two of them, those two angels, saved our lives."

Lauren's fingers lingered in my pubic hair. I started to become aroused.

"What are you going to tell Adrienne? I mean about Peter and Lisa?"

"I don't know. I think Adrienne's known about them for a while. About the affair, I mean. From what they both said, maybe Peter was coming back around. But if there're any details Adrienne needs to know, I've decided that I think you should be the one to tell her."

She took advantage of my vulnerability, pinched a clump of hair, and yanked.

ACKNOWLEDGMENTS

To cynics who whine that there are no gentlemen left in the publishing business and to writers who moan that there just aren't any editors around like there used to be, Al Silverman offers convincing evidence to the contrary. To say I'm grateful for his guidance and friendship doesn't come close.

I wish to sing the praises of others at Penguin, too, especially Michaela Hamilton, my inspiring editor at Signet. Elaine Koster, Barbara Grossman, Carolyn Carlson, and Joe Pittman have earned my deep appreciation and respect, as has my publicist, Matthew Bradley, who somehow manages to fashion quilts from whatever scraps of fabric happen to be available. Thanks, too, to Jory Des Jardins and Trilce Arroyo for keeping me on track.

I had invaluable help outside of New York, too. I received law enforcement and forensic education from Stephen Adams, John Graham, Tom Faure, Terry Schlenker, and Virginia Lucy, medical guidance from Drs. Stan Galansky, Terry Lapid, and Robert Greer, and theatre instruction from Rodney Smith, Curt Hancock, and Jane Dettinger. Jonathan Jackson talked to me about woodworking, John Olson guided me through the Washakie, and Tom Schantz taught me, among other things, about literary box canyons and invisible men. If some of their lessons failed to stick, blame me, not them.

As is usually the case, family inspired me. This time, special thanks to my nephew, Jesse White, and niece, Teal Purrington, and to my sister, Elizabeth White, on whom I first practiced my tall tales.

As is always the case, love makes it all possible. I thank my entire family, especially Alexander and Rose, and my mother, Sara Kellas, for their constant support.

I feel incredibly fortunate to count as friends many of the people mentioned above. Other friends whose counsel and support have been immeasurable along the way include a pair of fine writers, Harry MacLean and Mark Graham, a valued colleague, Elyse Morgan, and the couple who gave me the key to door number one, Patricia and Jeffrey Limerick.

Thanks, all.

Don't miss
Stephen White's latest thriller
Remote Control
soon to be published by Dutton

The police were cordial to her at first.

But everything changed when each cop in turn discovered that Lauren had asked to speak with a lawyer. Malloy had warned her it would. She knew it would.

Her friends in the department could no longer be overtly friendly.

Her enemies could now be openly gleeful.

You ask for a lawyer, you are guilty. Rule of thumb in the detective bureau. "There are exceptions," Sam Purdy had told her once. "They only prove the rule."

She hadn't bothered to disagree with him. She had been a prosecutor back then, not an arrestee. Not an *offender*.

The blizzard outside felt warmer to her than the chill she experienced when they arrived at the police department.

After asking three different times, Lauren was finally given permission to phone her husband, Alan Gregory. She placed the call from a gray flannel cubicle in the Detective Bureau. She had already surrendered her watch and wondered what time it was.

Alan knew the time. When the phone rang, the clock on the microwave in their kitchen in Spanish Hills east of Boulder read 8:54.

He, too, had been late getting home. Expecting Lauren

to follow him at any moment, he had showered, fed the dog, and started dinner. When Lauren didn't arrive, he grew more anxious. He stared down the lane searching for her car and tried, unsuccessfully, to raise her on her pager and her cell phone, dialing each number twice.

Out loud, he asked the dog if she knew why Lauren was so late. Emily, a big Bouvier des Flandres, looked at him curiously, wondering if he was offering a walk. He tried to lay the blame for his wife's tardiness on the blizzard. But given the events of the last couple of days, the storm was not a comforting culprit and he was worried.

A big pot of water for pasta had been simmering for thirty minutes already, and needed to be refreshed.

"Hello, it's me," she said breathlessly.

The somber tone of Lauren's greeting alerted Alan that something was wrong. "Hi," he replied, attempting to mask his nerves. "You're real late, what's up? You having some problems with the snow?"

"Alan—oh, God—I'm in trouble. Maybe serious trouble. But it's not the snow. I need you to come to town, okay?"

He placed his wineglass too close to the edge of the kitchen counter, then reached back to move it farther away. "Are you all right? What happened?"

"No, no . . . I'm not . . . all right, that is. But I haven't been hurt. . . . You need to pay attention, okay? Stay with me here. They won't give me much time to talk with you."

"Of course. Who won't give you much time? What the hell's going—"

"Before you leave to come down here, you have to

track down Casey Sparrow for me. I think you'll find her phone number in—"

Any remaining calm Alan possessed disappeared. "I know her phone number. Jesus, why do you need to talk with Casey?" Alan was a clinical psychologist, and Casey Sparrow had served as guardian *ad litem* for one of his young patients.

"I may have some legal problems. It's real important that you find her and talk with her."

"What kind of legal problems? Is this about work? Why do you need Casey?"

But he was already thinking he knew what it was about. *Why does anybody need a criminal defense attorney?*

"I'm at the police department, I'm being held for questioning . . . in a shooting. You're my first phone call since they took me into custody, and it's beginning to look like I'm going to need some help getting out of this. I want Casey. The cops are being pretty hardass with me, playing it strictly by the book. The whole situation is a little complicated right now, to say the least."

A shooting? Struggling to stem a tornado of panic, Alan didn't know what to say. The chaotic events of the last few days spun in rewind and replayed in his mind. This whole mess had started with a shooting, and now, it seemed, it was going to end with one.

The moment of silence lingered into seconds, the poignancy ripe, Alan's mind consumed by static.

"Have you been arrested?"

"Technically, yes."

It struck him that his usually precise wife was being vague.

He reminded himself to listen, to use his professional skills. Calm, Alan, calm. Hear her out. She'll tell you what you need to know.

"What happened, Lauren?"

"This isn't the best time for me to tell you that. Maybe we'll be able to talk later."

"You think someone is listening to you right now?"

"It's possible, yes."

"I can't believe this."

She said, "The police are saying that I shot a man. So things are an absolute disaster for me, legally."

Alan guessed the fact about the shooting was not in dispute with whoever she feared might be listening.

"They think you *shot* somebody?"

"Yes."

"Did you?"

Silence.

"You don't even have a *gun*, Lauren."

More silence.

"Do you?"

"Later, sweets."

He thought about lightning striking twice. "You can't tell me what's going on, can you?"

"No."

"Is the man dead?"

"Not yet. But apparently he's critical. They say it doesn't look good for him. I don't know whether or not to believe them."

Alan swallowed. This was his D.A. wife wondering if she could trust the police? *Jesus.*

"Did this guy attack you? What was he doing to you?"

What a night this was turning out to be. What the hell were you doing with a gun?

"No. It's not like that. He never got that close to me. It's not like that at all. He was almost half a block away from me when he fell."

To Alan, it sounded as though Lauren were admitting the basic facts. "Where did you get the gun? Why did you shoot it? What on earth is this all about?"

She exhaled audibly before she said, "You know," her voice barely a whisper.

Yes, he did.

"Your friend?"

"Yes."

Emma. *Damn.*

The level of complication jumped by the tenth power. He had been praying that this Emma mess might just go away.

"Jesus. Is she hurt?"

"I don't know. I don't think so. I haven't seen her since this morning. You know that she missed that motions hearing this afternoon? So I don't really know how she is. I was hoping you knew something. That would help me know what to do."

He did. But her caution was contagious, and he didn't want to talk about Emma on the phone.

He asked, "Is Sam there? At the police department?"

"I haven't seen him. But they're mostly keeping me in an interview room by myself. Everybody's come down here to be part of this. To the police department, I mean. The chief is here, the commander, the legal counsel, half the detective bureau. I'm not sure they really know what to do with me, given that I'm a D.A.

and everything. Most of these people like me, Alan. They seem truly upset that I've asked to speak to an attorney. They want me to tell them something to make this go away."

"But you can't?"

"You know better than anyone what's at stake. Her vulnerability right now . . . ."

"Does Roy know that you've been arrested?" Royal Peterson was the elected D.A., Lauren's boss.

"Maybe, probably. I haven't spoken with him yet, but I'm sure someone has tried to find him and let him know what happened."

"If the case isn't Sam's, whose is it?"

"Scott Malloy picked it up. But I'm guessing that one of the detective sergeants will run the show on something like this. God, I hope I get lucky on that." Malloy was someone Alan had met but didn't know well. The detective who was not there, Sam Purdy, was a good friend.

Alan thought, *it's a little late for lucky.* "What do you mean, 'get lucky'?"

"It's a chain-of-command thing. There are two detective sergeants in the general investigation division. One of them is that guy I had that trouble with on the ride-along, back when I was a baby D.A. Remember? I'm just praying that he's not the sergeant who supervises this."

Alan did recall the story about the fateful ride-along. Lauren had caused the man a passel of trouble by supporting a brutality complaint a citizen had lodged against him.

"Is Malloy cutting you any slack?"

"None. He's been . . . businesslike. Respectful. Everyone's polite and apologetic, but they seem to want to make sure that they're not doing anything that will let them be accused of giving me special treatment." Her voice softened finally, reassuring Alan that she really understood the gravity of what she was facing.

"I'm so sorry, sweets. Who caught this in your office? Has anybody been by?"

"Elliot." Elliot Bellhaven was one of Lauren's favorite colleagues in the district attorney's office.

"That's good, right?" He tried to make his voice sound encouraging, but it felt trivial and silly.

"He stopped in and said hello. He was nice, but it won't make any difference. This will go upstairs immediately and then to a special prosecutor as soon as Roy can arrange to get one appointed. The commander of the detective bureau came by already, too, and he said he would permit me another call after this one. I'll use it to call Roy."

Alan exhaled through pursed lips. "You're sure this isn't just going to go away?" Alan wanted to hear that it was all a big mistake.

"No, not tonight it isn't."

"God."

"Honey?"

"Yes."

"I need my medicine. Any my syringes, too. You know where everything is? Don't forget the alcohol wipes."

"Of course. I'll call Casey first, and then I'll be right down. I love you, Lauren."

"Yes," she said. "Alan, there's something else—"

"What?"

"My eyes," she whispered.

"What?"

She stayed silent. This was a secret, too, from whoever might be listening.

Oh, shit. She'd woken that morning with some intermittent pain when she moved her right eye. "More pain?"

"Worse than that."

Only one thing worse.

"You're losing your vision again?"

"Yes." Her voice was firm, but he heard a crack in it.

"One eye or both?"

"Much worse in one than the other. But both now."

"Blurry?"

"In one. A big hole in the center of the other."

"You'll need steroids, honey. Right away. You know Arbuthnot is going to want to get started immediately, while the inflammation is fresh." Alan knew how aggressive her neurologist was about visual exacerbations. He also knew how much his wife despised IV steroids.

"Right now what I need is Casey Sparrow. The IV can wait. Please hurry. And bring the checkbook from my brokerage account. Casey may want a retainer for this."

"Casey will wait for her money."

"Bring it."

"Where is it?"

"Top right-hand drawer of my desk. It's the one with the gray cover."

The line went dead.

He said, "I love you."